## SUE CHAMBLIN FREDERICK

From Madison County

# THE MAN SHE CALLED DARLING

SUE CHAMBLIN FREDERICK

From Madison County

# THE MAN SHE CALLED DARLING

WORD JEWELS PUBLISHING

# ACKNOWLEDGMENTS

There is much joy in remembering the 1950's. The 50's culture created times that will forever be remembered as 'the good ole days.'

In *The Man She Called Darling*, Madison County is alive and well with authentic memories, its characters as real as this morning's sunrise.

My thanks to Teenie Cave, Sheriff Simmie Moore's daughter; Sandra Chamblin, Lon Terry's great-granddaughter; Phyllis Williams, Lum Townsend's daughter; the Washington's, Townsend's, Sapp's, Gaston's, Davis', Gibson's and, of course, Dr. Frederick Bush, Madison County's illustrious country doctor and Dr. James Aubrey Davis, the County's memorable veterinarian.

*Cowboys have always been my heroes.*

For Roy Columbus (Lum) Townsend
Born February 20, 1921 - Died May 9, 1985

*One of Madison County's greatest cowboys.*

# PROLOGUE

DooRay wondered where the angels were. Quite curious, he searched through endless dark passages, up and down, around corners, all the while turning his head and looking for some kind of light. *There had to be angels somewhere.*

From far away, the faint sounds of music drifted closer. Not the sound of trumpets. Nor harps. In the cool dark, he strained to hear, cocking his head to the right, then the left. *Country music? Hank Williams? Hank Williams was in Gloryland?*

A bright light flashed through his closed eyelids. Had he arrived in Gloryland, the same place Hank Williams played his guitar? Had he traveled all this way only to hear Hank sing *My Bucket's Got a Hole In It?* He struggled to shield his eyes from the hot light, but his hand was too heavy to lift. No matter how hard he squeezed his eyes shut, the light remained.

And there was Hank again. *Your Cheatin' Heart* boomed from the heavens, the sound deafening, as though a huge megaphone was mounted atop the highest cloud. Then, a soft, cool sensation of floating. *Come on, Hank, let's sing together. I saw the light, I saw the light.*

*Praise the Lord, I saw the light. No more darkness, no more night.*

# PART I

DOORAY

# CHAPTER ONE

In the early morning, DooRay left the Donnelly farmyard and hurried across the wide field that bordered Ran Terry's cypress pond. He moved quickly, an urgency, as though the pond was the proverbial mansion on a hilltop, that same mansion where streets were paved with gold and where angels strummed their glorious harps. His bare feet quickly skirted the rows of corn, his narrow footprint depicting long toes that grasped the dirt like miniature plows. His goat Murphy trotted behind. *The fish were biting and waiting for him.*

The sapling-thin black man headed due west, passing under the shade of century old oaks, taking care not to snag the end of his cane pole in the low-hanging limbs covered in moss. When he approached the bottom of the hill, he could smell the dark, swampy water, the pond's fish unaware that a cane fishing pole, held with absolute precision by a one-armed, but skilled fisherman, was about to swing a hook in their direction. DooRay sang as he walked, his high baritone voice sweeping the morning air with *Jesus, Jesus, sweetest name I know,* and landing in the gentle hills of Madison County.

DooRay had fished in the pond's cool shade for years, favoring a cypress stump, flat on the top, that was just right for sitting. There were years he didn't fish, years he had left his beloved Madison County and fought the Germans in World War II. The tall man with cave-black skin sometimes pondered the tragedy of his missing arm, the memory of it laying shriveled up and ragged in the mud of an artillery field. There were times he'd forget he had no left arm and, in a flash of color, imagined it back where it was supposed to be. He decided it was a trick of the mind, perhaps like a hallucination.

It was when he slept that he envisioned his arm back where it was before it was blown away by an artillery shell, and dreamed of playing softball or dressing up to cat around in downtown Madison on Saturday nights, looking for a pretty woman. Sadly, at the end of his dream, his arm disappeared, and he knew no woman wanted a one-armed man who used his toes like fingers.

"Git a move on, you old goat. Don't you know them fish is waitin' for us." DooRay slapped the hind end of Murphy and clucked his tongue. "A body'd starve if they waited on you." Murphy didn't bother to change his gait; he knew his master would wait on him no matter how slow he was.

In a quarter mile, the pair entered a stand of towering bald cypress, some over a hundred feet in height and, most likely, over a hundred years old. They maneuvered around the woody projections of cypress knees that rose from the earth as if gasping for air. Only a few steps farther and DooRay felt the cool water cover his feet. He looked behind him and watched Murphy's hooves sink into the dark water. He knew the goat liked the pond as much as he did.

Beside a small river birch, DooRay eased to a standstill and listened to voices filtering in short bursts through the trees, a cackling of laughter. Then, the unmistakable odor of cigarette smoke wafting in the muggy air, through the shade and then hanging in a thin haze above the still water.

DooRay eased back a few feet, tugging on Murphy. "We gots to go," he said quietly, a slight tremble in his words.

From the darkness around the pond, about thirty yards away, a man in denim overalls jumped from a log and moved in DooRay's direction. "Hey, nigger!" Water sloshing all around him, the man waved his arm. "Get over here, boy!"

DooRay turned away. "Going home," he said over his shoulder, taking a quick step in the direction of the Donnelly farm. He heard water splashing behind him and knew the man was running toward him. DooRay turned and watched the man climb on a flat cypress stump and point at him.

"Cain't you hear good?" he called, twisting his flushed face into ribbons of hate. "I said get over here!"

His heart thumping in his chest, DooRay scrutinized the angry face. The man's nose seemed squashed against his face, like a boxer's nose. Ears that were truly cauliflower ears stuck out from his head, uncovered by the cap he wore. His body held a bulky weight as he balanced on the stump and sent a bullet-like stare across the pond to DooRay. He growled as he lifted a whiskey bottle to his lips. He drank long, then capped the bottle. "I ain't tellin' you agin, nigger."

Murphy nudged DooRay's leg. There's trouble here he seemed to be saying. *Let's go home.* DooRay felt the same fear he felt that day in September of 1944, in that ditch three miles north of Lucca, Italy, as his patrol began to advance toward the Germans. He had fought hard, his two arms holding his rifle, leading his all Negro patrol into enemy territory.

At the edge of the pond, the drunk man close, DooRay felt his heart race. His one arm hung by his side, his fingers touching the top of Murphy's head. The man hollered to another man who crept up behind him and propped his foot on the cypress stump. "Would you lookie here, Spit. I wonder how this nigger would swim with only one arm. I say we throw him in the Withlacoochee and find out."

Spit nodded. "Now, that's a deal, Freddie." His laughter was drunk shrill, echoing into the dark recesses of the pond.

DooRay heard his feet suck out of the mud as he quickly turned and began to run, Murphy at his heels. It was then that the whiskey bottle soared through the air and slammed into his head, sending spurts of blood across his shoulders. As he fell, he heard a gunshot and watched as Murphy stumbled and fell beside him. Just before his eyes closed, he heard his beloved one-eared goat release a weak cry. DooRay reached out and placed his hand on the goat's face. "Gone be alright, you ole goat."

# CHAPTER TWO

The cool of an early morning breeze swept through an upstairs window of the stately Donnelly house and settled in the shadows of Essie's bedroom. She had stirred earlier when she heard the faint sounds of DooRay's raspy voice drifting across the gabled roof of the house, her eyes remaining closed, but her face smiling as she pushed deeper under the covers. *Catch a lot of fish, DooRay.*

The farm girl wanted to return to the dream, the dream about the Irish doctor and his sing-song accent as he cajoled her into climbing aboard a sailing ship and sailing to Ireland. "I can't go!" she wailed. "Ireland is too far away."

Still, the strong arms of Robert Gray lifted her from the wharf and thrust her onto the deck of a ship, his lips finding hers, his hands tightening around her waist. "No, lassie. Come away with me and let me show you the world."

Essie yelped in her sleep, struggling to leave the sailing ship and the hot breath of the Irishman. "Let me go!" she cried.

Then, an awakening. Her eyes searched her bedroom. She was alone, no Irishman in the room, no sailing ship. Only the sound of Killer, the yard rooster, crowing from atop the wellhouse, the hens clucking busily nearby.

From the farm lane came the putt-putt of a tractor, its engine in a chug-chug rhythm as it swung under the oak tree at the end of the porch. The motor went quiet and Essie heard Emmett Gaston. "Essie, need to talk to you and DooRay."

She jumped from the bed and crossed her room to the south window. "Hey, Emmett. I'll be right down."

Essie slipped on a pair of dungarees and an old shirt of her daddy's, the sleeves too long, the cuffs ragged. She rolled them up and shuffled into some yard shoes.

Down the stairs and into the kitchen, she found a pot of hot coffee on the stove, DooRay's handywork. She poured two cups and kicked open the screen door to the front porch. "Grab a rocker, Emmett."

Emmett, the farmer who leased three hundred acres of the Donnelly land, lumbered up the steps, his leaf-rake sized hands removing his cap. Essie heard the rocker groan as the rotund man, dressed in bib overalls, eased down onto the wooden slats and leaned back. "Heard you was back from runnin' all over Georgia." He reached out and took the hot mug of coffee.

"Oh, I've been back about a month. Good to sleep in my own bed."

"A body needs their own bed, for sure." He sipped his coffee, more of a slurp. "I heard you found your niece up there in Thomasville. Guess if it hadn't been for Hezikahah Pryor's niece, you'd still be lookin'."

Small town news travels fast. The story of Essie's missing niece had kept the town's citizens gossiping for months. It was true. Had Minnie Pryor not seen a picture of Jewell, there would never have been a diligent search for Jewell's daughter in Thomasville. Minnie had sworn she'd seen a girl who looked just like Jewell at one of Georgia's many plantations and the search began.

Essie listened to the squeak of the rocking chair while watching Killer scratch heartily in the farm lane. "Yes, it was at Minnie's insistence that we traveled to Georgia."

The big man finished his coffee and eased forward in the rocker. "I'm lookin' for DooRay this morning."

From the Bellville road a pickup truck flew past, heading east toward the Withlacoochee River, a dust cloud behind, its tires swerving in the dirt. "Somebody's in a hurry. Ain't seen that truck 'fore." Emmett watched until the red truck was out of sight. "Well, now, as I was sayin', where's DooRay?"

"Emmett, you know very well where DooRay is this time of the morning. Fishing over at Grassy Pond." She grinned at the big man. "He promised he'd catch a stringer of bream and bass for a fish fry tonight"

"I shoulda known. 'sides the Farmers' Almanac said it was just right for fishing in the early part of June. 'Course, DooRay don't need no almanac to tell him when to fish."

Essie laughed. "That's true. Anything I can help you with?"

Emmett's face became serious, a frown working its way between his bushy gray eyebrows. His false teeth clacked when he opened his mouth and pushed his way half out of the rocker. "Looks like we got us a panther. About three o'clock this mornin' a big one tore my chicken pen all to pieces and killed five chickens 'fore I could get me and my shotgun out the back door. Dangest thing. Oh, I had me a chicken hawk git one or two chickens over the years, but never had to bother with no panther. Big 'un, too."

"Oh, my. I'll certainly let DooRay know. We can keep one of daddy's guns in the tack room, just in case."

Emmett rose from his rocker. "Good coffee, Essie." He paused, his face melting into sadness. "Sure do miss seeing Jewell in church. She was an angel, for sure. I was out at Mt. Horeb the other day and walked by her grave." He shook his head and took a deep breath. "You got to pull out those cake pans and make the famous Donnelly sisters' buttered rum pound cake again, Essie." The farmer placed his *Ford* cap on his head.

"I know, Emmett." An image of cake pans sitting still and lonely swept into her mind, their emptiness sending a melancholia into the once happy kitchen of the Donnelly sisters' ancestral home. She stepped down from the porch with Emmett. "DooRay'll be home any time now and I'll let him know about that panther."

Essie moved back to the porch and watched Emmett pull himself into the tractor seat. He pointed across the barnyard as he cranked the tractor. "Might want to get that big rooster in the pen. He's ripe pickin's for that panther." He headed the tractor down the lane toward the Bellville road, then a right for the mile ride to Lon Terry's country store. Emmett was certain Lon had cut open the first watermelon of the summer, probably a big ole round *Cannon Ball*. He wanted to be there to get a slice or two and catch up on Pinetta's latest gossip.

Killer, the farm's resident rooster, pranced in circles nearby, his arching tailfeathers glistening in the morning sun. Essie noticed the old rooster had an eye to the sky as he chased after a horsefly, squawking the entire way.

Across the Bellville road, to the west, a peanut field sat prim in its ruler-straight rows, promising a peanut boil later in the year. A flock of cattle egrets gathered farther to the south, their white sleek bodies heading for Hoot Gibson's hayfield over in Hanson.

Essie's return to Madison County had been a heartfelt one, her search across southern Georgia for Jewell's daughter culminating into a glorious discovery, a discovery that would change not only her life, but that of Rose, Jewell's daughter, who, for eighteen years had lived only fifty miles from Pinetta.

Though Jewell's damaged mind did not remember the birth, the birth was revealed to Essie by Bootsey Birthright's 'slip of the tongue' on the Donnelly's front porch the previous summer.

"I'm surprised Jewell doesn't remember the baby," Bootsey had said, cake crumbs on her chin, on that June afternoon in the summer of 1956.

"Baby? What baby?" Essie had asked, her breath shallow.

"Jewell's baby." The old woman, Essie's mother's best friend, had waved her hand through the air. "Oh, I told your mama to tell you the truth, but she just couldn't do it. When Jewell got pregnant, your mama sent her up to me in Atlanta. Not to any finishing school in Switzerland. It was all a lie, Essie."

Even now, a year later, Essie's disdain for Bootsey Birthright ran deep. The woman had been a conspirator, a willing accomplice as Essie's mother Edith deceived not only her husband but also Essie. Essie would visit Bootsey, would tell her that Jewell's daughter had been found. The visit might heal some hurts, but it was Essie's mother, the mother who lay in the same cemetery as Jewell, who would never be forgiven.

Essie leaned back into the swing, her gaze toward the sky. She noticed a particularly small cloud, all by itself, and cast in a pink glow, almost dancing as it quickly changed shape and moved higher. *That you,*

7

*Jewell? I found your baby. It took me a while, but she was there waiting for us. Over in Thomasville, just as pretty as you please. Her name is Rose. She's coming to the farm, Jewell. And I'll teach her to make that buttered rum pound cake you like so much. Take her to the cemetery. We'll bring you roses. Some of mama's roses. You know, the yellow ones she got in Tallahassee.*

From the porch, Essie searched the fields to the west for DooRay, finding the tall majestic cypress at Grassy Pond, their tops flat, perhaps the perfect place for the tree fairies to have a tea party.

The wind picked up, and the tops of the trees at the pond swayed like a Vienna waltz. One last look at the field before Essie opened the screen door and walked into the house.

In the kitchen, she chopped onions for hushpuppies. When she looked at the clock, she was surprised. It was almost noon. *DooRay must be catching a lot of fish.*

# CHAPTER THREE

The sunrise in Thomas County swept across the sky, a sky the color of a bluejay's feather. The thin pink clouds stacked upon themselves as if creating a stairway to heaven. In Thomasville, Minnie Pryor boarded the Trailways bus headed east to Quitman on Highway 84 and then south, across the Florida state line to Madison County.

The trip was only fifty miles, a stop in Dixie, then Boston, where Trailways picked up freight bound for a station down the line. In 1957, life ran slow in the farmlands of south Georgia, a cycle of crops that broke time into pieces: digging for peanuts, corn shuckings, the cutting of hay and the loading of watermelons for shipments to northern cities.

Minnie's hands lay folded in her lap, the pair of white gloves on her small hands seeming out of place. *Only white women wear gloves*, she thought, '*cause they's afraid the backs of their hands 'll get freckles.*

Minnie, a prim and proper young black woman, sat erect, the rocking of the bus making her drowsy in the crowded back section. A small cardboard case that carried a few meager belongings, not the least of which was a letter from Essie Donnelly, sat on her knees.

"Girl, you goin' far? Maybe to Savannah?" The question came from across the aisle. A woman leaned closer, her stiff hair festooned with a yellow hat with small purple feathers on the brim. Her dress seemed too large for her, the fabric winding around her body like a tropical garden, printed with large red flowers, flowing tropical leaves and small yellow and green cockatoos. "Lots of folks goin' to Savannah. They's lots of houses to clean over that way." She raised a small cup and spat into it.

Minnie noticed the cockatoos on the woman's dress had no eyes. "No, ma'am. I'll be going to Florida."

"Florida!" the woman exclaimed. "Ain't no work in Florida. Those white folks down there cleans they's own houses."

The cockatoos didn't have feet either. "I'm visiting family," said Minnie.

The woman raised the cup again and spat. Minnie turned away while the woman wiped brown spittle from her chin. "Family's nice if they's good folks. Your family good folks?"

Minnie smiled at Tropical Garden. "Yes, they are."

"You know any white peoples down there? Like rich white folks you can clean they's house?"

*Oh, I know a white family.* Minnie nodded. "I have a friend. She's a white woman. Real nice."

"How much she pay you to clean her house?" The cup rose to the woman's mouth.

Minnie shook her head. "I don't clean my friend's house."

Across her bubble-shaped chin, Tropical Garden swiped her sweat rag vigorously and glared at Minnie. "You mean that white woman's your friend and you don't clean her house?"

"Yes, ma'am."

"How you know she's your friend? I don't think it be so, girl."

"Oh, it's so, all right. She gone send me to nursing school over in Tallahassee. And, that's a fact." Minnie raised her chin and pulled her cardboard case closer.

"Ain't no truth comin' outta your mouth, child. No white woman's gone do that for no black girl."

On the fringes, Minnie felt a slight irritation. She squared herself and faced Tropical Garden. "Yes, ma'am, she is. She wrote me a letter and says if I comes to Madison County, she gone pay for my college education."

"Well, la tee dah, nigger girl. That white woman sho 'nuf is your friend."

"Yes, she is." Minnie eased back in her seat and watched the highway, saw her little town of Boston, Georgia, slide by, where only nine miles north, her father and two brothers sharecropped a hundred acres of farmland. Her brothers, Pitch and Orland, had cried when she left. "I'll be back," she said, "and I'll be wearing a white nurse's uniform."

She closed her eyes, her mind flitting here and there, but mostly dwelling on her escape from twenty-four years of farm work, serving the rich folks at Pebble Hill and Sinkola plantations in Thomas County, and then her miraculous friendship with Essie Donnelly.

Had it not been for a cane fishing pole, a stringer of fish and a haughty meeting with DooRay Aikens, she would still be cooking and cleaning for her two younger brothers and her father, as well as hoeing in a field of beans and okra. All admirable tasks, but, at age twenty-four, she wanted more.

DooRay had thought her snooty on that early spring day when he found her at *his* fishing pond. At first, she ignored him, her eyes fastened on the cork floating on top of the dark water. When DooRay huffed his way toward her, she looked up and saw the irritation on his face.

"Don't you know you be trespassin'? This here is Ran Terry's pond and he don't allow no fishing 'cept you got permission." He dipped his chin. "I 'pose you gone tell me you got permission?"

Minnie turned her eyes back to her cork. "That's a fine greetin' on this lovely June mornin'." Her voice was soft, like morning glories opening at sunrise. Her profile was regal – if not a queen, surely a princess in the vast farmlands of Madison County.

"This ain't 'bout a lovely summer mornin'," DooRay said evenly, no different than a game warden getting down to business. "All's I see is a stranger sittin' on my cypress stump and fishin' in my spot. Ain't nobody gone take my spot away." DooRay straightened his shoulders and stabbed the thick end of his cane pole into the dirt.

Minnie saw her cork bob once, then disappear. She set the hook and lifted the pole. A bream danced at the end of the line, its tail waving back and forth like a small flag. Catching the fish didn't deter her from a smug retort. "The way I see it, Mr. Skinny Man, is I got here first. If'n you got up at sunrise, you'd be in this spot 'stead of me." Minnie removed the fish from the hook and slipped it onto her stringer.

When DooRay saw the black girl's stringer of fish, his knees weakened. Not only did she steal his favorite fishing spot, she also stole *his* fish. At least a dozen fat bream and two bass hung heavily from the stringer.

He spat out angry words. "None your bidness what time I got outta bed this mornin', missy. You best head on down the road, or I'll go up the hill to Mr. Ran's house and have you toted off his land."

Minnie grinned. "Don't you know nothing, skinny man. Mr. Ran and me's been friends since I was in diapers. My Uncle Hez done work Mr. Ran's farm all these years and this here pond is like family to us Pryor's."

DooRay blinked and stared at the lovely face of the fisherwoman. Hezekiah's niece Minnie Pryor had, indeed, been a welcome visitor to Ran Terry's pond for years. She had, however, grown into a full-fledged woman. DooRay felt his heart thump. He stepped closer, his demeanor melting into submission. A slight smile began at the corners of his mouth.

"You fishing with worms or Vienna sausages?" His voice cracked. "Or bread?"

"Worms. I dug 'em this morning . . . 'fore your feet hit the ground, skinny man." She turned her head, a smile as wide as the Withlacoochee spreading across her pouty lips.

DooRay reached down and pulled the hook from the side of his cane pole. "You gone share those worms?"

The two had fished together until late morning, then walked to the Donnelly farm, Minnie's mule following, where DooRay introduced Minnie to Essie Donnelly, the prettiest white woman Minnie ever did see.

The bus slowed when it chugged up a hill, its motor grinding. Minnie opened her eyes just in time to see a roadside sign: Quitman, Georgia Population 458. The Trailways turned into a parking spot in front of the Piggly Wiggly, its air brakes whooshing into the quiet Friday morning. The driver, a gray haired man in uniform, whose name tag read *Eddie Westberry*, keyed the bus' microphone. "Quitman, Georgia. Rest stop.

Leaving in ten minutes. Get you a cold drink real quick like. Got a schedule to keep."

Tropical Garden left her seat and moved down the aisle. "Come on, girl," she said over her shoulder. "This here's Quitman and they gots the best Georgia peaches I ever did eat."

At the edge of the parking lot, a black man wearing a straw hat fussed over baskets of peaches, all arranged in rows on top of a long table. Minnie heard him call. "Fresh peeeeeeches. Get yo fresh peeeeeeches from ole Elroy Jackson." He sent his toothless grin across the parking lot, his black skin slick from the heat of the morning sun.

Minnie peered through the bus window. She'd get her peaches from Madison County. Then, she'd make a peach pie for DooRay Aikens. DooRay, the man whose missing arm did not bother her one bit, the man she planned to marry.

# CHAPTER FOUR

E ssie shredded a whole cabbage for coleslaw, Rana Terry's recipe, a little horseradish in it, a teaspoon of sugar and, of course, Hellman's mayonnaise. She slipped in a chopped green onion or two as well as a big fat carrot, shredded fine.

She couldn't bring herself to make a buttered rum pound cake as Emmett Gaston had suggested. Her heart was too tender after her sister's death. Making the cake without Jewell would splinter her in too many places, her memories already broken into little pieces that seemed to fade away with the passing of time.

Instead, she pulled out a new recipe from a friend in Suwannee County, Myrtis Brown Clark. She had met Myrtis in Live Oak at a Suwannee River Jamboree where a crowd had gathered to listen to little Benny Cox, Madison County's guitar playing, singing cowboy, only ten years old.

Myrtis, a lovely woman just a few years older than Essie, had brought her daughter, Bonnie. Together, they had spent a summertime Saturday eating watermelons, then a carrot cheesecake that had become a family favorite.

Essie read the recipe quickly, her mind wandering to DooRay, her ears listening for his melodious voice drifting across the corn field to the west.

The phone rang its four short bursts - Essie's ring on a party line of four people, all residents of Pinetta. Before Essie could say 'hello,' a voice boomed out. "Miss Donnelly, this is Thomas Fox in New York. So glad I caught you!"

Thomas H. Fox, the literary agent who had sold her novel *The Watermelon Queen of Madison County* to The Viking Press, had not been daunted when Essie broke her contract and returned the $10,000 advance to The Viking Press. His enthusiasm for her work had merely taken another route.

"Hello, Mr. Fox. What can I do for you?" Essie braced for the man's passion as a literary agent, whose energy had made many authors a star in the literary world.

"Oh, no, Miss Donnelly. It's what can I do for *you*!" he exclaimed. The man was out of breath, overwhelmed by his excitement. "Just heard from The Viking Press. They want to award you a $25,000 advance on your novel. It seems they are determined to publish your book. What's more . . ."

"Hold on, Mr. Fox. Did you forget our conversation about my novel? I'm not willing to publish at this time ——." Essie's voice had become shrill, a loss of patience with the man from New York City.

Mr. Fox's zeal spewed forth in laughter. "Ah, too late, Miss Donnelly. My assistant will be taking a flight out to Tallahassee within the next few weeks and will be knocking on your door very soon. Her name is Lola LaRue. She's an extraordinary editor of many famous novels and insists that your novel becomes a #1 bestseller. She'll have a contract ready for you to sign. I'll be in touch!"

"Mr. Fox . . . Mr. Fox." The man had hung up. Essie slammed the phone into the cradle. "Pushy New Yorkers!" *You go ahead and knock on my door, Miss Lola LaRue. And watch me send you right back to New York.*

# CHAPTER FIVE

S am Washington passed Lon Terry's country store and slowed for the
turn off the Bellville road onto the Donnelly farm road. He had
made this turn many times, not the least of which was a year ago, the
morning he had simply walked off the Madison County road gang. Jailed
for thirty days by Judge Earp for contempt of court, he could have paid
the $300 fine, but he was a hard-headed lawyer and a Washington from
Madison County, no room for clear thinking if you're mad. Judge Earp
had warned him twice. The third time was the last time. The Judge's
gavel swung hard and that was it. *Thirty days.* Thirty days for an
upstanding attorney who had defied Judge Earp one time too many.

On the twenty-ninth day of his 30-day sentence, Sam had decided he
needed some shade, a soft bed, a shower. He'd had enough of the road
work assigned to minimum security prisoners.

By some miracle, after he'd walked through a mocassin-infested
swamp, fought gargantuan mosquitos, and confronted a six-foot alligator,
he found all those cozy comforts at the Donnelly farm. After stripping
his muddy, tick-infested clothes, he had crept up the backstairs of the big
house and made himself at home. He did not, however, escape the wrath
of Essie Donnelly when she found him naked atop a frilly yellow
bedspread and snoring to high heaven in an upstairs bedroom.

The hard woman from Madison County had blasted him with angry words, a promise of a shotgun blast and another thirty days in jail. Even when he told her they had been friends at Pinetta's high school fifteen years earlier, she huffed her way to the telephone and called her Uncle Lester, who conveniently ran the prison work farm.

After heated threats from the mistress of the house, he had walked naked down the stairs, the Donnelly woman watching, a pillowcase with embroidered pink flowers hiding his most precious parts. Essie Donnelly didn't falter, yelled at him as he left the house and strutted down the lane to the county car where Lester Terry waited. The verbal barrage from Lester didn't hold a candle to Essie Donnelly's wrath. So much for high school friendships.

A year had passed, their non-relationship melting into a workable situation where, as long as he let her drive the bus, things worked in a suitable man/woman capacity. It was, however, Essie's trek to southern Georgia to find her dead sister's child that set in motion a slight parting of the ways. Sam felt abandoned by the feisty farm girl — it seemed he always ended up second in her life.

It didn't help that a handsome Irish doctor had moved into Sam's territory. Right from the start, it seemed as though Dr. Robert Gray had eased into Essie's life as slick as steamed okra, his deep attraction for her obvious when Sam saw them together at the Boston, Georgia, farm of Ollie Pryor. Perhaps he had read too much into the scene at the Pryor house. However, he still carried visions of Essie in her bed clothes, and blankets spread on the living room couch on that cold Saturday morning in March.

Life had since softened into a Madison County summer, fields plowed, crops planted and gentle rains that promised cool early June temperatures. Sam pulled up under the shade of a large oak tree at the east end of the long Donnelly porch, his eyes searching for Essie. He glanced up and saw her on the porch swing. His heart flipped slightly; she was his woman.

"Good afternoon!" he called. He placed his Panama hat on his head and walked across the yard to the porch steps. He grinned, "Do I smell a cake baking?" He reached into his shirt pocket and pulled out a cigar.

Essie watched the tall, slim lawyer jump onto the porch's edge, skirting the steps altogether, his hands grabbing the porch rail and swinging his legs high. Sam Washington was prone to unorthodox trivialities in his young life. Known for his impenetrable blue eyes and inscrutable countenance in the courtroom, it seemed the rest of his world was filled with a love for humor and candidness that sometimes unnerved an ordinary conformist who lived a life of tradition and conservation.

"It's out of the oven. Cooling."

Sam's blue eyes were smiling. "Dessert after the fish fry?"

Essie patted the seat beside her. "Come sit in the swing with me."

Sam unwrapped his cigar and sat beside Essie, the swing creaking. His long legs rested on the porch floor and he pushed them into a slow swing. "Pound cake?"

"Yes, dessert, and no, not a pound cake. A carrot cheese cake."

"What time is dinner?" Sam lit his cigar and puffed until a small cloud of smoke lifted in the afternoon air. He felt the warmth of Essie's arm next to his and reached over and squeezed her hand.

"Whenever DooRay gets here with the fish."

Sam looked surprised. "DooRay still fishing?" He looked at his watch. "It's 1:30. That's unusual. Never seen him fish this late in the day."

Essie nodded. "Me, neither. Think we should walk over to the pond?"

Sam left the swing, pulling Essie with him. "Let's go. Who knows, a moccasin might have got him. Can't be too careful."

Sam tugged Essie's arm gently, a curious urgency that caused him to quicken his steps, lift the barbed wire fence and step under it, Essie in front of him. "DooRay's probably up at Ran's house. Inez's got him cutting okra."

Their walk was quiet, with only the sound of bees in the wild flowers at the edge of the corn field. The June sun had started its descent to the west, leaving shadows beneath the oaks that lined the field. The smell of rich earth from a recent rain permeated the air and reaffirmed the cycle of seasons. Summer in Madison County produced bountiful crops, not the least of which were the best watermelons and cantaloupes in the south.

The field ran downhill, the southwest corner dedicated to a spring-fed, three-acre cypress pond that was home to fat bream and largemouth bass, as well as an abundance of cypress knees. If Ran Terry liked you and you were a Pinetta resident, you had free access to what the farmer considered world-class fishing. All you needed was a cane pole and worms. And, of course, a good fillet knife and some hot grease and corn meal.

Sam and Essie saw no sign of DooRay as they entered the shade of the tall cypress that comprised a good portion of the pond. Sam, a man with a perspicacious mind, in an instant, became anxious, an unsettling washing over him. He backed up a step and pulled Essie with him.

"What?" asked Essie.

"That's DooRay's cane pole over there." Sam pointed to the edge of the pond. "Essie, I want you to run up to Ran's house and see if DooRay's up there."

No questions asked, Essie quickly ducked under a strand of barbed wire fence and began running up the hill. Her heart thudded in her chest, her breath coming quickly. She didn't like the tremble in Sam's words.

# CHAPTER SIX

Essie bolted up the clay hill to Ran and Inez Terry's house, her thighs burning after only a quarter of a mile. The small house, nestled under large oaks whose heavy limbs provided cool shade, was at the top of the hill, a half mile away. Panting hard, Essie scrambled to the top, sweat dripping from her face. When she rounded the corner of the farmhouse, she found Inez holding a water hose that spewed water into a washtub, as well as showered about a dozen yellow ducklings swimming in the cool water.

"Inez," she called. "Have you seen DooRay this morning?"

The ducks scattered when Essie ran across the yard. Startled, Inez dropped the hose. "Essie! What in the world are you doing all sweaty and red-faced like that? Everything all right?" The woman picked up the hose and placed the end of it into the washtub and wiped her hands on her apron.

"Sorry, Inez. I didn't mean to scare you. Has DooRay been up this way?"

"Not this morning." Inez heard the screen door slam and watched as Ran Terry walked out onto the porch. "Honey, you seen DooRay this mornin'?"

Ran Terry, one of the five Terry brothers, shuffled to the porch edge, his bib overalls faded and covering a round belly. "No, I ain't seen 'em. Probably down at the pond fishin'."

Essie lifted her shirttail and wiped her face. "Just checking," she said. "I'll go on down to the pond. He's probably nearby."

"Want to take some squash with you? Got plenty. Corn, too." Inez reached for a basket.

"Thanks so much, Inez, but I'll come back later. Gotta look for DooRay." Essie turned and sprinted out to the clay road and began the half mile trek to Grassy Pond, her face troubled, mirroring her concern.

# CHAPTER SEVEN

Sam squatted beneath the tall cypress at the pond's edge. Footprints marked the black mud, a barefoot as well as a hooved print. *DooRay and Murphy.* Nearby a boot print. Two different boot prints. A scuffle in the mud and grass.

A few feet from the pond an empty whiskey bottle lay in the grass, alongside DooRay's cane pole. Sam leaned closer and saw blood spattered on the blades of grass. Then, a small wet area of pooled blood.

Sam Washington, an attorney by trade, was known for his quick mind as well as skill at deductions once the facts were laid out. He had, by no means, the long-held expertise of Sheriff Simmie Moore, but he had a mind that was clever, eyes that missed nothing, his prowess as an intuitive thinker pushing him into the status of a man to reckon with, whether it be in the courtroom, or in his daily life in Madison County.

He hesitated only a moment when he saw Essie duck under the wire fence. "Hurry, Essie. Let's get on up to the house." He backed away from the cane pole, the whiskey bottle and the blood spattered grass. "Let's get hold of Simmie Moore."

Essie half stumbled to Sam's side. "Simmie? What's going on?" Her eyes found the whiskey bottle. Then, the grass with the blood stains. "Where's DooRay?"

"I don't know, but certainly not here at the pond." He grabbed Essie's hand. "Let's go."

The two half-ran, half-walked to the Donnelly farm, an urgency creeping into their movements across the corn field. Sam heard Essie gasp and glanced her way, tugging her arm. Tears ran down her flushed cheeks. "We'll find the answer to all of this, Essie."

Essie stumbled and fell to her knees in the soft dirt. "Sam. Where are they? Where are DooRay and Murphy? He'd never leave his cane pole at the pond. I'm . . . I'm . . . "

Sam pulled Essie from the warm earth and held her. "Essie, let's think clearly. First things first . . . we'll call Simmie, begin a search and find DooRay . . . and Murphy. I need you to stay calm."

Essie sniffed and nodded her head, no longer the hard woman from Madison County. DooRay had lived at the farm for a year and was considered a family member. When lightning struck his little shack of a house the previous summer, burning into a pile of ashes, DooRay had walked down the Donnelly's farm lane on his way to Clyattville to live with his Uncle Mustard.

"Where you going?" Essie had asked on that cool May morning.

"Guess you hadn't heard, Miss Essie. Lightening done hit my house yesterday evenin' and burnt it up into a pile of black ashes. Murphy got singed a little bit. Wasn't nothing I could do it happened so fast."

"Oh, my, DooRay. I'm so sorry. That why you're going over to Clyattville?"

Murphy stuck out his long tongue and bleated softly. DooRay scratched the top of the goat's head. "I sure am. Looks like DooRay gone live with Uncle Mustard a while."

"Uncle Mustard? Mustard Aikens? Why, I know him!" Essie hurried down the brick steps into the yard, her bare feet crunching dried oak leaves. "Biggest thief there ever was. Worked for daddy one summer and stole everything he could get his hands on. Daddy shooed him off the place and told him to never come back. He's a mean rascal, DooRay. I can't believe he's your uncle, and you're gonna live with him."

DooRay scuffed his bare foot through the dirt and nodded. "Gots to do that, Miss Essie."

"Oh, no, you don't, DooRay. The old tack room at the side of the barn is a perfect place for you."

And there it began. During the summer of 1956, a one-armed black man became the man of the Donnelly farm, the maker of fluffy biscuits, the lard squeezed into the flour with one resolute hand, the white dough shaped with one skilled hand, slathered with butter with one gentle hand. DooRay Aikens, purveyor of all things good, had melded into a life on the Donnelly farm that rivaled the farm's ancestors, despite him not having a whole body. It was his mind and spirit that took over his missing arm and left him on a par with any farmhand on any farm in Madison County.

Sam and Essie raced across the yard and up the Donnelly house steps. "Essie, get one of your daddy's guns for me," he yelled as he picked up the telephone.

The operator answered when Sam dialed zero. "Hey, Mrs. Jones. Ring Sheriff Moore for me."

Sheriff Simmie Moore answered on the first ring. "Sheriff Moore." His voice was deep and steady. After decades of sheriffing for Madison County, Simmie was rock-solid, a sincere man whose love of the citizens of Madison County ensured his re-election. Then, again, no one ever opposed the popular sheriff.

"Simmie! This is Sam Washington. Need you to get over to the Donnelly place. Seems DooRay Aikens is missing. At first glance, there looks to be a scuffle down at Grassy Pond, where he'd been fishing."

"I'm on my way, Sam. Son Stokley might get there before I do. Believe he's in Pinetta. I'll radio him right now."

Essie took the stairs from the house's second level two at a time, and landed in the kitchen, where Sam paced the wooden floor, turning around when he heard Essie.

"Here you go, Sam." Essie handed Sam her daddy's favorite revolver, a Smith and Wesson .38 Special. Sam flipped opened the cylinder. Fully loaded, he snapped it back in place.

Essie pulled a box of cartridges from her pocket and placed them in Sam's hand. Sam noticed her hands shaking and, after placing the box in his pocket, he reached out and cupped Essie's chin. "Listen, here. We're in this together. I'll be by your side the whole way." He paused, noticing

Essie's tear-filled eyes. "I'm thinking we should trust that DooRay and Murphy are just fine." Sam gave her a reassuring smile. "We don't want to come to any conclusions when we don't have all the facts."

Essie took a deep breath, a half-smile on her lips. "You're right, of course. It's just . . . it's just that I want him home. Safe and home. That's all."

"I understand." Sam placed the revolver on the kitchen table, a frown across his forehead. The gun was the same gun Essie's sister Jewell had used to shoot George Barnwell the previous summer. Her first shot took off his ear. With the second shot, she hit him in the chest, dead center. Barnwell had made a mistake when he entered the home of two Southern belles whose daddy had taught them to be sharpshooters.

# CHAPTER EIGHT

From the dining room window, Sam watched two cars turn off the Bellville road and speed down the lane. In unmarked vehicles, Sheriff Moore and his deputy, Son Stokely, parked under the low hanging limbs of an oak tree and eased out into the yard.

Sheriff Simmie Moore, an affable man, wore no badge, no formal uniform, just plain clothes, khakis and a collared polo shirt. But, he did carry a pistol in the right front pocket of his pants. His wife, Monteen, removed the pockets of all his pants and replaced them with heavy sail-cloth to keep the gun secure.

Simmie's county car was plain, with no markings, a '56 Ford, whose tag read *35 County Sheriff* and was almost as fast as the moonshiners. He walked slowly across the yard, his deputy a few feet behind.

Sam left the house and walked out onto the porch. "Sheriff, thanks for getting here so quickly. You, too, Son."

Essie stood beside Sam. "Come on the porch, Simmie. Cooler up here."

Simmie and his deputy lumbered up the steps. Son Stokley, whose weight bordered on three-hundred pounds, might have been a big man, but he was agile. He wielded authority by his mere size, his presence foreboding when trouble was nearby. Son was Simmie's only backup, a position he carried with pride. The two presided over Madison County's citizens as though they were family. They were tough, but kind.

Sheriff Moore leaned against the porch rail and folded his arms across his chest. He was in a listening mode when he nodded to Sam. "Let's hear it, Sam. What's this all about?"

Essie broke in. "Simmie, DooRay left this morning around 7:00 to go fishing. I heard him talking to Murphy, then singing. You know how DooRay likes to sing."

Simmie cast a glance around the porch. "I'd say everybody likes to hear DooRay sing." He turned to Sam. "So what made you go looking for DooRay?"

"I arrived at the farm around 1:30 and Essie and I discussed DooRay and how he never fished so late in the afternoon. Most of the time, he's back to the farm by 10:00, at the latest. We decided we'd go check on him."

Simmie shifted his weight on the porch rail and glanced west where the tall cypress beckoned, their flat tops a dingy orange, a few crows catching an upwind and leaving their roost atop the trees. "You must have found something, Sam, or you wouldn't have called me. That right?"

Simmie squinted his eyes at Sam. "Tell me everything."

Sam cleared his throat, nervous and anxious, and became a lawyer in a courtroom. "You're right, Simmie. Essie and I approached the pond from the north side and saw DooRay's cane pole on the ground, half in, half out of the water."

Nearby, Essie nodded, her face grim. She wrung her hands and licked her lips, nausea rising in her throat.

"I sent Essie up to Ran Terry's house to make sure DooRay wasn't there visiting with Ran and Inez. While Essie was gone, I noticed various boot prints. Bare feet, as well as hoof prints, that I assume were DooRay's and Murphy's."

Sam seemed to struggle, swiping his hand across his forehead and biting his lip. "When I looked closer, I could see what looked like blood on the grass as well as a small pool of blood in the dirt. There was an empty whiskey bottle nearby." He held Simmie's eyes for a long moment. "No DooRay anywhere."

Simmie nodded and said. "Let's take a look." They left the porch and walked into the yard. It was obvious Simmie's mind was spinning, his mouth set in a grim line. He turned to Son Stokely. "You go on down the Bellville road to the south side of the pond, and see if there are any tire tracks or any indication someone's been parked there. Take pictures if you see tracks or anything out of the ordinary.

"Sam, you come with me and let's walk on down to the pond." Simmie walked a few steps and looked back at Essie. "Come along, too, Essie. May I assume Ran and Inez had not seen DooRay?"

"That's true, Simmie." Essie hurried down the porch steps and followed the two men to the fence, where they lifted the barbed wire and slipped through. The quarter mile walk to the pond seemed endless, realizing with every step that a tragedy was ever closer.

The search for DooRay Aikens, a beloved fixture in Pinetta as well as the whole of Madison County, would leave no stone unturned. The wide reach of the one-armed black man was limitless. His touching of hearts, his kindred spirit was known in every house, on every clay road, every farmer's barn, every steepled church, and all along the Withlacoochee River. DooRay Aikens was DooRay, the lionhearted, a champion, a man of courage whose goodwill served Madison County with legendary aplomb.

At the edge of Grassy Pond, Sheriff Moore examined the ground, knelt into the mud while his eyes swept the pond, its numerous cypress knees and finally the grass leading to the pond, where he found blood. Near the spattered blood was an area the size of a small watermelon. Dark and sticky, it, too, was blood.

When Simmie stood, he brushed off his pant legs and adjusted his hat. Sweat had formed on his upper lip, his cheeks flushed. "No doubt about it," he said to no one in particular. "Something's happened here and none of it good."

From the west side of the pond, Son Stokely pushed a strand of barbed wire close to the ground and stepped over into the field. He walked quickly, patting his pocket, then lifting his badge to his shirt and pinning it on. When Son Stokely wore his deputy badge, he was in police mode, a sure sign of his entry into a serious situation.

"Tire tracks, for sure. Somebody was parked on the south side of the road. Good tracks since we had rain yesterday." Son was panting when he stopped at the pond's edge. "Another thing. The owner of the vehicle chewed tobacco. There's tobacco spit all over the place."

"Get some good pictures?" asked Simmie.

"That I did. Looks like they were parked heading east, toward the Withlacoochee. Tire tracks showed them pulling forward onto the Bellville road. The tracks merged with others about thirty yards out."

"All right, let's get the word out. DooRay Aikens missing earlier today. Be on the lookout for suspicious activity as well as folks who don't live around here. In other words, strangers." Simmie appeared thoughtful. "Don't forget Murphy. Everybody knows that goat."

Simmie bent over and carefully lifted the whiskey bottle. Examining the label, he read out loud. "*Four Roses*, a Kentucky straight bourbon whiskey." He glanced at Sam and Son. "We got us a drinker, for sure. Didn't buy this whiskey in Madison County. Son, you drive to Clyattville and see if there's been any *Four Roses* sold over that way recently."

The sheriff pushed back his hat. "DooRay didn't walk away from here; he was carried. My best guess is whoever owned the vehicle parked on the Bellville road brought harm to DooRay. Murphy is another story. Can't imagine anyone carrying a goat anywhere. It's possible Murphy's somewhere in these woods since his hoof prints are all around here.

"I'll have Lum and George Townsend take their horses and do a search around these woods. Sam, you go on into town and get with the *Madison Carrier*. It'll be out tomorrow afternoon and I want it to carry a front page story about DooRay's disappearance. You know all the facts. However, don't mention the *Four Roses* whiskey bottle."

The four huddled a moment longer at the edge of Grassy Pond, the sun slipping farther west, leaving long shadows that preceded nightfall. An alliance had formed, the priorities cemented in the minds of four people who knew well their mission. *Find DooRay Aikens and his one-eared goat Murphy.*

# CHAPTER NINE

Long after nightfall, the Donnelly farmyard began to fill with citizens from across Madison County. The Agner's, Keeling's, Terry's, Townsend's, Gaston's, Sapp's, Gibson's, Wiglesworth's, Leslie's, Washington's – most from the northeast section of Madison County, and all friends of DooRay Aikens.

The men scattered around the barn where a bonfire lit up the night sky. Fred Glass arrived along with J. B. Hinton and Mutt Everett. The men smoked their cigarettes and chewed their tobacco, a few with a pint of moonshine in their pocket.

The Reaves brothers brought their bloodhound, Sniffer, a black and tan, its nose renowned in the county. Sniffer weighed eighty pounds, about six years old and knew the backwoods of the county like a bloodhound should. Give him a scent and he was off. A shy dog, he sat obediently by the legs of his masters, Booter and Feller Reaves, and watched the crowd, the folds of skin around his neck and chin somewhat humorous.

George and Lum Townsend tethered their horses by the well across from the tack room, the tack room where DooRay had lived since the previous summer.

Lum Townsend had a reputation as the best cow pony rider in northeast Florida. He was a true cowboy. He could train a horse in a matter of a few hours. *Trust.* It was about trust and Lum Townsend gave trust and accepted trust. The cowboy had a bum leg from a bone disease as a child, but never let his affliction keep him from riding.

Lum's horse was named Hickory, a gentle chestnut the color of tanned deer hide. A calm horse, he worked closely with Lum's two Catahoula Leopard hounds, Sport and Lep, to round up and pen cattle all across the farms of Madison County.

The gathering of men would stay all night and begin their search at daybreak. Rana Terry, Patti Crafton and Essie made pots of coffee and tomato sandwiches. The carrot cheesecake Essie had made for the fish fry was gone in a flash, as was the slaw.

Simmie Moore and Son Stokely arrived well into the night, returning from another ancillary search in the immediate area around the pond. Evidence was crucial in any crime and, there was no doubt about it, a crime had been committed.

"Listen up, folks." Simmie cast a deep voice over the crowd. "Let's break out into two or three-man teams and divide the search area as evenly as possible. I don't mind anyone carrying a weapon as long as safety rules are obeyed."

Son Stokely moved in and spread out a map on the long picnic table under a large oak tree. His flashlight provided enough light to show he had drawn a precise grid on the map. From east to west, from north to south, the black marker defined each area of about twenty acres each, each one identified A through J. Two hundred acres altogether, all surrounding Grassy Pond.

The sheriff motioned to the men who stood nearby listening. "Okay, each team come up to the map and get your assignment. Lum and George, since you're on horseback, I'd like you to scour the river banks, a half mile or so in each direction.

"The rest of you can cover twenty acres each, a total of ten teams. If we've got more than twenty men, muster up into threes. After we search this two hundred acres, we'll make another grid for more search areas."

Simmie looked at his watch. "Only an hour until daylight. Drink some coffee. Hope you're wearing good boots – lots of snakes this time of year."

The sheriff continued, one last comment.

"What are we lookin' for?" He scanned the crowd and his gaze lingered on the determined faces of the men before him. "We're lookin' for DooRay Aikens. We're lookin' for his goat Murphy. We're looking for tracks, or debris that might relate to DooRay's disappearance."

Simmie's voice softened, his hands upturned in question. "Could be he's hidin' in the woods, hidin' from some mean son-of-a-gun. Could be Murphy's hidin', too. We have reason to believe DooRay's injured. He might have collapsed somewhere nearby." Simmie paused and took a deep breath. "We just don't know . . . "

The sheriff held back some of his thoughts. He had to make a decision soon. Would they search Grassy Pond, wade out into the water and look for DooRay's body? Inside, the strong man trembled. He wasn't there yet; as strong as he was, he couldn't make himself think that was a possibility.

Sam Washington stood at the end of the porch, fatigue settling across his shoulders. An hour until sunrise. Beside him, Essie took his arm. "Come in, Sam. Let's lie down for a little while."

Sam followed Essie up the stairs to her bedroom and stretched out on a frilly yellow bedspread, feeling his tired body sink down into the soft mattress. "Isn't this the same bedspread I stretched out on last summer – the summer of the naked Sam Washington?" He laughed. "The summer of the shotgun totin' Essie Donnelly who shooed me off her farm?"

"The same one," Essie whispered, as the memory found itself in her heart. The summer of Jewell's death, the discovery of the baby she had birthed when she was eighteen, the return of Autrey Browning, the father of the baby, to Pinetta after almost twenty years.

Essie eased in beside Sam and closed her eyes. Voices from the search party filtered through the open windows. They were soft voices, a collective murmur across the farmyard, voices that melded together into one big lump of courage. The voices belonged to men who honored century old customs, that unwritten rule, that a neighbor help a neighbor.

In moments, Essie heard Sam's deep breathing and leaned her head on his shoulder. *We're coming, DooRay. We're coming.*

# CHAPTER TEN

D r. Frederick Bush parked at the end of the farm lane just as the morning sun sent faint light across the horizon. His gait was slow. A weary night delivering a baby in the Lee community had taken almost six hours and, even now, he knew he'd have to return soon to monitor the young mother, a fifteen year old, the girl crying and telling him all she wanted was to be a cheerleader, not a mother. Sadly, her youth was gone and she had entered a world of responsibility and the constant care of her newborn.

The country doctor stopped halfway down the lane and gazed at the gabled roof of the Donnelly house, the long porch sitting throne-like, as though its roots were entrenched before the birth of time. The porch, whose pine flooring seemed to wear an expression that fell somewhere between slumber and the prick of a thorn, reminded one of the memories that had been created there, under its sloping roof and where jasmine twisted wildly around the white columns.

Frederick Bush had delivered two babies in the stately house, sisters who grew up to be beautiful women, leaving behind a mother and father who now rested in the Mt. Horeb cemetery, not too far down the clay road north of the house.

He had pronounced one sister deceased at only thirty-three years of age, and watched her buried alongside her mother and father. Even as a young child, Essie, the remaining sister, had captured his heart, an old man who cherished what he considered the epitome of a strong woman, a woman who lived her life by her own rules, but prevailed in her quest to abide by the Beatitudes Christ set forth in the Sermon on the Mount.

And that was why the good doctor continued his walk down the lane and into the farmyard where dozens of men had assembled together in hopes of finding DooRay Aikens.

"Dr. Bush!" Sheriff Moore called. "Come this way, please." Simmie took off his hat and waved it high in the air.

The crowd of men parted and Dr. Bush eased past folks he'd known for years and stood beside Simmie. After a handshake, their voices dropped. "I don't know what we're going to find, Dr. Bush. Doesn't look good. It seems there have been some injuries. Most likely DooRay and his goat Murphy. Found blood around the pond and signs of a scuffle."

Dr. Bush nodded. "Let me know what I can do, Simmie. Just stay in touch through my office. I'll check in often."

"Thank you, Dr. Bush. Sun's comin' up and we're about to head out. There's some mighty good coffee over there on the picnic table. Might want to talk to Essie – she's taking this pretty hard."

Essie sat on the edge of the wooden picnic table, her shoulders slumped, her hands folded in her lap. She was in another place, her mind dark while her heart beat with a slow thud.

Dr. Bush ambled her way and smiled as he poured a cup of coffee. "Essie," he said gently. "When we find DooRay and Murphy, I'm hoping you'll bake a few cakes for us. Been a long time since I had a slice of your buttered rum pound cake." He sipped his coffee and when Essie looked up, he held her eyes, a steady, calming message hovering between them.

"Hello, Dr. Bush. Thank you for being here." She looked away and dipped her chin.

"Wouldn't be anywhere else . . ." he paused. "You're the strongest woman I know, Essie. Let's stay strong for DooRay."

The doctor saw a tear roll down Essie's cheek, a quiver in her chin. He patted her shoulder. "It's going to be alright, Essie," he said softly.

From the farmyard, George and Lum's horses broke into a gallop, their hooves beating softly on the lane to the Bellville road. Their dogs followed, leaving no doubt that George, Lum, Shorty, Lep, Hickory and Bucky were a team, not to be separated. They'd ride to the Withlacoochee and scour the banks a half mile in each direction.

From the side yard, five farm trucks started their engines and caravanned south to locate their grid and begin the search for DooRay.

Mutt Everett and J. B. Hinton lifted the barbed wire fence to the north pasture and the woods that bordered about ten acres of watermelons.

The Reaves brothers squatted on the dirt and talked softly to Sniffer. "Ya see here, Sniffer," said Booter, "this is DooRay's blanket. You sniff it real good."

Sniffer was a nose with a dog attached. His ability to identify smells one thousand times greater than humans, the dog's scent receptors captured DooRay's scent immediately. Sniffer picked up the trail and began tracking across the farmyard, his ears dragging the ground. He wouldn't stop tracking until the trail ended.

The brothers stood and stamped their feet. "Go get'em, boy."

Sniffer circled the farmyard twice, his nose to the ground, then shot out west, past the house and into the cornfield planted earlier in the spring by Emmett Gaston. The brothers followed, their feet whipping the ground, their long legs moving like thrashing machines.

On the porch, Sam looked to the skies. Dark clouds were forming in the west. Rain. Not good for tracking. Not good at all.

# CHAPTER ELEVEN

The Donnelly farmyard lay quiet except for the clucking of chickens in a nearby pen, and Killer, the farm rooster that scratched the dirt around the well, every now and then cocking his head looking for predators.

The sun hid behind gray clouds that were shaped like giant rutabagas, their flat bottoms swiped with purple hues and a yellowish gray color riding the tops. The clouds seemed to roll and turn within themselves, perhaps deciding if they wanted to release torrents of cool rain on the gentle hills around Pinetta, Cherry Lake, Hickory Grove and Hanson, as well as the winding Withlacoochee.

From the swing on the front porch, a vigilant Essie watched the lane to the Bellville road. Lightning flashed far to the west, chased by thunder. The search party would be returning soon with a report of their findings. Simmie Moore had set up camp by the barn, anxious for the reports when they came in.

At the end of the lane, a mule and rider plodded around the corner of the road and onto the farm lane, no hurry at all. The mule was a molly, with a short, thick neck and thin limbs, typical of the animal. The mule placed her small narrow hooves one in front of the other and soon stopped at the end of the porch.

"Minnie!" Essie cried, running down the brick steps and across the yard.

Minnie squealed and jumped off the mule and threw her arms around Essie. "It's me alright, Miss Essie. That be so!"

Fat raindrops chased the two women up the steps under the shelter of the porch, the wind blowing rain sideways. On the porch, they watched quietly as the downpour continued, a bolt of lightning arcing across the sky.

"Oh, my. Poor Sally. Can I take her to the barn?" Minnie watched rain pour off the mule's back. "She sure do hates to get wet."

Essie frowned. "That poor mule. You take her and I'll be right behind you with some dry towels. We're gonna get soaked."

Minnie jumped off the porch and grabbed Sally's bridle. "Come on, Sally." The two raced to the barn, Essie only a few feet behind.

The sound of rain on the barn's tin roof was deafening. Inside, Killer had taken refuge on top of an old ladder. Sally shook herself and opened her mouth in a happy grin.

"Oh, my." Minnie stamped her feet and shook her head. "Cain't believe we's so wet."

Essie tossed her a towel. "This will help." They dried themselves and found a place to sit to wait out the rain. A few birds had found a dry spot in the rafters and flitted around above them.

"Where's DooRay, Miss Essie. Don't see him nowheres." Minnie patted her face, her brown eyes wide and questioning.

*DooRay.* Of course, Minnie had not heard about his disappearance. She knew nothing of the involvement of Sheriff Moore, of the search party, of the blood found at Grassy Pond.

"Minnie . . . I'm not sure where DooRay is. He went fishing early yesterday morning and didn't return home." Essie tried to smile. "Got a whole bunch of folks looking for him right this very minute."

Minnie stared at Essie, her face unbelieving. "DooRay didn't come home? You mean he's been gone all day yesterday and last night, too?"

Essie slowly stood. "That's right. Nobody knows what happened. We found his cane pole at the pond."

"Well, what about Murphy? He gone, too?" Minnie's voice became harsh, an anger that demanded answers.

Essie reached out and placed her hand on Minnie's arm. "Murphy's missing, too."

The black girl stomped to the door of the barn and shouted. "Doo-Ray! DooRay!" A call that beckoned the thin, one-armed man with heart-felt urgency. If the search party couldn't find DooRay, then Minnie Pryor would. Her chest heaved as she called, "Murphy!" She hollered "Doo-Ray" again, her voice cracking, a sob on the surface.

"Minnie, lots of folks are looking for DooRay. And, they're going to find him. They've been searching since daylight, and it won't be long before they'll be back here with news."

Minnie pulled away from Essie and ran toward Sally, throwing herself onto her back, and grabbing the reins. "Miss Essie, I ain't staying in this here barn another minute while my friend is out there in the rain needin' my help." She kicked Sally in the sides and the mule jerked forward in a fast trot, out into the rain, her narrow hooves slapping the earth and throwing mud into the air.

Essie watched Minnie until she disappeared at the end of the lane, the rain whipping the mule and its rider. Lightning flashed, cracking like gunfire, and streaking across the dark sky into white heat.

The storm had moved east/northeast across the Withlacoochee River and into southern Georgia, taking the fast-moving clouds toward the ocean and leaving a limitless vision of blue skies across the county.

Essie left the barn and walked halfway down the farm lane, under tree limbs still dripping with rain water. She noticed there were no signs of Sally's hoof prints, all washed away by the deluge of rain. Her heart sank. The storm had not only washed away the mule's hoof prints, but also those of DooRay and Murphy. And, she thought with growing anxiety, any signs of who had harmed her beloved DooRay.

She turned and slowly walked back to the house and onto the porch where she sat in the cypress swing. Patti Crafton and Rana Terry would return any moment to prepare lunch for the search party, probably tomato sandwiches. She wondered if there were a few watermelons in the field north of the house that could be served. Her eyes teared. DooRay loved watermelon and tomato sandwiches.

# CHAPTER TWELVE

Sam Washington holstered Hubert Donnelly's Smith and Wesson and saddled up Lum Townsend's gentle white mare, Lady, and struck out across the Townsend's farmland south of the Donnelly's three-hundred acres and within two hundred yards of Grassy Pond.

Sam, despite his gregarious personality, both in the courtroom and out in the world, had a streak of wayward, almost mutinous, perspective on situations out of his control. His mind, turbulent and miles away from conformity, caused him to become a recalcitrant individual who had a hard time taking orders or acquiescing to the sway of a crowd.

Hence, his somewhat defiant decision to begin his own search for DooRay Aikens. He gently pressed his knees into Lady's belly and urged her forward along the Bellville road. Lum Townsend, Madison County's preeminent cattle rancher, had readily offered a horse to Sam, casually mentioning to stay away from Thunder, a disagreeable horse who could bite, kick and, generally, buck a good cowboy ten feet into the air.

Sam wondered why Lum kept Thunder as one of his round up cow ponies. "I don't get it, Lum," Sam had remarked when he stood outside Thunder's stall. "Why would you keep such a dreadful horse? He's not exactly a champion, you know."

Lum had become thoughtful while he reached out and rubbed Thunder's nose. Lum, a thin, lanky man, who walked with a limp, was never in a hurry to talk. He stepped up on a plank and removed a brush from a nail and began brushing Thunder's neck while the horse stood quietly behind the wall of his pen.

"Well, it's like this, Sam," he said, his voice deep and reflective. "Thunder's no different than a human. He's got his hang-ups. His peculiarities, his brooding. But, that's no reason to throw him away. I just try to understand him. Just like I try to understand people." Lum returned the brush to the nail and stepped off the plank.

He grinned at Sam. "Just like you, Sam. I understand why you want to go off by yourself to look for DooRay. Nothing wrong with that. We're all in this together, doing what we need to do." He looked over at Thunder. "And, this here horse? Why, he's a loner. Don't get into his space unless he wants you to."

The cowboy squinted his eyes at Sam. "You got your space, Sam. And nobody's goin' to bother you. Ride out and find DooRay and Murphy."

Lum walked out into the farmyard, his bad leg swinging his body to and fro, like a metronome a tad out of kilter. Sam watched him for a long while, a poignant thought crossing his mind: *the last of the Madison County cowboys.*

The lawyer-turned-cowboy guided Lady along the edge of the Bellville road, a clay road the color of a sweet potato, and looked for tracks of any kind. The discovery of tire tracks along the edge of the road by Son Stokely the day before proved significant. The tracks were definitive, a deep tread in the tire indicating a truck tire, its track wide and deep into the dirt. *Whoever owned this truck is the culprit*, thought Sam.

At no urging from Sam, Lady continued along the road, her tail swishing now and then. A half-mile into the search, he guided Lady across the road and south, into the vast stretch of woods bordering the Townsend's two-hundred acre farm. Lady weaved in and out of the trees while Sam kept his eyes searching for anything out of the ordinary.

On the trail, birds flitted across the path in front of them, but Lady

THE MAN SHE CALLED DARLING

didn't flinch. Only a few yards away, a rabbit casually hopped down the path in front of them, its white tail a beacon, as if saying *follow me, follow me*. Evidence of fallen trees lay around them, rotting and becoming rich humus over a period of years, insects helping the decomposition along.

Beneath a large maple, he reined Lady to a standstill and raised up in the saddle. His eyes swept the shaded land where pines, maples, oaks and hickory stood in harmony among the wood ferns. From the west, he heard distant thunder and knew a June storm was on the way.

A feeling of uneasiness pushed into his mind, the missing DooRay a blatant reminder of the fragility of life. His next thought was of Essie. Known as the hard woman of Madison County, it was not truly the real Essie. Sam knew her tenderness, her care of others. Knew DooRay was her heart, a man who completed the farm life she and her sister Jewell had lived prior to Jewell's death.

At that moment, deep in the woods, Lady stopped, nervously pawed the ground, then moved forward a few steps. She nickered quietly, a vibrating sound from her throat, and stepped backwards, then forwards. Another nicker, louder, her mouth open. She was communicating to someone or something as Sam kneed her gently and eased forward into the woods, his heart beginning to race.

"What's up, girl. Tell me. You take the lead." Sam grinned. Was Lady one of those old cowboy horses, like the Lone Ranger's Silver, Roy Rogers' Trigger? Did she have within her a reasoning mind, an understanding that surpassed a horse's typical intelligence?

It was evident that Lum had seen something special in this small white mare, only fifteen hands high, when he bought her. Sam imagined Lady rushing to get the fire truck to put out a house fire, stomping bandits who had robbed a bank. He laughed out loud. In a far away place in his mind, he heard a faint call, and tilted his head to listen. "Hi, yo, Ladeeeeeeeeeeeeeeeeeee!"

"Lady, I think I'm in love," he said, as he loosened the reins, relaxed his knees and sat back in the saddle. Lady acknowledged her rider's intent and pushed through the ferns and brush. Sure-footed, she knew exactly where she wanted to go.

About thirty yards away, Lady slowed to a stop and swished her tail. *Here,* she said, *here. Murphy is right here. Can't you see him?*

Sam saw nothing. He slid from the saddle and let the reins drop. "Okay, Lady. Let's take a look see." Lady remained still, waiting, her head arched.

From a few yards away, a sound similar to a baby's cry drifted from the underbrush. Weak and sporadic, the cry caused Lady to whimper and shake her head.

Sam walked slowly toward the sound, moving brush aside, searching. There is was again. Another cry. Only closer. And there, in a clump of wood ferns, lay Madison County's most beloved goat.

Easing to the ground by the old goat, Sam touched his face. "Well, look at you, Murphy," he said softly. "Looks like you've been into some trouble." Sam's hands ran over the goat's body, along his back where his hair was matted with dried blood. His legs were covered in mud; not a very pretty goat.

When Sam lifted Murphy's leg, a hole in his thigh oozed blood, a small wound but serious. "Looks to me like you took a bullet, you poor goat." Murphy tried to lift his head, but couldn't. He was panting, his body weak.

Sam stepped a few yards away and picked up Lady's reins. "Come on, girl. We've got a job to do." When he pulled Lady alongside Murphy, he rubbed the mare's neck. He whispered in her ear. "Do you kneel on command, Lady?"

Lum Townsend's horses were not ordinary horses. His skill in training them was renowned, not only in Madison County, but all surrounding counties as well. As Sam spoke to Lady, he tugged downward on her reins, her chin tucking into her chest. She backed up a few steps and, unbelievably, knelt and then lay down in the soft green ferns. *Bless you, Lum Townsend.*

Sam, astonished, praised Lady. "Good girl. Good girl." He next leaned over Murphy. "Hey, boy. Reckon you can stand up?" He placed his arms around the goat and gently pulled. "Come on, Murphy. Let's do this." Murphy bleated loudly in protest, but, with Sam's help, pulled himself to a standing position, his legs quivering.

In one swift motion, Sam positioned Murphy across the saddle. "Lady, rise and shine, you beautiful horse!"

Lady easily rose from her bed of ferns, the injured goat slumped across the saddle. The pairing was inexplicable. How did Lady know she needed to lie down, then carry the goat to safety? The white mare began a slow walk, Sam alongside her holding onto Murphy, and ambled through the woods, the path familiar to her.

A half mile farther through the woods, the tin roof of the Townsend horse shelter came into view. At the east end of a field, Argentine bahia grass rose a foot high, soon to be sweet hay, its tops blowing in the wind. Lady quickened her step; she knew the pasture was her home.

At the edge of the woods, Sam glanced west and saw black, rolling clouds, like a herd of buffalo, heading their way. "Come on, Lady. Let's get inside." They walked quickly, the wind picking up, the rain moving closer.

The mare, with Murphy across the saddle, eased into the small shelter where hay was stacked high around them, giving off a sweet, pungent smell.

Sam broke a bale of hay and spread it out, a dry bed for the injured goat. He eased the goat from the saddle and placed him gently on the hay, covering him with a horse blanket. He placed fresh water nearby. "You're gonna be fine, Murphy. Just hang in there. Dr. Davis will be out here soon and fix you up just right."

"Lady!" he called, grabbing her reins and pulling himself into the saddle. "Let's try to make it through the woods before the rain hits. Can you run, girl?"

Lady nickered, raising her head and seeming to feel Sam's urgency. "Was that a *yes*?" He pressed her sides with his knees and the mare lunged forward, across the field in a full run, her legs stretching long and sure, her hooves hitting the ground hard, kicking up dirt behind. Then, finding a trail as they entered the woods, she slowed to a fast trot, Sam giving her no commands. She knew exactly where he wanted to go.

Near the Bellville road, the black clouds unleashed torrents of rain, the raindrops fat and heavy. Thirty yards away, Lon Terry's grist mill came into view. Sam urged Lady into a fast trot, through the open doorway, and into the comforting sweet smell of grain. The rain whipped around them, while lightning struck with ferocious white light, the crack of it sounding like a bullwhip in the hands of an angry cowboy.

Sam patted Lady's neck and leaned back into the saddle. DooRay Aikens was on his mind. He was certain the beloved Pinetta man needed shelter, needed care, needed a little heavenly intervention.

# CHAPTER THIRTEEN

If ever there was a true cowboy in Madison County, it was Roy Columbus Townsend. Known as 'Lum' since birth, his expertise on a cow pony was heralded across several counties, as well as the San Pedro range where wild, scrawny cattle had the run of thousands of acres.

The cowboy would shy away if you asked him which horse was his favorite. But, everyone knew it was Hickory, a chestnut, sixteen hands high, with a white marking on his forehead in the shape of a naked woman. The image drew many a young teenage boy to Lum's horse pasture to see the 'naked woman.'

If you saw Lum on Hickory, his two Catahoula leopard hounds were nearby. There was Lep, gray and black spotted and shy until it was round-up time. Sport, a female, was slightly more gregarious than Lep, a perpetual grin on her long face. Their long, whip-like tails moved furiously when they were on the hunt. Nothing deterred them, except perhaps Lum's sharp whistle.

The somewhat rare dogs, not a true hound, but curs, had webbing almost to the end of the toes. The webbing was an asset in marsh land and water where the dogs trudged to rout cows. They were bred hundreds of years ago, thought to have been brought by the Native American Indians from Europe and Asia to track wild animals, and finally, in the northeast Florida ranges, they herded cattle, then penned them with the expertise of a bullwhip that was on fire.

Lep's eyes held typical Catahoula traits, one eye blue, the other a light brown with blue mingled throughout. Though bred to hunt wild boar, Lep and Sport seemed content to work alongside the cowboy. The two hounds completed Lum's roundup partnership: a soft-spoken cowboy, a gentle horse and two spirited hounds.

Lum rode east on the Bellville road, stopping at the old rickety bridge over the Withlacoochee. Still in the saddle, he looked down the middle of the steel-truss bridge and savored its memories. As a boy, he jumped from the wooden bridge and swam south down the slow-moving river until it reached a bend, where a white sandbar waited for a young boy to rest.

He jumped from the bridge long before a horse fell on him and crushed his leg. The injury kept him from ever swimming again. The horse, not the splendor of the blackwater river, became his best friend.

The early sun barely topped the trees that bordered the river, leaving long shadows in the soft morning. Lum surveyed the river, the northeast boundary of Madison County, its tea-colored water seeming to amble along with no place to go.

The banks were high, and cut out by limestone ledges that formed small shoals, a precarious river bank for humans, yet perfect access for wild animals. Off a small sandbar on the west side of the river, an alligator slid into the water. Hickory saw it, too, and swished his tail. "Gotta watch them gators, old boy. A big 'un would eat a horse real quick like!"

Lum laughed out loud and eased Hickory off the bridge, to the west side of the river and began his search for DooRay Aikens. Up high along the banks, he walked the chestnut slowly along the terrain where wild blackberries were abundant. The banks were thick with longleaf cypress, river birch, oaks and pines.

Rosemallow waved their pink flowers at river herons whose long legs disappeared into the dark water. Birds flitted in and out of the fringed branches of the river mimosas that lined the limestone ledges.

At a bend in the river, about a half mile on the trail, the forlorn shack of Tayki, an old Miccosukee woman, came into view. "Hello, the house!" yelled Lum, not wanting to scare the woman.

He reined in Hickory and sat quietly. The stillness was peaceful, only the chatter of birds. "Hello, the house," he called again, moving Hickory forward.

Tayki's shack was tucked into a deep cut-out in the river. If heavy spring rains brought the river high, Tayki carted the house, piece by piece, to higher ground. Then, when the water receded, she'd return, along with the debris that comprised her home.

Lum kneed Hickory to move on when a head popped out of the side of the sticks and lumber that simulated a wall. "What you want, horseman?" she asked, brusquely, no friendliness in her words, a rough voice carrying the wildness of an animal.

"Hello, Tayki." The woman had lived on the river for years, probably the only Miccosukee Indian left in the area. Though she wasn't a friendly sort, everyone in Pinetta knew her and referred to her as Miccosukee Mae.

Tayki didn't answer. Her wild hair covered her eyes, her mouth a straight line of coldness. She stepped out onto the bank and picked up a stick and threw it at him.

"Now, now, Tayki, there's no need for that." Lum stepped down from his saddle and tied Hickory to a small sapling. "Stay where you are, Tayki. I'm coming down."

"Ha!" Tayki hollered. "Don't want no company today."

"I'm not staying long," said Lum, grabbing the limbs of small trees to help him maneuver to her shack.

"No coffee for you. No food for you. Just old Indian woman." She picked up another stick and Lum watched it arc over his head.

"Just hold on a minute." A few more steps and Lum was on the white sand of the riverbank. "Settle down, Tayki. You know who I am."

Through half-closed eyes, Tayki stared at Lum, then sniffed the air. "You cowboy man." Her voice softened. "You bring Tayki meat?"

"No, no meat, Tayki. I'm here on business. Got some things I need to talk over with you."

Tayki hung her head, her chin resting on a dirty plaid shirt. "Tayki no steal. Tayki no go in barn."

Lum shook his head. "I'm not accusing you of anything."

Her mouth was a black hole when she opened it. No teeth, just wet, receded gums. "Tayki good woman." She wore a pair of old gray pants several sizes too big, a zipper in the front, a rope belt through the loops and the legs rolled up, exposing ragged socks the color of cow manure. Her shoes didn't match; one black, the other a dark brown with the toe cut out.

"Yes, you are," he said gently. Lum moved closer, the odor of the woman finding him. "Tayki, there's no problem. Don't worry. Just listen to me."

He looked around the campsite. Tayki's pet lay stretched out on a log near the water's edge. A black snake she had befriended many winters past. An odd friendship that had begun when the Indian woman found him curled up inside her shack when temperatures dipped into the thirties.

Lum cleared his throat. "Look me in the eye, Tayki. Have you seen DooRay?" Her eyes seemed endless black caverns, almost as if she was blind, the pupil the color of the iris.

The old woman huffed. "One-arm no fish here. I throw rock at him." She grinned, triumphant. "Tayki's river."

Lum nodded. "When's the last time you saw anybody on the river?" he asked. "Any river traffic? Seen anything unusual?"

The old woman's toothless gums glistened, her smile incongruous with her unfriendly behavior. "Nobody but Indian woman."

"You sure about that? Nobody messing around the river?"

"Nobody." She licked her lips and pulled a can of snuff from a side pocket. "You go now."

Lum nodded. "You see anything, walk on up to Mr. Terry's store and let him know."

"You go now," she said again.

Lum started back up the riverbank, his back turning when her raspy voice followed him. "You seen Cat?"

Lum shifted on the top of the bank and looked down at her. "Cat? No, no cat."

Tayki looked around above him, up into the trees. "He gone two days."

"If I see your cat in the woods, I'll bring it to you." He paused. "What's his name?"

The woman grinned. "You no bring cat. Panther. Sleep with me. Keep me warm. Cat bring you here. Eat you."

A high-pitched peal of laughter shot through the woods, making the hair on Lum's neck stand straight up. He hurried to Hickory, shoved his boot in the stirrup and swung his leg over the saddle. Hickory was nervous; the old woman's laughter had spooked her, obvious as she dug her hooves in the dirt and sprinted into the woods.

The search along the woods that lined the river carried Lum a mile south. A diligent search proved fruitless. Nothing unusual in the woods. A few old campsites from years past. A moonshine still, rusted and dilapidated, lay scattered in a clearing. The ghost of times gone by drifted from the earth and into the tall trees above. He was certain if he scoured the earth, he'd find arrowheads from the many Indian tribes who frequented Madison County in the 1800's.

Lum led Hickory back to the Bellville bridge and met up with his brother, George, who had searched the woods to the north. Right away, he noticed his brother fidgeting in the saddle

"Not a blasted thing," said George. "Nobody's been camping, fishing. Nothing."

Lum leaned forward in the saddle and swiped a horse fly from Hickory's neck. "I talked with Tayki. She sees and hears everything on this river, but says she ain't see DooRay or anyone else."

"I can't believe she was cooperative. Usually, she throws rocks at me if I get near her camp." George glanced west. "Hear that thunder? Let's get on back to the Donnelly barn before there's a downpour."

Lum looked at his watch. "Gettin' near noon. Everybody's probably reported in. Let's go see what's happening."

The two men turned their horses west, down the Bellville road, leaving the calm river and its Miccosukee guardian. Lum shifted in his saddle.

"George, it's been over twenty-four hours since DooRay left to go fishing. There's not too many places he could be around here without somebody knowing about it."

George nodded in agreement. "You reckon somebody has DooRay at their house, taking care of him? Hiding him?"

The two brothers rode side-by-side for a long moment without talking. "Could be," Lum finally said, his mind anxious, the disappearance of DooRay settling hard in his heart. He felt DooRay had gotten into some kind of trouble with someone unknown to him or, for that matter, anyone else in Madison County.

"Simmie's probably already talked with most everybody about a stranger passing through. Let's mention it to him, anyway."

Lightning flashed in the distance as if Morse code. Flash. Flash. Flash. And, then the boom of thunder rolled across the sky.

Hickory flicked his ears and picked up speed when George's horse Bucky eased in front of him. At that moment, the two horses shot forward, their hooves pounding into the clay road, their necks stretched out.

Lum kicked Hickory's side, leaned low in the saddle and clicked his tongue loudly. George took off his hat and slapped it on Bucky's rump. The race was on.

Hickory in the lead, his tail flying, when Bucky eased up on his rear, George waving his hat wildly. Hickory was not to have it. His muscled forelegs lunged forward and gained ground, leaving Bucky at least a length behind.

Bucky, his shorter legs pumping hard, picked up speed and, in moments, was neck to neck with the big chestnut. George leaned forward and whispered in Bucky's ear. "Beat that no-good rascal and I'll give you extra feed tonight."

# CHAPTER FOURTEEN

The rain passed quickly, leaving the Bellville clay road slick with thick mud. Puddles dotted the lane to the Donnelly farm, while rain dripped from the many crepe myrtles and dogwoods that stood along the edge of the nearby woods.

The search for DooRay had come to a standstill as members of the search party straggled in, some drenched, unable to find shelter in the woods. They gathered around the picnic table near the barn and waited for the remainder of the search party to arrive. Hot coffee made the rounds as the men recapped their search.

Son Stokely wiped rainwater from the table and laid out the grid map of the area searched. He marked off each section as the men reported in. "Got to hear from Lum and George." He paused. "Haven't heard from Sam Washington, Mutt Everett, J. B. Hinton, and, let's see . . . the Reaves brothers and Sniffer."

From the lane, Simmie Moore pulled his car to a stop. Wet clay smeared the sides of his 1956 black Ford, a sure sign he'd been down the Bellville road at a significant speed.

The sheriff's face bore grim lines as he slowly walked to the farm-yard. "Just met up with Sam Washington coming across the road at Lon's grist mill. He tells me he found Murphy about a mile south of here, over on the Townsend property. Said the goat had been shot. Almost dead."

The men looked at one another, their thoughts racing. Whoever had shot Murphy was a mean rascal and certainly capable of hurting DooRay. Their faces turned into granite, leaving no doubt anger brewed within them.

Simmie sat at the picnic table. Weary, he put his head in his hands for a moment, then continued. "I radioed for Dr. Davis to go out to the Townsend place and take a look at Murphy. He's on the way there now."

Coming down the lane, Sam and Lady sidestepped the puddles and ended up beneath the trees in the back of the house. Sam let Lady's reins fall to the ground while he swung out of the saddle and headed for hot coffee and the latest news. He was weary, but found himself encouraged at having found Murphy.

"Any news?" he asked, looking at Son. He grabbed a cup and poured coffee.

"Not a thing. We've got a few folks still out, but due in any time." The big man shook his head. "It's like DooRay done been swallowed by a hole in the ground." He glanced west. "'Course, the Reaves boys haven't reported in. No telling where Sniffer has taken them."

"One thing's for certain," said Ivy Wiglesworth, who had just returned to the Donnelly farm. "Any tracks have been wiped out by this rain." He slapped his hat against a tree and water flew in every direction.

"That's true," said Simmie. "But, that dog is amazing. He can hold a scent even if it rains and then pick it up again somewhere. Don't count him out."

Mutt Everett walked up behind the group of men. He'd been in the northern grid, all the way to the Mt. Horeb church. His pants were covered with sticktights, a water mark up to his knees.

"That was a toad strangler, weren't it? Didn't last long, but it dumped a bucket or two." He moved into the crowd, his attention keen.

"Tell everybody about Murphy, Sam," said Simmie.

Sam nodded and stepped closer to the picnic table. He reached out and touched the part of the grid that was Townsend land. "Here's where I started."

His finger stabbed the area of the Bellville road where Son Stokely had found tire tracks. "I moved up Bellville about a half mile and crossed over into the woods. Lady and I took it kinda slow. You know, checking everything out. Wasn't too far into the woods that Lady nickered several times." Sam chuckled. "I knew it was horse talk, for sure."

He glanced over at Lady and pointed. "That's a smart horse over there. She led me right to where Murphy was stretched out in a bed of wood ferns."

Sam gathered his thoughts for a moment. "The old goat was quite weak and, after examining him, I discovered he'd been shot."

"Shot!" yelled J. B. Hinton. "Who'd shoot DooRay's goat?" J. B.'s ears turned red, his eyes blazing. "Stuff like that don't happen 'round here." He stomped in a circle, balling his fists by his side.

"Now, hold on, J. B. We'll figure this out." Simmie held up his hand. "Go on, Sam."

Sam took a deep breath. "I could tell Murphy was hurtin', real weak. I laid him across Lady's saddle and took him to the horse shelter over at Lum's. It was only a half mile away. He's over there now."

"You reckon he'll be alright, Sam?" Lon Terry, quiet and brooding, straightened his large Stetson hat.

"Don't know, Lon. We'll see what Dr. Davis says."

From the farm lane, two horses approached, their riders hunched in the saddle. Wet and tired, George and Lum Townsend trotted to the barn and left their horses tethered at a railing. The rain had caught them a half mile from the Donnelly farm, despite the speed of their horses. Fast moving, the front had moved into south Georgia.

"Come on over," called Son. "You're the last ones in 'cept for the Reaves brothers. Anything to report?"

George and Lum crossed the farmyard, Lum's limp prominent. The brothers gratefully reached for coffee and moved into the circle of men.

Lum shook his head. "Nothing of significance. We covered a lot of ground along the river, George to the north. Me, south." He sipped his coffee.

"I met up with Tayki." Lum looked around the group. "All of you know Miccosukee Mae. After she attacked me with a stick or two, she told me she knew nothing. Hadn't seen DooRay. I asked her to let us know if she saw anything unusual on the river."

George stepped in. "But, you all know how the old woman is. She keeps to herself. She won't be telling us anything. It's *her* river. She throws rocks at anybody who comes around and then runs and hides in the woods, taking that damn black snake with her, all wrapped around her neck."

"Don't be too hard on her, George. She's cranky sometimes – possessive of her river," said Lon.

Simmie pointed to Son. "Everybody accounted for?"

Deputy Stokley smoothed out the grid map. "Looks like everybody's reported in 'cept that bloodhound, and the results are the same for everyone: no clues as to DooRay's disappearance. Of course, Sam found Murphy."

Simmie commented. "Finding Murphy tells us whoever's involved has a weapon. It's possible Dr. Davis will find a bullet in Murphy's leg and we'll go from there as far as identifying the gun."

The group of men spoke quietly among themselves, concern on their faces. "What's next, sheriff?" called Durward Sapp, a farmer east of the Donnelly farm.

Simmie Moore knew the men were all thinking the same thing. Just didn't want to say it. And, as sheriff of Madison County, it was up to him to broach the subject: Whether or not to drag the pond for DooRay's body.

"Well, folks," Simmie's voice caught. "We've done a lot of searching . . . "

The sound of loud barking came through the woods from the east. The Reaves brothers dipped under a barbed wire fence, a leash around Sniffer's neck. Wet and covered with mud, Sniffer flopped down in the grass along the fence where the brothers attached his leash to the fence post and joined Simmie at the picnic table.

The two brothers, Booter and Feller, were out of breath. They'd been tracking for hours. There wasn't a dry spot on them. Mud covered their boots, pants, and shirts. Splattered with mud, their faces were unrecognizable.

Mutt handed them coffee. The men quieted and moved in closer. "Glad you're back safe," said Simmie. "Reckon you've been just about everywhere in this county," he said with a half-smile as he glanced at their muddy faces.

Fred Glass handed the brothers a big bandana. Booter swiped his face, revealing scratch marks across his cheek. "Dang near went up to Kentucky and back," he said, tossing the bandana to Feller.

Booter laughed. "We couldn't keep up with that dog. Seems like Sniffer just wanted to run."

"That so?" Simmie glanced over at the bloodhound. He was as muddy as his handlers. Stretched out on the grass, he was unconcerned with the drama unfolding around him.

"Here's what we think, sheriff." Booter finished his coffee and motioned for more. "Old Sniffer done taken DooRay's scent real good. Took us straight to the pond, Mr. Ran's pond at the bottom of the hill. He messed around the pond for quite a while, moving all around it. Looks like he got confused when he got to the south side of the pond. He worked hard around the Bellville road area when he picked up a strong scent. He followed that scent down the Bellville quite a way, then cut north, about a half-mile from the river. Then, he cut east to the river and stayed on the trail up and down that river bank for a mile or so."

"Right!" said Feller. "Seems like he wanted to jump in the water."

Booter scratched his head. "Then, the trail went as cold as a beaver's tit. Old Sniffer stopped dead still and wouldn't go no farther."

Feller shrugged his shoulders. "That's when we headed back here. Got caught in all that rain. Couldn't find a dry spot anywhere. Lightning 'bout cooked us."

Simmie nodded, his mind traveling in many directions. Finally, he glanced at the circle of men. "Anybody have any questions?"

"What do you think all this means?" asked Moses Robinson.

"I'll tell you what it means," yelled Paul Ellington from across the farmyard. "It means DooRay done been kidnapped."

From the porch steps, Essie walked into the group of men and glanced at the tired faces. "I've been listening a while," she said quietly. Her lips quivered. "DooRay's gone. That's all there is to it."

Sam stepped by her side and touched her shoulder. "We're not giving up, Essie."

She looked up at him, her brow furrowed. "Think we should go ahead and drag Ran's pond?"

# CHAPTER FIFTEEN

Rana Terry, Shirley Crafton and Cora McLeod placed platters of corn on the cob, fried chicken, sliced tomatoes and bowls of acre peas with steamed okra on top on the picnic table in the farmyard.

Essie slid a large bowl of potato salad across the table and wiped her hands on her apron. Gallons of sweet iced tea lined the table along with two apple pies baked by Inez Terry, blackberry dumplings from Shirley Wiglesworth's kitchen, a chocolate cake baked by Gladys Robinson and a batch of oatmeal cookies just out of Essie's oven.

The men filled their plates, talking among themselves about the missing DooRay. There was much speculation about who had brought harm to the beloved one-armed black man who for years traversed Madison County in an old wooden cart pulled by his goat Murphy.

Rob Crafton, the front of his shirt covered with cookie crumbs, had been quiet during most of the discussions. It seemed, though, that he had carefully put together a scenario he believed to be the answer to the ongoing mystery as to the whereabouts of DooRay Aikens.

"I'm a thinkin' this," his gruff voice bellowed across the table. "If'n DooRay was fishin' at the pond, it's quite possible a gator got him."

"A gator," yelled George Townsend. "Ain't no gator knows how to shoot a gun. Yer forgettin' that old goat done been shot."

"That's right," said Paul Ellington, shoving a fork full of apple pie in his mouth. "It seems to me we've got to search that pond, for sure. 'Cause somebody shot him and threw him in the pond. We'll find DooRay alright. And a bullet in him, too, I bet."

Fred Glass jumped from the table and slammed his fists together. "Don't you go talkin' that kind of nonsense, Paul. I, for one, ain't thinking DooRay's dead." He glared across the table. "Talk like that doesn't do anybody any good."

Simmie lifted his hand. "Boys, let's be civil. We have no answers right now." He paused and looked skyward. Another round of dark clouds continued to move in. Full of rain, they would cover Madison County within the hour. "We have very little to go on. We've got Murphy with a bullet in him. We've got a bloodhound who found DooRay's scent near the river. And, that's about it." He turned to Lon Terry.

"Lon, I've been thinking about any strangers in the area. Anybody in your store lately you hadn't seen before?"

The Irishman, his red hair streaked with gray, wiped his mouth and shifted his brown eyes to the sheriff. He pushed his glasses further up his nose. A tall man, freckled from head to toe, Lon became contemplative for a long moment. "Come to think of it, there was two fellas bought some chewing tobacco 'bout 7:00 yesterday morning. They was from . . . Alabama, I believe."

Lon cocked his head. "Hey, Rana!" Rana Terry looked his way. "Those two fellas come in early yesterday at the store? You see 'em?"

Rana, a short, round woman with brown hair and known for her macaroni and cheese, nodded. "Sure did. They was drivin' a red pickup truck. Not from 'round here."

"Hey!" hollered Emmett Gaston. "I seen that truck fly past the Donnelly's yesterday mornin' . . . I'd say 'bout 8:00."

Simmie and his deputy, Son, exchanged glances, their minds going to the tire tracks on the edge of the Bellville road, near Ran Terry's pond.

"Looks like we got us somethin' else to go on," said Ivy, looking around the group, his Adam's apple extending as he looked up to the sky. "'Course, with all this rain comin' in, we're at a standstill, I'd say."

From the farm lane, a pick-up truck eased forward and parked alongside Fred Glass' tractor, only a few feet from the barn. A dog's head popped out of the open window on the passenger side, his attention on Sniffer, who slept peacefully by the fence. Rufus, a black and tan Beagle, was Dr. Davis' long time companion on his house calls. The dog lifted his nose and sniffed the air and wondered if there was any chicken left for him.

Dr. James Aubrey Davis, Madison County's long-time veterinarian, both small and large animal, spoke to his dog. "Stay in the truck, you hear. Don't want you gettin' into any trouble." He patted the dog on the head, his wide pendant ears silky smooth, and walked across the farmyard.

"Hello, gentlemen," he said, removing his hat and swiping his hand across his hair. He then pointed to the picnic table. "I sure hope you saved me a slice of that there cake. Is that Gladys Robinson's chocolate cake?"

"Come fix a plate," called Rana. "Plenty left." Rana found a clean plate and handed it to Dr. Davis. "Try some of Shirley's blackberry dumplings, too."

Dr. Davis grinned. He'd been up since daylight. A calf to deliver, the little thing stuck for hours. Then, a pony's ear had to be sewn together. Seems a barbed wire fence got him.

The reputation of the gregarious doctor ran far and wide, his most renowned accomplishment being the repair of Hoot Gibson's bull, Romeo, who was totally remiss in his performance capabilities the previous summer. The two-thousand dollars Hoot paid for the bull seemed wasted, all his cows lonely and neglected as the eighteen hundred pound bull moped in the corner of the pasture the entire summer, totally impotent.

Had it not been for Miccosukee Mae's mysterious gray powder, which Dr. Davis had administered in Romeo's food, the bull would have gone to slaughter. Romeo became known as the "the miracle bull," his prowess as a lover unsurpassable.

Dr. Davis poured sweet tea and found Sheriff Moore leaning against a fencepost. "Afternoon, Simmie. You look mighty tired. Lot going on and this weather isn't helping, is it?"

"Jim." Simmie nodded. "Had a lot of rain. More comin'."

Dr. Davis glanced over his shoulder, then turned back to Simmie and lowered his voice. "Got something for you." He reached in his pocket and pulled out a spent bullet. A small piece of metal, a tad larger than a pencil eraser, lay in the doctor's hand. "Took this out of Murphy's thigh. It was lodged half-way between the thigh bone and the main muscle. Surprised it didn't go all the way through."

Simmie picked up the metal and examined it carefully. "The lab boys over in Jacksonville will take a good look at this. Few evidence bullets are intact, but this one looks pretty good for finding some rifling."

The sheriff slipped the bullet into his shirt pocket. "Tell me about Murphy."

Dr. Davis chuckled. "That's one tough goat. I was able to anesthetize him and remove the bullet with no problem. Patched up the wound. He lost blood after he was shot, but it clotted real good."

The doctor looked away for a moment, then back to Simmie, questioning. "What about our friend DooRay?"

"Don't know, Jim. We've got a few leads and we'll pursue them as soon as we can. Looks like two fellas passed through here yesterday morning. We'd like to talk with them if we can find them."

Jim Davis nodded. "Let's hope we can find DooRay soon. I'm troubled, Simmie. Things like this don't happen around here."

Simmie looked over at the crowd of men around the picnic table. "We've got some good neighbors here, Jim. Everyone of them friends of DooRay. If they have anything to say about it, they'll find DooRay."

"Well, one thing's for sure. Old Murphy is gonna make it. I gave him some good medicine. He's over in the Townsend horse shelter. Might want to have somebody check on him in a few hours. He's sleeping real good right now. He drank a pretty good amount of water before I left, just before those meds kicked in."

"Thanks, Jim. We'll probably bring him back over this way after awhile. I'm certain Essie will want to tend to him. I'll send some fellas over later."

Dr. Davis reached out his hand. "Keep me posted, Simmie. I've known DooRay and his family these past thirty years."

"I'll do that, Jim." Sheriff Moore slapped Dr. Davis gently on the back. "Thanks for mending Murphy."

The doctor laughed. "Can't let anything happen to that old goat." He scooped up a slice of chocolate cake and grinned at Gladys. "Moses sure is a lucky fella."

Dr. Davis ambled to his truck, gave Rufus a pat on the head and guided the truck down the farm lane and to the Bellville road.

Simmie removed his hat and walked around the back of the house and to the fence on the west side of the farmyard and looked out over the cornfield. He felt a weariness overtake him as he reached out and grasped a fencepost, felt his body sink as he lifted his foot and placed it on a strand of barbed wire. Then, the anger hit him. His body shuddered as the heat rose up through him. *I'll not drag that pond, DooRay. I want to hear you sing again.*

# CHAPTER SIXTEEN

Lightning flashed in the distance, its light running across the dark sky like racing white wolves in the night. Mountainous clouds pushed from the southwest, across the warm gulf, picking up abundant amounts of rain and unfurling it across Madison County.

The Donnelly's farmyard lay empty and quiet. Killer crouched atop the wellhouse where rain pounded his feathers. Still and unmoving, his once elegant tail drooped into an unknown sadness. His hens nearby, they roosted for the night, only an occasional soft caw.

The front porch swing moved slowly back and forth, its occupant pushing it with a bare foot, watching the rain and feeling the slow beat of her heart. When lightning flashed, Essie kept watch on the end of the farm lane. She imagined seeing the tall, lanky DooRay ambling toward her, his arm lifting in a wave. *Hey, Miss Essie, I done brought you some fish.*

"Come on home, DooRay," she said, her plea lost in the night, not heard by anyone, the words softened by the falling rain. She felt herself tremble. If she stayed awake all night, she'd be able to see him walk down the lane, just at daybreak, when the sun touched the tall cypress on the Withlacoochee. She'd hear his baritone voice sweep down the lane.

Yes, that's what she'd do. She'd stay awake and wait. Put a light on in the barn. Check on Murphy every few hours. She had bedded him down at dusk, an hour after the Townsend brothers carried him to her barn. Dr. Davis had done a good job doctoring the old goat. Murphy was full of good medicine and sleeping like a baby.

Then, she'd make a cake. DooRay's favorite cake. A pineapple upside down cake. She'd put extra pecans in it. She'd keep hot coffee on the stove with lots of sugar nearby.

But . . . first, she wanted to . . . pray. *A DooRay prayer.* To Almighty God. *Walk with me, dear Lord. I'm so weary and afraid. Give me strength to carry on, and wisdom to bear the pain . . .* Essie fell to her knees and released the tears that she had held back throughout the day. Her body shook and swayed, a low moan escaping her throat and floating into the black sky.

Rain blew across the porch. Cold and wet, Essie drew her body into a ball and closed her eyes. The night closed in around her and pushed her further into a deep cave. No sounds. Just the darkness. Then, a soft light. She slowly opened her eyes and smiled. There was DooRay. "Why, DooRay, you have two arms."

# CHAPTER SEVENTEEN

The soft gray light of dawn found Essie unmoving, her sleeping body still curled on the long front porch, her mouth open, a gentle whiffle escaping with each breath. Rain dripping from the porch roof played a rat-tat-tat on the large leaves of the caladiums that lined the porch steps, while nearby a single frog croaked loudly.

A fly landed on Essie's cheek and she slapped at it. "Shoo," she said, opening her eyes, almost at once wondering what day it was and where she was. Her face pressed the boards that lined the porch floor. She turned her head and looked up and saw the jasmine twisted around the porch columns.

Then, she remembered. *DooRay. Murphy.* She struggled to her feet, stiff and sore, and moved slowly to the swing. She wanted a cup of coffee. She hadn't brushed her hair in two days, nor bathed. She then felt the grit of her unbrushed teeth.

She leaned back in the swing and stretched her legs. She had sent Sam home in the early evening of the previous day. Unwilling to contend with the tragedy at hand, she wanted solitude. Sam's presence brought everything into reality; she didn't want that. She wanted to flee, wanted to deny that DooRay was missing. Sadly, when Sam left, she had floundered and realized how fragile she was and finally acknowledged the extent of her grief.

Essie looked up when a blue jay squawked above her, his body entwined in the jasmine, only his head exposed. Perhaps there was a nest.

In the yard, in the mist of early morning, there was motion. A gray thing moving with stealth, as if floating through the air; up, then down. Essie squinted her eyes and wondered if she really saw what she saw.

She rose from the swing and leaned on the porch rail. Closer she went, while watching a form settle in the middle of the yard. It hovered there, as gray as the sky, and blended into the earth. Essie wondered if it was a living thing or perhaps a mirage that had descended from an unearthly place.

Curious, she walked down the porch steps and observed 'the thing' coming to rest, a body forming. Eyes, nose, mouth. *Tayki!*

"Tayki! What are you doing?" Essie moved closer. Tayki rarely left her river shack, preferring the company of Slick, her six foot long black snake, to the friendship of humans. The Miccosukee Indian was harmless, though eccentric. She had lived along the Withlacoochee for decades, eating fish and raiding vegetables from nearby farms. Her favorite pastime throwing rocks at river traffic occupied most of her time.

Edging closer, Essie smelled the stench of the woman and hesitated "Tayki!" Essie yelled. "Open your eyes!"

The Indian woman was a left-behind, her family moving south to the Everglades when she was a little girl. Only ten years old, she hid in the woods on that winter day in 1907 and watched them go. She would not leave her river, the crooked river named the Withlacoochee. She knew the river's heartbeat, saw its life in the fish, turtles and alligators and remained there. As an adult, she bartered with Lon Terry at his general store. She brought him fish in return for salt, cornmeal and lard.

One day she handed Mr. Terry three freshly dressed chickens in exchange for nails and burlap sacks. The tall Irishman looked at the chickens for a long moment. Finally, he gave Miccosukee Mae a wry smile. His gruff voice eased out slowly. "Three of Miss Rana's chickens come missing early this mornin'."

Tayki lifted her dark eyebrows and shrugged. "Chickens no like Miss

Rana. Run away from home, maybe." She folded her arms and stared into the Irishman's brown eyes.

"Miss Rana fed them corn morning and night. They loved Miss Rana," he quipped, his skin turning red at his neck.

A quiet few minutes followed. Tayki's gaze settled on the head of a stuffed mountain goat mounted on the back wall of the store. She seemed to have an ethereal conversation with it before turning back to Mr. Terry.

"Miss Rana no sing to chickens. You must sing to chickens for them to be happy." She paused, chewing on the soft end of a palmetto frond. "They run away because they sad."

Lon Terry scoffed. "I'll take these chickens and give you one pound of nails and a half dozen burlap sacks."

Tayki smiled her toothless smile. "Hammer, too?"

"No hammer, Mae! If I was you, Mae, I'd not discuss this with Miss Rana."

Essie slammed her hands together in a loud clap. "I said open your eyes, Tayki!"

Slowly, Tayki opened them and she stared at Essie. The Indian's eyes were many colors: the iris of her right eye dark green, flecked with gold and black and slightly off center. The pupil focused over Essie's right shoulder and wavered as if looking for a passage to another land.

Tayki's left eye, smoky gray with blue streaks, found Essie's face. She stared, her pupil sharp and seeing. She had come back from that other place, the place far away, the place from long ago.

"DooRay dead."

Essie leaned forward. Her voice a harsh whisper, she said, "What did you say, Tayki?"

Tayki spoke again, her raspy voice lifting. "I say DooRay dead."

Essie lunged forward and grabbed the old woman's long hair and yanked her head backwards. "No, he's not," she screamed. From somewhere deep inside, Essie brought forth a snarl. "Shut your mouth! Don't you say that again."

Her gums empty of teeth, Tayki opened her mouth and emitted a low, quiet laughter from her chest, rumbling, escaping from her throat and, finally, breaking into the still morning. "Or, maybe, DooRay alive."

The strange eyes closed but the grin returned. "Or, maybe, DooRay dead," Tayki said, flinching back away from Essie.

Essie jerked Tayki's head back again and leaned into her face, her hand wrapped tightly around her dark hair. A guttural sound, deep and menacing, formed into words. "Take me to DooRay."

After a long moment, Tayki opened her eyes. "You follow me to river."

Essie released the straggly hair and stepped back, panting. "I'll get my car. You're riding with me."

Tayki slowly stood, her body crouched and bent into uneasiness. "Tayki no ride in car."

Essie grabbed Tayki's hair again and yanked her forward. "Yes, you are."

Parked near the barn, the Pontiac glistened with rain water. Killer scratched the earth nearby and skittered away when Essie hurried to the car, pulling a protesting Tayki.

"Get in," Essie commanded, opening the car door.

Tayki resisted, fright on her face. "No ride in car."

"Oh, yes, you are!" A frenzied Essie pushed Tayki, but the old woman grabbed the edge of the car door. Then, dropped to the ground, unrelenting.

Almost crazed, Essie fell to the ground alongside Tayki, tears running down her cheeks. "Tayki," she whispered, "we have to go to DooRay." A wildness in her eyes, she grasped Tayki's chin. "Please, Tayki, we have to hurry. DooRay needs us."

Tayki stared at Essie and reached up and removed the farm girl's hand from her chin. She examined Essie's face a long moment, her mismatched eyes taking in every detail. Finally, her body slumped. "Tayki ride outside car to river."

Essie, her heart beating wildly, frowned. Confused, she stammered. "Outside . . . outside the car?"

Tayki pointed. "Up there."

*Up there?* Essie glanced to the top of the car. "On top of the car?"

Tayki grinned. She nodded vigorously. "Fly like bird."

The 1948 Pontiac left the farm lane with Tayki firmly attached to the front fender, one hand gripping the hood ornament, the other waving in the air. The Indian's long hair caught in the wind and blew behind her like a horse's tail.

She began to chant unknown words into the sky, where they melded with the clouds and went to places not known to others. She sang songs to the Universe, perhaps to Chief Arpiucki, while she danced the green corn dance with him, young and free again.

It was two miles to the Withlacoochee. Down the wet clay road toward Bellville, where the river divided Florida and Georgia and wound its way quietly into memories of times past. The tires on the Pontiac slipped sideways, then forward, as the wet clay grabbed at the black rubber. Essie slowed and cussed at the old woman who hollered at the wind and shook her fist at the demons who followed her.

The river in site, Essie slowed the car and watched as Tayki pulled herself up and stood on the wide fender of the Pontiac, her shirt tail flapping in the wind. She lifted one leg, then the other, and began to dance. Her face to the sky, she called all her sisters and brothers, her snakes, the wild animals that roamed the vast woods around the river and wrapped her arms around them, speaking softly with words unknown to others.

The old Pontiac slowly slid to a stop along the side of the road near the old bridge, a narrow and decrepit passageway that oversaw the dark river and its myriad of secrets. The keeper of the river, Tayki jumped from the Pontiac's fender and landed in a crouched position atop the steep bank, her eyes open, searching.

# CHAPTER EIGHTEEN

A bolt of lightning struck nearby, its flash bright with anger. It was followed immediately by cannon-like thunder, the sound rumbling down the flatness of the river for miles, then fading into a quiet murmur.

Tayki shrieked loudly and cursed the sky in a distant language, her body gripping itself, then becoming as still as a statue, as if turned to stone. Her eyes closed, saliva trickled from the corner of her mouth.

From a few feet away, Essie grabbed a pine cone and threw it at her. "Get down that bank, Tayki. Where's DooRay?"

Tayki remained still, a gurgling in her throat. Finally, she turned and glared at Essie. "Quiet. Tayki thinking. Tayki see things. You shut up."

"What things? What things do you see?" Essie growled. She picked up another pine cone. "Come on." She threw the cone hard, striking Tayki in the chest. "I'm not telling you again, you old woman. You show me where DooRay is or I'll stomp you into the ground."

Tayki held up her hand and closed her eyes again. "I see One-arm. He's sleeping with alligator."

Essie grabbed Tayki's arm and pulled her down the steep bank, almost tumbling into the water. They landed on white sand, along the limerock edges of the bank, Essie's head scraping the side of a small river birch.

Tayki jumped to her feet and began a zig-zag walk to her shack, laughing with each step. "You hit head on tree, stupid white woman."

Blood trickled down Essie's forehead and into her eye. She pulled up her shirt tail and wiped the wound dry. She silently cursed Tayki as she followed her down the riverbank.

Tayki's shack was a quarter mile south, along the edge of the slow-moving river. They passed river mallow in bloom, and finally rounded a sharp bend that was the front yard of the Indian's shack.

Essie glanced at a log, a tree that had fallen in the river, about fifteen feet long. There, on the end lay a shiny, black stretch of snake.

"No touch Slick. He asleep."

"Don't worry. I don't touch snakes."

Tayki laughed again. "White woman just stomp on poison ivy."

At the shack, Tayki stepped onto the first rung of a homemade ladder that had been nailed into a nearby tree. A water oak, tall and leaning, provided a perfect vantage point for the Miccosukee woman's observance of river traffic. "Come," she said, gruff and commanding, as she pulled herself from one rung to the next.

Reluctantly, Essie did as she was told and followed the woman up the tree. At about twenty feet, Tayki moved out onto a thick limb, her body lying prone, pointing her boney finger. "One-arm," she said, matter-of-factly. She shrugged. "He dead." She turned and lifted her eyebrows at Essie. "Or alive."

Essie, her legs trembling, pulled herself onto a limb and pushed aside small branches to give herself a line of sight. She peered down the river, her heart thundering in her chest. Only a hundred yards away, on a snow-white sandbar on the opposite side of the river, lay the black body of DooRay Aikens, unmoving. Shirtless, he lay on his stomach, his left shoulder armless. A deep cavity where his arm should have been, lay exposed.

Essie shrank back. Her hand covered her mouth to stop the scream that waited in her throat. There, alongside DooRay, lay an eight foot alligator, as black as DooRay's skin. The gator's upper teeth lay exposed, despite its closed mouth. Eyes closed, it was if the reptile thoughtfully wondered what to do with the black man who lay within one foot of its smiling mouth.

# CHAPTER NINETEEN

The scream found its way into the quiet morning. Full of anguish, Essie's long, loud piercing cry awakened the river as though a giant predator had been unleashed, soon to devour every living thing.

Scrambling across the limb and to the top rung of the tree ladder, Essie pushed her body into a free fall, plunging fifteen feet to the ground below. She landed hard, her breath swooshing from her lungs.

Above Essie, crouched on a limb, Tayki considered the sprawled woman below her and chuckled. "White woman so stupid. I see no wings on your back."

Essie sucked in air and slowly stood. "DooRay," she croaked. "Got to get to DooRay." She turned and began running along the riverbank, brush slapping her face, a vine catching her ankle and sending her tumbling into the water.

Behind her, Tayki sashayed along the white sand, Slick around her neck. "No hurry, stupid girl. Dooray dead," she called. Slick eased from around her neck and slid down her chest onto the bank. He slithered into the water where a rotten log formed a perfect vantage point for the reptile, whose eyes feasted on a large frog at the end of the log.

Essie crawled from the water onto the riverbank and rested on her knees. She looked up at Tayki. "Get out of my way." Her eyes burned with hatred. She would kill the old woman if she said *DooRay dead* one more time. She would chop her body into little pieces and feed them to the fish. Then, she would burn her shack and all the things that remained of the crazy woman.

Essie lingered on the bank. Water dripped from her hair, the abrasion on her forehead oozing blood. Where had her Christian heart gone? She had murder on her mind, the teachings of Christ buried somewhere deep and perhaps unretriveable. Her fingers twitched while her teeth ground together, an explosive rage simmering within her.

Tayki stared at Essie, her mismatched eye wavering, looking for focus. Silently, Tayki lifted her right foot and slipped off her shoe, a man's shoe. A shoe that in no way resembled the shoe on the other foot. She then removed her left shoe, a blatant act of defiance spreading across her face.

Essie rose to her feet, watching Tayki. Unsteady, she twisted the end of her shirttail and river water rained on her feet. She waited.

Tayki reached up and removed her shirt, exposing small sagging breasts no bigger than fried eggs. She pulled her rope belt from the loops and let it drop to the sand. Her pants were zippered. She slid down the metal tab and, in only seconds, became as naked as the day she was born.

Her burnished skin the color of rawhide, Tayki dove into the dark tea-colored water and disappeared, leaving behind a pile of dirty clothes, her shoes and her rope belt. She also left behind Essie Donnelly, whose eyes were riveted on the sandbar, the smiling alligator and the still body of DooRay Aikens.

# CHAPTER TWENTY

Tayki's body sliced the surface of the water as though she were a knife. Thin and hard, she disappeared instantly, her powerful arms carving a path through the tannin-colored water to the sandy bottom.

She swam effortlessly for twenty yards, soon followed by a travel companion who eased alongside her, so close she could touch it. A river cooter, its large webbed feet moving smoothly, turned its yellow-striped head toward Tayki. The dark eyes spoke to the Indian woman.

Sixteen inches long, the cooter was a female, thirty years old. Though ordinarily shy, the streamlined body bumped Tayki and extended its long neck. *Shall we race*, she seemed to be saying.

Tayki kicked harder and shot ahead of the colorful carapaces that housed the turtle. Her lead was short-lived. The surprising strength of the webbed feet pushed the turtle past her, and Tayki grinned as it wiggled its tail and swam faster.

The two incongruous friends broke the surface of the water together, high into the air, ending in a loud splash. "Ah, Yellow Face! You beat Tayki again!" The Indian woman continued her swim with the river cooter beside her. They had been friends for years; a motley pair who knew the Withlacoochee as no other.

In her peripheral vision, Tayki saw Essie standing at the water's edge, only twenty-five yards away. Laughter bounced across the water. "Ha. You no can fly; you no can swim either, white woman."

Yellow Face slipped beneath the surface of the water, her webbed feet guiding her to a small cove on the opposite bank. The turtle had seen the stranger, seen the white legs half-way in the water.

Earlier, Essie had slipped off her bluejeans and now watched as Tayki swam leisurely toward the sandbar. "I can swim," she yelled. Her face twisted in irritation. "I can do anything you can do, Tayki."

Tayki laughed again. "Come. We talk to Tail." She beckoned her with her skinny arm, one bare breast breaking the water as she waved.

"Tail?" called Essie. Her eyes riveted to the woods across the river. Suspicious, she looked behind her and then down the riverbank that led south. "Who is Tail?"

The Miccosukee woman shrieked loudly and slapped the water with her hand. "Oh, you so stupid. You no can fly, you no can swim and you no can talk alligator talk."

She dipped beneath the surface and disappeared once again, only a ripple left behind. Essie screamed at the place where Tayki had been. "Tayki," she yelled. "I'm going to snatch you bald headed, you hateful old woman. I'm coming after you."

Essie dove into the water, her anger swinging her arms into rhythmic strokes toward the sandbar. She was a mighty swimmer and covered yards in seconds. Her strong legs kicked in cadenced form, quickly leaving behind the Withlacoochee's river bank.

The sandbar waited. As did DooRay; dead or alive. Essie would swim the river, confront the alligator and shelter her friend no matter the consequences.

She covered the remaining yards with ease, her focus locked onto the alligator. Nearing the sandbar, her feet felt the bottom of the river, and she pushed herself to a standing position, water covering her knees. She wasn't sure, but it seemed, at last, that the alligator had opened his eyes. Somehow she knew they were fastened on her.

Only a few yards away, Tayki surfaced and tread water. A low, cooing sound, almost a lullaby, drifted across the river to the sandbar. Her words, though not understandable, were tender, perhaps even cajoling, and, finally, a fervent pleading.

Essie stood spellbound. Paralyzed with wonder, she watched as the alligator rose up on all four legs and walked to the edge of the sandbar, closer to Tayki. He was listening to her, his head moving slightly up and down, perhaps in rhythm with the Indian woman's melodic exchange with him.

"Tail. You go," Tayki said softly. The gator hesitated, his mouth open slightly. He turned his head and looked at Essie, then back to Tayki. Slowly, he backed into the water and sunk down below the surface. With a swish of his tail, he was gone.

*DooRay.* Essie clamored up the sandbar and fell to her knees beside DooRay, her heart thudding. She reached out and, with a trembling hand, touched his cheek. "DooRay," she whispered. She leaned closer and placed her arms around his sand-covered shoulders.

Then, she gasped. And listened. She listened to DooRay's soft snore. A blowing of air through his mouth. Glorious air.

# CHAPTER TWENTY-ONE

Indeed, DooRay could not swim with one arm, but he could float. He lay on his back, his gaze on the sky above him. He watched gray clouds move swiftly east as Tayki and Essie swam alongside and gently guided him toward the river bank.

"Lawd," he said, a smile on his face. "I sho glad to see you, Miss Essie." He glanced at the ugly Indian woman. "You, too, Tayki."

The three glided to the water's edge, unaware that the river cooter followed them far below the water's surface. A naked Tayki climbed up the bank first, her thin body rippled with muscles. DooRay grimaced and turned his eyes away. He'd never seen a naked Indian woman.

Essie held onto DooRay's arm and, together, they stumbled onto the bank. "I've got you, DooRay. Take it easy."

"I gone do that, Miss Essie." He moved carefully beside her, his bare feet finding leverage in the sand.

Tayki ran ahead, rounding a bend, and finding her pile of clothes. By the time, Essie and DooRay approached her shack, she was buttoning her shirt and pulling on her mismatched shoes.

Essie found her bluejeans and slipped them on. "Can't swim in bluejeans," she said, as if apologizing for her bare legs. "Come on, DooRay. I've got the Pontiac parked at the bridge."

"Yes, mam. DooRay sure is tired."

From the door of her shack, Tayki grinned and held out a pair of scissors. "Here."

"What for?" Essie asked.

"Jewell's scissors." Tayki looked at the ground, not meeting Essie's gaze.

Essie took the scissors and examined them. Jewell's sewing scissors. "Where did you get these?"

Tayki shrugged. "On porch."

"You stole them?" Essie glared at the worn face, into the mismatched eyes.

"Tayki no steal." The Indian woman countered Essie, the uncentered eye catching the opposite side of the river.

"Pretty scissors." She reached inside her shack and pulled out a darning needle, a skein of yarn, a pack of needles and a fan with a picture of Jesus printed on one side and the words *First Baptist Church, Pinetta, Florida*, printed on the other. A smile grew slowly. "All pretty."

Essie felt herself soften. "Please keep them. I have more." She looked at Tayki a long moment. "Thank you, Tayki, for finding DooRay."

The toothless mouth opened wide and revealed her bare gums. It was the Indian woman's best smile. "Thank you for ride on car. Tayki fly."

DooRay and Essie slipped inside the Pontiac at 10:30 in the morning, a long missing sun easing from behind the fast-moving clouds, and headed slowly back to the Donnelly farm.

DooRay, his empty shoulder exposed, sat quietly for a few moments, then turned to Essie. "They's some bad people out there, Miss Essie. They done hurt me and throwed me in the river."

Essie reached over and held out her hand. DooRay placed his right hand into hers. Essie squeezed his hand and sighed deeply. "I know, DooRay." On the sandbar, she had seen a wound above his right ear, gaped open and crusted with blood.

"They done shot Murphy and – "

Essie shouted. "DooRay! Murphy's fine. Dr. Davis sewed him up and he's back home in the barn."

Laughter poured from the black man's chest. "That's a tough old goat, all right. Ain't no bad man gonna git the best of him."

DooRay stared out the car window, at the Townsend farm in the distance, cattle egrets walking behind cows, searching for insects. His chin quivered as he gasped for breath. Then, the sobs came. Like a loud croaking frog, the sounds of sorrow spewed forth as the black man leaned over and placed his head on his knees, a vision of the two men filling his head. Their bloodshot eyes, their whiskey gut and their hateful snarl as they called him *nigger*.

*The bad people.* Essie breathed deeply. The image of DooRay being thrown off the Bellville bridge, his body hitting the water, raced across her mind. *Murphy.* A bullet piercing the handsome goat and his body faltering as he tried to run.

*The bad people.* Essie felt the heat on her face, the rapid beat of her heart. *She'd find the bad people.* And when she did, she'd ignore her Christian teachings, forget any traces of compassion or forgiveness. On the Bellville road, in the Pontiac with DooRay beside her, she felt her body become steel, her mind hard and unrelenting. *She'd find the bad people.*

At 11:00, Sheriff Moore and his deputy, Son Stokely, drove down the farm lane. Essie had called Simmie as soon as she had returned to the farmhouse. She then settled DooRay on her mother's brocade couch, one of her father's soft cotton shirts on his thin body. She promised him breakfast, thick-cut bacon, fried eggs and hot buttered grits. DooRay said he'd make the biscuits. Essie refused his help; she would make the biscuits for her beloved friend.

# CHAPTER TWENTY-TWO

S heriff Simmie Moore emanated calm. His trademark, readily recognized by the citizens of Madison County, classified him as a distinguished intellectual property. Or better said: Sheriff Simmie Moore, *Genteel Man, Bearer of Big Gun.*

At 5' 10", somewhat stocky, his body seemingly turtle slow, the sheriff carried within himself an acute awareness of what some folks deemed *the naked truth.* Simply said, Simmie's ability to assimilate facts in a situation was lightning fast, as though he had a sixth sense.

Simmie Moore admitted to himself that he purposefully curbed his analytical expertise, choosing instead to shuffle facts from here to there, and then back again. His ability to collect data was renowned – nothing escaped his pursuit of *the naked truth.*

When he arrived at the Donnelly farm that morning at 11:00, he seemed disheveled, his eyes puffy and bereft of sleep. His night had been spent in turmoil: one of his citizens had been the victim of a hate crime.

DooRay Aikens, a gentle, one-armed black man, had been assaulted and thrown off the Bellville road bridge. His goat had been shot. Sheriff Moore had seen the blood-soaked ground, the empty whiskey bottle and the bullet wound in Murphy, Madison County's beloved goat.

He parked his 1956 Ford near the front porch of the Donnelly house and waited for Son Stokely to unload his large body from the front seat of his Madison County deputy's car. Son, Simmie's best deputy in all the years he had been sheriff, ambled into the farmyard and eyed Killer, the Donnelly's resident rooster.

Killer didn't like Son. Perhaps it was Son's size or even the deputy's way of walking that intimidated the rooster. The rooster countered the only way he knew how. Killer skittered sideways, throwing his three inch spurs in the air and airbrushing Son's leg. Son laughed. "You ole rooster. You're headed for the pot, for sure."

Killer pranced in a circle for a few moments, then ran to the barn. Evidently, he knew what the word "pot" meant.

Sheriff Moore looked up when he heard the front screen door open and watched Essie walk out on the porch with a tray of iced tea. She was a lovely Southern woman, although perhaps covered by a soft patina that hid her fits of temper and tendency to be hardheaded.

"Good morning, Essie." Simmie walked up the porch steps and found his favorite rocker. Son followed him and leaned against the porch rail.

"Mornin' to you, Simmie. You, too, Son." She served their glass of tea and found a seat in the swing. "You look tired, Simmie." Essie noticed the sag in his face. He must have been called out during the night or taken his dogs coon hunting.

"Everything's good, Essie. I'm thankful DooRay's been found. I'm anxious to talk to him." He glanced at his deputy. "The sooner, the better. Of course, you gave me some of the details when you called."

"Let him rest a while longer, Simmie. He's been through so much." Essie pushed the swing with her foot and peered across the Bellville road at the vast fields. A tractor moved slowly across a field to the west, hilling rows that were as straight as broomsticks.

"I understand." Simmie pulled a small notebook from his shirt pocket. "Tell me about Miccosukee Mae showing up here at daylight."

"I'll keep it simple, Simmie. Tayki saw DooRay on a sandbar about one-hundred yards from her shack. She walked the two miles over here and ended up in the front yard." Essie pointed. "Right in that spot right there. She told me about DooRay's body. Didn't know if he was dead or alive. Just knew he was there. And, of course, you know the rest. Glad you answered your phone."

She gathered her thoughts and looked back at the lawman. "Where do we begin, Simmie." Essie released a half smile, but only for an instant.

The sheriff knew what she was thinking because he knew Essie Donnelly. Her tenacity was well known across the county, as well as her indefatigable pursuit of all things right. He would never skirt issues with her. She was just as much a seeker of *the naked truth* as he was.

Simmie found himself choosing his words carefully. He'd better not falter when it came to the farm girl; she was afraid of nothing.

"Well, Essie, the way I see it so far is that DooRay happened on some folks at Ran Terry's pond. We found two sets of shoe prints, some tire tracks at the edge of the Bellville road, next to the south side of the pond.

"We have a bullet that was taken from Murphy's leg. Don't have a lab report on it yet. There was a whiskey bottle on the ground. *Four Roses* brand. Blood was in the grass about fifteen feet from the edge of the pond."

Simmie paused and sipped his tea. "That's about it. After we talk with DooRay, I'm certain we'll know a lot more." He cleared his throat. "From those tire tracks, we think the vehicle was a truck."

A few quiet moments passed, the porch swing moving back and forth. Killer skittered across the front yard and hid behind an azalea bush, a soft cawing escaping from his open beak, perhaps in attack mode waiting for Son Stokely.

Essie nodded thoughtfully, her eyes half-closed. "They had to be strangers, Simmie. The folks who did this. Nobody in Madison County would harm DooRay." She frowned. "What about Lon Terry's two customers who bought chewing tobacco?"

"Interesting. Neither Lon nor Rana had seen them before."

Essie left the swing and leaned on the porch rail. *The bad people.* "Let's let DooRay sleep for another hour. He'll be rested and ready to answer any questions."

Sheriff Moore eased up from the rocker. "I'm thinking Son and I will go on down to the river. Talk with Miccosukee Mae. We'll be back in an hour or so." He glanced at Essie. "By the way, I ran into Minnie Pryor at Terryville late last night. She'd been out searching for DooRay most of the day. Said she was going home to get some rest and she'd be by to see you later today."

He hesitated. "Hope you're makin' a buttered rum pound cake today."

"I'll probably be in the kitchen later. I'll whip up something delicious."

Essie walked down the steps with Simmie. "You're going to see the old Indian? I hope she's not naked."

# CHAPTER TWENTY-THREE

The first indication that Tayki was nearby was the rock that sailed past Simmie's head. The second clue was the panther that screamed from the top of an oak tree, the same tree that Tayki straddled and from which she spit a well-aimed mouthful of snuff in Son's direction.

"Dang blast it, Mae. Come down from that tree! Leave your friend up there or I'll shoot him." The sheriff shook his fist at Miccosukee Mae. "And if you spit at us again, I"ll put you in jail for a night or two."

An ear-shattering screech split the air as Tayki threw another rock, this time catching Son's shoulder. He cursed and picked up the rock and threw it at the tree. "I'm coming up that tree after you, Mae."

A hyena laugh caused chills to run up and down Simmie's back. "You come down right now, Mae, or I'm gonna shoot your friend."

Quiet filled the river banks. Only a few yards from Tayki's shack, the sheriff slipped his hand in his front right pants pocket. His .38 grasped in his hand, he waited. Finally, Tayki shimmied down the tree, brown snuff at the corners of her mouth.

The deputy glared at Tayki, another rock in his hand. "Mae, you can't be throwing rocks at the law. People go to jail for things like that."

Tayki shot Son an aloof glance. "Tayki no like you. My panther eat you one day."

"Don't threaten us, Mae. We're here on official police business." Sheriff Moore, his face grim, gave the Indian woman his most piercing stare.

Tayki turned her head and spat into the river, a smile inching its way across her lips. She jerked her chin in Son's direction, a rumble of laughter in her throat. "That boy too big to climb tree."

Simmie pulled out his notebook. "Mae, Essie tells us the two of you pulled DooRay off a sandbar this morning."

Tayki barked. "Why you call me Mae? My name Tayki."

The sheriff hung his head, exasperated. "Okay . . . Tayki. Tell me about DooRay."

Tayki seemed to grow an air of importance. She straightened her shoulders, lifted her chin and looked down her nose at the lawmen. "One-arm a black man."

Simmie glanced at Son, then back to Tayki and nodded. "Go on."

"Sometime One-arm dead, sometime One-arm alive. Sometime, I tell Tail to eat One-arm. Sometime, I tell Tail to leave One-arm be."

"Tail?" Simmie began to fidget, an apprehension building. "Who is Tail?" He looked at Son. Son shrugged.

"My friend," said Tayki, rather flippantly.

"What friend?"

"Gator," said Tayki, matter-of-factly, giving Simmie and Son a look that said 'you stupid.'

Son rolled his eyes. "So, the first time you saw DooRay was on the sandbar early this morning?"

Tayki nodded and pointed. "Sandbar."

Simmie and Son both appraised the sandbar in the bend of the river, about one-hundred yards south.

"About what time was that?" asked Simmie, beginning to write in his notebook.

Up high in the oak tree, the panther climbed down a few feet, right above them. Watching. Occasionally, his pink tongue swiped around the edge of his mouth.

"When fish start jumpin'." Tayki calculated time the only way she knew how.

Simmie took a deep breath. "Sunrise?"

"When light rise that way." Her brown, crooked finger lifted and pointed east.

"Did you see anyone around the river yesterday morning?"

Tayki wrinkled her brow. Thoughtful, she looked skyward. "No. Tayki go look for mushrooms in the woods. No here."

"I see. So, you heard nothing unusual, saw nothing strange?"

Again, the Indian woman looked skyward. Searching, thinking. "Smell something."

"Smell something? Like what?"

Tayki narrowed her eyes. "Whiskey."

"Whiskey?"

Miccosukee Mae sniffed the air. "Tayki smell everything. I come back from woods and smell whiskey in the air."

Simmie turned the page in his notebook and wrote for a few moments, then looked up at Tayki. "Can you think of anything else that might be helpful."

They waited. Son kicked the dirt with his shoe. Simmie rocked on his heels. The river flowed slowly south, its water cool and on its way to its confluence with the Suwannee River.

"Music."

"Music?"

"Tayki hear music."

"Where?"

Tayki grinned and looked skyward. "In the air."

Simmie sighed deeply and sauntered away from Tayki, not turning his back to her. Son did the same thing. Just as they opened their car doors, the panther jumped out of the oak and swished his tail. Tayki picked up another rock, glaring at the men. "Tayki's river."

After he had received Essie's phone call early that morning, Sheriff Simmie Moore called off the search for DooRay. Thus, began the dubious task of finding whoever had harmed the gentle black man.

# CHAPTER TWENTY-FOUR

The Donnelly farm lay serene, a slight breeze, and Killer finding a dust hole by the barn and becoming quite docile. Murphy slept soundly in the barn, the medicine given to him by Dr. Davis leaving him without pain. The goat had eaten and seemed to be improving.

Around Noon, Dr. Bush arrived. He was there to fulfill the promise he made to Essie: *When you find DooRay, I'll be there.*

The good doctor climbed up the porch steps, his worn black bag in his hand. He'd delivered just about every baby in Madison County, stitched every wound, and set every broken bone. There wasn't a family who hadn't lovingly given him eggs, hams, chickens, corn, peaches, watermelons and, best of all, bottles of the best corn liquor that was ever made.

"Essie!" he called as he took off his coat and sat in a rocker. He was weary, as usual. Two babies delivered in the night as well as the search for Rufus Tootie's wooden leg. The babies were easy; the search for the wooden leg not so easy. Why Rufus thought a doctor should be called because he lost his wooden leg was confusing to Dr. Bush. Of course, the consumption of a gallon of homemade wine might have corrupted Rufus' judgment.

The missing leg turned up in the outhouse. It seemed Rufus' habit of removing the leg while indisposed was the culprit. When Dr. Bush left the Tootie's house, Rufus was asleep on the couch, cradling his leg.

The screen door slammed. Essie carried a slice of cake and a glass of tea. "Dr. Bush, so glad you're here. DooRay is just about awake. Take a moment to eat some cake."

"Thankful you called me, Essie." He reached for the tea and cake. "I'm anxious to see his head wound."

"Oh, it's a mess, Dr. Bush. Split wide open but clotted real well."

"Probably needs stitches. But, that's okay. I'm a good seamstress." He grinned and took a bite of cake. "Oh, your buttered rum pound cake. Been a while."

Essie nodded. Jewell's death the previous July changed many things. When Jewell was alive, they baked dozens of rum cakes, all of them consumed by friends and neighbors. Sadly, Essie had found it difficult to bake without her sister.

At Dr. Bush's last bite of cake, he glanced at Essie. "Looks like you have quite an abrasion on your forehead."

"Fell at the river. Nothing serious." Essie brushed her hair from her face. "It's not bleeding anymore. Be a scab is all."

Dr. Bush nodded. "Assume you put some kind of antiseptic on it."

"Of course." She cast a wry look at the doctor.

Handing Essie his empty cake plate, Dr. Bush stood from his rocker. "You think the patient is awake?"

"I think so." Essie opened the screened door and led Dr. Bush into the house. "DooRay, Dr. Bush is here."

DooRay, stretched out on Edith Donnelly's brocade couch and covered with a blanket, slowly sat up. Essie handed him a glass of iced tea. "Thank you, Miss Essie. Hello, Dr. Bush. Looks like you all the time patchin' this here fella up."

Dr. Bush pulled a chair closer to the couch. "That's what I'm here for, my friend. I want to take a look at that head of yours."

"Yes, suh. DooRay done been knocked clean out."

Dr. Bush opened his bag and pulled out a small flashlight. "Let's take a look." The wound was on the right side of DooRay's head, above his ear. The gash was about three inches long, the impact splitting the skin like a watermelon. Blood oozed out behind the clotted wound.

"Well, young man, it appears to me that you were hit by a mighty hard object. That's quite a gash."

DooRay nodded. "It sure does hurt. Gave me a big ole headache."

Dr. Bush gathered a handful of gauze and doused it with alcohol. "Reckon we better clean it up a bit 'fore I put some stitches in your head."

"Stitches?" DooRay's eyes widened.

"Yep. Afraid so. That's a messy cut. Take about twelve or so stitches, I reckon."

A horn honked and a car pulled under a shade tree and parked. Sam Washington emerged, a smile on his face. Essie had called him earlier and told him DooRay had been found. The Madison County attorney considered DooRay one of his best friends, their man talk in the barn while Sam smoked cigars was one of their favorite pastimes.

He stepped onto the porch and into the sitting room where Dr. Bush worked diligently. "Now, I'm going to deaden the area around this cut, DooRay, with some lidocaine, which is a local anesthetic. It'll decrease the bleeding, too. You won't feel a thing. And this is a small needle. Small but sharp." He leaned in with a syringe.

Sam grimaced as he watched. He glanced at Essie and frowned. He motioned to Essie's scraped forehead, a question in his eyes. She shook her head. "No problem."

Sam Washington. His entry into her life had been a tumultuous one, but she had discovered he was more than just a friend. She knew he loved her, his pursuit of her steadfast. She was the one who vacillated between friendship and romance. *What was she afraid of?*

"Sixteen!" exclaimed Dr. Bush. "Sixteen stitches, DooRay." He patted DooRay's shoulder. "That is the best stitching I've ever done! But, I'm afraid it will leave a big scar. Won't have any hair there, for sure."

DooRay grinned. "Didn't feel a thing, Dr. Bush."

"That's good. Now, here's what I want you to do. You've had a traumatic forty-eight hours, and I'd like to see you right here on this couch for the rest of the day." He looked at Essie. "That alright with you, Essie?"

"Just fine, Dr. Bush. That way, I can keep an eye on him."

"Well, I'll get out of here then. Got to go check on Columbus Townsend."

"Columbus Townsend? Who's that, Dr. Bush?" Sam scratched his head.

Dr. Bush laughed. "I'm talking about Lum Townsend."

"Columbus? Why did his mama name him Columbus?"

"Wasn't his mama who named him. His daddy had a favorite bull named Columbus."

"Lum is named after a bull?" Sam laughed and slapped his knee. "I can't wait to call Lum by his given name."

"You do that and he might put a knot on your head. Anyway, seems like he got tangled up in a barbed wire fence late yesterday evening. Horse is fine, but he isn't." He closed his black bag and looked at DooRay. "Might have to do some more stitching before this day is over, DooRay. Lum will be glad I practiced on you."

DooRay reached out his hand. "DooRay sure does thank you, doctor." His voice trembled. "You sure does know how to use a needle."

"I'm just glad you're back home safe and sound, DooRay. Essie will be a good nurse. I'll check on you in a day or two. See you folks later." He left the Donnelly house whistling a tune about the streets of Laredo and a cowboy wrapped up in white linen.

Sam pulled up a chair. "Where's my slice of cake?"

"Coming right up." She left the room and heard Sam ask DooRay about his injury. She laughed when DooRay replied that he was upset that no hair would grow in the area of his injury.

Out in the yard, a car door slammed. Sheriff Moore and his deputy, Son Stokely, hollered through the screen door. "Can we come in, Essie?"

Sam jumped up and opened the door for the lawmen. "Come on in, sheriff. You, too, Son."

"Hello, Sam." Simmie glanced at DooRay. "Well, you're a sight for sore eyes, DooRay."

"I'm mighty fine, sheriff."

"That's good to hear." Simmie fingered his pocket and pulled out his notebook. "You feel up to answering some questions, DooRay."

DooRay glanced at Essie. "That okay wif you, Miss Essie?"

"It's a good idea, DooRay. I'm sure Sheriff Moore is anxious to get as much information as possible."

DooRay leaned back on a pillow. "It okay if ole DooRay lie down. I's feelin' a little woozy."

Simmie noticed blood seeping through the bandage on DooRay's head. "You go right ahead, DooRay. I'll make this as quick as I can." Simmie settled in a chair next to the couch. Son leaned against the wall to the right of the screen door. He didn't need a notebook; he had a sharp mind that devoured and stored information swiftly as well as accurately.

The sheriff leaned closer to DooRay. "DooRay, first of all, we want you to know we're sorry this has happened to you. And, we're relieved you're back home and in good hands.

"Also, I want you to know, as sheriff of Madison County, I'm going to do everything in my power to find the culprits who did this to you."

DooRay closed his eyes. He saw two men. He saw hate. He saw Murphy slam into the dirt. Saw the goat's eyes pleading, asking a question. *Why?*

"Yes, suh. They be bad people."

"So, you went to Ran Terry's pond early yesterday morning . . . "

"Me and Murphy. We's gone catch us some fish. Ain't gone bother nobody. Just me and him.

"I gots there and heard some men's voices. They laughin' and talkin' like they had sense. Next thing I know, they's hollering at me. Not friendly. I figure me and Murphy better head on back to the barn." DooRay involuntarily grimaced, the memory painful.

"Then, one fella done throwed a whiskey bottle at my head. I hit the dirt and then my goat hit the dirt, too. I heard a gun fire just 'fore I fell into a deep well. No light. No sounds."

Simmie turned a page in his notebook. "What happened next?"

DooRay closed his eyes again. He spoke without opening them, as if talking to himself. "Yes, suh, that sure was a black place I be in. When I wakes up, I'm a floatin' down the river on my back, looking up at the rain. Just as pretty as you please. That dark water carries me a ways, them raindrops hittin' me hard, like pecans falling from a tree."

The sitting room stilled, the vision of DooRay floating down the

Withlacoochee vivid in everyone's mind. Simmie leaned closer. "Go on, DooRay," he said softly.

The black man opened his eyes and looked around the room. His face was troubled, his mouth trembling. "I ain't never floated 'fore. Guess the angels just pulled me along."

The black face softened. "I singed me a little song while I be floatin'." He then placed his hand over his eyes while his sweet baritone voice swept the room, lilting, beseeching. *"Be not afraid, 'tis I, 'tis I. The storm can't harm my trusting soul, for Jesus walks the waves that roll. His voice I hear, which calms my fear. 'Tis I, be not afraid."*

No one spoke. The words of the one-armed man's hymn hung in the air, a soft peace touching the sheriff, his deputy, Sam and Essie. DooRay lay fast asleep, his breathing slow and steady. He was at Ran Terry's pond, a fish on his cane pole, his goat Murphy nearby.

At dusk, Minnie and her mule, Sally, ambled down the farm lane, the clop of Sally's hooves sending a slow, tranquil sound across the yard. Minnie tied Molly to the porch rail and climbed up the front steps of the Donnelly house.

"Miss Essie," she called.

Essie peeked out the screen door. "Hello, Minnie. I'm so glad you're here. DooRay's been asking for you."

Along about midnight, Essie climbed the stairs to her bedroom, her body weary, her thoughts of Tayki. Had it not been for the old Indian, DooRay might not have been found. Her treatment of Tayki had been harsh. She had been unkind, hateful and impatient with her. Tomorrow, she would go to the river, tell her she was sorry for her behavior. Maybe, take her a present of some kind. Perhaps some fresh eggs or a watermelon. She would ask Tayki to forgive her.

# PART II

ESSIE

# CHAPTER TWENTY-FIVE

June ended softly, the corn tasseling in the Townsend field to the south and the Gaston field to the west. July's heat pounced upon Madison County and blew its hot breath across the Donnelly's front porch, the hand fans from the Pine Grove Baptist Church seemingly useless.

Minnie tended DooRay, pampered him with cool drinks, tomato sandwiches, and banana pudding. She curried Murphy like he was a baby and, had DooRay let her, she would have put a ribbon on top of his head, between his horns.

Sheriff Moore came by and updated DooRay and Essie on his progress in finding the men who had assaulted DooRay. He'd shake his head and lament – *this case has gone cold.*

"Cold?" Essie had asked. "What do you mean, Simmie? You've got tire tracks, a spent bullet and DooRay gave you an excellent description of those two hoodlums."

"I know, I know, Essie. But, everything's come to a deadend. The spent bullet Dr. Davis took out of Murphy has no readable markings."

The sheriff pulled his pipe from a pocket in his cotton shirt and packed it with tobacco. "I'm thinkin' we'll find something soon." He struck a match and puffed vigorously.

The fragrance of Captain Black and Carter Hall tobacco filled the air and the sheriff who 'always got his man' shook his head. "This is an aggravatin' thing, Essie. It's tedious work, lots of things have to come together. And, that takes time."

Essie stewed the days away, her anger subsiding, but ever present. Her mind would not rest: *the bad people were out there somewhere.*

July 4th, a Thursday, Independence Day, arrived on a hot, cloudless day. Essie fried chicken and made chicken gravy for a pot of mashed potatoes. Sliced tomatoes and cucumbers lined a large platter, lots of salt and pepper. Warm blueberry cobbler from Caroline Sapp's blueberries waited on the stove for vanilla ice cream.

On the Donnelly front porch, Pat Boone sang *Love Letters in the Sand*, the radio turned low – Sam asleep in the swing.

Near the barn, Killer scratched in the dirt, his glorious tailfeathers catching the mid-day sun. Murphy chased him until he flew to the top of the wellhouse, his rooster eye glaring at the frisky goat. The bullet wound in Murphy's leg had no affect on his agility. He had yet to pull the wooden cart, but he would before the summer ended.

At the picnic table, Essie spread out a tablecloth, white with large red geraniums. She wore a soft yellow sleeveless dress with tiny buttons down the front. She was and always would be the watermelon queen of Madison County.

Minnie left the tack room, Murphy following her. "Miss Essie, you let me set that table for you."

"Please do, Minnie. I've got everything ready inside." The two women walked across the farmyard, through the back porch and into the kitchen.

"My, everything smells so good. DooRay's hungry, for sure." The young black girl picked up a stack of dinner plates and napkins. "That man is feeling real good. I changed his bandage and everything's just about healed."

"That's right," said Essie. "Dr. Bush checked him the other day and said he's fully recovered."

"Uh, huh. That be true, Miss Essie. He be a blessed man."

"Well, he's blessed to have you, Minnie. You've taken such good care of him – I think that's why he's done so well. You're going to make a wonderful nurse."

Sam straggled across the yard from the front porch. "I smell some fried chicken."

Almost at the same moment, DooRay ambled from the barn. "Did I hear somebody say dinnertime?" He walked slowly, his tall, thin body ramrod straight, his shirt sleeve pinned up where his left arm should have been.

At the picnic table, Essie and Sam sat across from each other, relaxed and thankful. Essie asked Minnie to bless the food. Heads bowed, Minnie, her voice soft, began to speak. "Dear Heavenly Father, we . . ."

From the front yard, someone hollered. Shrill and loud, the voice rose. "Anybody home?" Then, from the back screened door, a woman waved furiously. "Well, it looks like I arrived at just the right time."

She clacked down the porch steps in her 5" stiletto heels, carrying a large, shiny patent leather bag, black and white striped. Her hair, a bright copper, hung to her shoulders, Jayne Mansfield style.

At the bottom of the steps, she jacked up the front of her tight red dress and tried to cover a significant amount of cleavage. Unsuccessful, she simply bounced her way to the picnic table and greeted everyone with a wave, or perhaps it was just a flitter of her fingers, her blood red fingernails at least a half inch long.

She sat on the bench by Sam and looked around the table. "Where's my plate?" her large blue eyes questioning. She shrugged her shoulders, the pillow tops of her breasts heaving up, then down.

Sam, unable to speak, stood from the bench and half-ran to the house. Essie watched him go, then turned to the stranger now sitting at their table. *Uninvited.*

"I don't believe I know you," Essie said cooly, her eyes unwavering as she regarded the movie-star face, the red pouty lips and rouged up cheeks.

The redhead fluttered her eyelashes and flashed a Hollywood smile. "What? Mr. Fox didn't call you and tell you I'd be here today? I'm Lola LaRue."

*Lola LaRue.* The literary agent who made stars out of writers. Thomas

H. Fox's most prized asset, he had told her. Why, Lola LaRue would make millions for Essie with her novel *Watermelon Queen of Madison County.* But first, she must eat some fried chicken and mashed potatoes.

Sam returned with a plate, fork, knife and spoon and a glass of ice for the prized asset who set with her cleavage piled higher than the mashed potatoes she was about to put on her plate. He fumbled nervously, almost spilling the tea he poured for her. He glanced from the tea glass to her cleavage and back again. No wonder he ended up spilling the tea.

"Ah, yes, Mr. Fox," said Essie. "I made it clear to him that I wasn't interested in publishing my manuscript at this time. So, I suggest you – ."

"Oh, no, honey. I'm gonna stay right here 'til I get you to sign on that dotted line." Lola LaRue picked up a drumstick and licked her full lips. "I didn't fly all the way from New York City just for your fried chicken."

Essie lifted her chin and released a fake smile. "Is that right?"

# CHAPTER TWENTY-SIX

Essie watched the 5" stiletto heels sink into the dirt as Killer chased Lola LaRue to her car. The literary agent rolled down the car window and shook her fist at Essie. "I don't care how long it takes, I'm not leaving Madison County until we have a deal!" The New Yorker whipped her car around and sped down the farm lane in her rented 1957 Ford Thunderbird convertible, dust whipping up beneath the car.

When the sun hit her streaming copper hair, the strands flowed hot, like a flame thrower. In seconds, Miss LaRue turned onto the Bellville road, her pink convertible shimmying wildly as she gave the car a hefty amount of gas. No doubt about it, the New York woman was Thomas Fox's prized asset.

The porch swing moved slowly, Essie pushing it gently. A slight smile playing along her lips. Her trademark hardness had surfaced. Not only surfaced, but threw itself gladly at the woman from New York City, who obviously had underestimated the woman from Pinetta, Florida.

Had the buxom woman spoken gently, gently like a southern woman, perhaps her task would have been much easier. *It would delight me, Miss Donnelly, if we could discuss your wonderful novel Watermelon Queen of Madison County. I find it so delightful and worthy of recognition.*

Her fate was sealed when she threw a chicken bone in the yard, then asked one-armed DooRay to slice her a piece of the watermelon that sat in the shade under a nearby oak tree.

In a rocking chair across from the swing, Sam lit a cigar and turned on the radio. Sonny James' *Young Love* came across the airways. *They say for every boy and girl, there's just one love in this whole world . . .*

"What's wrong with your eyes, Sam?" The swing moved back and forth. Essie waiting.

"Huh? What do you mean?"

"They're bloodshot. Perhaps tired and strained."

Sam shrugged and blew out cigar smoke. "Don't know why."

Essie stilled the swing, her breath slow. "Oh, I know why."

"You do? Why?" Sam sat forward in the rocker, his eyes questioning Essie.

"Too much ogling Miss LaRue's breasts overworked your eyes." There was no smile.

Sam shot up from the rocker. "Now, Essie. That was unnecessary. I've never even *seen* your breasts and there was Lola, all dolled up, just askin' for a look-see. What was I supposed to do?"

Sam began a courtroom pace up and down the porch, his cigar in and out of his mouth in quick puffs. "For that matter, we've been together for a year and we have yet to even make love. I've been a gentleman, and have honored you all this time."

Sam threw his cigar into the yard. "I'm a man, Essie. You seem to forget that. For that matter, I'm always way down on your list. 'Oh, let's go find Jewell's baby.' And I can tell you what's coming next!"

Sam slammed his fist on top of the porch rail, his face twisted in anger. "You're thinkin', 'Oh, let's go find DooRay's assailants. Let's become Sheriff Moore's deputy and scourer the world to find the rascals who hurt your DooRay."

He slung the rocker aside and stood over Essie, his breath hot, his face flushed. "I'll tell you what, Essie. Here we are in our mid-thirties. I want to get married; I want to have children."

His voice went quiet, a whisper. "Well, maybe it's not *you* who's in my future."

The farm boy who had become a lawyer left the porch and flung himself into his car, his pent up frustrations spilling over. The engine roared and the car bolted down the farm lane, turning left on the Bellville road and heading for . . . *somewhere*. He'd cross the Withlacoochee, and find himself in Georgia, where he'd find a cold beer and look at any dang breasts he could possibly find. And if that caused him to go blind, then so be it.

# CHAPTER TWENTY-SEVEN

J ust after dusk, a quarter moon topped the tall cypress east of the Donnelly farm and spread its light like vanilla frosting across the fields to the south, a soothing light that promised to perhaps unveil night fairies flying amongst the clouds.

Fireflies danced wildly in the nooks between the trees, then chased one another, their flashing lights all about love. Across the farmyard an owl called from the top of the oak tree by the barn, an answer coming from deep in the woods to the north.

The cypress swing that had been built by Essie's grandfather held many memories, not the least of which was the kiss Sam had given Essie the previous summer, on a soft June night filled with a certain magic.

Essie sat quietly, a gentle push of the swing, her thoughts wandering like a lost puppy. *Sam.* His desire for a family was evident. He wanted to marry her, have a dozen children and live happily ever after. *And why not?*

Essie's three-month sabbatical to her daddy's fish camp on Cherry Lake the previous fall was her way of mourning Jewell's death. *Seclusion. Solitude.* She had excluded Sam from her life in order to mend, to cope with the loss of her sister. Sam thought he should be at her side, helping her grieve by simply being nearby.

Perhaps he had forgotten who the farm girl was. *Independent. Head-strong.* The most iron-willed person he had ever known. His reaction to her need for solitude was one of anger. She had shut him out.

The crowning blow came when Essie declared she would search for Jewell's baby. A baby born and given away. A baby who was now seventeen or eighteen years old. A baby that was somewhere, unknown.

Again, Sam had been placed second, maybe third or fourth, in Essie's life while she began the difficult search for Jewell's child.

Knowing Essie as he did, Sam knew Essie would pursue DooRay's assailants. Was he giving up on her? Giving up on the auburn-haired farm girl who had so enthralled him? He had been captivated not only by her strengths, but her tender care of those she loved. She was afraid of nothing, a hothead at times who dazzled him with her fierceness. Then, beneath the hardness, he had discovered a deep reservoir of compassion, as well as generous amounts of integrity. *She was his girl, his ideal woman.*

Essie admitted to herself that she assumed responsibilities that perhaps were not hers to assume. Yet, it was that same compassion that gave DooRay a home when his house burned. He was now a part of the Donnelly family, her adult child.

Along about midnight, the July moon sat centered in the sky above the Bellville road, soon to begin its westward journey. The night became still. Even the fireflies had quieted their light, the whippoor-wills hushed, the owls silent as a coolness settled over the Donnelly farm.

"Miss Essie." DooRay eased up the porch steps. "I's wantin' to see if you alright." He sat in a rocker near Essie. "Ole DooRay couldn't sleep. Looks like you cain't either."

"We're just two night owls, aren't we, DooRay?"

"That be so. My mind jus' won't quit. It's gallopin' around like a wild horse. I tries to stop it, but it keep on goin'."

"You've been through a lot, DooRay, but, as time passes, you'll get back to the old DooRay. You reckon?"

DooRay rocked quietly for a few moments, a deep sigh as he looked up into the night sky, the moon looking back. "Yes, ma'am. This old body and mind just needs some time."

"DooRay, you're not old! You're my age and we're only thirty-five." Essie laughed softly. "We've got a lot of living to do."

Neither spoke, the rocker rocking and the swing swinging, a calm place where the fragrance of night air, corn stalks and cut hay drifted from the nearby fields. It had been this way for more than a hundred years, the only changes being the people who now plowed the fields, who planted the corn, and who hoped a hundred years from now, things would be exactly the same.

"Miss Essie. DooRay done had a memory." The black man's breath came slow, a hesitation that preceded his thoughtful homily.

Essie watched the same moon DooRay watched. "A memory? Want to tell me about it?"

In the midnight darkness, DooRay turned toward Essie. The rocking chair stilled, the noise of the rocker's movement settling on the wooden planks of the porch and creating a fervent moment of anticipation. The black man's words were a whisper, a whisper that was perhaps evidence of a subtle reluctance to leave his throat. Perhaps the whispered words were a prophecy waiting to be revealed.

"Miss Essie, DooRay done thinks he seen those bad peoples before."

# CHAPTER TWENTY-EIGHT

DooRay *done thinks he seen those bad peoples before?* Essie jumped from the swing. "Where? When?" she shouted. The soft patina that Sam declared had covered the farm girl from Madison County vanished. Essie stood above DooRay and commanded him to answer her question, her words as sharp as Killer's spurs.

DooRay flinched. "Now, now, Miss Essie. Hold on."

*Hold on?* The men who knocked DooRay unconscious with a whiskey bottle, put a large gash in his head, shot Murphy, and then threw the one-armed man into the Withlacoochee, could not be put on hold. Essie placed her head in her hands and stood silently. But only for a moment.

She took a long, slow breath and expelled it. "Of course, DooRay. Let's sort this out," she said softly. Essie returned to the swing and waited.

DoRay cleared his throat, rocked and gathered his thoughts. "Yes, ma'am. They was here. Last summer, not long after DooRay moved into the tack room. They was salesmen. Remember? Done give you a bag of seed. Believe it was corn. You told those mens to go see Mr. Gaston 'cause he lease all your land."

A deliberating quiet filled the Donnelly's front porch, while Essie gave DooRay's words long and careful consideration. *Seed salesmen.* The swing moved back and forth, the chains creaking in harmony with a chorus of crickets.

Suddenly, Essie jumped from the swing. "Come on, DooRay."

DooRay slipped out of the rocker and followed Essie down the porch steps through the dark yard. She outpaced him in a half-run to the barn. He grumbled to himself. "They's no tellin' what that woman is thinkin'."

In the barn, Essie turned on the barn lights, then shoved aside rakes, hoes, a basket of old gourds, burlap sacks full of feed corn for the chickens and finally a crate of old flower pots.

DooRay heard her mutter, *"those bastards,"* as she rolled an old tire straight out the barn door. The tire was followed by a small rusted wagon stacked with canning jars.

Again, words of maleficent intention were flung with anger. *Sons a bitches.* The soft patina had not only worn off the watermelon queen of Madison County, but it had disappeared into a black hole the size of Montana and exposed the woman who would, without the slightest bit of compunction, find *the bad people.*

"Got it!" Essie screamed. She leaned over and grabbed a five pound bag of seeds, brushed off the cobwebs and a dead cricket. "Don't know why the mice didn't get to this."

She tossed the bag on top of a wooden table. "Look here, DooRay. *Alabama Seeds.*" She read the label: *Consistent Yields, Corn, Silage, Soybeans, Alfalfa. Seed #PB5630 - 86 Days Until Harvest. Not for Resale. Sample Only.*

"*Alabama Seeds.*" Essie's eyes gleamed. A wrong would be righted.

DooRay nodded and rubbed his chin. "Reckon we better call Sheriff Moore and tell him 'bout this?"

"No! No need, DooRay. I'd like to study this a little more. No worries." Thoughtful, she added. "And don't tell Sam." At that moment, Essie knew she'd not tell Simmie Moore nor Sam, not tell them of DooRay's epiphany, his recall of a memory that would surely unearth and expose *the bad people.*

*Alabama Seeds. Two salesmen. Beware. You will soon encounter Essie Donnelly of Madison County.*

# CHAPTER TWENTY-NINE

The moon, indeed, found the far western sky, turning over the sentry of the earth to the sun, which rose in glorious oranges, pinks, and deep lavender over the tops of the trees that lined the Withlacoochee River. The sunrise met with clear blue skies that promised a hot July day, a day just right for cold watermelon and, of course, tomato sandwiches.

Atop the wellhouse, Killer crowed loudly, as befitting his important duties in the Donnelly farm yard. He, not the rising sun, officially announced the new day. A pompous, feathered bird, he considered himself the finest rooster in all of Madison County. His cone and two wattles were flame red, his tail feathers sweeping high in glorious colors that even Monet could not duplicate.

Essie, still in bed, heard Killer, then the sound of a car moving down the farm lane. She stumbled to the bedroom window and saw a pink Thunderbird. *Lola LaRue. Not getting out of bed for that woman*, she thought, and climbed back under the covers.

A horn trumpeted for five minutes, but Essie ignored it, got up and brushed her teeth, then cursed the Thomas H. Fox Literary Agency. She would call Simmie Moore and have Miss LaRue arrested for . . . for exposing her breasts. Or, perhaps run out of town for eating five pieces of fried chicken and two bowls of blueberry cobbler, both with ice cream, at a private July 4th picnic, to which she wasn't invited.

Sam's flirtatious behavior toward Miss LaRue was still fresh on Essie's mind. The very idea that Miss LaRue would return to the scene of the crime was outrageous! When Essie had picked up the big butcher knife that Sam had used to cut their July 4th watermelon and waved it in Lola LaRue's face, it should have been quite obvious that Miss LaRue was an unwelcome visitor.

Yet, there she was, sitting in the pink Thunderbird, the horn blaring and, most likely, her ample bosom pointing skyward. And, what were her parting words when she shook her fist at Essie? *I don't care how long it takes! I'm not leaving Madison County until we have a deal!*

Essie walked to the window and stared at the pink car for a long moment. There was only one thing left to do. *Shoot her.*

She left the bedroom, moved down the stairs and into the kitchen. DooRay had left coffee simmering on the stove, its aroma comforting. She found her favorite cup, dainty bone china with tiny pink roses entwined around the rim. *Jewell's cup.* She felt a moment of sadness as she filled the cup and watched the steam rise. *I miss you, Jewell.*

The blaring horn quieted. From the porch, Essie heard the creak of the swing. *Oh, no, you . . . you Yankee!*

She ran to the screened door and slung it open.

And there, smiling sweetly, was Miss Lola LaRue – Thomas H. Fox's prized asset, the procurer of million dollar contracts, the star-maker, and a New York nightmare with a size 42DD bust.

"Good morning, Miss Donnelly," said the copper-haired woman. She dipped her head and looked up through her long, black eyelashes. "I said I'd be back." Her face exploded into a cunning smile.

An unsmiling Essie sat in a rocker and sipped her coffee. "Miss LaRue, your tenacity will not work here."

Lola crossed her legs, a red pair of shoes, all criss-crossed with straps, harnessed her not-so-dainty feet. The enormous breasts that so intrigued Sam Washington hid beneath a tight green blouse whose buttons strained to keep her bosom hitched.

"Why, Miss Donnelly, your lack of confidence in my abilities is hurtful." She pressed her painted lips together. "My only goal is to ensure your writing talent does not go unnoticed."

Lola wrinkled her brow and continued. "Tell me. What is so awful about becoming a famous author? Accumulating wealth?" Case closed, the smug literary agent leaned back in the swing and crossed her arms.

At that moment, Killer jumped from the yard onto the porch rail, his spurs shining dangerously in the morning sun. A soft gurgling sound traveled from his throat. The colors in his right eye flickered nervously as he eyed Miss LaRue. Killer's intuition was uncanny; how could a rooster sense malevolence?

The prized asset of the Thomas H. Fox Literary Agency stiffened, her eyes glued to Killer. She glanced at Essie, then back to the rooster. "Will that chicken hurt me?"

Essie almost laughed. "Only if I tell him to do so." She stood and walked to the porch rail. "Go on back to the barn, Killer. I'll call you if I need you." She gently tapped the rooster and he flew off the rail.

Behind her, Lola breathed a sigh of relief. "Thank you."

In the rocker once again, Essie's focus returned to Lola. "I don't doubt that your interests are sincere, Miss LaRue. But, in the end, these are my decisions, not yours. When and if I decide to go forward with the publication of my manuscript, I'll certainly do so."

Essie lifted her chin, a sign of resolution. "I'm afraid your trip from New York has been totally squandered. Please let Mr. Fox know my decision." She paused. "And no more surprise visits."

Huffy in her reply, Lola arched her perfect eyebrows. "Your decision is idiotic. A renowned literary agent, a stellar publisher and a lucrative contract has been laid at your feet and, yet, you put your nose in the air and spurn it all. You're not very bright!"

*You are not very bright.* Perhaps it was now time to shoot Miss LaRue. Drag her body out onto the Bellville road and then run over her with the pink Thunderbird. Then, allow the buzzards to dispose of the detritus that remained. If there were any further remains, they could be shipped back to New York, to the Thomas H. Fox Literary Agency. Essie would send the box with a pink ribbon around it, the same color as the Thunderbird.

From the Bellville road, a car turned down the lane. *Sam.* He parked near a grove of pecan trees, far away from the pink Thunderbird. Perhaps a disassociation that would redeem him from his breast gawking of the previous day.

His walk was slow. Head down, he ambled to the front porch and remained at the bottom step. Sam Washington was a handsome man. Tall, blue-eyed, a smile that was warm and engaging, he was perhaps Madison County's most eligible bachelor.

"Bad time?" he asked. Cigars poked from his shirt pocket, his love for smoking on the Donnelly's front porch his most favorite pastime.

Aloof, Essie glanced his way. "Suit yourself."

Sam's eyes darted to Lola, then back to Essie. "I think I'll go out to the barn and check on DooRay." He didn't wait for a reply as he left the steps and moved toward the barn.

Essie stood and leaned against the porch rail, only a few feet from Lola. *You are not very bright.* "Miss LaRue, your brashness offends me. Shall we say goodbye before I whip your ass?"

Essie's question was posed with a sublime softness. Beneath that softness was a controlled anger. The hard woman had spoken and if Miss LaRue had the tiniest bit of intelligence, she would sprint from the swing and jump into her pink Thunderbird and fly, yes *fly,* down the farm lane to the Bellville road and then to the Tallahassee airport.

Lola threw her head back and laughed like a donkey. "Oh, you don't mean that, now, do you, Miss Donnelly?"

"I'm afraid I do, Miss LaRue."

The donkey woman's screams could be heard within a half mile radius of the Donnelly farm. The pitiful sounds then trailed the pink Thunderbird as it vanished down the Bellville road toward Madison.

From the barn door, DooRay and Sam watched the dust settle on the farm lane. Essie glared at them and stomped up the porch steps.

Back inside the house, she poured herself a second cup of coffee and once more admired Jewell's bone china cup. She noticed one of her knuckles was scuffed, an abrasion that had turned red. She paused a moment, then smiled as she began to wonder if all the women from New York City could run as fast as Lola LaRue.

# CHAPTER THIRTY

The afternoon yielded a comfortable peace as Sam puffed his cigar, his seat on the picnic table a perfect place for man talk. DooRay sat beside him and began telling him the story of the alligator that napped with him on a sandbar in the middle of the Withlacoochee River."

"Yes, suh, Mr. Sam, I floated down that riber and next thing I knowed I landed on a big ole white sandbar. I said, 'oh, lawd, thank you.' 'Cause I done be so scared, so tired. My head felt funny and foggy, like I had no mind at all. I hit that sandbar and crawled up it like it was a mattress. A soft mattress just waitin' for ole DooRay."

"Go on, DooRay." Sam struck a match and lit a second cigar. His eyes swept the house looking for signs of Essie. The cold shoulder she had given him earlier had hurt. Of course, he'd not been too kind during their confrontation of the day before. And all because of Lola LaRue's breasts.

DooRay scratched his head. "It was along about dark, I suppose. I don't 'member them mens throwing me off the bridge, I jus' 'member them talkin' 'bout it before they hit me in the head over at the pond. Yes, suh, in the head, and I felt myself gone to *Gloryland*. Yes, suh, Glory-land." DooRay paused and took in a breath. "I reckon I came back from Gloryland when I hit the riber. I jus' don't 'member."

Murphy trotted to the picnic table and nudged DooRay. "Hey, you ole goat." Clouds covered the sun and left the barnyard in shadow. Afternoon showers were on the way. They'd come from the west and carry warm rain to Madison County's cornfields and watermelon patches.

DooRay reached out and scratched Murphy's head. "Yes, suh. I musta floated down that riber all day and I'm thinkin' that sandbar done found me. Last thing I 'member before falling asleep is seeing the moon comin' up."

DooRay laughed. "I sho wasn't thinkin' 'bout no gators. The next time I opened my eyes it was daylight, and lo and behold, an alligator was jus' a few feet away, looking at me."

Sam shook his head. "I can't imagine your thoughts, DooRay."

The first raindrops began to fall, and Killer and Murphy both ran to the barn. DooRay jumped off the picnic table. "Oh, I knowed my thoughts alright. I jus' closed my eyes and went back to sleep." The black man laughed and sprinted for the barn.

The rain lasted two hours, pummeling the tin roof of the barn and sounding like marching soldiers. Sam and DooRay continued their conversation for another hour, then said goodbye when Sam ran out of cigars.

It was 4:00 in the afternoon when Sam left the Donnelly barn, not too early for a cold beer. He wanted no part of Essie's 'Lola LaRue' conundrum, so he ignored the house as he walked to his car. A cold beer would be much safer than confronting the hard woman from Madison County.

On the banks of the Witchlacoochee, on the Georgia side, Mozelle's relished their reputation for fried catfish dinners and *hard* liquor. The catfish was fresh, right out of Black Bayou Lake in Louisiana. The liquor – *always fresh.* Mozelle's was a place where folks, mostly locals, enjoyed the friendly atmosphere as well as a cold seventy-five cent beer.

The parking lot was crowded, mostly pick-up trucks, a few motorcycles. Occasionally, a tractor or mule would belly up to a nearby river birch. Inside, Elvis Presley's *All Shook Up* played on the jukebox, not too loud. The aroma of hot grease hung in the air, along with cigarette smoke and the smell of perfume. Sam found an empty seat at the end of the bar and ordered a Pabst Blue Ribbon, a beer around since 1872, lovingly named after Captain Pabst, the brewery's president.

The bartender placed a cold beer in front of Sam and said, "Enjoy."

Sam sipped his beer. He was troubled, his thoughts not of his conflict with Essie, but of the perpetrators who had harmed DooRay. The Negros in Madison County were an important part of the community, well respected and acknowledged as contributors in many ways to the economic well-being of the county.

DooRay was beloved by all who knew him. His distinguished service in World War II won him recognition by the Army, his gallantry in action awarding him a Medal of Honor. The loss of his arm in battle was a huge contribution by a simple man who simply did his duty. To assault DooRay with the intent to kill him by throwing him off the Withla-coochee bridge was not taken lightly by those who knew him, as evidenced by the fervent search for him by the citizens of Madison County.

Sam reminded himself to get with Simmie Moore regarding the progress of the case. It didn't escape him that Essie's interest in the case was as intense as the sheriff's. She'd clean her daddy's gun, load them and have them within easy reach. The apprehension of the culprits would become her most impassioned priority.

Sam asked the waitress for a serving of hot hush puppies. The jukebox changed to *Star Dust* by *Billy Ward and the Dominoes*, its soothing melody evoking a feeling of loneliness. Another sip of beer as Sam looked into the mirror behind the bar. It reflected the entrance to the bar from the outside, the door squeaking each time it was opened, then a clunk as it closed.

Just as his hushpuppies arrived, the door squeaked and in walked a stunning woman, her lips painted bright red. She wore a tight blue, v-necked sweater. Skin-tight bluejeans ran down her legs to a pair of 5" heels, shiny silver. *Well, howdy do, Miss Lola LaRue.*

# CHAPTER THIRTY-ONE

Lola LaRue knew she was beautiful. Every head turned as she sauntered through the large room, around the small, square tables and finally to the end of the bar. She leaned over and put her perfect behind 'on stage.' She knew every pair of eyes in the room lusted after her. She propped her elbows on the bar, squeezing her breasts together into a lovely, deep pile of cleavage, each luscious inch reflected in the mirror facing her.

She had yet to see Sam at the opposite end of the bar. Instead, her eyes gave a coquettish glance to the bartender, along with a seductive smile. "How about a cold beer," she called. "And a glass."

The bartender, a skinny fellow named Hank, practically performed flips as he ran down the bar with a beer and glass in his hands. "Yes, ma'am. Here you go." He lingered a moment while she poured the beer into her glass. "How about some fried catfish?" he asked, hopefully.

Lola scrunched her face. "*Catfish*? I don't eat *catfish*. What about oysters on the half shell? I'd like some of those Apalachicola oysters."

Lola looked at him slyly. "The big ones." A laugh followed. Again, that seductive smile.

Hank's face dropped. "Oh, no, ma'am. We don't serve oysters. Potato chips?"

The New York City femme fatale took a long, slow sip of her beer. "I'll pass." It was then that Lola's gaze traveled down the large wall mirror and rested on Sam Washington. She tilted her head and grinned. "Hey, farm boy! Let me buy you a beer."

Her abrasive voice carried across the room and every head turned. *The buxom redhead wanted to buy someone a beer.* But who? They watched with envy as she sashayed toward the end of the bar in her silver shoes. She walked slowly, her entire body feasted upon by anyone who wasn't blind.

Just as Sam finished his hushpuppies, he turned. "Miss LaRue."

Without a moment's hesitation, she said, "Please call me Lola."

"Lola," said Sam. Refusing to leer at her cleavage, he reached for his beer and took a long drink. He hoped she didn't see his hand shaking.

"So, what about it? Another beer?" She slid next to him, her perfect derriere finding the barstool. The fragrance of her perfume wafted into his nostrils and he steeled himself to keep from swooning. *She was all woman.*

"No, thanks. One is plenty." He heard the bar door squeak and then clunk. A chill went up his spine as his back stiffened. With his luck, Essie would be standing in the middle of the room holding one of her daddy's guns. *A gun used for killing.*

He glanced quickly into the mirror. No one he knew. He quieted his heart and picked up a chip. "I assume you're heading back to New York?" His words were spoken with a soft casualness. *No, he didn't hear screaming in the Donnelly yard earlier that day, didn't see the pink Thunderbird convertible fire down the farm lane, its occupant shaking her fist in the air.*

After Miss LaRue's altercation with Essie, he desperately wanted to check her body for any broken bones, bruises, swelling or injuries in general. Thankfully, he kept his eyes on Hank and the myriad of beer bottles. One glance at the dazzling body would net him fifty years in the Essie Donnelly jail. He'd not risk it. *Period.*

Lola smiled sweetly. "Of course not. I'll return with a contract and insist Essie sign it." Her expression was one of complete and utter confidence.

Sam twirled his barstool toward her. He knew it was dangerous, but he was totally flabbergasted. There was no denying the doggedness of the woman. Tireless, her resolve was unlimited. She would traverse the tallest mountain, swim the mighty oceans and, in the end, sell her soul to the devil to persuade Essie to sign on the dotted line.

It was a mystery to him how Lola LaRue could subject herself to Essie. Granted, the book contract was a truly extraordinary opportunity for Essie, but 'no' was 'no.' If Essie Donnelly said 'no,' then the proverbial team of wild horses could never drag her an inch in a direction she didn't want to go.

"I think that's a poor decision, Lola. Essie is not a moveable object. If I were you, I'd head on back to New York." Sam finished his beer and stood from the barstool.

"Hey! Not so fast. Let's forget about Essie for a moment." She oozed sexiness. It came from every pore of her body and washed over Sam like a rushing tide. He stood in absolute stillness, feeling her breath on his face.

Lola slid from her barstool, her breasts brushing across his chest as she moved from the bar. He felt her heat and could almost hear his heart racing. "Forget about Essie?" he asked.

"Yes," she said, reaching up and stroking his cheek. "Just you and me."

Sam grinned and removed her hand from his cheek. "Lola, I don't think Essie'd like sharing me with another woman." He stepped away, but turned back toward her. "And, frankly, Miss LaRue, I don't want to be shared."

Sam pushed open the bar's squeaky door and heard it clunk behind him. Outside, the evening sky was ink blue, the quarter moon lighting the way to his car. The waters of the Withlacoochee rolled by, night sounds echoing from the nearby woods. Sam Washington, the man who loved Essie Donnelly, found himself laughing. *Oh, if Essie only knew he had had a close encounter with the indefatigable Miss Lola LaRue.*

# CHAPTER THIRTY-TWO

The sun barely up, Essie poured fresh coffee. Nearby, a bowl of fresh eggs sat in the center of the kitchen table. The hens had been laying regularly, despite the hot weather. She heard Killer crow for the third time as she walked out on the front porch and found the swing.

Essie's night had been fitful, a tossing and turning that left the bed linens twisted, the bedspread on the floor. Her mind chased demons the entire night, confronted them with anger and devoured them with fire.

Her squabbles with Sam had frayed her and left her spent. Perhaps it was conflict within herself that was the problem. *Why did she struggle so?* It was evident that she was a complex woman, but at age thirty-three, why wasn't she more content? More settled? Less angry?

She realized her frustration was perhaps well founded. Her mother's partiality toward Jewell should have wounded her over the years. Nonetheless, it did not – it simply made her a strong-willed, independent woman. She was afraid of nothing, accepting her hardness as an asset, one that provided her with the necessary tools to live her life. Decisive. Driven. And, most important, thanks to her father, her mental acuity.

Her frustration, in large part, was the realization of her mother Edith's shallowness, her lack of depth. In the end, Edith's own selfish need for perfection in her life had placed Jewell's pregnancy and the birth of a baby in a precarious situation. Essie would never forgive her.

Her mind's turmoil was recognizable. Essie knew she must confront her unrest, mend the uncertainty, attack her tumultuous life as though it were a deadly enemy.

*Bootsey Birthright.* Yes, she'd resolve her issues with the woman who conspired with Edith Donnelly to take Jewell's child away from her. *Heavens, no!* Essie's mother would never allow the Donnelly's reputation to be tarnished by a baby born out of wedlock. Edith considered herself royalty in Madison County – how could she be the mother of a daughter who had had sex before marriage?

Since last summer, upon the discovery of the baby's existence, Essie had wanted to find the child. But, her mother was dead and there was no information to be had. *Except for Bootsey Birthright*, her mother's best friend.

Under the pretense that Jewell was in a finishing school in Switzerland, Edith had sent her to Atlanta, where Bootsey was the all-girls school administrator. Together, Edith and Bootsey plotted to give the baby away. *Here. Want a baby? Here's one. Take it. It's yours.* Given away like a bushel of corn, or a watermelon.

Bootsey had refused Essie's request for information on the circumstances surrounding the baby's birth. It seemed the information had died with Edith. Essie had begged her mother's best friend to help her. Bootsey Birthright had been steadfast in her refusal.

As yet, Essie had not told Bootsey she'd found Jewell's child. But, she would. *That very day. Rose* was her name. Rose and her mother, Annalee, planned a visit to the farm soon. *Your daughter's coming here, Jewell. To the farm. To the place where you were born and lived all your life. We'll bring you flowers.*

Simmie Moore's 1956 Ford turned onto the farm lane toward the Donnelly house. Perhaps the sheriff had news. It could be that he had found the two men who had thrown DooRay into the Withlacoochee. He parked and walked across the yard. His pipe rested in his shirt pocket and he fingered it as he stepped onto the porch.

"Good morning, Essie. Got some more of that coffee?" He pulled off his hat, his black hair parted perfectly and combed to one side. Only forty-seven years old, Simmie Moore was not only good at his job, he was also handsome.

From the farmyard, DooRay's clear baritone voice lifted high in the air, the hymn familiar. *Softly and tenderly, Jesus is calling . . . calling for you and for me.* He rounded the corner of the house, followed by Murphy, with Killer riding the goat's back. "Good mornin', sheriff."

"Hello, DooRay. Just the man I want to see." He eased into a rocker and pulled out his pipe.

"Come on the porch, DooRay, and let's have some coffee."

DooRay grinned. "Yes, ma'am, Miss Essie. That'd be good. Biscuits and jelly, too?." He opened the screen door and they headed for the kitchen, while Murphy and Killer wandered off into the yard, Murphy's hind leg a little stiff.

Back out on the porch, DooRay and Essie served hot coffee and a plate of biscuits, still warm.

Simmie packed his pipe. "I'm thinkin' another hot day." He began a slow rock and lit his pipe. "How are you feeling, DooRay?"

"I'm better every day. Minnie's been a good nurse."

"I'm certain she's the best. She cares a lot for you, DooRay."

"She sho' do."

"By the way, DooRay, when Son and I met up with Miccosukee Mae to talk to her about anything she might have seen or heard, she gave us two odd clues. Don't really know what they mean.

"She said she wasn't on the river that morning. Said she was out in the woods gathering mushrooms. But, while she was in the woods, she heard music. When she returned to her shack, she got a distinct smell of whiskey." Simmie scratched his head. "How in the world she smelled whiskey and heard music, I don't know."

Essie nodded. She hoped DooRay would not mention the *Alabama Seeds* salesmen as she contemplated Simmie's conversation with Tayki.

"Whiskey, huh?" The black man watched his goat for a long moment, his eyes squinting, deep in thought. "Sheriff, DooRay don't 'member nary a thing after I was hit in the head.

"I woke up floatin' down that riber." He looked at Essie, his eyes shadowed, thinking about *Alabama Seeds* and the two men who gave her the sample bag of seeds.

Simmie nodded. "You remember hearing any music?"

DooRay raised his eyebrows and stared wide-eyed at Simmie. His eyes shifted to Essie. At that moment, he remembered the blaring radio from the previous summer, the memory buried until now. The seed salesmen had left their truck doors open, the radio playing country music at full volume.

"No suh. I was gone to Gloryland till I floated down the Withlacoochee." DooRay closed his eyes, remembering.

"I understand, DooRay." He paused and flicked a fly off his khaki's. "That was one tough interview. That old Indian woman's panther was up in the tree, his yellow eyes watching us. She called him *Cat* and said he'd eat us if she asked him to."

"Panther?" said DooRay. "They's a panther killin' chickens all around here, sheriff. Reckon it's Cat?"

"That's right, Simmie," said Essie. "Emmett Gaston lost about a half dozen chickens to a panther about a week ago. Said he shot at him, but missed."

"Well, these woods are full of panthers. Could be *Cat*."

"I done got me a gun out in the barn. I'll use it if'n a big ole cat mess with my chickens." DooRay finished his coffee and stood. "Gots to go water the chickens." He stepped off the porch and hollered across the yard. "Come on, you two rascals. Let's go take care of the chickens."

Murphy and Killer raced across the yard. DooRay was their best friend.

"Thank you, DooRay. I'll see you later in the week. If you think of anything that might be helpful, let Essie know and she'll give me a call."

Simmie stood and placed his empty coffee cup on the porch rail. The sheriff was a deliberate man, and his failure to solve the case was troubling him greatly. "Essie, I'm doing my best. You know that, don't you?"

Essie left the swing and patted Simmie on the shoulder. "You're the best man I know to solve this mystery, Simmie. Just give it some time."

Despite Simmie's frustration, Essie had no intention of telling him about *Alabama Seeds*. No, she'd handle that on her own. *Yes, there she was again.* That hard woman who had no problem righting a wrong, no matter the consequences.

Inside the house, Essie picked up the telephone and dialed the operator. "Hello, I'd like to place a long distance call, please. Andalusia, Alabama. 565-2300. Thank you."

A cheerful voice answered the telephone. "Alabama Seeds."

Essie didn't hesitate. "Hello, I'd like to know when a salesman for your company will visit Madison County, Florida."

"Sure. I'll transfer you to Sales."

Essie heard a click, then a loud, southern voice. "Willard Jones, Territory Sales Manager. How can I help you?"

Essie could hear a gasp between each word, a raspy voice that made her think he was a smoker. "Hello, I'm wondering when one of your salesmen will be visiting the Madison County, Florida, sales territory?"

"Uh, let's see here." Essie heard papers shuffling, then an unmistakable drag on a cigarette. "Well, that'd be the fourth week in July. July 22nd through July 26th. First appointment is at the Davis farm out on Highway 145."

"I see," said Essie. July 22nd – only two weeks away. "Which salesman is that?"

"Same one as always. Malcolm Maxwell. 'Course, everybody calls him *Spit*. Big tobacco chewer."

*Well, well, Spit, looks like you and I will be crossing paths very soon.*

The sound of a trotting horse echoed through the barn, then fell silent, followed by a clang of stirrups and the soft blowing of air from a horse's mouth.

Lum Townsend led his horse Hickory to the water trough, the chestnut drinking heartily. To his right, the door of the tack room stood propped open with an old bucket, and a smiling DooRay ambled out into the farmyard.

"Mr. Lum, you're a sight for sore eyes."

The cowboy slapped Hickory on the rump and the horse found a patch of grass near the fence row. "I was going to say the same thing about you, DooRay." Lum extended his hand and gave DooRay a warm handshake.

A grinning DooRay motioned to the picnic table. "Come on over here and sit a spell."

Lum obliged and the pair saddled up to the benches, their backs to the warm sunshine. "So glad to see you doing well, DooRay. Everybody was worried about you for a while there."

"Oh, ole DooRay done be fine, but I thank you for your concern. Folks have been mighty good to me."

DooRay shuffled his feet and turned to Lum. "I wants to thank you and George for ridin' 'round in these here woods trying to find me and Murphy."

"We wouldn't have had it any other way, DooRay. And that's what neighbors do when there's trouble – look out for one another."

"Yes, suh. You folks did 'actly that." DooRay's voice broke and he turned away.

Lum reached out and gently slapped the black man's shoulder. "You're family, DooRay. Don't you ever forget that."

# CHAPTER THIRTY-THREE

After her retirement, Bootsey Birthright had moved to Madison. Her house, a cottage-like design, was small but charming. Bootsey and Edith, best friends since elementary school, had considered themselves the principal leaders of the elite in Madison County. Edith, married to a wealthy farmer, or so she thought, and Bootsey, a graduate of Barnard's under-graduate program. Then, on to Columbia, where Manhattan had become her playground.

In New York, Bootsey picked up uppercrust habits which prepared her for her administrator's position at a prestigious all-girls college prep boarding school in Atlanta.

Bootsey's illustrious education and acclaimed career did not, however, provide her with integrity. She lied, conspired and broke the law when she, at Edith's direction, gave away Jewell's baby.

Essie knocked softly on the wooden door. At her feet, a yellow cat rubbed against her legs. She reached down and rubbed its back. The little red collar's bell tinkled when the cat jumped onto the wicker furniture.

Another knock, louder this time. At last, a harsh voice from inside. "Who is it? I don't want any Girl Scout cookies! Nor, do I want to donate to the Madison High School's cheerleaders. Get off my porch."

A hateful woman, Bootsey also lacked social skills. Essie called through the door. "It's Essie Donnelly, Miss Birthright."

Immediately, the woman yelled through the door. "I don't know any Essie Donnelly."

Essie took a deep breath. "Edith Donnelly's daughter."

"Edith's dead. Been dead."

"That's true, Miss Birthright. But, this is her daughter."

A long moment passed and Essie almost knocked again. Then, another retort from the old woman. "The pretty daughter?"

Essie bit her lip. When and if Bootsey opened the door, she would slap her, yank her hair and spit on her.

Finally, Essie said. "I brought you a pound cake, Miss Bootsey." She had no pound cake, and she also had no patience.

The door slowly opened and revealed the pompous Miss Birthright. Her bright blue eyes had faded, no longer bursting with light. Her hair had not been combed; where did the prim lady go?

"Where's the pound cake?" She frowned at Essie, then pursed her lips. "Do you know what I do to girls when they lie to me?" She sneered and began to close the door.

"Wait! Miss Bootsey, I want to talk with you about Jewell." Essie placed a hand on the door.

"Jewell who?" Bootsey looked puzzled. "Are you Jewell?"

"No, I'm Essie. Jewell died."

"Does Edith know?"

Essie leaned against the doorframe and sighed. "Everything's fine, Miss Bootsey. Maybe I'll bring you a pound cake tomorrow. And some vanilla ice cream."

The old woman smiled. "That would be lovely." The door slammed shut, almost catching Essie's fingers. Startled, she lingered a moment, watching the yellow cat jump off the porch and run into the hedge. A nearby mockingbird fussed at the cat and flitted through the air above him. A slight breeze brought the fragrance of gardenias from the yard next door, perhaps an omen.

Bootsey Birthright was no longer a nemesis in Essie's life. Essie had let her go, had acknowledged Bootsey's mind was incapable of reason.

At last Essie was free, the pain of betrayal lifted. *I found the baby, Miss Bootsey.*

Essie left Madison and drove north along Highway 145 to Pinetta. The ride home was bittersweet.

# CHAPTER THIRTY-FOUR

I t was nearing late afternoon when Essie turned the old Pontiac down the farm lane. She held her breath and looked for the pink Thunderbird, which was nowhere to be seen. Relieved, Essie walked to the mailbox and gathered the mail. In the front porch swing, she leaned back and listened to the geese at Grassy Pond. The sun had moved behind the tall cypress trees that bordered the pond, leaving long, deep shadows along the edge of the cornfield.

A Western Auto flyer, a seed catalog and two pieces of personal mail lay in Essie's lap. The first letter was in a pink envelope and written in dainty cursive.

*July 3, 1957*

*Dearest Aunt Essie,*

*I am writing to you to let you know Mama and Daddy have told me about my birth mother. They said it was a miracle that Mama met you at the rose parade in Thomasville. Mama said you told her I look just like my real mother. I know we met at the rose parade, but I didn't know you were my aunt. I can't wait to see you again and hear all about my mother. Mama is going to call you to talk about our visit to Pinetta sometime this month. Thank you for searching for me. I love having an Aunt Essie.*

*All my love,*

*Rose*

*A miracle.* Yes, it was. If Minnie hadn't seen a picture of Jewell and declared it was a girl she had seen at one of the Thomasville plantations, Essie would never have found Rose. *Your daughter is coming to the farm, Jewell. She'll see your yellow bedroom and visit the cemetery. We'll put some roses on your grave. And, Jewell, we'll sit in the grass and talk to you and tell you how much we love you.*

The second envelope, the handwriting bold and forthright, as well as unrecognizable, held no return address. *Essie Donnelly, Pinetta, Florida. Intriguing,* she thought.

And there it was. As much a love letter as a cocky Irishman could write.

*My dear lassie,*

*By now, you are probably back home and enjoying the summer at the Donnelly farm. It has not been the same here in Thomasville without the auburn-haired beauty I met on a cold night back in March. In the middle of the night, if I recall. I also recall your feisty commands to this jaunty fellow. Of course, I gladly succumbed to your spell.*

*Archbold Hospital has me in their cardiac unit, to which I am totally devoted. The surgery for Pitch went well. But, I'll update you when I see you, which will be very soon.*

*On a cold March day*
*I saw her there*
*And knew*

*That her auburn hair*
*Would weave a snare*
*That caught me unaware*

*Robert Gray, Your Obedient Servant*

Essie read the letter twice. And smiled. The memories came flooding back. Awaking the good doctor in the middle of a cold March night in Boston, Georgia. Demanding him to save Minnie Pryor's life. Talking together late into the night. And, she watched while he fell in love with her. *Dr. Robert Gray, handsome Irishman.*

Her feelings confused her. While reading the letter, the beat of her heart quickened. And what did he say? *I'll update you when I see you, which will be very soon.*

Essie tucked both letters away and went inside the house. In the kitchen, she hesitated. A large vase of fresh flowers sat in the middle of the kitchen table. She saw daisies, lilies, roses, gladiolus, and baby's breath in glorious colors. *Sam.*

She quickly opened the card.

*Dear Miss Donnelly,*
*Please forgive my brash behavior. I apologize for assuming it was*
*a requirement for you to agree to a contract with the Thomas H.*
*Fox Literary Agency, as well as the publisher. Of course, the deci-*
*sion is yours. The choice is yours.*
*I feel I have been insensitive to your needs and ask that you*
*pardon my actions.*
*There is no change in my belief that your novel is worthy of publi-*
*cation and will garner you recognition as a talented author.*
*Watermelon Queen of Madison County is a poignant story that*
*should be shared with readers everywhere.*
*Sincerely,*
*Lola LaRue*

*Is this card a forgery?* Essie laughed out loud. *Lola LaRue apologizing?* She stepped back and admired the flowers. *Be candid, Essie. A trick? Was Miss LaRue really apologizing, asking for a pardon?*

Essie would concede one thing and one thing only: Miss LaRue knew how to change the game. The flowers and a conciliatory note opened the door – but only slightly.

Evening came softly. Across the Bellville road, the last glimmer of the sunset touched the Townsend pastures, where cattle settled for the night, a lonely soft bellow now and then.

In minutes, the light faded and darkness fell. A whippoorwill called from the woods, perhaps an invitation to go courting. Another melodic call. Yes, there would be courting under the July moon.

Essie slipped out on the front porch and found her 'thinking' spot on the swing. *Where was Sam?* His absence was unsettling. It had been two days since she'd heard from him. She stood and walked to the porch rail, a longing in her heart. She heard the whippoorwill again and felt the nudgings of despair. *Perhaps she should go to Sam.*

# CHAPTER THIRTY-FIVE

Another night of turmoil, of pacing in the long upstairs hallway and finally finding the front porch around 3:00 a.m. Essie's mind raced at quantum speed, landing in giant piles of anxiety that seemed insurmountable.

*Bill and Mike Washington.* She had to talk with them. Confronting *Spit* would not be easy, not for what she had in mind. Over the years, it was the Washington boys, Sam's brothers, who supported her in her pursuit of justice.

In March, in Boston, Georgia, *Fat Belly,* a degenerate, had slaughtered a black sharecropper's pigs – a sow and her eleven pigs – in retaliation for Essie's removal of the 'whites only' sign on Fat Belly's shack of a store on Highway 84. She had to right that wrong, but not without the Washington's. She had threatened to cut off Fat Belly's testicles, an act not approved of by Bill or Mike. They did, however, help her tie up the deplorable man while she had a little chat with him.

The brothers had always been her backup, the prowess she needed in case it was necessary. Bill and Mike were God-fearing, integrity-laden men. They were also men who did not like to see the underdog trampled upon. Hence, their cooperation when it came to seeking justice. Bill's level headedness and Mike's adeptness when using his .38 were huge assets.

There were other attributes that could not be ignored. The men had courage, were brave and daring when called for. Mike's backbone could have been construed as cockiness, mostly when he twirled his .38.

Bill, soft-spoken but fearless, held Essie and Mike to a certain standard. Between the three of them, they could handle most anything. An encounter with Spit and his partner would be a piece of cake, or so she thought.

At 5:00 a.m., Essie climbed the stairs to her bedroom and fell into a fitful sleep. Dreams plundered her mind, captured a naked Irishman who crooked his finger at her and beckoned her to make love to him. She felt her resistance weakening and sauntered toward him, pulling off her clothes.

It was then she awoke, Killer's crow loud and irritating. Her heart thundered in her chest. Breathless, she jumped from her bed. *Robert Gray*. In the dream, she had made passionate love to the handsome Irishman. Had kissed him longingly, her body feverish with desire.

She quickly dressed, stumbled down the stairs and found a cold pot of coffee on the stove. Glancing at the clock, she realized she had slept until 9:00. Unheard of for a farm girl who had awakened with the chickens each morning her entire life.

"DooRay," she called from the back porch. She clamored down the steps and trotted across the barnyard. Murphy dashed from the barn and followed her to the tack room. "DooRay," she called again.

"Yes, ma'am, Miss Essie."

"Where are you, DooRay?" Frustrated, Essie glanced down the fence line, the wellhouse and finally called again. "Where?"

"Up here, Miss Essie." DooRay had climbed the oak tree on the east side of the tack room, his legs hanging from a large limb, where he sat and looked at her. *How could a one-armed man climb a tree?*

"What are you doing in that tree?"

"Oh, DooRay done be makin' a hide-out."

"A hide-out? What for?" Essie, frustrated, peered up into the tree.

He grinned and swung his legs. "I figure I can sit up here and wait for that ole panther that's killin' chickens 'round here."

"You mean sit up there with a gun . . . all night?" Incredulous, Essie walked around the tree, her neck craned to see DooRay's hide-out.

"Well, the way I see it, I can sleep up here with a loaded gun and when that cat come sneakin' by to have some of our chickens for dinner, I'll give him a pellet or two in his hind end."

Essie rolled her eyes. "DooRay, what if you fall off your hide-out? You'd break your neck, for sure."

"Don't you worry none, Miss Essie. I fought in the Big War and I sure as rain gone fight a panther without breakin' my neck."

Essie huffed and shook her head. "Where's the gun?"

DooRay pointed. "Right there. I got it all rigged up. See this here twine I got tied around the trigger? Why, I can lean back in my hide-out and when I sees that big ole panther, all's I has to do is pull the twine."

Essie scanned the oak tree. Finally, she saw a board with a notch cut out of it, the gun's barrel wedged neatly inside and pointing directly at the chicken pen.

"Well, DooRay, that's daddy's shotgun! That thing has no choke on it! You fire that and it will kill every chicken in that pen. It's pointed right at them."

There was silence from the hide-out. DooRay's legs stopped swinging. The oak tree stilled. Finally, DooRay ducked his head and, sad-eyed, glanced down at Essie. "Miss Essie, you knowed I only gots one arm. I cain't shoot this shotgun 'less I got twine running down to that trigger."

For the first time ever, DooRay sounded prickly, like a bear with a sore head. He'd figured out how he could shoot a gun with just one arm, and he was dang proud of it. It seemed to him that Essie had overlooked his ingenuity and been insensitive to his disability.

The mistress of the Donnelly farm became thoughtful, gazing at the board with the notch in it, the position of the gun, the twine tied around the trigger. And, lastly, the firing path of the buckshot. Exactly what was the spread of the pellets? *Goodbye, chickens.*

"All right, DooRay. I guess that panther doesn't know what he's in for." She walked away and left DooRay in the tree, his legs dangling down, a smile on his face.

# CHAPTER THIRTY-SIX

It was only a few miles to the Washington farm. Through Pinetta, then north on Highway 145, the farm covered hundreds of acres, saddling up to the Withlacoochee River on the western most acreage, the waters flowing south, eventually reaching its confluence with the Suwannee River, near Live Oak.

Essie's earliest memories at Paul and Julia Washington's farm were peanut boils and cane grindings. Their three sons, Bill, Sam and Mike were important to the farm's success. Sam's career had shifted from the farm to attorney. Mike was still in college, and Bill was his father's right arm when it came to managing the farm. Essie had known them her entire life, their families entwined through church, school and farming.

Essie drove slowly, gathering her thoughts. Of course, she could not share her plans with Sam. He would admonish her, refuse to be a part of anything that was in the least bit unlawful. *Unlawful?* Sometimes things just had to be done in an unlawful manner. At least, that was *Essie's law*.

It was true she should have turned over evidence to Sheriff Moore. And, eventually, she'd provide him with all the information she had gathered. DooRay's realization that the men who had assaulted him were the same men who had been at their farm the previous summer, representing Alabama Seeds, was a stroke of good luck.

Essie had to admit her plan to confront *'Spit'* and his cohort was self-serving. Justice beyond the criminal justice system had always been Essie Donnelly's modus operandi, her methodology based on pure common sense. Not to mention, her extensive knowledge of guns, and the skill to use them, always an asset in any situation.

Her fearlessness, as well as her innate characteristic of righting wrongs, was not thwarted by the court's process of legally determining guilt or innocence.

The assault on DooRay had affected her greatly. Then, an obvious attempt to kill him by throwing the one-armed man off the Bellville road bridge, had placed her in a revenge mode. The thought of finding his body in the Withlacoochee River and then burying him was unthinkable. No, she'd not let the opportunity of confronting *Spit* pass her by.

Essie parked near the Washington's barn and honked the horn. Mike, out of college for the summer, moved from behind a tractor and waved. Essie slipped out of the Pontiac and stepped over a pile of cow manure. "Got a cow loose, Mike?"

Mike grinned. "A calf. Slipped through the pasture fence early this morning. She's back with her mama." He wiped his hands on a work rag and walked her way.

"What's got you out this way?" He narrowed his eyes. "We both know very well anytime you drive out here, you're in trouble and need help." He laughed. "Or, at least, need backup. Am I right?"

Mike, handsome and energetic, moved into the shade of the barn and sat on a bale of hay. Essie followed and sat near him. "Mike, do I really have that reputation around here?" she asked, smiling.

"Ha! You're dang right. Essie, you have been trouble your entire life. I can't tell you the number of times . . ."

"Mike, please! What are you saying? That I'm stubborn? Impulsive? A hot-head? Mentally deranged?"

Still laughing, Essie blurted. "Of course, I'm trouble!" Then, softly, "But I feel I've always been led by the right reasons." Essie looked away, her gaze finding the old house where the Washington's had lived for decades. Barely audible, "I've got to do this, Mike."

Mike sighed deeply and leaned back. "Okay, let's have it. Will this require breaking the law . . . again?"

Essie turned and grinned at him. "Possibly."

"Will it require the use of a gun?"

"Possibly."

Mike shook his head. "Do I need to get Bill in on this?"

Essie stood and brushed hay off her bluejeans. She found a nearby stool and pulled it closer to Mike. "Possibly." She gazed at him, her face turning hard. "I'm pretty sure I know who assaulted DooRay and threw him into the Withlacoochee."

Mike became quiet. He leaned over and picked up a strand of straw and stuck it in his mouth and chewed awhile. "That right? Who? And how did you find them?" He spoke a little too casually, an indication he knew what was to follow. Why panic at this point?

"DooRay found them. He's sure he recognized his assailants. He remembered two men stopped by the farm last summer and left a sample bag of seed corn. They were from Alabama Seeds out of Andalusia, Alabama."

"Seed salesmen? What were they doing at Ran Terry's pond?"

"Up to no good. Drinking, goofing off. Two reprobates who thought it would be fun to throw a harmless, one-armed black man off the bridge on the Bellville road." Essie swallowed hard.

She continued. "Not only did they bust DooRay's head open and shoot Murphy, they decided to have a little more fun. Throwing him off the bridge was probably the most fun they'd had all year."

Mike nodded. "You sure about this?"

"Of course. DooRay's recognition of them was certain. One of them is named *Spit*."

"*Spit*? Think maybe they've been to our farm?"

"Don't know. They're scheduled to work the Madison County area the week of July 22nd, calling on the Davis farm sometime during that week."

Mike sent her a frown. "So, you're gonna hijack them somehow?" He laughed. "Lasso them, drag them naked all across Madison County? Tar and feather them? Ride them out of town on a rail, their hind ends dragging the dirt?"

Essie gave Mike a long, cool look, staring him down and making him squirm a little. "This is a serious matter, Mike, and I assure you these evil-doers will receive their just punishment."

"But, Essie! That's not up to you. That's up to Simmie Moore to handle the proper way. Apprehend them, arrest them, press charges. Why do you have to be such a vigilante?"

Essie found herself getting angry. She refused to be denied the opportunity to confront Spit and his cohort. "Because Sheriff Moore's process would be too easy for these rascals." She paused and watched a barn cat climb a tall stack of hay. In moments, she heard the mewing of kittens.

She turned back to Mike. "I'm going to do this without your help, if I have to, Mike," she said softly.

Mike knew Essie Donnelly well. He knew she'd handle things in her own way. What way, he didn't know at this point. "You know I'm in, Essie," he said quietly." He stood from his seat on the hay bale. "Let's go talk to Bill."

Bill Washington had always seemed to take on the role of pacifier whenever the situation called for a calm, low-key individual who kept a cool head. That is, in most circumstances. His involvement in Essie's shenanigans was one of respect – respect for a woman whose judgment was sound, although her methods in resolving conflicts were sometimes questionable, and definitely unorthodox. He admired her quest to do the right thing – always. Her defense of those she loved was well grounded. No stone unturned, she would right a wrong and fulfil her responsibilities as a protector of those who were in need, especially those she loved.

They found Bill in a corn field, atop a tractor pulling a harrow. Mike whistled loudly and Bill took off his hat and waved to them as they bellied up to the barbed wire fence and waited.

Bill shut off the tractor and walked across the field to the fence. It was a slow walk, a walk perhaps with a little bit of trepidation.

Madison County's renegade woman flashed Bill a dazzling smile, a sure sign of an upcoming entrapment. He smiled back. Essie was really a man in a woman's body. She was also a true, lovely Southern belle . . . until she was riled. It was then that her hands balled up into fists, her face contorted in anger, and her mind went to a place called retribution.

"Hello, Bill. Got a few minutes?" Essie lifted a strand of barbed wire while Bill, taking off his hat, ducked under it.

Bill fanned himself with his hat. "Let's go sit in the barn." Without speaking, the three headed for the barn and found seats on hay bales. The barn fan spun loudly, and stirred the hot air.

Bill leaned over and placed his elbows on his knees and clasped his hands. And waited. He noticed Essie had that look about her. She was on the warpath and headed for a reckoning.

Mike was the first to speak. "Bill, Essie's trying to solve a little problem and she needs our help."

"A little problem? Essie?" Bill send a half-grin to Mike, then turned to Essie. "What is it this time?"

Essie stammered. "I . . . I'm on the trail of the two men who harmed DooRay, threw him in the Withlacoochee. I figured you and Mike might like to help me wrap it up." *Wrap it up?* Essie's words painted her proposed undertaking with a casual indulgence.

Bill nodded, an uneasiness prickling the back of his neck. "Wrap it up? How so?"

The barn air smelled like a hay field, its bales of hay stacked high and dry. A baby calf lay in a nearby stall. Hand fed, it would stay safe in the barn until steady on its feet. His mama wouldn't feed him.

"Not sure," replied Essie. "I just know these two men work for the Alabama Seed Company out of Andalusia, Alabama." She repeated the details she had told Mike earlier, and carefully watched Bill's face.

"So, you're going to have a little chat with them? Does this involve testicles?" Visions of Fat Belly, Essie's most recent caper, were fresh. No doubt about it, it was Essie's threat to remove Fat Belly's testicles that brought justice to the victims of his misdeeds.

Essie stared wide-eyed at Bill. "I do not solve every problem with the removal of testicals." She jumped from the hay bales and paced the barn. "This is ridiculous. All I'm asking you two to do is be on standby in case I need your help."

"And you want us carrying guns?" Pragmatic Bill. He wanted to know the entire plan before he made any commitments.

"Well, what do you think?" Her words were heated. "They shot Murphy with a gun so I'll assume they carry guns. Do you want to be my backup *without* guns?"

Bill's words were conjoling. "Essie, we'll be there for you. Just don't want anybody to get hurt. I understand you're leaving Simmie out of this, but it's a dangerous thing to do."

"Are you afraid, Bill?"

"You know I'm not, Essie. I'm just being cautious." He slapped his knee for emphasis. "And don't anybody dare let mama and daddy know what we're doing."

Essie left the Washington farm, drove to the highway, and counted the days until the week of July 22nd. Fourteen days. She'd visit Dave Davis and find out when the Alabama Seed salesmen would visit his farm. Then, she'd figure out a way to have a little chat with Spit and his buddy. That's all. *Just a little chat.*

Paradoxically, she knew she would never catch them if she thought like an ordinary person. She was a 'good ole' boy' kind of thinker who was not a criminal expert in any way. But, there was one thing she did have and that was perseverance. And perseverance was deadly if you were Essie Donnelly.

# CHAPTER THIRTY-SEVEN

Had a poem been written about the town of Pinetta, one word would have described it perfectly. *Small.* Yet, inside its clay road boundaries, and its many outlying farms, there was the sound of soft heartbeats, a gentle pounding that affirmed the existence of life, the state of being.

Over the years, it was likely that no citizen had given any thought to the town's architecture. It was as though the town had just 'poked' up from the earth, here and there. The houses, the churches, the buildings sprouted like random thoughts that seemed to attach to one another and create a town.

Pinetta's small town architecture extolled its black and white checkerboard house near the railroad tracks, its small inventory very much in demand as it was mostly sweets and snacks for children who walked home from the nearby Pinetta school.

Across the tracks, an open-sided shack-like building west of the train depot was aptly called the 'cucumber house.' Farmers brought their wagon loads of cucumbers to the building, where they were graded and then trucked to the Roddenberry Pickling Company in Cairo, Georgia. Ivy Wiglesworth kept everything organized and running.

Like the seed in the center of a peach, the Pinetta train depot held together the mountains of watermelons from Madison County farms, getting them loaded on trains headed north. Farmers pulled their wagons loaded with Cannon Balls, Crimson Sweets and Charleston Gray's by horses and mules, as well as trucks for shipment to Valdosta. In Valdosta, they were shipped farther north to the big cities. There was no telling where a Madison County watermelon ended up.

Essie passed the train depot and drove across the tracks where J. T. Woodward's store sold essentials as well as the best ice cream in the county. Next, the Allen store, the drug store and Coody's meat market. The drug store served as the post office, having been in the Allen store until it closed.

Essie pulled back across the tracks. *What was she doing? Looking for Sam?* He wasn't at Webb's Barber Shop, nor chatting with Jack Woodard at his garage. She pulled the Pontiac back onto Highway 145 and headed for the Bellville road. She wondered if Sam was huddled up somewhere with the buxom Lola LaRue. *No, no, he wasn't.* Not Sam.

She drove slowly and passed Vernon Smith's house as she turned onto Highway 150. She was in a nostalgic mood, her memories vivid. Born and raised in Pinetta, her most unforgettable memory was the 1948 flood. The Withlacoochee had overflowed, as well as Cherry Lake. The waters reached almost to Hickory Grove.

At the Donnelly house, the Bellville road had been impassable, water levels up to five and six feet. Many properties were destroyed, but the fishing was good. The Donnelly house escaped the high water, its foundation high on a clay hill.

Essie slipped by Terryville where Lon Terry stood at the gas pump talking to Paul Ellington. He waved and she saw his freckled face smiling. She glanced across the road and watched his Tamworth hogs rooting in the mud. Lon always kept a water hose atop the fence and sprayed cool water into the pen during hot summer months.

Essie felt lost without Sam. Maybe she took him for granted. His last words to her . . . 'well, maybe you're not in my future' were hurtful. Perhaps his absence was a 'cooling off' period, a time to reassess their relationship.

*What if they married? Why not?* She found herself daydreaming. *Children? A family?*

She slowed at the farm lane and guided the Pontiac to the barn. She looked up to see if DooRay was in the oak tree, his fingers attached to the twine that was hooked to the trigger of the powerful shotgun. She didn't see him. Surely, he had not fallen and broken his neck.

Murphy trotted to meet her, a ritual that she appreciated. Killer wasn't far behind. The rooster sprang forward and jumped onto Murphy's back and held on. They were a humorous pair. Add DooRay to the mix, and it was a circus.

"DooRay," she called. She soon heard laughter. Across the field north of the barn, two figures walked slowly through the run-away watermelon vines. One was DooRay, a walking stick in his right hand, his deep voice rumbling across the field. Next to him, a tall man wearing a hat, carried a watermelon on his shoulder and whose laugh she had heard before.

# CHAPTER THIRTY-EIGHT

*The Irishman.* The closer he got, the faster her heart beat. A flitter in her chest, an anticipation, caused her to take a quick breath. As she watched his slow trek across the field, the memories came flooding back.

A cold March night, a loud knock on the good doctor's door at 3:00 a.m. in Boston, Georgia. His sleepy appearance, wearing plaid boxer shorts. His Irish accent. Then, his frustration with the farm girl who asked him . . . no, who *demanded* that he follow her to the Pryor farm to save the life of Minnie Pryor.

Dr. Robert Gray had saved Minnie's life, a spider bite that had almost killed the young woman. And, in just over a week's time, the doctor had melded into the Pryor family as though the universe had shifted, had sent him there to do more than administer to Minnie. The young Pryor boys, Pitch and Orland, Minnie's brothers, were also in need.

Dr. Gray's pursuit of the repair of Pitch's club foot had become a passion. The poverty in the family was also a concern. It was obvious the doctor's Hippocratic oath had been taken with heartfelt devotion. *Into whatsoever house I enter, I will enter to help the sick.*

*First do no harm* and all the ethical principles of the oath had, indeed, become Dr. Gray's mantra. At the Pryor house, his medical skill had been parlayed into *heart* care, an acknowledgment that he was needed far beyond the physical care of Minnie Pryor.

Essie felt a gentle tug on her heart. The Irishman had had an impact on her life. But, she couldn't truly define it. His care for her had gone well beyond platonic and she knew it. Just didn't know what to do about it.

And, here he came into her life once more. The same handsome, dark-haired man, his perpetual smile and that funny accent that came from across the sea.

Dr. Gray hollered across the field. "Ah, there's my lass. Oh, how I've missed ye." He waved, almost dropping the watermelon. Laughing, he spoke to DooRay. "My friend, do ye see what that woman does to me?"

At the fence, Dr. Gray shifted the watermelon to Essie and the two men crawled under a strand of barbed wire. Once under the fence, Dr. Gray grabbed the watermelon and placed it on the ground. It was then that he swooped Essie off her feet and twirled her around. "Ah, it's you! My auburn-haired lass with the sharp tongue. The farm girl who doesn't let a man boss her around." He sat her down and grasped her shoulders and simply looked at her.

His voice softened. "I don't know how I did without you these past three months, lassie. We have lots to talk about."

"That we do, Dr. Gray. That we do." Essie words were spoken with a genuine admission, an acceptance of the effect the good doctor had had on her life.

She glanced at DooRay. "DooRay, I see you've met Dr. Gray, the doctor who saved Minnie's life."

DooRay, his grin unstoppable, nodded vigorously. "Yes, ma'am, I surely did. We's had a good talk while you was gone." He pointed to the watermelon, at least a twenty-five pounder, his eyes gleaming with delight. "Ain't this the prettiest watermelon you ever did see?"

He glanced at Dr. Gray, pointing to the elongated, greenish gray watermelon. "This here is a Charleston Gray, sweetest watermelon there ever was."

"Absolutely," Essie said with enthusiasm. "Shall we get it nice and cold." She leaned over to pick up the long watermelon, but Dr. Gray reached it first. "Got it, lassie."

"DooRay, I'll get us some iced tea and tomato sandwiches in a little bit."

"Yes, ma'am. You knowed DooRay likes tomato sandwiches. I be waitin'."

Essie and Dr. Gray walked together to the house, up the back steps and into the Donnelly kitchen, where Dr. Gray placed the watermelon on the kitchen table.

"Before we go any further," he said, with some seriousness. "My name is Robert Gray. You may call me *Rob*." He grinned. "How does that sit with you, Miss Donnelly?"

Essie became flustered. "Well . . . I have no problem with that . . . it's just that . . . "

"What? Lassie, whether you care to remember or not, you and I have been through a lot together. I consider you a friend, a good friend." He dipped his chin, his expression one of adoration.

"Of course, we have." She pulled the tea pitcher from the refrigerator. "I . . . don't have a problem with calling you *Rob*."

Essie poured two glasses of sweet tea, lots of ice, and led the way to the front porch. *The important porch.*

It seemed most of life was spent on the porch. Babies rocked. Old men dipping their cinnamon snuff. Old ladies dipping their peach snuff. The deep discussions of crops and rain. The latest gossip heard at church. A passionate kiss. Some romantic fondling between lovers. And, of course, favorite bible verses, read over and over again,

Essie had written most of her novel, W*atermelon Queen of Madison County,* on the front porch, the clack of the keys on her Royal typewriter blending with the sounds of farm life.

Edith and her friends exploited the porch as though it were the most private place on earth, their gossip trapped in the summer winds and blowing safely out of earshot.

And, now, for the first time, an extraordinarily handsome man from Ireland sat in her swing, holding a glass of Southern sweet tea, looking as though he was born to be the master of the Donnelly farm. He pushed the swing slowly, his eyes surveying the yard, the fields across the Bellville road, and finally coming to rest on his auburn-haired lass.

"Let me hear about Pitch . . . Rob." Had calling the doctor by his first name placed their relationship onto another level? *More personal?* Or was it just the next step in solidifying their friendship? She waited, somewhat unnerved. *She had missed him.*

"Pitch, that fine boy, has been put through a series of extensive testing. Many x-rays by Dr. Christoph Meyer. As you may remember, Dr. Meyer is a renowned orthopedic surgeon. He took on the case gratis, which is a miracle somewhat of itself. His analysis and prognosis is complicated, but workable."

Rob sipped his tea. "With his father's permission, Pitch had surgery a few weeks ago. Then, a long stretch of physical therapy." He smiled at Essie. "I do believe that boy will be able to play basketball at some point. Dr. Meyer is that good."

Essie nodded. "How is Pitch dealing with all this?"

"Oh, my man Pitch is overjoyed. I spent a lot of time with him during his testing, and it's obvious he's looking forward to a new leg, one that will allow him to walk normally. It may be a little shorter than his left leg, but not much. It was a complex procedure, but amazingly successful."

Another sip of his tea, a stopping of the swing, and Rob leaned forward. "Essie, you haven't asked me why I'm here." His face was solemn, his eyes beseeching.

Rob Gray, a frank and imploring man, held her eyes with his own. He devoured her beautiful face, her deep brown eyes the color of dark rum, her flushed cheeks, her sweet smile and waited.

Essie's rocker became still as she returned his stare. "As you said in your letter, I assume it's to catch up on each other's lives. Especially, Pitch's progress." She lifted her chin, "Am I wrong?"

Rob sighed deeply and began to push the swing again. "No, you're not wrong. But, there's more." He smiled but it quickly faded. "What about this Sam fellow? He still around?"

How uncanny. *Still around? Not for a few days.* At this moment, she couldn't answer his question. "Sam's quite busy with his work. Travels occasionally." She looked away, watched a squirrel eating acorns in an oak tree, then a woodpecker climbing upside down on a tall pine tree on the farm lane.

Rob chuckled. "You know what I meant by my question, Essie. And you know exactly why I'm here."

He drank the last of his tea. The good doctor thought about their time together at the Pryor's in Boston. He was happy being with a family, but especially happy with the farm girl who had captured his heart. He would not easily give her up.

"I know what you mean." She rose from her rocker. "We neglected to put that watermelon in the refrigerator. Shall we do it now?"

Rob glanced at the other end of the porch as Killer flew to the porch rail and cocked his eye at the stranger.

When he turned back to Essie, he said, "Come here and sit with me, Essie." Spoken softly, but firmly, the Irishman had, just that very moment, made some things very clear.

Suddenly, Essie remembered her dream of the previous morning. The Irishman naked and beckoning her to come to him. Essie, pulling off her clothes, her body hot with desire. Perhaps her dream was a glimpse into the future, whether she believed it or not. Whether she wanted it or not. Almost in a haze, Essie looked longingly at Dr. Robert Gray, and felt the pain of emotion in her heart.

Rob left the swing and, in three strides, pulled Essie into his arms. He kissed her softly, one hand in her hair, the other cradling her cheek. She kissed him back, a fevered kiss full of heat, and the unmistakable, delirious feelings of passion.

The tears came as her body slumped into Rob's arms. "Please. Please, let me go." Rob gently pulled his arms away, only to have Essie place her head on his chest and sniffle her way to calm. He pulled her close, rubbed her back and smoothed her hair away from the tears.

He rocked her gently. Once again the front porch had witnessed the frailties of life, a gamut of emotions that encompassed two people who, unbeknownst to them, had become much more than they had bargained for.

"It's okay, lassie. Have a good cry." Long moments passed until finally they left the porch and found the watermelon where they had left it.

"I see absolutely no reason why we can't eat a hot watermelon, do you? Rob thumped it and declared it perfectly ripe. "Did you know when one has tasted a watermelon, one knows what angels eat?" He glanced at Essie. "A quote from the brilliant Mark Twain."

She laughed. "A hot watermelon. Never heard of such a thing. But, we can try it. But, let's make some tomato sandwiches and pour more tea."

The two worked quietly, Rob washing the tomatoes and placing them on a cutting board, Essie handing him a sharp knife. And there, in the Donnelly kitchen where the essence of life had moved from the front porch to the kitchen, life continued on. Just different people, different conversations and, of course, a different watermelon – a hot one right out of the field.

# CHAPTER THIRTY-NINE

Late afternoon drifted to the farmyard picnic table. A platter full of tomato sandwiches, with lots of mayonnaise, salt and pepper, and a new pitcher of iced tea were arranged on a yellow tablecloth, its edges scalloped in red. And, of course, the twenty-five pound watermelon took center stage.

The sun had begun to settle across Madison County, leaving a few hours of daylight in its wake. Lum Townsend's cows grazed in the field across the Bellville road, their cuds full of lush grass. Afternoon rains had been plentiful, a good thing for farms in the county.

"Miss Essie, I do believe thems the best tomatoes I ever did eat. Sweet as candy. Somethin' else I'd like to eat and that's some good ole sweet corn. I reckon I'll crawl through the fence and pick some of Mr. Gaston's golden queen corn."

Essie laughed. "Well, if you find some golden queen, let me know. You might do better looking for silver queen." She winked at Rob. The Irishman had probably never heard of either one.

DooRay joined her laughter. "I knowed it had somethin' to do with royalty. I's get us some sweet corn and we's have us a corn on the cob party. DooRay ain't never been to a corn party." He became thoughtful.

"Maybe we's ought to invite that old Indian woman. Only she cain't bring her panther or that big ole black snake."

"Panther? Isn't that a wild animal? Snake?" Rob frowned. "Who is this woman?.

Essie pressed a napkin to her lips. "DooRay, do you mind if I tell Rob what happened to you?"

"Naw, I don't mind." The black man picked up another sandwich. His eyes downcast, he murmured, "Sure glad to be alive."

Essie began. "The Indian woman is a Miccosukee woman who remained on the river, the Withlalcoochee, when her family migrated to south Florida, to the Seminole tribe. That was some years ago. She was only ten years old. Everybody knows her and calls her Miccosukee Mae."

Behind DooRay, Murphy nudged DooRay and he reached over and scratched the goat's head, yanking his horns. Murphy, absent one ear, butted him softly.

"It's a long story. Two men assaulted DooRay a while back, then threw him into the Withlacoochee River, just two miles down the road, east of here. Miccosukee Mae found DooRay on a sandbar in the river. Pretty much saved his life."

Rob listened intently. "Is that how DooRay got that wound above his ear?" The doctor had noticed DooRay's injury immediately, but didn't say anything. He did take a good look at it, noticed the three inch scar and wondered how DooRay had been injured.

"Two men accosted DooRay at a fishing pond about a quarter mile west of here. Threw a whiskey bottle at him, knocked him out. Shot Murphy. It was pretty harrowing. Then, they took him to the Bellville bridge and threw him in the river." Essie's voice broke. "He can't swim with one arm."

Rob nodded, absorbed the information and glanced at DooRay. "You're a tough man, DooRay."

DooRay laughed. "One thing's for sure. Ole DooRay can float." He chomped a big piece of watermelon. How he could grin and eat watermelon at the same time was amazing.

"So, what about this panther and snake?" Rob leaned back, knowing it would be a good story.

Essie began slowly. "Living her life on the river and being an Indian – by the way, her Indian name is Tayki – she is exposed to every wild animal on the river and seems to make friends with them. Talks to them. The panther is *Cat*. Sleeps with her. As does *Slick*, a six-foot black snake that she carries around her neck. She's strange, but harmless."

Rob stared in disbelief. "Sleeps with a panther named *Cat*?" He shook his head. "I'd like to meet her someday. Not get too close to her, mind you. Meet her from a distance."

By sunset, the platter was void of tomato sandwiches, the tea pitcher empty. The watermelon had deep cuts into it, but leftovers would be served the next day.

From the front yard, a voice called. "Anybody home?"

Emmett Gaston was met by Murphy and the goat followed him to the picnic table. "Glad I caught you folks." Emmett looked at Rob. "Howdy. My name's Emmett Gaston. Don't believe I know you." He reached out and shook Rob's hand.

Rob stood and shook Emmett's hand. "Robert Gray."

Essie moved down the bench and made a place for her neighbor. "Emmett, there's not a bite of food left on this table except some watermelon."

"Not a problem, Essie." He eyed the watermelon. "That one a my watermelons you got there? That's a *Charleston Gray*. Can't believe my neighbor is stealing my watermelons. Guess I ought to call Simmie Moore."

Emmett let out a holler and belly laughed. "Just stopped by to let you and DooRay know that ole panther tried to get into my chicken pen again last night. Hadn't been for my yard dog barking up a storm, that ole cat might have succeeded. Chased him off with a blast from my shotgun." He glanced at DooRay. "Be on the lookout, DooRay. He'll eat every one a your chickens."

"Wait a minute," said Rob. "Is that Miccosukee Mae's panther, *Cat*?"

"That ole woman has a panther named Cat?" Emmett pulled off his farm hat and scratched his head. "Now, ain't that somethin'."

Essie waved her hand. "These woods are full of panthers. I don't think it's Cat."

DooRay, wide-eyed, his head swiveling back and forth between Rob,

Essie and Emmett, rose from the table. "Well, it looks like ole DooRay gone sleep in his hideout tonight."

"Hideout?" Emmett asked.

"Yes, suh, Mr. Emmett. I got me a hideout in that oak tree over yonder. Put me a piece of plywood across two limbs and got me a bed. Gone sleep up there tonight with my loaded shotgun."

Emmett narrowed his eyes. *How is a one-armed man going to hold a shotgun, aim it and fire it?* "You be careful, DooRay. Panther's are dangerous. They'll attack a man as quick as they'll eat a chicken."

"Oh, I's got it all figured out. Yes, sir, I'll be waiting on that killer cat."

Emmett replaced his hat and bid good night. "You folks have a nice evening. Mae's waitin' on me. She's frying chicken livers for dinner. Love them thangs."

Emmett hurried across the farmyard and jumped in his old pick-up and headed down the lane. He dearly loved fried chicken livers.

At nightfall, Essie and Rob returned to the front porch. She in the swing; Rob in a rocker. The night sky was clear, empty of clouds, a near full moon high above.

"Your farm is just as you described it to me. You left nothing out. Not DooRay. Or Murphy. Or Killer. Nor the beautiful farmland."

"It's home. I've been here my entire life. Almost went to New York late last year, but changed my mind. More important things to do."

"Like find Jewell's daughter?"

"Yes. And I found her. Her name's Rose and she looks just like Jewell. She'll be visiting soon."

"That was quite a miracle, wasn't it?"

Essie pushed the swing and watched fireflies in the nearby woods, east of the house, along the lane. "Yes, it was," she said, barely audible.

Rob rose from the porch rocker. "I'm staying at the Hotel Madison on Range Street. Guess I'd better let you get some rest. Thanks for those tomato sandwiches. And watermelon."

In the dark, Essie couldn't see his face, but knew he wanted to stay. To make love to her. To tell her he loved her. "Well, it's wonderful to see you again."

Rob reached out his hand. "Come here, lass." And, she did.

# CHAPTER FORTY

E ssie heard the whippoorwills outside her bedroom window, their call beckoning. The notes were musical, like a soft drum beat that sent a perpetual message of love. Her breathing was slow. A calm had swallowed her and placed her into a pleasant cloud of tranquility. She closed her eyes and waited for dreams of Robert Gray, which she knew would come.

In the large oak tree by the barn, DooRay's hide-out spread between two thick limbs. A sheet of old plywood, wedged tightly into the crevices, formed a perfect place in which to observe the chicken pen, where a dozen or so chickens roosted, thoughts of a killer panther on the loose the furthest thing from their mind.

An old quilt and pillow softened the plywood. DooRay adjusted the shotgun, ensuring it was wedged firmly in the notch in the board. The twine traveled from the gun's trigger to DooRay's fingers. He was ready. Alert, he found himself listening to night sounds. The lonely bawl of cattle seemed to ricochet from one field to the other, ending up in Lum Townsend's pasture to the south.

DooRay heard the wings of an owl, a flapping sound that carried across the barnyard and into a nearby tall pine. Tu-whit tu-whoo it called, answered by another owl some distance away.

Soon, DooRay was lulled into a peaceful sleep, the twine still grasped in his hand. The chickens roosted undisturbed and unafraid. *DooRay Aikens would keep them safe.*

It was near daylight when DooRay opened his eyes. Next to him, he heard the sound of soft breathing and occasional whimpers, like a sleeping baby. Across his chest, he felt the foreleg of an animal resting heavily on his body. Slowly, he turned his head and looked into the sleepy yellow eyes of *Cat*. The panther yawned, then closed his eyes and snuggled closer, a deep sigh escaping his throat.

# CHAPTER FORTY-ONE

"I declare I was sound asleep. Next thing I knowed, I felt this hot breath on my face and when I opened my eyes, there he was – that killer panther staring at me with those hateful yellow eyes. I said to myself, it's now or never, DooRay Aikens. Right then, I said, *'boo'* and that big ole cat jumped from my hideout and skedaddled into the woods."

DooRay took a deep breath, almost panting, his arm waving and pointing like a maestro at the symphony. "Ain't no killer panther gone git DooRay's chickens." He slapped his knee for emphasis.

Essie squinted at DooRay. "Were you afraid, DooRay?"

"Naw, ole DooRay ain't 'fraid a nuthing." He paused, then looked off into the distance. "Only thing bothers me is I wonder if'n that old cat has fleas." He jerked his head towards the hideout. "Bet they's fleas all in my quilt and pillow."

Essie tied an apron around her waist and walked back to the house. "Come pour yourself some coffee, DooRay. We'll check for fleas, if you want."

DooRay followed Essie into the house, mumbling to himself. "I's have me a talk with that ole Indian woman. Tell her to keep that panther a hers at the river. Next thing I knows, that ugly black snake a hers be sleepin' wif me, too."

"I'm making biscuits this morning, DooRay. Maybe some thick sliced bacon. You have a good meal and you'll feel better. Fig preserves, too."

The black man sat at the kitchen table and scratched his head. "If'n I have fleas, I gone have a thing or two to say to Miccosukee Mae. Cain't a man live in his castle and be nice and clean."

Essie felt the laughter coming, tickling her chest, lingering in her throat. "I'm sure everything will be just fine, DooRay. Let's be thankful Cat didn't bother your chickens." She dumped flour in a large wooden bowl, followed by cold lard. "No need to talk to Tayki. I'm planning to visit her before Dr. Gray comes this afternoon."

"Well, you gives that woman a piece a my mind, Miss Essie. A law abidin' citizen in Madison County ort to be safe from a panther crawlin' in his bed. 'specially if'n he gots fleas."

Breakfast was fresh eggs from chickens the panther didn't eat. Grits, hot biscuits and some thick-sliced bacon. Fig preserves with buttered biscuits got DooRay calmed down somewhat. His eyes remained watchful as though the panther was hiding under the table or behind the refrigerator. He flinched at every sound. "These biscuits are almost as good as mine, Miss Essie." He grinned at her as he picked up his fourth one.

"Say, Miss Essie, I like your friend, Mr. Gray. He's mighty fine, all right. Mr. Sam like him, too?"

Essie hesitated. *Sam?* "He's a good doctor, DooRay. Minnie was very lucky to have him care for her."

"I'd say so. She say good things 'bout that man." DooRay leaned back in his chair. "Miss Essie, I sure do like Miss Minnie. She's a good woman. Says she gone be a nurse."

"Oh, she is, DooRay. Going to nursing school in Tallahassee in September. She'll be over later this afternoon and visit when Dr. Gray comes, and we'll discuss her education."

"Mighty fine." DooRay rose from the table, scratching his arm. "Dang fleas." He stepped out the screen door, "Fine breakfas', Miss Essie."

The chains holding the porch swing creaked softly, a slow rhythmic sound that broke the morning quiet and made one think of primitive music. Constant, the sound echoed from one end of the porch to the other and then back again. *Lola LaRue was back.*

Essie slung the dish towel across the back of a chair, untied her apron and threw it on the kitchen table. She hurried through the sitting room and out the front screen door. *And there she was.* The woman who would not go away. The woman who would not take 'no' for an answer. The woman who vowed she would not return to New York without a signed contract from Essie Donnelly.

"Don't think a vase of flowers will get you a signed contract, Miss LaRue!" Essie's hands were on her hips, a stance that said she was immovable, her words not quite a shout, but close to it.

Lola continued to swing, her hot pink pumps shining brightly in the morning sun. "Miss Donnelly, the note I wrote to you was very sincere. I meant what I said. I want to start over with our . . . our relationship."

"Relationship?" Essie rolled her eyes and threw herself into a rocker. "We have no relationship. You, Miss LaRue, have invaded my home, my privacy and my peace of mind."

Lola lifted her eyebrows in surprise. "I do believe I apologized to you in my card. Isn't that enough?" *There it was.* That same arrogant attitude, a haughtiness wrapped around each word, commanding and superior. Her ostentatious display of par excellence behavior was offensive, demeaning and, without a doubt, not welcomed by Essie Donnelly.

It was the South, a place where one's comportment was defined through their treatment of others, an aura of genteel character and spirit evident in their very being. The woman from New York expelled emanations of a hard heart, with not the slightest of reservations.

Essie's jaw tightened, her teeth clamped together. "Let me understand you, Miss LaRue. A vase of flowers and a sincere note card wipes the slate clean? Allows you to return and begin your bedevilment all over again?

"What do I need to do? Shoot you? Call the sheriff?" Essie stared at the New Yorker through blazing eyes. She felt herself flinch, an ardent inclination to lose every ounce of gentility her Southern body and mind possessed, and pounce upon Miss Lola LaRue.

Lola sighed deeply, closed her eyes and leaned back into the swing, perhaps coming to some kind of conciliatory conclusion. Without opening her eyes, she spoke. Softly and slowly, words drifted from the swing, across the porch and into the summer morning. Her face was peaceful, serene. A beautiful woman, and now even more beautiful.

"I have wonderful memories of my farm days. My mother and father had a dairy farm. Some goats, too, and, of course, chickens. My two brothers and I lived an idyllic life – hard work, but happy.

"Sometimes, during my hectic life in New York, I'd give anything to smell the inside of that old barn. Sweet hay." Lola laughed quietly. "I even miss the smell of cow manure. It was just . . . just so . . . " She let the thought fall unfinished, unable to find the perfect words.

"Daddy had a favorite cow. A Jersey named Geraldine. He loved that cow. Said she had more butterfat in her milk than any cow he had ever owned. He pampered her and, of course, we kids did, too." She gently pushed the swing, her eyes still closed. It was though she was alone, her thoughts free and uncensored.

"One day – this was in the mid-thirties – the Great Depression, of course. A man came by and asked daddy if he could paint an advertisement on the side of our big red barn. 'What kinda advertisement?' my dad had asked. The man said he represented the Bloch Brothers Tobacco Company and wanted to advertise '*Chew Mail Pouch Tobacco*' on the side of his barn."

Lola finally opened her eyes, smiling at Essie. "We lived on Highway 33, right outside Oblong, Illinois. Not too far from Vincennes, Indiana. Lots of traffic on that highway passed right by our barn."

A summer breeze picked up Lola's Jane Mansfield styled hair and ruffled it, giving her a tossed look, perhaps that of a country girl instead of a well-coiffed New York woman. Her gaze swept the fields south of the farmhouse, a far-away look that took her back to her childhood.

Then, laughter. "So, daddy told the man 'no.' Said he wanted the company to paint the name of his favorite cow on the side of our barn. He wanted *Geraldine* painted in big, tall letters across the barn wall. Well, of course, the company man said no and left none too happy."

The porch paused and fell into a soft respite that savored the moment, the only sound was the creak of the chains on the porch swing and the squeak of the rocking chair.

"That's a sweet memory," said Essie. A fly landed on Lola's bright pink shoes. Lola watched it crawl around for a few moments, then slapped at it. Essie wondered if they had flies in New York.

"Well, that's not the end of the story." Lola grinned at Essie. "Every story has to have a good ending." She rose from the swing and leaned against the porch rail. Killer scratched in the yard, his wattles swinging back and forth.

"The next morning, my daddy got out a tall ladder and placed it against the barn wall and proceeded to paint *Geraldine* across the side. Took him four days."

Lola turned and looked at Essie, her expression one of regret. "Sometimes, it's these memories that keep me sane in that big city called New York."

Her voice changed, a confession brewing in the words. "You see, Miss Donnelly. The reason I want to publish *Watermelon Queen of Madison County* so badly is because it's also *my story. Farm girl wants to leave the farm and see the world.* Your story is a poignant memoir and I love it."

Lola drifted down the length of the porch and back again. Thoughtful, she returned to the swing and began a slow push, her face serene.

Essie had been lulled into a compassionate place. Lola's memories had soothed her, had taken the harshness out of the redhead and elevated her to the dignity and softness of a Southern woman. A very rare occurrence indeed.

"Well, I guess I'll get back to Tallahassee and catch the next plane to New York." Lola stood from the swing. "Thank you for your time, Miss Donnelly. It's been a pleasure despite our differences."

Essie left her rocker and faced Lola. "I appreciate your candidness, Miss LaRue. Thank you for letting me see a little bit of your soft side. I . . . I didn't think there was one." She gave her a sheepish grin.

"It's okay. Sometimes we get lost and forget about the important things. Please stay in touch and when you feel you want to publish your wonderful manuscript, you know where to find me."

Essie hesitated. "Tell you what, Miss LaRue. I'll sign that contract for the publication of my manuscript, but I don't want to go to New York anytime soon."

Lola looked surprised. "Really?"

Essie nodded. "Really."

The two women conferred for a few moments, Lola grabbing her briefcase and pulling out two sets of documents. "You won't be sorry! This is a great story."

The pink Thunderbird convertible zoomed away from the farmhouse, its occupant's red hair flaming in the sun. Her hand shot up holding the documents, waving them wildly. Her squeal could be heard all the way down the Bellville road.

In a few hours, Essie's telephone rang. It was the Thomas H. Fox Literary Agency, the renowned agency that would have her book published. "Miss Donnelly," Thomas Fox yelled. "I just heard from Miss LaRue. Congratulations! You've made a marvelous decision! This is great news."

"Thank you, Mr. Fox. Miss LaRue was . . . was quite accommodating. At last, she and I kinda bonded. I didn't realize she was raised on a farm and was a farm girl just like me."

The silence at the New York end of the telephone was ominous. "On a farm?" Mr. Fox's words were hollow.

"Yes. In Illinois."

"Miss Donnolly, Miss LaRue was born and raised right here in New York City."

# CHAPTER FORTY-TWO

S am's heated words still rang in Essie's ears. *Maybe it's not you who is in my future.*

The fifth day since his departure from her front porch had brought Essie into a serious scrutiny of their relationship. Her feelings were mixed. Her hardheadedness had caused her to say 'Let him pout.' He was just as stubborn as she. Angry and frustrated with her, he evidently needed a 'cooling off' period where he could think things through.

Sam was an incredible man in many ways. His devotion to her had never been questioned. His tenacity had kept his pursuit of her strong. He loved her or, at least, he thought he did. They must, at some point, resolve their issues. Or, go their separate ways.

There was no doubt that Essie's unwillingness to commit to marriage was the source of Sam's frustration. Essie's lack of commitment had gone on too long as far as the farm boy turned attorney was concerned.

Dr. Robert Gray's presence at the Donnelly farm had complicated things greatly for Essie. For everyone, the players swam in indecision, confusion and discontent. And, it was all about *love. Love should not be so complicated.*

Yet, it was. And, it was certainly time for Essie to make decisions that would remove her from the immobility of indecision.

Sam's tenure in Live Oak at the trial of Stanley Barnwell had kept the midnight oil burning. Change of venue had been decreed by the courts, Judge Earp presiding. The publicity in Madison County regarding the assault charges against Barnwell for DooRay Aikens' injuries in May of 1956 had deemed the high-profile case be moved to Suwannee County.

Criminal prosecution of the attacker in DooRay's case would demand financial restitution.

Barnwell's attempted murder of Sam Washington by burning down the barn where Sam slept was being handled by the State Procecutor. The evidence was overwhelming: Barnwell was going to prison for life.

Despite Sam's late night hours and the tedious work on DooRay's case, in the back of his mind his thoughts were of Essie. He had made a decision. He'd ask her to marry him . . . *one more time.* If she was reluctant, it was clear to him that the relationship must end. Perhaps she didn't love him enough. Perhaps marriage and family were not important to her.

He turned out his desk light, leaned back in his chair and closed his eyes. Sam loved Essie deeply. Was he prepared for the hurt he knew would come if she didn't accept his proposal? Of course, he could go on, but it wouldn't be easy. She was in his blood, and, most definitely, wrapped around his heart.

Sam had spent the past five days in heart-felt turmoil. He rose from his chair and closed his office door. It was well after midnight. Tomorrow, he'd go to the farm, sit on the front porch and share his thoughts with Essie. *Marry me, girl, or I'm leavin' on the midnight train to . . . somewhere.*

# CHAPTER FORTY-THREE

The Withlacoochee ran quiet, its dark waters smooth, only a swirl here and there as Tail patrolled the banks and looked for his breakfast.

A half mile from the Bellville bridge at the Florida/Georgia state line, Tayki's shack teetered on the river's high bank, its construction a jumble of sticks, tree limbs, and various scrap wood scavenged from nearby farms.

The Indian woman had stripped an old outhouse of its tar paper roof and transported it to her castle on the crooked river. The shack housed not only Tayki, but also Cat, her companion of many years and, in cold weather, Slick, her six-foot long black snake, found a warm place between the myriad of Tayki's collections.

Cat, a hundred fifty pound Florida panther with a lovely tan coat and creamy underside, lay on a large branch overhanging the river, his yellow eyes watching Tail, the eight foot alligator who had recently slept with DooRay on a beautiful white sandbar. Cat swished his tail, his throat rumbling.

"Stop that, Cat!" Tayki threw a pinecone at the panther and climbed the tree. She sat on a limb parallel to Cat's and spoke softly. "Tail your friend. No eat Tail."

Cat looked at Tayki, then back to the alligator. He'd not eat the alligator, but perhaps he'd ride Tail's back for a moment or two. Just to let him know who was king of the Withlacoochee River.

Along the banks, Essie found her way to Tayki's shack, a stench finding her nostrils and causing her to cough. "Tayki," she called.

Tayki had seen the farm girl as soon as she skirted the bank from the bridge. She laughed at the white skin and the fancy clothes Essie wore. She narrowed her eyes. Essie carried a bag. Maybe full of rocks to throw at her. Tayki shrunk back into the tree.

Essie called again. "Tayki."

Cat growled, his tail swishing slowly back and forth. All he had to do was spring from the limb and the woman would vanish. Instead, he cringed when he heard Tayki say 'no.'

At the shack, Essie glanced across the river, down the river bank and into the nearby woods. She tilted her head upward and found Tayki watching her, a grin on her face.

"Silly white woman climb tree and try to fly again?"

Essie ignored Tayki's sarcasm. "Come down, Tayki. I have some things for you."

"Rocks?" asked Tayki. Her glance flitted from the bag to Essie.

"No rocks. Nice things. Come down."

"Can Cat come, too?" Found in the woods in his den, Tayki had cared for the little spotted kitten almost from birth. Weak and starved, he barely survived.

"No! Leave him in the tree."

"Hateful woman." The Indian woman crouched on the tree limb for a moment. She mumbled something to Cat and then extended her foot to the first rung of the make-shift ladder. She came down swiftly as though afraid to turn her back on Essie. When she reached the ground, she quickly turned and grinned at Essie. "Tayki no fly like white woman."

Essie backed up a few feet. Tayki might spit on her or yank her hair. "Come sit on the river's edge with me. I have a present for you."

Tayki glared through the mismatched eyes, the eye off-center catching the river behind Essie. "Present?"

"Yes. A gift."

Tayki circled Essie, a suspicious half-crouch bending her body. In the nearby oak tree, Cat walked farther out on the limb and watched. "You give something to me to eat?"

"Many things. Yes, to eat."

Tayki held out her hand, never taking her eyes off the bag. "Give."

Essie reached into the bag and pulled out a small box of beautiful brown chicken eggs. "DooRay sends these to you."

Through her dissimilar eyes, she beheld the eggs with wonder. Could she count? Did she know the box held an even dozen. Slowly, she smiled her toothless smile, the gums glistening. "One-arm give Tayki?"

Essie nodded. "Take them."

Tayki dipped her chin. "Tayki love One-arm." She reached out and grasped the box, her brown, gnarled fingers holding tightly. "More?"

Essie laughed. "Yes, more." She reached into the bag and pulled out three hair clasps, each one a different color. They had lain in Jewell's dresser for the past year, untouched. Yellow, blue and purple. "I'll show you."

Essie moved closer. "Bend over a little, Tayki, and let me put one in your hair." Essie opened the clasp and waited.

The old woman looked confused, a little dubious. She shook her head 'no.'

"Look, Tayki." Essie reached up and pulled her auburn hair together and closed the yellow clasp. "See. Beautiful."

Tayki grinned and swept her straggly hair together and leaned over. "Tayki beautiful."

Essie attached the purple clasp to her dark hair, sweeping it high on Tayki's head. "Yes, Tayki beautiful."

Tayki closed her eyes and tilted her head to the heavens. She lifted one foot, then the other and began a slow ritual dance, turning in circles, a sing-song chant that told her ancestors Tayki was now a beautiful princess.

"More?" Tayki asked.

Essie reached down into the bag one more time. Jewell's scissors and a skein of pink yarn. "For you," she said softly.

With longing, Tayki reached out and rubbed the scissors. Her eyes found Essie. "Bochonkom tayke?"

Essie didn't know it, but Tayki had just asked Essie if she could touch her. Essie stilled and Tayki placed her hand over Essie's heart, then to her own heart. She leveled her stare at Essie. "White woman no stupid."

The two women sat by the river's edge for a while, Tail across the river on the eastern bank. Cat still in the tree above them. Slick, who had been hiding in the shack, slithered down the bank and wrapped himself around Tayki's neck and slept.

"Tayki, I'm wondering about Cat. There's been a panther killing chickens all around the farms in the area. Do you . . . "

"Not Cat!" she said. "My Cat no like chicken. He like wading birds. Rabbits and white-tail deer."

"I see. Well, he did pay us a visit late last night."

"How you know it Cat?"

"That's easy, Tayki. Cat climbed up the tree where DooRay slept and lay beside him. A wild panther would never do that."

Tayki jerked back. "Cat sleep with DooRay?" Then, a peal of laughter shot from the old woman's mouth. Shrill like a thousand seagulls crying, the sound carried down the river and into the nearby woods. She rocked back and forth, wiping tears from her cheeks. The purple clasp popped from her hair, leaving it spread across her face and shoulders.

Then, a stillness as the Indian woman slitted her eyes at Essie. "Cat have fleas. DooRay have fleas now."

Frustrated, Essie stood from the river bank and began walking back to the car, her bare feet sloshing in the cool river water. Only a few feet away, she turned. "I'm just trying to warn you, Tayki. Somebody might shoot Cat. Tell him not to leave the river."

She continued on, only to have Tayki rush beside her. She reached out her hand and caught Essie's arm. "Cat see men throw DooRay into river."

Essie flung around. "What? How do you know that?"

Miccosukee Mae grinned, only a pink tongue in her mouth. *She talked to animals.* "Cat tell me he pee in truck."

Astonished, Essie stared at Tayki. The woman appeared complacent, a knowing crossing her face and settling in her eyes. From the oak tree, Cat hissed and paced a tree limb, his tail swishing back and forth.

A hoarse whisper left Tayki's throat, her body seeming to shrink, wrapping itself into ropes of muscled sinew. "Cat kill two men if he want to," she said, matter of factly, a hint of a smile forming on her thin lips.

# CHAPTER FORTY-FOUR

A t high noon, the sun centered itself in a bright blue sky, no rain to cool the July heat. Emment Gaston's farm hands gathered watermelons in the field to the north and loaded them on waiting trucks. They'd end up at the train depot in Pinetta, then loaded onto a freight train bound for cities far away.

Murphy drank from a large bucket near the well, Killer nearby watching. DooRay piddled in the tack room, the presence of fleas a worrisome thought as he swept the floor of runaway hay. He hummed softly, talked to the angels and hoped Essie was baking a pineapple upside down cake for him.

The farm lay quiet, its heartbeat slow and easy, like the slow walk of a mule grinding sugar cane. A puff of wind stirred the leaves in the pecan trees east of the farm lane, a soft rattling sound that spoke of a bountiful harvest.

Inside the Donnelly kitchen, Essie stirred cake batter. Glad to be rid of Lola LaRue, she whipped the batter furiously, irritated at the deceitful woman who had presented herself as a sweet farm girl, a farm girl incapable of lies. *Imposter*!

Essie would eventually go to New York, work the promotional circuits so touted by Miss LaRue. *The New York Times bestseller list will have your novel at the very top,* Lola had proclaimed. There would, however, be a few changes made on the publishing contract as well as her relationship with the fake farm girl.

Essie grabbed an iron skillet, smeared the bottom with butter and brown sugar and turned on the oven. She lined the bottom with cherries, pecans, and pineapple slices before pouring in the golden cake batter.

The sound of a car crunching acorns on the farm lane drifted through the front screened door. Essie slipped the cake into the oven and wiped her hands on her apron. In forty minutes, DooRay would be eating his favorite cake.

On the porch, she watched Simmie Moore amble across the yard and up the porch steps. "Hot enough for you, Simmie?"

The sheriff of Madison County removed his hat and found a nearby rocking chair. "Whew! Can't remember it being this hot. Probably near ninety-five degrees."

"That calls for some iced tea, Simmie. I'll be right back." In the kitchen, Essie gathered glasses, ice and a pitcher of tea. Back on the porch, she handed Simmie a glass and found a spot on the swing.

The mistress of the Donnelly farm contemplated Simmie for a long moment, waiting for the lawman to perhaps begin a conversation that addressed the current status of his investigation.

She found herself in her usual contemplative state of mind, a deep brooding that kept her focused on the two men from Alabama Seeds. She'd not falter; the men who harmed DooRay would not escape her wrath. As she watched Simmie, she knew his adherence to the law would prevail, a process that he could not alter. That was the man he was.

Yet, she had no qualms at all about breaking the law. It was true – she was a renegade, a vigilante woman prone to righting wrongs regardless of laws. Where did that come from? Somewhere in the Universe, had she been assigned the task of righting wrongs?

*What about the pleasure . . .* yes, the pleasure of seeking justice. No, she'd not cut off the testicles of the Alamaba men, but she'd delight in watching them . . . .

"Essie, I've gotten a lead on the perpetrators."

Essie lifted her eyebrows, a ringing in her ears. *Really?* "Oh?" She leaned forward, her heart racing.

Simmie nodded. "Jack Woodard said two men came by his garage in the early morning and asked him to air up their tires. They were in a red truck, big all-terrain tires. Said they were from Alabama."

"Alabama? What were they doing in Madison County?" Of course, Essie knew what they were doing in Madison County. She looked away, afraid Simmie would see the pretense in her eyes.

"Not sure. I'll keep digging. About that whiskey bottle we found at the pond, Son made a trip to Clyattville and was unable to determine if there were any purchases of *Four Roses* whiskey. They could've bought that whiskey between here and Alabama, so that's a lost cause."

The sheriff pressed tobacco into his pipe. "I was hoping the article in the Carrier would generate some clues. Not heard a word from anyone. These men are ghosts, for sure."

Sheriff Moore rose from the rocking chair and lit his pipe. A long draw before he blew the smoke into the air. "I'm wondering how dangerous these men are." He took a short puff. "Anybody who'd throw a one-armed man off a bridge can't have too much of a conscience. I reckon he'd do just about anything." Simmie held Essie's eyes with his own for a long moment. Was he sending her a warning?

Simmie thanked Essie for the iced tea and meandered down the porch steps. He stopped and glanced back to the porch. "By the way, Emmett Gaston tells me a panther has been after his chickens again. Says Micco-sukee Mae has a pet panther. That true?"

"Just an ole cat. Stays around her shack most of the time. I wouldn't worry too much about it."

Simmie nodded. "Emmett seemed concerned. Said he goes to bed with his shotgun every night." The sheriff waved goodbye and guided his Ford down the farm lane. He turned left on the Bellville road. Perhaps a ride to the Withlacoochee River and the bridge where DooRay was thrown into the water and left to die.

Essie leaned against the porch rail and watched Simmie's car until it was out of sight. She knew what the sheriff didn't know. The two men were seed salesmen from Alabama Seeds and, yes, they had no conscience. Her chance of confronting them before Sheriff Moore deter-mined who they were was slim. Simmie was like Booter and Feller's bloodhound Sniffer. He'd stay on the hunt until he found the culprits.

Inside the house, Essie pulled the cake out of the oven and placed it on top of the stove to cool. She returned to the porch, a copy of *Peyton Place*, worn and faded, in her hand. She had read the novel the previous summer, a fitful, frustrating story of a small town whose occupants never seemed to be happy.

She had compared herself to the women in the story and decided she was not like them. They were weak, lost women, their lives in turmoil.

Was her life in turmoil? She closed her eyes and pushed the swing, lulled into thoughts of Sam. She seemed unable to separate herself from him, admitting he was as much a part of her life as if they were married. Yet, they had not made love. *Desire? Did she desire him? Yes, she did.*

*Commitment.* Fulfilling that desire would also mean commitment. That's what she was afraid of – *commitment.*

*The Irishman.* The tall dark-haired doctor, as much a master of romance as any Romeo, had written a poem in the letter he had sent her. He wrote that she had caught him in her snare.

*Snare?* If so, it was unintentional, an oblivious state of mind, a lack of awareness that made her unaccountable for any feelings the Irishman may have had for her. In her dreams, she may have stripped herself naked and made love to him, but it was *only a dream.*

No doubt about it, she was in dangerous territory. *Torn between two men?* Her heart pulled in one direction and then the other. *On second thought, it could be that she was just like the women in Peyton Place!*

The lyrics of *In the Garden* drifted into the shade of the front yard just moments before DooRay rounded the corner of the house. *I come to the garden alone . . .*

Behind him, Murphy tagged along, Killer riding his back as though the old goat was a chariot. DooRay reached up and scratched his head. "Dang fleas."

"DooRay, I suppose you smelled that cake I just took out of the oven!" Essie laughed. Just who was DooRay? A farm hand? A tenant? She watched his pine-sapling body climb the steps and find a rocking chair. She knew who he was – her dear friend, a family member who somehow helped fill the emptiness left by Jewell. His words had soothed her on many late nights when she grieved Jewell's death, when she couldn't sleep and paced the porch for hours. "Come on, now, Miss Essie," he had said. "Gots to pray to our Lord for peace."

She'd prayed all right, but in the middle of prayer, she'd collapse into sadness, a grief beyond consolation.

"Yes, ma'am, I done smelled that cake. Hope it's my favorite." He began rocking the chair, a grin crossing his black face. "They's nothin' like a sweet cake to make everythin' alright in this here world." He chuckled, his eyes scrunching up into a line of laughter. "Sure hopes I don't have to share any of that cake with nobody."

Suddenly, DooRay raised up from the chair and peered out into the yard. From the lane, the Irishman's black car turned into the drive and slowly found its way to the shade near the barn. "Dang," said DooRay. "There goes my cake."

DooRay had hardly returned to his rocker when another car turned into the drive. *Sam Washington.* He parked his car near the crepe myrtles, whose hot pink blossoms heralded the joy of summer. "Well, I'll be," he whispered to himself, "looks like ole DooRay's luck done turned bad."

The swing on the porch stilled, as well as Essie's breath, as she watched Sam walk toward the porch. From around the corner, Rob Gray headed their way. The earth seemed to stand still as both men stopped and stared at one another.

# CHAPTER FORTY-FIVE

S am Washington's blue eyes clouded, a reckoning perhaps that threw him into a well of uncertainty, a spinning of his mind that wrapped itself around confusion and doubt and left him rooted in despair.

He could not take his eyes away from Essie. She, too, seemed to face an accounting, falling all at once into the realization of truth. She opened her mouth to say something, but Sam never heard it. He quickly returned to his car and left the Donnelly farm, perhaps for the last time.

Rob Gray stood for a long moment in the shade of a nearby oak tree, not sure of his welcome. He called across the yard. "My lass, shall I return another time?" His words were soft, an understanding embedded in each one. He saw her distress, and it was clear to him that perhaps he was the cause of it.

Essie rose from the swing, her auburn hair caught in a soft breath of wind. The hem of the long skirt she wore fluttered around her legs as she walked to the edge of the porch. "Yes. Another time, Rob."

She watched him go, the same breeze catching his black hair. He pulled his car to the drive, his arm thrown out the window in a final wave. He found the Bellville road and headed toward Madison and away from Essie Donnelly.

The stillness of the porch emitted a melancholia, inching across the old wood like a fungus that could not be stopped.

DooRay, who had shrunk back into his rocking chair, glanced at Essie. "Everythin' gone be alright, Miss Essie."

She turned, a deep sigh escaping. "No, DooRay. It's not alright."

Minnie Pryor arrived in late afternoon and DooRay shared the pineapple cake with her. They sat together on the picnic table and watched Murphy prance around the farmyard with Killer on his back. Yes, they were definitely a circus act. DooRay told Minnie Miss Essie was not feeling well and would visit some other time.

Essie had retired to the coolness of her bedroom, the hard woman of Madison County succumbing to the pain of heartache. She floundered in despair as she paced the wood floors and muttered to herself. But, she would not tarry long.

# CHAPTER FORTY-SIX

Dave Davis farmed two-hundred acres off Highway 145, only three-quarters of a mile from Hanson. His fields lay in magnificent rows of corn as far as the eye could see, tasseling and promising a bumper crop. His tobacco fields lay farther west.

Essie followed the narrow dirt road, passing a pasture full of fat beef cattle, mostly Angus, a few yearlings following along. The farmhouse lay quiet in the late afternoon, the sun easing down behind the trees that ran along the western horizon. The haybarn, corn crib and mule lot stood shaded and still. Dave's mule Queen ambled along the fence line and curiously watched Essie.

If the Alabama Seed salesmen kept to their schedule, they'd visit the Davis farm the week of July 22. But, which day? Dave liked to talk and, sooner or later, Essie'd have the answer to that question.

Dave waved from the barn as Essie pulled up. She parked the Pontiac alongside a tobacco wagon and crossed the farmyard to the old barn, its siding a weathered gray, probably a hundred years old. Inside, the smell of hay was sweet and carried the fragrance of sunshine.

"Hello, Dave. Good to see you," she called.

Dave was a big man, tall at six feet. He wore a green khaki shirt and overalls, along with a brimmed canvas rain hat. His brown brogans were worn, but still rugged. Dave's laughter was contagious – not a day passed that he didn't have a joke to tell.

"Well, if it ain't Essie Donnelly." His greeting was affable, typical of the gregarious man who said the word 'damn' in almost every sentence he spoke. "Ain't seen you in a damn long time, Essie."

A fine man, Dave had known her father well, the family hard-working and an integral part of the Pinetta and Hanson community. Essie lamented her less than honorable approach in acquiring the information she needed to confront Spit and his partner.

She could outright tell Dave her intent, but to include him in her surreptitious intention to confront the Alabama men would muddy the water and perhaps subject him to potential danger. As much as she'd like to be forthright, she held back, unwilling to expose her friend and neighbor to anything she considered the least bit menacing.

They meandered out of the barn to the barbed wire fence bordering the field to the east. "Yes, it's been a while, Dave. How's the family?"

"Oh, Lillian's doing just fine. Wally's helpin' her put up pears. Tree was loaded this year." He pulled a Camel from a pack in his overall pocket. "Bobby drove the girls into town to pick up some things for their mama."

"That's good to hear. Corn's looking good."

He lit the Camel with his big farmer hands and waved the smoke away from his face, a thousand wrinkles chronicling his many years in the sun. "That's a fact. Damn near dried up till those April rains come up."

Idle conversation, Essie thought, as she struggled to approach the dates of the seed salesmen's visit. "Emmett Gaston has leased my three hundred acres for the past few years. Mostly corn and watermelons." Essie casually glanced at the stand of corn. "What kind of corn did you plant this year?"

"Oh, same as always. Makes good corn." He shifted his weight and jerked his chin to the nearby field. "Yes, sir, that just might be the best stand of corn I've ever planted."

"Must be good seed." Essie sensed Dave's enthusiasm for his corn crop and listened attentively. He was considered one of Madison County's most successful farmers.

He nodded his head vigorously. "Gotta have good seed to start with or you ain't gonna git any damn corn. That's all there is to it." Dave hiked up his overalls and reached for another Camel, his large fingers hardly fitting into the open pack.

"Where do you purchase your seed?" Essie swiped her hand across her forehead, perspiration beginning to drip down her face. Before he could answer, Essie said. "Let's get back into the shade of the barn, Dave. This July heat is smothering me. Besides, I see you have a big fan running and that'll cool us off quick."

Dave laughed. "Why don't you come on up to the house. I bet Lillian's got something cold for us to drink." He lumbered across the farmyard, Essie following. "'Sides that," he said, "she'll give you some pears. She stayed up all night peeling the damn things." Dave never answered her question about the seeds.

Lillian's kitchen was filled with Mason jars on every inch of her countertops. Wally, only eleven years old, grumbled as he washed a sink full of pint and quart glass jars. "Daddy, I don't even like pears. Why do I have to wash these jars?"

"Now, now, Wally. You help your mama. Them's a lot of pears, alright. But, you'll appreciate them this winter. There's nothin' like a hot pear cobbler."

"It's so good to see you, Essie." Lillian handed her a glass of sweet iced tea. "Bet you don't like your tea as sweet as Dave, but it's good and cold."

"Thank you, Lillian. I'd say it's close to a hundred degrees out there in that farmyard."

"At least a hundred. Have a seat while I fill these jars. I want you to take a few quarts for your pantry."

"How kind of you. You know I'll enjoy them." Essie looked around the kitchen, her gaze falling on a big John Deere calendar hanging on the wall by the window. The month of July's calendar picture depicted a little boy wearing a big straw hat, his hands wrapped around the steering wheel of a John Deere Model 8010, six-cylinder diesel tractor.

Dave's #730 Johnny Popper worked just fine, its two cylinders almost musical as it crossed his fields and promised to work harder than any big diesel.

From the kitchen table, Essie read the July calendar, her eyes finding the week of the 22nd. And, there it was. Written in bold letters in the July 24th block: *Alabama Seeds.*

*Well, hello, Spit. Looks like you and I have a date on the 24th of July. That's a Wednesday. Don't be late.*

# CHAPTER FORTY-SEVEN

Dusk in Madison County was like no other, its softness like a peaceful mist spreading far and wide. Slowly, the light faded across the gentle hills, and the remaining shadows melted into a sublime darkness.

On Highway 145, Essie left the Davis farm. But not before Dave and Lillian had loaded her car with canned pears and mayhaw jelly. The Davis' were not unlike all the farm families who lived in Madison County. Generous and kind, their lives were hard, but close to the earth, the significance of God and family prominent.

She continued past Pinetta, north toward Valdosta. In a few miles, she turned left onto the Washington farm road and drove a short way, then parked. Alone with her thoughts, she found herself wanting to see Sam.

By 8:00, a few stars had poked the sky and still she sat watching the lights in the Washington house. She needed to let Bill and Mike know about next Wednesday and the visit Spit would make to the Davis farm.

Essie glanced at the lights in the top of the barn where Sam used the loft for his bedroom. She felt a longing, unable to untwine herself from the man who had loved her since he had seen her in the yellow dress on the homecoming parade float so many years ago.

And, why would she want to leave Sam by the wayside?

Had the relationship with the Irishman been such a gentle, friendly persuasion that she had succumbed to his captivating charm without any misgivings?

*What hold did he have on her?* Confusion set in. Essie admitted one thing she knew for sure. She didn't like any constraints or demands in her life. And, Sam had been guilty of both.

*There it was again – her rebelliousness.* Her unwillingness to be dominated. Suddenly, her heart thudded. A truth spilled out as clear and true as spring water. *She would never marry.*

Essie left the Washington farm lane and turned on the Bellville road. Driving slowly, she watched a cloudless night sky and the many stars' that lay untethered, just sitting there, each one the magic of creation.

At the farm, she turned left onto the narrow lane and parked the Pontiac near the end of the front porch. A waning moon cast a soft light on the barn roof where an owl perched and surveyed his surroundings. When Essie opened the car door, she heard the creak of a rocking chair and saw DooRay sitting on the porch, his chair moving back and forth.

"Lawdy, Miss Essie, ole DooRay 'bout give up on you. You missed some good tomato sandwiches, for sure." DooRay's gravelly voice held laughter, its sound soothing.

"Oh, I'll always come home, DooRay." Essie climbed the steps and settled in the porch swing. One of Lum Townsend's cows bellowed for its calf, a sad, lonesome sound.

"I knowed that, Miss Essie."

"Where's Murphy?"

"I reckon he's settled in for the night." DooRay glanced her way. Something was on his mind. He let out a deep sigh. "Miss Essie, I been thinkin' 'bout somethin' pretty hard."

The porch swing stopped. Essie breathed the night air and waited. Only a few feet away, DooRay continued rocking, his one arm resting in his lap. "You know them bad peoples?"

"I do," she said.

"I reckon you ain't told Mr. Simmie about that seed bag, has you? 'Bout them mens visitin' this here farm last summer?"

In the dark, Essie shook her head. "No. I haven't, DooRay." The cow across the road bellowed again. *Where was her calf?*

The black man nodded slowly. "Ain't nobody gone catch those bad peoples if'n the sheriff ain't knowed about it." He rocked slowly, thinking.

Perhaps DooRay had been born an analytical individual. Thoughtful, he chewed on things quietly. His intelligence lay hidden in his lack of proper grammar, lay in his inability to go beyond his physical disabilities and, of course, held back by the culture of the times.

Interestingly, his high school education had been completed, his mama a stalwart proponent of reading, writing and arithmetic.

In World War II, his blackness was overlooked to some degree as was his lack of refinement, which allowed him to expose his penchant for leadership. After the war, perhaps his heritage and the loss of his arm had prevented him from pursuing a better life.

*Ain't nobody gone catch those bad peoples . . .*

Essie contemplated DooRay's declaration. It was obvious he had examined her decision to withhold information from Sheriff Moore. As yet, he had not come to the reason for her doing so.

"Oh, those men will be apprehended, one way or the other."

"Now, Miss Essie, you ain't gone do nothin' foolish, are you?"

The rocking chair stilled and Essie knew DooRay was watching her. "DooRay, there are just some things I have to do on my own." *Yes, on her own.* There it was again – a compelling need to right a wrong.

"What you gone do?"

Harboring a deep sigh, Essie left the swing and spied Jupiter low in the southern sky along with the last quarter of a waning moon. Unrest settled on the farm, a discontent that swallowed any semblance of happiness and left emptiness in its place.

She had no idea what she was going to do. She knew she wanted to see the 'bad peoples' faces, their hate, their evilness. It was then that she'd know what to do. Look into their eyes and wonder why they had thrown a harmless, one-armed man into the Withlacoochee River.

Finally, she answered DooRay's question. "I don't know."

She turned from the porch rail. "This is something I can't let anyone else handle, DooRay." Essie paused and, in the dark, tried to see the black man's face. The innocent, kind, loving face.

"You see, DooRay. This is personal – they did this to *you*. And, you're part of my family. How can I not resolve this in my own way?"

It was then that Essie decided she would not involve Bill and Mike Washington. Although they had committed to help her confront DooRay's assailants, she'd go it alone.

"Good night, DooRay."

Essie left the porch, walking down the steps and to the farm lane. Her walk was slow, deliberate. How many times in her life had she walked this lane, troubled? Hurting?

At the edge of the Bellville road, she looked east toward the Withlacoochee. Her thoughts building on one another, she turned her face skyward, then smiled. The stars were endless in the dark sky, seeming to multiply as her eyes slowly focused and her body relaxed.

No, there would be no need for Bill and Mike this time. It would be just her and DooRay. DooRay Aikens would be given an opportunity to confront the *bad people*.

Essie wandered back down the farm lane and wondered which of her daddy's guns she liked the best. She knew DooRay liked her daddy's shotgun.

# CHAPTER FORTY-EIGHT

A fitful night. In the dark bedroom, Essie called out Sam's name. A plea. It had been five days since she'd seen him, and then for only a moment. It was when she had watched Sam's steely stare, his eyes glaring at Robert Gray, and then at her. A confusion. His stare questioning. *Why was the Irishman at the Donnelly farm?*

His face had been full of hurt, perhaps a breaking of his spirit. But, how would she know? She'd find him tomorrow. Go to the courthouse. There would be no more unanswered questions.

And what about the Irishman? He, too, had stayed away after he and Sam had crossed paths. The complexity of their relationship in the forefront, for whatever reason, she didn't want to let Robert Gray go.

The turmoil in her mind swept away any reasonable thought and pushed her into indecision. Bewilderment followed, a need to flee the incongruities of her life and seek a gentle peace.

Finally, she closed her eyes and sought sleep. From the open window, a soft breeze caught the thin curtains and brought the sound of a distant train. The last thing Essie remembered before a deep slumber was Sam's kiss. His lips soft, he had held her and whispered, '*You're my girl, Essie Donnelly.*'

A shotgun blast exploded in the night, the sound deafening. A loud squawking. DooRay hollering. Murphy's shrill cry! A scream from a wild animal.

Essie ran down the stairs, grabbed a flashlight and was out the back door. "DooRay!" she called.

From the hide-out in the tree by the tack room, DooRay cackled loudly. "Lawdy, Miss Essie. I done shot me a panther."

"Where? Where is it?" Essie scanned the yard, the beam of the flash-light finding nothing out of the ordinary.

"Don't know 'actly. I jus' pulled this here twine on the trigger of my gun and pow!" DooRay bellowed from the hide-out. "I reckon that rascal's blowed all the way to the Withlacoochee and maybe into Georgia."

"DooRay! Get down outta that tree and show me that panther!" In the farmyard, Essie circled the chicken pen, then along the fence line. Behind her, DooRay scoured the farmyard, Murphy trailing him. From his roost atop the wellhouse, Killer flapped his wings. Not seeing a rising sun, he stuck his head under his wing and crouched low. He'd not move until the sun was up.

"Ain't seen nothin'," said DooRay.

"Well, I see something. Look here. There's blood on this barbed wire. And, here. Are these tracks?"

"Could be." DooRay squinted and leaned close.

"You shot a cat alright. Look at these prints. And there are drops of blood all around."

DooRay knelt on the ground. "That be true, Miss Essie. Ain't no doubt 'bout it. They's a wounded panther done skedaddled away from this farm." He looked up at Essie, his eyes wide. "Reckon we ort to chase after him? Kill him dead?"

Essie pondered DooRay's question for a moment. "I don't think that would be a good idea, DooRay. Let it go for now. We'll be watchful. Don't think he'll be back."

"That could be, Miss Essie."

"You put up that gun and I'll go make some coffee. It'll be daylight in an hour or so."

DooRay scratched his chin. "Could be that panther was Cat, the old Indian woman's friend."

"That's possible. What alerted you to the panther?"

"Well, it was like this, Miss Essie. DooRay done be sleepin', but I done had one eye and one ear open, just in case. I heard this here scratching sound comin' from the chicken pen. And, there it was, running his claws up and down that old post. I even seen him lickin' his lips gettin' ready to eat them delicious chickens. That's when I pulled that twine on the trigger of your daddy's shotgun. And blam! Why that gun jumped in the air ten feet. Only thing that stopped it was a big ole tree limb. It come back down with a wallop. That's when I heard that panther scream."

Essie deliberated for a moment. "I hope it wasn't Cat. Tayki would be devastated. She'd probably come down here and throw rocks at us for the next one hundred years." She turned and walked back to the house. "Come get some coffee, DooRay. Why don't you make some biscuits for us."

Inside the Donnelly kitchen, coffee perked while DooRay squeezed Crisco through snow white flour. "Yes, suh, I like shootin' yo daddy's gun alright. It gots this hair trigger. Sure needs to be pointin' in the right direction when it goes off. Don't want to shoot no human."

# CHAPTER FORTY-NINE

Around 8:00, the party line rang its four short rings. Essie, in the swing drinking her third cup of coffee, hurried through the screen door and picked up the receiver. "Hello."

"Ah, it's my lass." Robert Gray's Irish voice boomed through the phone. "I must extend my apologies, Essie. I'm back in Thomasville. I received an emergency call from Archbold Hospital right after I saw you last. Seems the cardiology staff has been shortened by the death of one of their residents. As a result, I've been working eighteen hour days." He caught his breath. "Enough about me. How is my beautiful lassie?"

Essie became hesitant. The Irishman's voice was lilting, beckoning and pulling her closer. "Everything is fine. DooRay's recovering. So is Murphy."

"Stop! I want to know about *you*!" Rob laughed, teasing her with his words.

Essie smiled into the telephone. "No problems here on the farm."

"You!" the good doctor yelled. "I want to know about my lass." More laughter.

"I'm very well," she said. What could she say? Say she missed him? Say she was confused? Say she spent sleepless nights in a quandary of doubt?

"That's good to hear. As soon as this dilemma is resolved here at the hospital, I'd like to return to Madison County. Or, for that matter, you could visit Thomasville. Perhaps we could go to Boston, Georgia, and visit Ollie Pryor and the boys."

He was slowly pulling her in, inch by inch. With each beat of her heart, she knew there was something there. But, what was it? Admiration? Respect? Love? It was as though she had two hearts, each one beating separately against the other, spreading discord in her mind, a rivalry between the good doctor from Ireland and the Madison County farm boy who had loved her since he saw her on the homecoming float so many years ago.

"That all sounds lovely, Rob," she said, a softness in her words.

"But?"

Of course. But what? "I'm still caring for DooRay."

"Not a good reason, Essie. DooRay will be fine. This settles it – if you won't come to Thomasville, I'll come to Madison County."

"Well . . . " Essie began.

"Can't wait to see you, my lassie." And, the good Irish doctor hung up.

# CHAPTER FIFTY

A rock whizzed by her head and Essie knew Tayki was nearby. Another one followed, landing at her feet. She then heard a surreptitious cackle coming from the woods. How far could the old woman throw a rock? How deadly was her aim?

"Tayki!" Essie turned toward the woods, only a few yards from the Indian woman's shack. She glanced around for Slick. He could be anywhere, hanging from a tree limb or curled on a river stone in the sun, his shiny black skin jewel-like.

"Don't you throw another rock, Tayki, or I'll give these fresh eggs to my neighbors." Essie used her meanest voice. "You hit me and I'll call Sheriff Moore."

Silence. A breeze rustled leaves from the many trees that lined the riverbank. A bird called. A blue jay in a tree near the shack jumped on a higher limb and stared at Essie, cocking its head and squawking loudly.

In the early morning light, a figure moved with stealth from tree to tree, finally jumping into the open. Tayki grinned at Essie, a cunning shape to her toothless mouth. "How many eggs you bring Tayki?"

"Twelve."

"Where?" She stepped closer, her eyes sweeping Essie.

"Right here." Essie leaned over and picked up the egg carton from the grass. "Fresh this morning. DooRay gathered them for you."

"One-arm?" *The black man who slept with Tail had gathered eggs for her?*

"Yes. DooRay."

"Open box." Tayki sniffed the air, her eyes closed. She lifted her arms and opened her eyes, shaking her head vigorously. "Yes. I take eggs."

Essie closed the lid on the egg carton. "How will you cook these eggs, Tayki?"

"Cook?" She scrunched her brows. "No cook."

"You eat them raw?" Essie glanced toward Tayki's shack. Surely, the old woman could somehow cook over a fire. Boil water. Roast meat.

Tayki grinned. "Put in hot sand few days. Good." She licked her lips, her tongue almost black.

"Oh." Indeed, the white sand along the bank became hot in the July sun. Essie shuddered slightly. She'd cook her eggs on her stove.

Essie moved into the shade of a river birch. "Tayki, where's Cat?"

"In woods. No see today." The mismatched eyes in the brown face skirted the woods, flickering back to Essie. "Why you ask?"

Essie nodded. "I thought I should let you know there was a panther at the farm early this morning. Tried to get our chickens."

"Not Cat." Tayki raised her chin and folded her arms across her chest. A small petite woman, she looked defiantly at Essie, while a hard line formed across her mouth.

"Are you sure?"

"Tayki sure. Cat has lady friend in woods." She gave a sly grin and raised her eyebrows. The sun caught her pupils and Essie saw her own reflection.

The sound of water splashing echoed across the river. Perhaps kids jumping off the Bellville bridge or river otters. "DooRay fired on the panther. Not sure how bad he was hit, but we did see blood on the fence and ground."

Tayki flashed her eyes at Essie. "I ask Cat when I see him." Her eyes strayed to the river again and the woods around them. "Cat my baby.

Found him in den with his eyes shut. No mama. I feed him. Seven winters now."

"I see. When you . . . you . . . talk to him, make sure he knows to stay away from the farms around here. Somebody'd shoot him if he's killin' chickens."

Tayki grimaced. "Cat no kill chickens," she said, her lips twisted as she spoke. "No say again."

Without another word, Tayki ran to the tree ladder and climbed the tree. Out of sight, she curled around a tree limb. From the ground below, Slick slowly crawled up the tree and wrapped himself around a limb near her, his head resting on her shoulder.

"I'll put your eggs in your . . . house," called Essie. She walked the few feet to the shack and placed them at the doorway. Her glance inside caught Tayki's meager possessions. A smooth walking stick leaned against a large tree branch. A rusted tire rim with a mound of pine straw on top took prominence in the middle of the small room. The tailgate of a truck stretched across a tin wall in the back, next to a shock of weathered corn stalks.

A string of pine cones hung from a makeshift rafter, adding a slight air of festivity. Fish bones lay piled on top of an overturned wooden crate, along with river stones as smooth and polished as fine silver.

And there, in the dark corner, lay *Cat*. Stretched out and snoring softly, his paws began to quiver. He was dreaming, his sleek body running through the woods, chasing his love.

# CHAPTER FIFTY-ONE

Madison County touched the Georgia border in northeast Florida, not too far from Tallahassee in the panhandle, with Valdosta to the north. The town of Madison's citizens walked its streets in quiet harmony, walked in the same kind of comfort they felt at home. There was fellowship here, a familiarity that endeared folks to each other, as well as to the businesses, churches, and the small mom and pop eateries that cooked and served food just like grandma did.

Essie parked the old Pontiac on southwest Range Street and walked past the telephone company, which was across the street from The Arcade, on Pinckney Street, a block off U. S. 90. The telephone company had a large plate glass window on the front of the building and the switchboard operator, Mrs. Jones, waved to Essie as she passed by.

At the corner of U. S. 90 and north Range Street, the Four Freedoms Park lay in hushed reverence. Essie stopped and read the bronze tablet. The park's tribute to the freedoms of speech, worship, from want and fear, was signified by President Franklin D. Roosevelt to Congress in 1941. The park and its four freedoms manifested itself in the small north Florida town as well as its citizens.

The park was dedicated to Captain Colin P. Kelly, Jr. from Madison, a military pilot in World War II who died at twenty-six years old when his plane exploded over the ocean. Only six years older than Essie, he had graduated from Madison high school, gone on to West Point and then into the war. He piloted a B17C in the 19th Bomb Group and was shot down by the Japanese on December 10, 1941. Essie remembered him well, her mother and father close friends of the Kelly family.

From the park, Essie walked to the courthouse on Base Street. Her daddy had taken her to town on most Saturday's, never failing to point out the neo-classical design of the courthouse. Built in 1913 and, to this day, prevailed as it was originally built. No additions, no renovation in years past, it remained as it was in the early part of the century, simply a place where folks who lived in the county did their legal business.

Sam Washington's duties as prosecuting attorney for the State of Florida kept him busy, the court cases coming one after the other. It was at the courthouse, looking for Sam, that Essie found Jeanette, Judge Earp's secretary for many years.

Essie poked her head around the doorway to Jeanette's office. "Good morning, Jeanette."

Jeanette, a pretty brunette, looked up from her work. "Essie! What a nice surprise. How are you?"

"Doing well. On errands this morning." She paused. "And looking for Sam."

"Oh, my. Not here. He's in Tallahassee."

"Tallahassee?" So that's where Sam had been since he'd run into Rob Gray. Essie contemplated the discord that was mounting between her and Sam, a slow parting that gnawed away at her heart. Exactly where did their relationship lie? She admitted she was the one who straddled the fence. And, had straddled it much too long as far as the farm boy turned attorney was concerned.

She must sort out her feelings. Get rid of the turmoil. Sam was right. She had put him second in her life. She couldn't deny his claim. After all, her priority for the past three weeks had been the *bad people*.

On her way out of Judge Earp's offices, Sheriff Moore climbed the regal steps of the courthouse and met her at the large wooden doors.

"Hello, Essie. Just thinking of you."

Essie smiled and hoped Simmie did not see the untruths in her eyes, the lies she was getting ready to tell. "Good afternoon, Simmie. You doing okay?"

"Somewhat," he said, with a tinge of frustration. "I just spent the past two hours going over DooRay's assault case. It looks like a dead end, Essie. I've pursued every clue available. The bullet in Murphy's leg was not enough to identify. The whiskey bottle turned up nothing. That dang red truck is nowhere in this county."

Simmie released a deep sigh. "I feel like I've let you and DooRay down. All I can do is keep trying."

Essie glanced at the flagpole, its flag furling and unfurling, lashed by a July breeze pushing its way east. What was it that DooRay said? *If'n you don't tell the sheriff 'bout them seeds peoples, how he gone catch 'em?*

She found herself hesitating, a catch in her throat, a lie forming and building bigger than she wanted it to. How could she deceive the sheriff of Madison County, a trustworthy friend whose care of the county's citizens was renowned throughout northeast Florida.

When she turned her eyes back to Simmie, he appeared to be resigned, had accepted the facts as they were. But, she knew Simmie well. He would not give up, would not allow DooRay's assailants to go untethered. It was just a matter of time before his tenacity paid off.

Essie understood *tenacity* – she feasted on it, swilled it, devoured it. She wouldn't let the rule of law deny her the opportunity to right a wrong, especially against DooRay Aikens.

She paused while her untruthfulness burrowed itself into her conscience and fermented there. In the end, vengeance won out. "You haven't let us down, Simmie. We know you've done your best. Something will come up."

*Essie Donnelly, you are going to rot in hell.*

From Madison, Essie took Highway 145 to the Davis farm and a conversation with Dave Davis. Only days until the Alabama Seed salesmen's visit to Dave's farm. And Essie had a plan for Spit and his cohort. *A very special plan.*

# CHAPTER FIFTY-TWO

The lane to Dave's farm covered a mile, a country mile, broken up by gentle curves and slight rises in the road's mixture of dirt and clay. The ruts in the lane spoke of years gone by, each bump a memory of a wagon filled with watermelons or corn. She could almost hear the plod of the mule's hooves, the creak of the wagon wheels.

As she topped a small hill, she saw the top of the barn roof, a dull tin, and then guided the Pontiac around a soft curve. The farmer's fields of corn were abundant, the corn stalks at least six and seven feet high. Ample rains had blessed the Davis farm as well as all of Madison County.

Dave sat on his tractor, easing it into the barn. When he saw Essie, he waved, a grin pushing his face wide like a slice of watermelon.

Essie parked under Lillian's dogwoods and called "Hello, Dave," as she slipped inside the barn and waited while the farmer climbed from the tractor.

The rim of Dave's cap was soaked in sweat, as was his face and shirt. "Whoopee," he squealed. "Glad to get off this damn tractor. Hottest July I ever did see. I'm ready for some a that cool fall weather."

"Don't blame you, Dave. Maybe we'll get a cool shower this afternoon." Essie glanced around the barn. An old tom cat walked the board atop a stall, then stopped to scratch on a post. Half his tail was missing, the four remaining inches flipping back and forth like a metronome.

From the house, Dave's son Wally hollered, "Daddy, mama said to come eat lunch."

Dave waved to his son. "Be there in a minute. Tell your mama to set another plate."

Essie sat on a nearby milk can. "Dave, I was wondering if you'd do me a favor." She noticed the worn face, a sign of fatigue around his eyes. He'd probably been up since before daylight.

"Why, sure. Let me have it." Dave leaned against the tractor tire.

"If I remember right, the Alabama Seed folks are calling on you next week. That true?"

"They'll be here alright. Come 'bout twice a year. They always got new, improved seeds. Love to show 'em off."

"I was wondering if you'd send them over to my place. As you know, Emmett Gaston leases my three-hundred acres, and he's been complaining about seed failure. Thought maybe I could help him out and do a little research for him on his corn crops."

*A smooth liar you are, Essie Donnelly. I do believe you're going straight to hell.*

Dave shook his head. "Oh, my, crop failure ain't nothing to sneeze at, Essie. I done had my share of corn gone bad. 'Course, most of the time, it has to do with drought or too much rain. Seeds is important, too. Bet ole Emmett'd appreciate your help. Ain't nothin' dumb about Emmett — he's been farming as long as me."

From the house, the screen door slammed. "Daddy, mama said if you don't git up here right now, she's gone feed everything to the hogs." Wally, Dave's youngest child, stood a moment, shading his eyes from the sun. "She made carrot cake, daddy. Your favorite."

Dave pushed himself away from the tractor tire and ambled toward the house. "Wouldn't want Lillian to throw out a carrot cake, would we?" They heard the screen door slam shut. Dave chuckled. "Lillian sure is particular about lunch not gettin' cold."

"I think most women are that way." Essie swiped at her face as a wasp zipped close and hovered. "So, Dave, you'll send those representatives of Alabama Seed on over to the house?"

"Yep. No problem, Essie."

Essie smelled fried pork chops before they were halfway to the Davis house. A memory drifted by. Fastened to the aroma of Lillian's fried pork chops, the memory took her to her mama's kitchen and eventually to the front porch where she'd set an overflowing dinner plate on her knees, her iced tea glass beside her on the wooden slats of the swing. She'd push the swing gently and pop a slice of tomato into her mouth, followed by okra, and then a big bite of cornbread.

Her mama had fussed at her. "A true lady would sit at the dining room table, Essie. Look at your sister Jewell. She's a genuine southern lady. Napkin in her lap. Her left hand properly placed."

*Oh, mama. Why didn't you love me just like I am. Daddy loved me. He praised me every day. "That was a great shot, Essie. Now, try to hit a pine cone up in that pine tree near the barn."*

Indeed, Lillian Davis' carrot cake was prize worthy. She served Wally two slices when he promised to clean out the hen house. Dave wanted a second slice, but Lillian held back. "You know the doctor wants you to keep your sugar down."

# CHAPTER FIFTY-THREE

From the Davis farm, Essie turned the Pontiac onto Highway 145, heading north, the sun beginning its decline to the west. Her thoughts rambled, an inability to sort things out regarding Sam. She chastised herself for placing Sam on the edge of her life, in the fringes of her mind.

In Pinetta, she took the Bellville road east, past Lon Terry's general store. As she passed, she saw his Tamworth hogs rooting in the cool mud in their pen across the road from the store. The little store was dark, but in the waning light, she saw Lon and Rana on the front porch of their small house. She honked the horn and waved.

Evening shadows fell across the Donnelly farmyard, framing Killer's silhouette on top of the well house. Nothing stirred in the chicken pen despite the ruckus from the previous evening.

In the calm of the night, the front porch waited and promised comfort, a small utopia of summer sounds, a soft breeze and the joy of solitude.

It was at the top of the steps that Essie smelled smoke and then saw the soft glow of Sam's cigar. She stilled while her eyes found him in the swing. She didn't know if he could see it, but she sent him a smile. "I'm glad you're here," she said, a softness in her words that assured him she had missed him.

"Come sit by me," he said, his words low, but somehow commanding. He patted the seat of the swing and waited. His long legs stretched before him, and slowly pushed the swing as he puffed his cigar.

Essie moved across the length of the porch, a lightness in her steps. No words were spoken when she sat beside him. Sam placed his arm around her and gave her a gentle squeeze.

The swing moved back and forth, a summer night's melody in the creak of the chain and the occasional tap of ashes off the end of Sam's cigar. Heat lightning danced across the sky, flashing to the same beat as Essie's heart, then fading away.

Next to her, Sam's body was warm and smelled of aftershave, a light fragrance of woodberry. From far away, a hound dog bayed, the sound mournful. A short shriek sounded to the north, in the woods on the other side of a watermelon field. Most likely an owl.

"I didn't see your car. Where did you park?"

"Other side of the barn. Wanted to show DooRay some knives I picked up in Tallahassee."

Sam tapped the end of his cigar on the nearby porch rail.

"You know what I'd like to do, Essie?" Sam's words drifted into the evening air, floated there and waited. His breath came slow, a delicate patience that wound itself around his heart and squeezed.

"I'm listening," said Essie.

Sam removed his arm from around Essie's shoulder and leaned forward, his forearms on his knees. Appearing thoughtful, he seemed to withdraw, a remoteness surrounding him while a decision brewed deep inside.

At last, a deep breath. "Tomorrow's Saturday. I'd like for you and I to get married." He leaned back into the swing. In a voice barely audible, "I've loved you longer than I can remember. There seems to be no part of my life that I didn't have you in my thoughts. In my plans for the future."

The tall man eased from the swing and leaned against the porch rail, his arms folded against his chest. "Where is your heart, Essie? Is it always going to be this farm? Or something else? Any place except me?"

Sam moved down the porch to a rocking chair and faced her. The soft light from a sky full of stars and a full moon fell on Essie's face, and Sam could see the brightness of her eyes.

His courtroom voice continued, probing, but gentle. "Essie, I can't love you anymore than I already do. It's a love that compels me to not give up on . . . us."

The porch, the place where life seemed to unfold like roses in the warmth of a new spring, found Essie silent, Sam's words sending his hunger, his endless aching need for her, into her own heart.

Was her heart afraid of heartbreak, afraid of waking, afraid of opening and allowing Sam's love to swaddle her, to surround her? She seemed immoveable, confined to indecision.

"Essie?" Sam tossed his spent cigar into an empty flower pot and waited.

"Sam, I need a little time."

"No, Essie. No more time."

Sam rose from the rocker and stepped to the swing. His hands gently pulled her to him and held her there. "Marry me, Essie."

# CHAPTER FIFTY-FOUR

The mule's hooves slowly clopped into the soft clay, a muffled sound that made one think of distant thunder. Sally was an old mule that had been down many roads, pulling wagons loaded with sugar cane or tobacco, but, best of all, circling a mill whose rollers ground sugar cane to make a clear, sweet juice that would soon be boiled into sorghum.

It was a slow, arduous task for the mule to walk in wide circles for hours around the mill, but at least she didn't have to pull a heavy load. Sally was a dependable mule with no bad habits. Never kicked or bit.

It was, however, in her younger years that Sally was a racing mule. At county fairs, she could run a half mile in 58 seconds, an awesome feat for a mule. Her then owner made money off her until one day Sally refused to race, her large eyes glazed over. The mule was tired.

In her later years, she was content to carry Minnie Pryor down the Bellville road to the Donnelly farm where she knew the black man kept sweet molasses grain in a bucket near the fence. Even had Minnie not guided her, Sally would have found her way past Grassy Pond and past the Townsend cornfields to the shade of an oak tree by the Donnelly barn.

Minnie didn't hurry the mule, but gave her free rein along the winding road, past Lon Terry's general store and grist mill, where the Irishman's hogs rooted in the mud.

In her hand, the young black woman grasped a letter, a confirmation that she had been accepted into a nursing school in Tallahassee. She had squealed so loudly when the mailman delivered the letter that her Uncle Hez had come running in from the field.

"Lordy, Minnie. I thought a snake done got you." He wiped the sweat from his face."

Minnie had shown the letter to her daddy's brother. "Look here, Uncle Hez. I'm going to nursing school."

Nursing school. No more work in the hot fields. No more plantation work in the big mansions in Thomasville. She'd study hard, make good grades and wear a white uniform and cap and all because of Essie Donnelly.

On the farm lane, Minnie guided Sally to the barn where Murphy ran out to greet her. Killer was close behind. The goat liked Sally's company, often times nudging the old mule into a pasture, where they grazed together.

"Well, it's a good mornin' when I sees a pretty girl in the sunlight." DooRay took the mule's reins. "You're pretty, too, Sally." He slapped the mule on her belly and helped Minnie to the ground.

"Ain't long 'fore Miss Essie gots breakfas' on the table."

Minnie glanced toward the house. "I'm hungry, alright."

"Come on. Let's go get you a cup of good coffee." DooRay sauntered down the worn path, his long legs ending in bare feet that knew the way to a good meal.

At the back porch, DooRay hollered through the screen door. "Miss Essie, I got Minnie here. She sure 'nuf is hungry."

From the kitchen, Essie pulled a pan of biscuits from the oven. "Everything's ready," she called. "Just need to put jelly on the table."

"Smells good in this here kitchen, Miss Essie. Ain't nothing like bacon and eggs. Fresh eggs, too. Them hens been laying right nice." DooRay paused and shook his head. "If'n that panther don't get 'em."

DooRay was a gentleman and carefully poured coffee for Minnie and handed her a ceramic cup painted with yellow roses.

Essie laughed. "DooRay, that panther's not coming back here. That shotgun will see to it." She thought of Cat asleep in Tayki's shack.

"Miss Essie, I have good news for you." Minnie pulled out the acceptance letter from the nursing school. "I'm goin' to nursing school."

Essie clapped her hands and grabbed Minnie. "Oh, Minnie. You did it! You passed every test they gave you and you're on your way! I'm so proud of you."

"Yes, ma'am. I'm a little bit scared."

"No need to be scared of anything, Minnie. As smart as you are, you'll do just fine." Essie paused. "You know what the hardest part of this is going to be?"

Wide-eyed, Minnie stared at Essie. "What?"

"I've got to teach you to drive."

"Drive? Miss Essie, I don't even have a car."

Essie sat down at the table. "I've been thinking about that. I bet that old Pontiac out there will be just right for you."

"Your Pontiac?"

"That's right. You'll be able to come home on weekends and holidays. Every college girl needs a car, Minnie."

The kitchen quieted. DooRay hung by the back door and listened to girl chatter. Minnie was leaving. He felt a lump in his throat. Minnie, the girl who stole his favorite fishing spot, had become his best friend. Had nursed him after the bad people had hit him with a whiskey bottle and then threw him in the Withlacoochee River.

He felt sadness as thoughts of her far away in Tallahassee pressed into his heart. He thought her beautiful, her smile sweeter than July's watermelons. And her hands. Long slim fingers that had worked the fields as he had. Long hot summers and aching backs. Still, she appeared genteel, her skin the color of autumn acorns.

She caught him watching her and saw the ache for her in his eyes. Had his feelings for her been hidden somewhere, covered up by his lack of wholeness? Yet, when he came home from the war without an arm, his mama had told him that hearts become stronger when a body is not complete. And his mind? His mama said it would sharpen and compensate for the absence of fingers and a hand.

Minnie smiled at DooRay, seeming to say *don't worry none. I'll be back.*

"DooRay, come sit down. Let's eat some breakfast." Essie pulled out chairs and poured orange juice.

Minnie placed napkins on the table, along with salt and pepper. "Did you make this corn cobb jelly, Miss Essie?"

"No, I didn't. Miss Mary Chamblin made that jelly. Gave me a few jars." Essie placed a platter of fried eggs on the table. "Eggs are getting cold."

It was the best of times. Those simple moments that melded lives together, stayed stuck in memories like the stick-tights on socks and made the prospect of getting old a pleasurable thing.

The sound of bees in the crepe myrtle trees by the back porch drifted through the screened door and brought with it a promise of the sweetness to come. Hens clucked, a soft bray from Sally.

Minnie glanced across the table at DooRay. His eyes were downcast as he fiddled with an uneaten biscuit on his plate.

"What's wrong with you, skinny man?" Her words were soft, poking at DooRay like the frilly end of a dog fennel. "The way I see it, we've got to go to Mr. Ran's fishing pond before I leave. Have us a big fish fry."

Essie saw DooRay flinch. He hadn't fished since the bad people split his head open wide with a whiskey bottle and then threw him into the Withlacoochee. There was fear in his eyes. Perhaps the same fear he felt in Italy, on the battlefield where he left his arm in a muddy ditch and struggled to survive.

Across the table, DooRay lifted his eyes and looked at Minnie. It was then that Essie realized DooRay's deep love for Minnie. *Could a one-armed man living in a barn ever be loved by the lovely Minnie Pryor, a soon-to-be nurse?*

"DooRay," Essie said gently, "a stringer of fish will make a perfect dinner tonight."

A long silence while DooRay buttered his biscuit and then spooned jelly across it. "Don't feel like fishin', Miss Essie. I think me and Murphy gone go ridin' in the cart. Maybe go to Mr. Lon's and get a RC cola."

The black man rose from his chair. "'cuse me. I got some bidness in the barn. Thank you for breakfas'." DooRay left a half eaten biscuit and a full cup of coffee and slowly left the kitchen. The screen door gently shut, the boards squeaking as he walked across the porch, down the steps and out into the farmyard to the barn.

Minnie watched DooRay leave. Perplexed, she glanced at Essie. "Miss Essie, what's wrong with that man?"

"Oh, Minnie. DooRay doesn't want you to leave. You two have been through a lot together this past month. He's going to miss you quite a bit."

Minnie nodded. "Well, truth be known, I'll miss him, too. He's the best friend I ever had."

Essie sipped her coffee, her eyes lingering on Minnie's lovely face. "Minnie, are you aware that DooRay thinks of you as more than a friend?"

# CHAPTER FIFTY-FIVE

A flash of gray caught Essie's peripheral vision. Then, another. She placed a wet sheet across the clothesline and pinned it carefully. Behind the sheet, out of sight except for two mismatched shoes, Tayki stood silently.

Essie sighed. "I know you're there, Tayki, I see your shoes."

Still no movement. Just a black shoe and a brown shoe, with the toe cut out. Red socks crumbled around the old Indian's ankles, revealing skinny legs that were the color of dark tea.

Essie reached in the clothes basket and pulled another sheet to the clothesline. The gray shadow moved behind the next sheet.

"What do you want, Tayki? Are you hungry?" Essie squeezed a clothespin onto the line. Again, she looked down at the pair of shoes. "Coffee?"

She heard a giggle. Then, a hand tapped the sheet from the other side. From the other side of the sheet, two shoes moved to the end, and a head popped out.

Tayki grinned at Essie. Her hair was held back in one of Jewell's clasps. She wore a faded yellow skirt that came to her knees, along with a blouse the color of a John Deere tractor. Her eyes were bright in the wrinkled face. "Tayki pretty."

Essie laughed. "Yes, you're pretty." She straightened the wet sheet and stuck another clothespin on the line. "Why are you dressed up? I've never seen you in a skirt."

Tayki twirled around, her shoes clomping loudly. Was she performing an Indian dance or was it a happy twirl? "Tayki's birthday."

"Birthday? You know your birth date?" Essie narrowed her eyes. "How do you know?"

"Oh, you so stupid." Tayki frowned. It seemed Essie was no longer the Indian woman's friend. Tayki stomped away a few feet and turned. "The spirits come and tell me."

"The spirits?" Of course, the spirits. Tayki heard voices and spoke to, those voices. A complex woman, Tayki's mind went far beyond the mind of a mere earthling.

Essie picked up the clothes basket. "If you promise not to take anything, you can come in the house and get coffee and biscuits. Then, we can sit on the front porch."

Tayki deliberated, her mismatched eyes straying around the yard and then to the house. The green eye with gold flecks found Essie. "Sweet cake?"

Essie smiled. "But, of course. I have some left-over apple cake."

Tayki grinned until her eyes almost squinted shut. Essie wondered how the old woman would look with teeth.

The two women climbed the back porch steps and found the Donnelly kitchen full of all the aromas from breakfast, the bacon, the toast and, of course, coffee.

"Please sit at the table, Tayki, and I'll bring you coffee and lots of sugar."

Tayki snickered while she sat and smoothed her skirt, taking a moment to pull up her red socks. She placed her hand over her mouth and snickered again. "Tayki want everything. Big cake."

Essie placed a bone China cup on the table along with its matching saucer. Small, delicate green leaves fell across the rim on the saucer. The cup had larger green leaves entwined with soft purple violets. She filled the cup with coffee, adding lots of sugar.

"Here you go, Tayki."

Tayki admired the cup. Then, snickered one more time and looked up at Essie. "Birthday cup?"

Essie found Tayki's good eye and smiled. "Just for you."

The apple cake had been baked the day before. Mary Lou Buchanan had dropped it off on her way to Cherry Lake from Hickory Grove. "I was thinking of you and DooRay, Essie," she had said. "I'm just so glad DooRay's recovered and things are going well." Mary Lou, a fine neighbor, made the best cakes in Madison County.

Tayki ate silently except for the loud slurp from her bone China coffee cup. Without a word, she reached for another slice of cake, picking the baked apples from the top and filling her mouth.

Then, suddenly, she jumped from her chair. "Tayki go. Birthday over." She plowed through the screen door, then stopped abruptly on the steps of the back porch. She turned and yelled. "Tayki see red truck. Smell whiskey. Hear music."

Then, she was gone.

# CHAPTER FIFTY-SIX

*he red truck.* Essie stood on the back steps and watched Tayki run
from tree to tree, a gray whirlwind with blurs of a yellow skirt and
green blouse. The Indian woman's stealth seemed other-worldly, a spirit
that came to the earth perhaps only when needed. The last glimpse of the
gray shadow wrapped itself around a large pecan tree to the east of the
farm lane, blending with the wide trunk before disappearing into the
woods.

Perplexed, Essie searched the tack room and barn looking for
DooRay. When she didn't see Murphy or the wooden cart, she glanced
around for Killer. It seemed the three had left the farm, DooRay's thirst
for an RC cola a clear euphemism for a need for solitude, an escape from
the realization that Minnie was leaving Madison County.

Tayki's mysterious announcement that she'd seen the red truck,
smelled whiskey and heard music was disturbing. Were the *bad people* in
Madison County? If so, why were they at the Withlacoochee - a crime
scene that almost ended in DooRay's death.

Waves of anxiety spilled into Essie's thoughts. She vacillated back
and forth between anger and maybe . . . fear. She found herself formu-
lating a plan. Indecision surfaced when her anger demanded DooRay
Aikens be given an opportunity for vengeance.

But, what about DooRay? Did DooRay require retribution to ease his pain? *An eye for an eye, DooRay?*

Essie wanted to go to the river and talk with Tayki. The old Indian woman was eccentric, a peculiarity amassed in a body that was almost unearthly. Tayki jumped from her spirit world to her life as the guardian of the Withlacoochee River and then back again. Essie's dilemma lay in how to sort out the spirit world and the river world when it came to believing what the Indian told her. She'd go to the river early the next morning.

But, first, she'd wait for DooRay's return and tell him about Tayki's visit. They'd sort it out together. Essie, DooRay, Murphy and Killer.

The mailbox was full of seed catalogs, a magazine from *Good Housekeeping* and a personal letter to Essie. She didn't recognize the handwriting, a smooth cursive that was large and flowing across the envelope. The return address was simply *'Thomasville, Georgia.'* A small sticker of a sunflower was stuck to the back flap of the envelope.

She settled on the porch swing and opened the letter.

*July 10, 1957*

*Dearest Essie,*

*I hope my letter finds you well on that big farm of yours. I'm certain you have had a wonderful summer in the country and have enjoyed all the good things that summer brings.*
*Rose and I have checked our calendar and decided on the dates we can visit the Donnelly farm. We hope these dates are agreeable to you.*
*July 17 - 19 will be perfect for us as it will not conflict with Rose's travel to Athens for her first year of college. We shall arrive by Noon on the 17th and depart after breakfast on the 19th.*
*Please let me know your availability.*
*I wish for you to know that Rose is anxious to see you, her beautiful aunt, and learn all she can about her mother Jewell. Rose assures me that my husband and I have been wonderful parents,*

*but that her biological family is important, too. I am so pleased that Rose has accepted this new chapter in her life with such an amazing maturity.*

*I anticipate your reply. My telephone number is CA 6-1797.*

*Most affectionately,*
*Annalee Montgomery*
*421 S. Hansell Street*
*Thomasville, Georgia*

*Jewell. Your daughter Rose will visit the farm next week. I'll show her your room, your yellow room where everything is just like you left it. We'll sit on the front porch - Rose can sit in your chair and I'll tell her all about you.*

*Then, we'll go to the Mt. Horeb cemetery and put flowers on your grave. Some of mama's roses - the Sunrise Sunset that you liked so much. You remember - the fuchsia-pink with the apricot centers?*

*I'll show her how to bake the buttered rum pound cake. We'll serve it on mama's Glenlea China, the one with the tiny pink and blue flowers. Do you think daddy would mind if we used the last of his Pusser's Gunpowder Proof rum?*

*And Rose's father? I'd like to tell her about Autrey Browning. I know if he was alive he'd want to meet her. If he wasn't buried in Texas, we'd visit his grave, too.*

*I'm so excited, Jewell.*

Late afternoon showers formed in the west and brought blustery winds that blew the corn sideways in Lum Townsend's field across the Bellville road.

Just before the fat raindrops fell, Murphy trotted down the farm lane pulling the old wooden cart, DooRay standing and swaying back back and forth inside, holding tightly to the reins with his one hand. Killer barely managed to grasp the goat's back as the cart whipped around the edge of the barn and stopped.

The rain came in torrents, drumming the tin roof of the barn with sounds as loud as a passing freight train. From the end of the porch, Essie watched all three duck into the barn just as the wind blew a limb across the farmyard, narrowly missing Killer's beautiful tail feathers.

She settled in the porch swing and felt soft sprays of rain blow across her face. It was Saturday – the day Sam wanted to get married. Her throat ached and then she felt tears.. The tears turned into sobs. No matter where he was, she'd find him tonight and ask him to wait for her just a little while longer.

# CHAPTER FIFTY-SEVEN

Essie called Annalee and confirmed their arrival on Wednesday. "Come hungry," she had said. "I'll have a wonderful lunch ready for you and Rose."

Rose would sleep in Jewell's room and Annalee in her mother and father's room down the hall. Both lovely rooms, her guests would be treated with good old Southern hospitality.

Essie's mother had been the ultimate hostess, meals always served on her Glenlea China, silver place settings and Irish linen tablecloths. The crystal she used was Swarovski from Switzerland. Edith Donnelly had bragged that she had traveled to Switzerland to purchase it.

The rain tapered off and left clear skies to the west where the sun eased toward the horizon. The front porch dimmed as rain dripped from the roof into the caladiums. The chain on the swing creaked softly, as did the frogs that hid beneath the azalea bushes.

Essie heard DooRay before she saw him, a soft humming that sounded like an angel hovering in the rain-washed sky. He rounded the corner of the house and eased up the brick steps. "Evenin', Miss Essie." He sat in his favorite rocker and crossed his long legs.

"Hello, DooRay. How was your cart ride?"

DooRay was thoughtful for a moment or two. "Well, old Murphy was feelin' quite lively and when I said 'giddy-up, you ole goat' he took off like a chicken on fire. Yes, suh, that's some goat. He done healed real good from that bullet wound."

The black man croaked a throaty laugh. "Killer done fell off twice. Mad as a hornet. Had to stop and let him jump back on, his feathers all ruffled up. Murphy thought it was funny. I done think he did it on purpose. Startin' and stoppin' with a jerk like that."

Essie laughed along with DooRay. "Guess Dr. Davis fixed his leg just right. A bullet can't stop that goat." She eyed DooRay. A hint of sadness remained on his face, despite his flight from Minnie and her plans to go to Tallahassee.

Essie wondered if DooRay had healed as well as Murphy. Dr. Bush was right; no hair had grown over the long, whiskey bottle scar on the side of his head. The emotional scars were hidden, simmering somewhere in DooRay's mind. His float down the Withlacoochee, the encounter with Tail, the eight foot alligator.

The remaining sunlight slipped behind the tall cypress at Ran Terry's pond. A few cattle egrets flew west, disappearing into the softening sky. A whippoorwill began its call from the north field, where crickets burrowed beneath the watermelon vines.

"DooRay, when Tayki was here this morning, she told me she saw the red truck."

# CHAPTER FIFTY-EIGHT

"The bad people is back?" DooRay whispered, eyes widening. He sighed deeply, closed his eyes, a slight twitch in his one hand. The rocker stilled and, within it, sat a man whose life had hung in the balance, saved only by his ability to float, even in a semi-conscious state.

A lone white sandbar had captured his body from the deep, dark waters of the Withlacoochee and held him, while all around him the woods were alive with the sounds of a summer night.

On the dark porch, just a few feet away, Essie heard DooRay's breathing. Shallow, short breaths that puffed into the air, perhaps laden with fear.

"DooRay, what are you thinking?" Essie asked, with as much calmness as she could muster.

A sound came from DooRay's throat. Was it anger? A conciliatory acceptance of the troubles that were to come?

Finally, "All's I can say, Miss Essie, is we ort to let Mr. Simmie know. That's what a sheriff does. He gets the bad peoples." An adamant resonance sounded with each syllable as DooRay struck the air with his fist.

No words were spoken as they each struggled with their own thoughts. As much as Essie wanted to confront DooRay's assailants on her own, she must respect DooRay's feelings, which were quite clear. *Let the sheriff handle the bad people lawfully.*

Then again, without the least bit of compunction, the word *vengeance* crept into Essie's mind for the hundredth time. Vengeance had been there from the beginning. Festering, boiling, growing, it fed her need to right a wrong on behalf of someone she loved, someone whom she considered part of her family, and that need far surpassed DooRay's stance of following the law.

Quietly, Essie spoke. "I find it odd that Spit and his cohort have blatantly returned to the river. Do they think their act was insignificant, of no importance – so much so that they had no qualms about showing their faces in the county? That bashing your head with a whiskey bottle and throwing you in the Withlacoochee was just a . . . a morning of fun? That there would be no repercussions for their ruthless behavior? That your life had no value to anyone?"

Suddenly, Essie stood from the porch swing, her words twisting into a hot fury. "And, what will the courts do? Will they charge them with a misdemeanor? Fine them for being a public nuisance? Give them three months in jail for aggravated assault?"

Essie's throat seized, the pain of hurt and anger forcing her to step down from the porch, unable to contain her outrage.

Tears running down her cheeks, she looked up at DooRay. Just above a whisper, she said, "DooRay, those men meant for you to drown. They wanted you dead. They threw a harmless, one-armed man into the river knowing you could not swim."

DooRay heeded Essie's words as he watched her in the darkness, watched her pace through the wet grass and fling her arms through the air. It was then that he was certain she'd never tell the sheriff the bad people had returned.

# CHAPTER FIFTY-NINE

It was near midnight when Essie eased the Pontiac down the farm lane toward Pinetta, a waning full moon finding its way across a clear, ink blue sky. She headed west on the Bellville road, barely missing a deer that loped across the road in front of the car, followed by a spindly-legged fawn. Essie slowed as the pair disappeared into the nearby woods behind Lon Terry's gristmill.

At highway 145, with the Pontiac's windows rolled down, Essie hesitated, the night air cool after the late evening rain. Slowly, she turned north where the Washington farm's two hundred acres lay in quiet repose.

Essie felt her heart beating wildly. S*am.* He'd said *'tomorrow is Saturday. Let's get married.'* It wasn't the first time he'd asked her to marry him, but somehow she thought it might be the last.

It was *still* Saturday and Essie remained a single woman. She gave herself a wry smile and looked at the car's clock. Just a few minutes before midnight. She wondered if the opportunity to accept Sam's offer would expire when the hands of the clock struck twelve. Perhaps she appeared flippant, instead it was just a moment of analytical thought.

The farm lay serene, the house and the outbuildings silhouetted by soft moonlight. The evening rain glistened on the leaves of the crepe myrtles. The barn where Sam lived was dark, his loft high above bales of sweet hay, the rooms seemingly empty. From the Washington home, the faint strain of Eddie's Arnold's *Make the World Go Away* drifted through the open windows.

Essie parked along the fence line, only a few feet from a small herd of black Angus cattle. The cattle stared at the car, a few tails switching back and forth. They became nervous and began to move away from the fence, several small calves kicking their legs in the air as they followed the herd. A few cows snorted and shook their heads in a hasty retreat.

The moon that sat among a million stars led the way to the barnyard, where a myriad of farm wagons, trucks, harrows and plows sat in shadowed silence. The odor of manure swept the air from a hog pen a quarter of a mile to the north, near the winding Withlacoochee River.

Inside the barn, Essie quietly climbed the ladder to Sam's loft. A slow climb full of trepidation, she held tightly to the ladder and, one by one, stepped onto the rungs. *Closer. Closer.* And, then the voice of Sam Washington.

"I heard the Pontiac when you turned onto the lane." His voice was calm, perhaps resigned. He never knew what Essie Donnelly was thinking.

Essie paused at the top of the ladder, the doorway to the loft a few feet away, nestled in a small landing. The door was open and soft light streamed across the landing and fell on the auburn haired woman who had come to bargain with Sam Washington.

*Yes.* That's the way it would be – *bargain.* Seek an understanding. Declare a truce, perhaps. And, then . . .

Essie could hear Sam's footsteps as he approached the doorway. From the top of the ladder, she took one last step onto the landing and saw the man who had proclaimed his love for her.

Their eyes met, his clouded with a slight weariness, a worrisome look on his face that made the handsome man seem vulnerable. Of course, he was vulnerable – he was at her mercy. A man in love was always in peril. The whole world knew that when a man was exposed to the wiles of a beautiful woman, a man in love was defenseless.

*Essie's eyes?* They were full of hunger as she stepped toward Sam, her arms reaching out. A small gasp escaped from her throat, and in one swift movement, Sam swept her into his arms.

# CHAPTER SIXTY

Barely daylight, a heavy mist hung across the Bellville road, the sun hiding deep in the eastern horizon. Only a few soft rays escaped the tops of the tall cypress that hugged the ever-moving With-lacoochee.

The tires of the Pontiac crunched across the scatter of acorns that lay across the farm lane beneath the limbs of several large oaks. A scurrying rush of squirrels indignantly swished their tails while the Pontiac moved over their breakfast.

Early morning shadows fell across the front porch of the Donnelly house where heavy dew dripped from the edge of the roof. Essie parked and walked across the wet grass onto the brick steps of the porch, her eyes finding DooRay sitting in the shadows in his favorite rocker, his eyes closed. She wondered if he had been in the porch rocker all night, waiting for her return.

"DooRay?"

"I's awake. Just restin'."

"Have you been here all night?"

DooRay slowly opened his eyes. "Yes, ma'am. This here rocker done held me like it was my mama." He smiled and his gaze lingered on Essie before finding a hummingbird zipping to a feeder. "Mornin' time is

DooRay's favorite time. I gets to say good morning to the sun, to the sky and, 'specially to my friends."

"Your friends?" Essie leaned against the porch column, a half smile on her face.

"Yes, that be right. Murphy and Killer. If'n you'd been here earlier, you'd a heard Killer crow like he was a mighty lion. Ain't never seen him so big and puffy on top a that well house. I reckon he's the king of the farmyard, for sure."

At that moment, Murphy trotted around the corner of the house, the absence of his right ear a rather interesting feature, an anomaly that set him apart from all other goats. His master had one arm; Murphy had one ear. It was clear that they belonged together.

The old goat merely wanted to be near his master. He began to graze along the edge of the wide yard, Killer sitting atop a fence post nearby. DooRay eyed the pair and chuckled.

Essie eased up on the porch rail and swung her legs back and forth. No words were necessary. DooRay knew where'd she'd been. She caught his dark eyes watching her, no judgment in his soft study of her.

"DooRay, I'm going down to the river to see Tayki. I want to know more about the red truck she saw. Want to go?"

DooRay left the rocker and stretched. He appeared thoughtful before stepping down from the porch. "I reckon ole DooRay gone stay at the farm." He walked a few steps away and turned back. "I be here when you get back."

A single ray of sunlight broke the heavy mist and fell across DooRay, the light settling on his face, while around him the mist seemed to darken. Essie stilled and watched DooRay's body almost levitate. *Was he an angel?* She blinked and the sunlight faded.

"DooRay, don't leave." she said, as she jumped from the porch rail and stood on the steps. "Why haven't you been fishing? It's been well over a month since we've had good fried fish, and some of those hush-puppies you like."

The black man lifted his chin and stared at the farm girl. His lips seemed to quiver before he spoke. "It's the red truck, Miss Essie. You knows them bad peoples are still out there."

Murphy and Killer followed DooRay's slow walk to the barn. The rooster's legs had no knees, and he ran stiff-legged like a man with wooden legs. Murphy trotted behind DooRay and nudged his backside. DooRay ignored both of them. He had a lot on his mind.

Sam had held her through the night. Her sleep had been fitful, full of whimpers that sounded like kittens mewing. He soothed her, rubbed her back until he, too, fell asleep. They both dreamed. Sam's dreams were of courtroom fights with other lawyers and heated words with a judge. Essie's dreams were of running. Always running. Running to catch someone or running from someone?

She woke up several times and wondered where she was. *In Sam's arms.*

*Their bargain?* She had come to bargain, but to bargain with a lawyer was not an easy thing. Sam's stance was black and white. No muted, obscure agreements between them. Either she would commit to marriage or he would walk away. His words *'have your cake and eat it, too'* stung. Awake in his arms, she thought of him walking away from her and the heartache it would cause.

She closed her eyes just as light seeped through a small window in the barn. It was then that the tall handsome Irish doctor stampeded into her dreams. *Well, hello, Lassie,* he crooned.

# CHAPTER SIXTY-ONE

The Withlacoochee ran quietly, the dark rum-colored water warmed by mid-day sun, its limestone banks covered with lush vegetation that reminded one of the tropics. The sound of a large sturgeon slapping the water echoed down the river like a clap of thunder and told the river the fish was king.

Near the old iron bridge on the Bellville road, about two miles from the Donnelly farm, Essie parked the Pontiac and maneuvered the steep bank of the river with ease, ending up at the water's edge.

At the top of a high bank, only a quarter mile from the Bellville road, Tayki had built her mansion, which was surrounded by tupelo trees, swamp mallow, oaks, cypress and maples. Her responsibility as guardian of the river was most likely an innate eccentricity, one she inherited from her Indian ancestors. The Miccosukee woman loved the river as well as the river creatures. Her ability to survive for decades in the vast woods surrounding the river touted her intelligence. Her ability to throw well-aimed rocks with amazing accuracy depicted just one of her incredible skills.

Essie walked along the shore and prepared herself for an onslaught of rocks or the sound of malicious laughter coming from the trees. She listened intently for Tayki, only to hear the chirping of birds and the occasional chatter of squirrels.

"Hello," she called, nearing the Indian's shack. "Tayki! Where are you?" She climbed the riverbank, pulling on small trees to lift her up. Her finesse in the woods was almost as proficient as Tayki's.

At the doorway to the shack, Essie peeked in, only to find it deserted. She glanced at the large oak that towered over the dwelling, but saw no sign of Tayki or Cat.

From atop the bank, she scanned the east side of the river for Tail and saw only a few spindly-legged water birds searching for minnows. Thinking Slick might be sunbathing, Essie glanced at the half-submerged log. There was no snake to be seen.

The woods behind the shack and to the west ran for miles before thinning and turning into lush farmland filled with corn or peanuts. She knew Tayki occasionally raided the fields belonging to the Townsends for food and any other treasures she might find.

Walking a few yards into the woods, around trees and through thick brush, Essie stopped at an old abandoned logging road that ran north and south, parallel to the river.

She gazed south, down the length of the road until it met a bend, then saw nothing but trees. Perhaps Tayki was mushroom hunting. A breeze swept through the trees, the sound of rustling leaves filling the quiet. It was then that she heard the motor of a vehicle.

At the sound, she turned south again and, through the trees, saw the front end of a red truck. The vehicle's big tires lumbered down the abandoned road slowly, low hanging tree branches slapping the truck's windshield.

*The red truck. Well, hello, Spit.*

Essie's eyes locked on the truck. Her body tensed, but she didn't move. She stood vigilant, her jaw tightening. She felt her teeth clamp together . . . and waited.

For a fleeting moment, she thought of her father's guns, their power-fulness as well as their beauty. She also thought she would like to have one at this moment, a moment that had become somewhat serendipitous, unexpected, an encounter with *the bad people*. If she had a gun, she wondered if there would be a duel – the bad people and the farm girl from Madison County. She almost smiled.

In the middle of the logging road, her body had become leaden. The truck could run over her before she'd move. She stepped forward as the truck ambled the final few yards and stopped.

*Spit* had a face only his mama could love. He stepped out of the truck, a grin showing yellow teeth plastered across his face. "Howdy!" he called, stepping from behind the truck door and easing a few steps toward Essie.

From the passenger side of the truck, another man emerged. Red-faced and bleary eyed, a whiskey bottle in his hand, he leaned against the truck's fender and grinned at Essie.

"Hello," said Essie. Her eyes narrowed. "You folks from around here?"

A grinning Spit shook his head. "Naw. We're from Alabama. Here doing a little fishin' and huntin'."

"That right?" Essie inched a little closer, her heart racing.

"How 'bout you? You from around here?"

Essie deliberated a moment, glanced into the woods, then back to the men. "No, I'm from up in Georgia."

"What're you doing out here in these woods?" Spit casually turned his head and Essie watched as tobacco juice the color of manure flew into the woods.

"Oh, my husband and I are mushroom hunting," Essie lied.

"Mushroom hunting? Ya'll don't have mushrooms up in Georgia?" Doubt spread across Spit's face.

"Not this many," Essie said easily.

Spit raised his eyebrows. "What kind you lookin' for?"

"King Boletus. Porcini."

Spit, his body tank-like, removed the cap from his head and ran his hand across his hair. He replaced it carefully, all the while watching Essie. "Where's your husband?"

Essie waved her hand in the direction of the river. "Down the river bank a few yards. He'll be along in a short while."

Spit sent his tobacco juice about six feet into the brush. "He huntin' mushrooms, too?"

Essie nodded, a nervous patter in her chest.

Spit's companion burped loudly and threw his empty whiskey bottle into the woods. He turned away from Essie and sent a stream of pee onto the trunk of a nearby tree. When he turned back around, he lost his balance and his body slammed against the truck. He cursed and crawled into the truck seat.

"So how often do you visit this area for hunting and fishing," Essie asked, feigning curiosity.

Spit stepped closer and Essie could clearly see the face DooRay had described. Here he was at last – the perpetrator, the man who had needed a little Saturday morning excitement to begin his day, and he had chosen DooRay Aikens, a one-armed black man who would never hurt a fly.

Essie felt the heat rise in her chest, her throat seized as she watched the man whose maleficent act had almost killed DooRay.

"Oh, Freddie and me get over this way every few months or so. We sell seed and fertilizer to farmers in the area, mostly Madison County." He paused and spit again – no wonder they called him 'Spit.' "Came over early to fish a little. Gonna camp here for a few more days, then we got to do some real work next week."

"Camp on the river?" Essie scoured the woods for Tayki. *Where was she?*

Freddie climbed out of the truck and pulled a new whiskey bottle from the truck bed and drank long. Another loud burp, another pee.

"Yep, there's a big ole sandbar down by that bend in the river. Beautiful white sand. Perfect place to set up a small tent. Campfire. Paradise."

Essie noticed a Jon boat poking out of the truck bed.

Essie digested Spit's words. *Big sandbar at the bend in the river.* Tail's sunning spot. The joy she felt at that moment was sinful. The two men would camp in the backyard of an eight foot alligator – an alligator who was as much a river guardian as Tayki. It was hard for Essie to suppress a smile.

"Sounds heavenly," she said, sweetly. "Well, good luck with your fishing. I've got to rendezvous with my husband." Essie turned and began walking back to the river, a shiver forming along her back. *She had just been with the bad people.*

# CHAPTER SIXTY-TWO

E ssie hurried along the river to the bridge where she had parked the Pontiac, her mind in a thousand different places. *The bad people.*

*Should she tell DooRay?* Tell him she had seen the bad people, had spoken to them. *Should she tell Simmie Moore?* The Madison County sheriff whose reputation as a lawman was above reproach. Yet, despite her respect for him and his position, she continued to deceive him. Were her daddy's guns clean and loaded? *Yes, they were.*

And Sam? He would visit in the late afternoon and perhaps stay for dinner. It was possible his visit was an overture to the end of their relationship. Then again, was it a prelude to a new beginning? *What was wrong with her? The man loved her deeply.*

Filled with anxiety, Essie climbed the bank from the river's edge, crossed the old iron bridge and eased into the Pontiac. She sat for a moment, then smiled. Perfectly balanced on the edge of the dash, a smooth, round rock the size of a golf ball stared back at her. *Tayki.* The river guardian. The Indian woman who talked to creatures.

Essie sped along the Bellville road for two miles until she reached the farm lane, then whipped the car to the right and followed the lane to the barn.

"DooRay," she called, slamming the car door and trotting to the tack room.

A voice floated from high above. "Up here, Miss Essie. High in the tree where could be some angels 'round. Cooler up here. Nice breeze." The black face was covered with a wide smile.

Searching the massive branches, Essie found a grinning DooRay perched on the floor of his hide-out. "Come on down and drink a cold glass of iced tea with me, DooRay. We've got to talk. Your rocker is waiting for you."

Crossing the farm yard, her thoughts tumbling, Essie saw a car turn onto the lane. *Simmie Moore.*

*Damn!* It was going to be a day filled with blatant lies, one after the other. *How could Madison County's watermelon queen, mistress of the Donnelly farm, writer of a soon-to-be #1 novel, become a liar?* Her body sank. *Maybe, just one more little lie.*

For an honorable woman like Essie Donnelly, integrity was more important than a good corn crop. More valued than a prize black Angus cow. To what depths had she sunk, she didn't know. Her nature was that of a pit bull – she would hang on for dear life to what she deemed the right thing to do. To her detriment, the chance that she was misguided never occurred to her.

As she watched the sheriff step out of his car and wave to her, she called a greeting. "Hello, Simmie."

At that same moment, it was quite clear to her that she was going to tell as many lies to Madison County's illustrious sheriff as necessary.

The Donnelly front porch provided a cool respite from the furnace heat of July, its two large paddle fans whirling beneath the high ceiling in perfect harmony. The giant oak trees that shaded the house kept the sun at bay, while a stiff breeze from the west ran down the long porch and chased the humid air.

The screen door slammed behind Essie as she brought a tray of glasses filled with iced tea. DooRay had collected his favorite rocker and settled himself near the swing. Simmie liked the Adirondack chair and its wide arms and eased himself into its cushioned seat. He removed his hat and placed it in his lap.

"Here you go," said Essie, handing out the iced tea. She cornered the swing and moved aside a copy of Carson McCullers' *The Heart is a Lonely Hunter*, the first novel she'd read after *Peyton Place*. Her love affair with words had created her own novel *Watermelon Queen of Madison County*. She thought of Lola LaRue and the literary agent's quest to make her a renowned author. Essie was acutely aware, however, that her life on the farm had become more important than being listed on the New York Times best seller list.

Essie sipped her tea and glanced at Sheriff Moore. He was watching her, his intelligent eyes reading her, perhaps assessing the farm girl's possible knowledge regarding DooRay's assault. As a law officer, he was acutely aware of body language, eye movements, and of someone's efforts to deceive.

Simmie knew Essie well. And that was why he was sitting on her front porch, his antenna high. He saw that she was nervous, a little too chatty as she told him Emmett Gaston had yet to kill the panther that was raiding his chicken pens. She told him Tayki had had a birthday. The tell tale clue was she never asked how the investigation was going regarding the assault on DooRay.

And on and on. He waited until she caught her breath.

Simmie smiled. "Some folks over in Clyattville tell me they've seen a red truck parked at Mozelle's on several occasions in the past week."

Essie stared at Simmie, unblinking. That made sense. The Alabama men were in the area. Hunting and fishing, they said. Mozelle's was the perfect place for them to buy liquor and eat good fried catfish.

"Do you plan a stake-out of some kind?" Casually, Essie crossed her legs and kept her eyes on Simmie. She'd not flinch. She was reminded again that she was withholding pertinent information. She could be charged with obstruction of justice. She could go to jail.

"Not so much a stake-out as keeping an eye out. We'll drive by often, especially at night. Got some folks over there who'll call me with information. Of course, Mozelle's is in Georgia. Don't want to step on any toes."

Simmie reached in his shirt pocket and pulled out his pipe. He scraped the bowl with his pocket knife, then stuffed it with his favorite tobacco. When he put a match to it, the tobacco flared and the sweet aroma of fragrant tobacco caught the air.

DooRay sat unmoving, his eyes downcast. Simmie noticed the black man's quiet composure. "DooRay, how're you feelin'?"

Simmie did not miss DooRay's quick glance to Essie. "As fine as can be, Mr. Simmie. Miss Essie and Minnie done take real good care of me."

"Been fishin' any?" Simmie drew long on his pipe. Once again a sweet fragrance was puffed into the air.

DooRay's shoulders slumped. "Naw. Done been too hot."

The sheriff knew the black man almost as well as he knew Essie. "DooRay, I've never known you to find an excuse not to fish," Simmie said, with subtle jest.

Essie stopped the movement of the swing. "Simmie, DooRay's dealing with a little apprehension about what happened and staying clear of Grassy Pond."

Simmie nodded, his gaze on DooRay. "Have you talked with Dr. Bush? Maybe he can help."

"No, suh. Just . . . just stickin' close to home." He looked up and sent a forced grin. "Ole Murphy and Killer and me as happy as can be. Right on this here farm. Gots plenty to eat, a place to sleep."

"Glad to hear that, DooRay." Simmie placed his hat on his head and stood from the chair. "Essie, I'll keep you posted on any activity at Mozelle's. I've already talked with the sheriff of Lowndes County and he's aware of everything."

The sheriff moved slowly down the brick steps. "I'll be seeing you folks later. Thanks for the tea, Essie."

Half-way to his car, he turned back and glanced at Essie. "You don't happen to have any new information on this case, do you? Maybe from Tayki?"

Essie felt DooRay's eyes on her. He'd hear her lie.

"Not a thing, Simmie. Not a thing," she said smoothly.

# CHAPTER SIXTY-THREE

The porch lay quiet except for the lowing of Lum Townsend's cattle. Essie and DooRay watched the sheriff drive down the farm lane and turn toward Pinetta. Most likely, the lawman would stop at Lon Terry's general store and the two men would revere their duck hunting escapades.

The paddle fans on the porch's high ceiling whipped the air, both DooRay and Essie appreciative of the stiff summer breeze tunneling through the long porch. Acorns from the limbs of the towering oak trees pinged the roof and caused a frenzy among the many squirrels who chased them with glee.

Essie's troubled mind leapt from one dilemma to another, leaving her in a myriad of formidable quandaries. Out of the corner of her eye, she saw DooRay watching her, his large, sad eyes questioning. Somehow, the black man knew. He knew that, once again, she had withheld information from the sheriff.

DooRay possessed an innate ability to perceive the thoughts of others with an uncanny accuracy, his intellect far exceeding his persona of a disabled black man who lived in the tack room of a barn and gathered eggs from the chicken pen, raked pine straw with his one arm and made prize winning biscuits.

DooRay's inarticulate speech did not determine the quality of his mind. Hence, he was not to be judged by his manner of speaking.

Once again, Essie chastised herself for not giving DooRay the opportunity to confront his assailants. Regret beat in her like a second heart. *She had to tell him everything she knew – that was all there was to it.*

Essie took a deep breath. She would relinquish control of the revenge she had harbored. She would bequeath to DooRay the right to whatever retribution he deemed necessary.

The farm girl struggled for words. "DooRay . . . I need to tell you something."

DooRay sent a questioning glance to Essie. He continued to rock back and forth slowly, forward and backward, and waited. He was a calm man. Deliberating and thoughtful, he held Essie with a beseeching stare.

Essie turned away from his watching eyes and to the squirrels as they gathered acorns. Almost to herself, she said, "Spit was at the river."

The rocker stopped and DooRay leaned forward, closer to Essie. Closer to the words she was about to say. "You done talk to him?"

Essie nodded and shifted her face back to DooRay. "He was there with the other man."

"What those mens doin' at the river?"

"Camping. They plan to fish the Withlochoochee and hunt some. But, first, they're going to spend the week calling on their seed customers. Then, come back and camp for three or four days."

DooRay hung his head. His words came softly, not accusatory. "I see you didn't tell Mr. Simmie."

There it was again – DooRay's mastery of getting to the core of a situation. Plain and simple. He was holding Essie accountable.

"That's . . . that's true," she said, weakly.

Silence followed. Murphy rounded the corner, Killer close behind. They both chased squirrels, then rested in the shade of the dogwoods that lined the farm lane.

DooRay drank the last of his iced tea, his thoughts forming, and at last spilling out into the July air. "Miss Essie, what you gone do?"

DooRay's question jolted Essie. *What was she going to do?*

She pushed the swing hard, exposing her anxiety. Her chest rose and fell as her breath caught. Finally, a deep sigh. "DooRay, I don't know what I'm going to do." She paused and found the dark eyes of her friend.

Moments passed. Then, "But, I'll tell you what I'd like us to do."

DooRay's eyes widened, his attention square on Essie Donnelly. "What's that, Miss Essie."

Eyes closed, Essie half-smiled, a dream-like smile that softened her face and put her into a thoughtful fantasy. When she opened her eyes, she grinned at DooRay.

Her words were barely audible, but filled with conviction. There was no doubting their importance. "I'd like to tie one of their arms behind their back and throw them in the Withlacoochee, just like they threw you. And see if they float. Or see if they drown."

Alarm covered DooRay's face. Then, riotous laughter. He slapped his knee and hollered. "Oh, my, Miss Essie. What a sight to see. Why those two mens would be one-armed just like ole DooRay."

He cackled again. "And, if'n they made it to the sandbar, old Tail would gobble them bad peoples up, for sure."

A sobering quiet. A hoarse whisper from DooRay as he leaned forward in his rocker. "You ain't gone do that, is you, Miss Essie?"

# CHAPTER SIXTY-FOUR

The sun was high in the sky as Sam left his barn loft at the Washington farm and drove through Pinetta, waving at the Falk boys as he turned onto the Bellville road. His tires grabbed the clay dirt and the car swerved a bit. The radio played Johnny Cash's *I Walked the Line,* and Sam sang along, his deep voice booming into the July air.

*Essie.* For the first time, she had come to him, open hearted, fragile, and needing him. She had unleashed tears, had trembled as he held her. The hard Essie had vanished, and a soft Essie had emerged, a rarity, and he wondered about the cause of it. The thought of lovemaking far from his mind. He was with a troubled woman.

She had slept in his arms, her body restless, a soft murmur now and then. When she stirred long after midnight, he had pushed her hair back from her face and spoke.

"Essie, what's got you so anxious?"

Eyes closed, "I've not been sleeping well, that's all," she lied.

"And, Rose and her mother visit a few days next Wednesday and Thursday. So much to do."

Sam had soothed her, but knew there were underlying causes for her turmoil. Had she spoken the truth, maybe Essie would have told him her heartfelt feelings about . . . *marriage.*

. . .

Terryville sat in the shade of large oaks, their branches spread wide. The little store hosted the best iced cream soda, the Vernors brand, in Madison County. Lon Terry stood at the Shell gas pump, gassing up his tractor, his large Stetson hat shading his Irish face.

Sam pulled onto the side of the road, next to the hog pen, and walked across the road. "Good afternoon, Lon. I suppose you know why I'm here, don't you?"

The tall, freckled man laughed his hearty laugh and screwed the top onto his gas tank. "Got one of them cream sodas waitin' for you. Let's go inside and get in front of the fan."

The two men shook hands and went into the small store where a large fan whipped the air around. The smell of feed, flour, leather boots, dungarees and old wood swept together like a recipe for happiness, leaving one to remember the scent for a lifetime.

"Come 'ear, boy." Lon reached into the cold box and pulled out a cream soda. He popped the top off and handed it to Sam.

"Thank you, Lon. Can't pass by here without stopping. Guess I'm addicted. Have one with me?"

"Oh, no. Rana'd skin me for sure. She says it's too much sugar. You'd think a sixty-five year old man could make his own decisions, wouldn't you?" Lon pulled off his hat and scratched his graying head.

"I'm thinking she's just looking out for you, Lon." Sam drank long, the cold sweet vanilla drink satisfying his thirst.

Lon stepped behind the counter and opened his cash register. Sam saw the tip of a gun barrel under a folded croaker sack by the register. "Look here, Sam." Lon handed Sam a small black and white picture.

It was a picture of Simmie Moore, Dale Leslie and Turner Davis and a few dozen wood ducks. A Labrador retriever stared into the camera. A duck hunter's dream, a stretch of water behind them. "Quite a picture. Those are three of the most prolific duck hunters in northeast Florida. That Miccosukee Lake?"

"Nope. Aucilla River. Simmie was just by here. Gave me this picture. Wants me to go duck hunting with him."

"You going?"

"If Rana lets me."

Both men laughed, the thought of missing a duck hunting trip with Simmie Moore was unthinkable.

"Simmie was just by here 'bout an hour ago." Lon put the picture away and closed the cash register.

"By chance, did he have an update on his investigation of DooRay's assault?"

"Said he'd gotten word that red truck they been lookin' for was over at Mozelle's. At least, he thinks it's the truck. Got Alabama license plates."

Sam's first thought when he heard this news was *Does Essie know.* Her tenacity was unparalleled.

"Could be. Did Simmie say anything about a stake-out of any kind?"

"No. But, I reckon its Lowndes County's jurisdiction. Don't know what Simmie's gonna do."

Sam left the little store, his cream soda costing ten cents. He would've paid a dollar.

At the Donnelly farm, he parked at the side of the barn. Nearby, Minnie and DooRay sat at the picnic table and watched Murphy butt a fencepost. Killer scratched in the dirt and made cawing noises, his eye always cocked to the sky.

DooRay lifted his one arm and waved. "Good to see you, Mr. Sam." DooRay knew Sam had been scarce around the Donnelly farm for quite a few days.

"Thank you, DooRay. I'm here for a fish fry. Hope you've been fishing."

DooRay's face clouded. "Naw. Ain't been to the pond."

DooRay's slumped shoulders and anxious face did not go unnoticed.

Sam turned to Minnie. "Hello, Minnie. Heard you were going off to school."

Minnie nodded, excited. "That's right. Nursing school in Tallahassee. Miss Essie wants to teach me to drive. Said she'd give me her old Pontiac."

"Teach you to drive? I've got to witness that, Minnie. That's a stick shift, you know."

"Oh, I drive Uncle Hez' tractor. I can sure change gears if I have to."

"When do you get your driving lesson?"

"The next day or two. Miss Essie said she's put me out there in that watermelon field and let me go." Essie pointed to the field to the north where old watermelon vines covered the ground.

Sam glanced at the fifteen acre field and decided Minnie would have no problem at all. "So, you'll have transportation in Tallahassee and can drive back and forth."

"That's right." She glanced at DooRay, smiling. "I got to come back to Madison County to check on this man."

Sam agreed. Again, he studied DooRay's face. "Something bothering you, DooRay?"

DooRay's eyes flitted to Killer. The rooster had made a dust bath and dirt flung in every direction as he fluffed his wings. DooRay's gaze never returned to Sam. His shoulders slumped.

"Naw. DooRay's jus' fine."

Sam, the courtroom attorney, barked. "No, you're not, DooRay. If you're not fishing, you're not fine."

DooRay flinched. The scar above his right ear bare, no hair covering the wound. Dr. Bush had done a good job stitching the skin together, but he could not guarantee the hair would return.

Finally, DooRay lifted his eyes. "You be right, Mr. Sam. That pond ain't the same anymore. Gots bad memories."

"Well, here's what I've got to say about that, DooRay. It's like falling off a horse - you just have to climb back on." Sam jumped from the picnic table. "Get some poles! We're all going to the pond."

Minnie grabbed DooRay's arm. "Come on, DooRay. Let's go fishing."

"Essie," Sam hollered.

The back screened door opened. "What's going on?" Essie eased down the steps holding a pitcher of tea.

"We're going fishing. Get your fishing clothes on. Gotta dig for worms."

And there it began. On a hot July afternoon, DooRay's healing simmered like sweet sugar cane waiting to make syrup. He baited his hook with a fat red worm and threw his line into the dark waters of

Grassy pond. The cork bobber floated only a few moments before it was pulled under and a fierce jerk pulled the line taunt.

Nearby, Sam, Essie and Minnie watched with wonder while the one-armed man fought a three-pound bass with a skill that was unsurpassed. DooRay whooped and hollered, "Come on, now, you big fish. You gobble that worm. DooRay wants to fry you up real nice. There you go. There you go."

He walked the pond's edge, working the fish and pulling it slowly onto land. "Yes, sir. Now, where's your brother, and your sister, and your uncle and your mama and daddy?"

A grin on his face, DooRay slipped the fish on a stringer and hunted for another big worm. "Yes, suh. Miss Essie, I hope you gots plenty of Crisco."

Almost dark, the sun erased from the horizon, they traipsed across Emmett Gaston's corn field and slipped under the barbed wire fence, a large stringer of fish grasped by one DooRay Aikens, fisherman extraordinaire.

Crossing the front yard, and in the dim light of dusk, Essie saw a figure standing on the porch steps, leaning against the balustrade, arms folded across his chest. The Irishman waved and stepped out into the yard, a grin on his face, light in his eyes.

# CHAPTER SIXTY-FIVE

If the moon held its memories, it would remember shining down on the Donnelly front porch and casting its light on Robert Gray and Essie Donnelly, his arms around her, his lips pressed softly against her cheek. The moon would have also lavished moon dust on the breathless moment, taking care to go slowly into the night.

But time had passed and now, as Essie stepped closer to the man who had taken more than a fancy to her, her heart thudded in her chest. *Robert Gray. The other man in her life.*

"Hello, Rob. This is a surprise." She hesitated a moment, her eyes unblinking, wide with questions. Behind her, Sam lingered beside DooRay and Minnie.

"Tis a big hello to you, too, lassie." He bounded toward her and, without hesitation, pulled her toward him into a warm hug. "At last, the hospital gave me a few days off and all I could think about was Madison County."

The Irishman caught Minnie's smile. "Ah, and there's my Minnie." He grabbed her and swung her around. "You're lookin' fine, my lass. I want to hear all about nursing school."

Robert Gray wasn't finished. He tackled DooRay next. "DooRay! You're looking well. How's that scalp wound?" The good doctor turned

DooRay's cheek and gave the scar a physician's scrutiny. "I'd say you're healed. No hair growing though." He slapped DooRay on the back.

And Sam. Stoic Sam. A cool gaze from the blue eyes that most people called his *courtroom stare*. He'd decided if the doctor tried to hug him, he'd kick the hell out of him. He backed up a step and waited.

Rob Gray, a lover of all humankind, grinned at Sam. Never formally introduced, he held out his hand. "Don't believe we've met. 'Course, I know who you are, lad."

*Lad?* He'd kick him for simply calling him *lad*. The gumption of the man was amazing. All that lad and lassie talk. Reluctantly, he took Rob's hand.

"Sam Washington," Sam said, then glanced at Essie. "Essie's fiancé."

Rob lifted his eyebrows, the dark eyes smiling. "Oh, my. Have you set a wedding date?" *So smooth.* He shifted his gaze to Essie, a longing in his eyes.

Sam stuttered. "Well . . ."

Essie broke in. "No, no wedding date . . . actually, there hasn't been a formal engagement." She cut her eyes to Sam. He was using his courtroom shenanigans on her, causing a fight to brew in her mind and slipping away from him just one more step.

There was no engagement ring on her finger. Once again, the thought of marriage intimidated her. She walked past everyone and climbed the porch steps. "Let's get those fish cleaned. I'll get the grease hot. Minnie, you can make the hushpuppies. Sam and DooRay, ya'll clean the fish. Rob, you chop cabbage for slaw."

She was at it again. The hard woman. The woman in command. *Don't push it, Sam Washington. I'm a free woman until I say differently.*

# CHAPTER SIXTY-SIX

DooRay's stringer of fish was filleted by Sam and DooRay out near the well, where the barn lights showed gleaming sharp knives scaling the fish, then slicing them into delectable pieces ready to fry.

On the back porch, hot grease bubbled, cornmeal lay salted in a large bowl and the Irish doctor gazed lovingly at the Madison County farm girl who had stolen his heart.

"My lassie, I visited in Boston with the Pryor's this past week. Pitch's surgery has improved his gait almost 100%, his walk near normal. Dr. Meyer is very pleased with the outcome. Pitch has been a good patient, doing all the exercises necessary to strengthen his leg."

"How about Ollie and Orland? Essie stirred the grits and readied the pan for Minnie's hushpuppies.

"Fine as can be. Ollie's crops have done well, especially the corn. Good rain. His new herd of pigs – Cheshire, I believe – is flourishing."

Essie handed Rob a cabbage and a sharp knife. "There's a cutting board on the counter. Quarter this cabbage and then chop real good." She placed a large crock next to the cabbage. "Put the chopped cabbage in this bowl."

Essie avoided the Irishman's eyes, afraid her heart would get lost in them. She remembered her dream. The one where he snared her and held her in a ship bound for Ireland. The thought of it made her heart beat faster, her throat seize up. She felt his presence dangerous. *Pure lust*, she thought.

Sam and DooRay stepped inside the screened back porch carrying a platter of fresh filleted fish. DooRay handed the platter to Essie. "Got some brim here, some bass and cypress trout. 'nough for ever'body. Ain't nobody goin' hungry tonight. Grease hot?"

Essie nodded and began flipping the fish into the cornmeal. She'd salt the fish good after it was fried. A meal fit for a king.

Sam eased into a corner of the porch, his arms folded against his chest. His jaw was tight, the line of his mouth straight and unmoving. He was going to have to fight for his woman. He glanced at Rob and instantly saw the Irishman's love for Essie, the dark eyes following her every move

The aroma of frying fish lifted across the Donnelly farm while Minnie dropped onion-laden hush puppies into a pan of hot grease, DooRay beside her. Nearby, Rob busily chopped a head of cabbage and softly sang an Irish diddy. *Where are me boots, me noggin', noggin' boots? They're all gone for beer . . .*

The Irishman's gaze frequently wandered to Essie, the auburn haired beauty who mesmerized him and kept his heart aflutter.

"Lassie," he called from the kitchen, watching her lift fish from the deep fryer. "The cabbage's chopped. What next?" He walked to the doorway. "A wee bit of salt and pepper? Some mayonnaise?"

"We need a little sugar and vinegar, too. Give me a minute and I'll finish up." Essie remained at the fryer, the dampness of the heat causing curls to form around her face. Her cheeks glistened with perspiration, a pinkness spreading across her face.

The Madison County homecoming queen was loved by two men. A storm was hovering, a turmoil that would cast itself into the middle of three hearts.

Essie turned over the job of frying the fish to Sam. "Here. Fry this last batch and we'll be ready to eat."

Minnie and DooRay arranged a high pile of hush puppies on a platter. "Miss Essie, you want me to set the table?"

"Go ahead and use those earthenware plates. The white ones." Essie pointed to the cabinet above the counter. "They're in that cabinet."

At the stove, Essie mixed a little vinegar and sugar, salt and pepper into a small pot and warmed it until the sugar melted. She then mixed it together with mayonnaise. "Here you go, Rob. Pour this over the cabbage and mix well."

A late evening quiet settled over the Donnelly's dinner table, where a feast of fried fish, hushpuppies, grits and slaw spread out like manna from heaven.

Minnie, the soon-to-be nurse who waited for DooRay to tell her his heart was hers, sat poised, her eyes downcast. She wanted him to tell her she was more than the woman who had nursed his wounds and soothed his hurts.

DooRay, the man who loved Minnie, but was too shy to tell her. The one-armed man who thought himself unworthy of her. The man who loved her from afar and believed she'd never want him.

Rob Gray, the man who had been thrown into Essie's life by sheer happenstance in the middle of a cold March night, buttered a hush puppy and sat dreamy eyed across from Essie. His love for her had become the most unassuming, natural thing in the world.

And Sam Washington. A tormented man who believed his love for Essie had been his destiny. The day he saw her on the Madison County homecoming float, capturing his heart, was the day he proclaimed his love for her.

And Essie. The farm girl who denied herself the intimacy of a relationship with Sam or Rob. The complexity of her heart and mind had overwhelmed her capacity to place herself within the confines of commitment. It was there that she must begin to change. How to effect that change was more than she could comprehend.

"So, about this engagement," began Rob, as he reached for his second hushpuppy.

# CHAPTER SIXTY-SEVEN

Tayki slipped onto the Donnelly front porch. An hour away from sunrise, she eased into the Adirondack chair and waited. Killer remained atop the wellhouse, his head under his wing, his duties as the king of the farmyard close at hand. Asleep in the tack room, DooRay dreamed about Grassy Pond and the bass he had caught. Nearby, Murphy lay curled into a pile of hay, his breathing slow and steady.

A warm morning breeze teased the leaves of the oak tree at the end of the porch. In the dimness of the morning, Tayki squinted her eyes. Across the yard and a hundred or so feet down the farm lane, a panther slowly padded toward the farmyard, its forelegs and hips rolling with muscle.

"*Cat?*" Tayki whispered. *Had he followed her the two miles from the Withlacoochee?* The cat stilled and, lifting its head, sniffed the air. Its mouth open, its tail swiped the air, a nervous twitch that revealed an orchestrated stealth.

At that moment, the panther's dark yellow eyes found Tayki, and, all at once, its forelegs pushed hard on the earth, its body soaring through the air, sending it to the edge of the front porch, only a few feet from Tayki.

*No,* thought Tayki. *Not Cat.* The panther had been stalking her, the

Miccosukee Indian woman, the hundred and ten pound river guardian, the old woman who talked to creatures.

Tayki had walked the two miles through the woods to the Donnelly farm, a walking stick in her hand as she maneuvered the thick shrubs and trees. She had been followed by a large panther, much larger than *Cat*. A male.

Now, a low growl found its way into the quiet morning as the panther crouched low, ready to spring to its prey. His yellow eyes locked on Tayki, the growl becoming louder and his tail switching with menace.

"You no eat Tayki," she said softly, her eyes watching his, unmoving. "You eat Tayki, I come back and feed you to Tail."

She saw the panther's eyes flicker, an understanding passing through them. She leaned forward. "You go now. Go before woman in house shoot you."

The panther slowly eased back down the steps, his eyes still watching Tayki. The growl had turned to a whimper, a soft mew that reluctantly acquiesced his power to the Indian woman.

Tayki watched the panther lope into the woods, the light of the morning sun catching his gleaming coat and sending him into a golden day.

In the Adirondack chair, Tayki watched the sun rise into the morning sky, the sound of Killer's vigorous crow announcing the day. From around the corner, Murphy trotted to the porch and looked up at her.

"Good morning, one ear," she said. "No ear you look funny." She caught herself. "You beautiful goat only one ear." Murphy ran back to the barn – it was time for DooRay to get out of bed.

The smell of coffee drifted through the screen door. "That you, Tayki?" Essie peeked through the screen. "Want coffee?"

"Coffee and big sugar," replied Tayki's, her words gruff.

Essie carried a tray with two coffees and some warmed over hush-puppies to the porch. "Hungry?"

Tayki grinned. "Tayki always hungry. No fish? I smell fish cooking last night. I eat cold."

"Cold fish? Be right back." Essie left the porch and returned in a minute with two fat brim. She'd put a spoonful of slaw and a plop of grits on the plate, too.

"Here you go."

Tayki pulled her legs into the big wooden chair and hunkered over her plate. She murmured obscure words as she rocked back and forth and ate hungrily.

Essie settled in the swing, sipped her coffee and watched Tayki. The old Indian was in constant motion, an energy that was from another world, a language that spoke to her ancestors and settled in some distant place.

"Tail eat good tonight," she mumbled, her toothless gums mashing fish and hushpuppies together.

"Tail?" Essie waited. The Indian woman spoke in riddles, the clues few and far between. "What about Tail."

Tayki leaned her head back and cackled loudly, bits of hushpuppy falling out of her mouth. Laughter shook her shoulders, her eyes squeezed shut.

Finally, her eyes opened and she turned to Essie. "Bad men set up tent on big sandbar." Another loud guffaw.

The swing stilled and Essie walked the length of the porch and leaned on the rail in front of Tayki. Breathless, she asked, "When?"

Tayki shrugged her shoulders. "Sun low."

"Yesterday?"

Tayki nodded. "Sleep on sandbar. I tell Tail no eat." The wrinkled face looked up and grinned. "Not yet."

Essie began to pace. Her niece Rose and her mother would arrive Wednesday at lunchtime. At last, Rose would step foot on the Donnelly homeplace. Their long-awaited visit had been highly anticipated. Jewell's child, a part of Jewell, would see her mother's ancestral home, the home where she had been born.

Essie's search for Jewell's daughter began across southern Georgia earlier in the year, with nothing but hope to guide her. She had left Sam, the 300-acre Donnelly farm and her treasured Madison County to find the child of her beloved sister. She had pursued the young girl with a tenacity that could only be driven by her love for Jewell, her late sister. *Your daughter's coming, Jewell.*

"Keep an eye on them, Tayki, but don't go near them. They're dangerous. They're supposed to be there for three or four days. Fishing, then hunting in the woods."

Tayki closed her eyes and began to rock her body. Again, she seemed to listen to the sounds of far-away voices, her chant rising and falling. Suddenly, she opened her eyes and stared at Essie, her one crooked eye staring off across the field. "Men very dangerous."

Murphy rounded the corner of the house and kicked up his heels as he pranced across the yard. Close behind, Killer strutted behind him.

From a lone pine tree at the edge of the west pasture, a hawk flapped its broad wings, flew high into the air, then circled the field before pushing its body into a slow, controlled dive. In seconds, it was upon Killer with his sharp talons, the force of his dive plummeting into the unsuspecting bird.

A loud cry pierced the morning as the large hawk lifted Killer and began to fly west across the corn field, struggling with Killer's weight. Running after them, Murphy emitted a mournful cry, his head lifted toward the early morning sky.

Tayki, her stringy hair flying behind her, jumped from the porch and ran to the fence. She waved her arms and shouted in an unknown language, the words penetrating the air like bullets.

Essie stumbled from the porch holding her daddy's rifle, fully loaded. She lifted it and aimed.

"No shoot!" Tayki shouted. "Bird bring Killer back."

Essie lowered the rifle and stared blankly at Tayki, her face flushed. Killer, the snake-killing king rooster of the Donnelly farm was a hundred feet in the air, feathers flying around him, his head twisting in anger.

The hawk, soaring with a wing span of four feet, dropped closer to the ground and spread his talons, releasing Killer to the ground. Killer tumbled to the earth in a flurry of feathers and squawks, ending up exactly where he had been snatched.

Tayki hovered over him, her chant low and somewhat pleading. The rooster jumped up and shook his body, feathers scattering all around him. He then strutted around the yard, his kneeless legs stiff. He was furious.

Murphy hurried to Killer's side as if to say *job well done*. Essie eased the rifle to her side and watched as the Indian woman shook her fist in the air at the disappearing hawk, her inexplicable words thrown once again into the Universe.

"Rooster good. Hawk feel bad. No mean to take Killer. Say bird too fat to steal." Tayki grinned and waved. "I go to river. Talk with *Tail*. And *Cat*."

"Tayki! Stay away from those men! They're dangerous. Just keep an eye on them. I'll see you the day after tomorrow."

Tayki slipped through the woods, east to the rising sun and the call of the Withlacoochee. Her ancestors walked with her, their conversations soft and soothing. Finally, the Indian woman rounded the trunk of a large oak tree and disappeared into the shadows.

Essie felt her words were lost as she called across the farmyard. "Thank you, Tayki." Essie was wrong. Tayki heard everything. She also saw everything. And now, as she hurried to the river, she heard the voices of the men. *The bad men.*

# CHAPTER SIXTY-EIGHT

The previous evening's fish fry had ended in scattered feelings, a simmering turmoil just below the surface in the Donnelly's dining room. Dishes had been cleared and washed by Essie and Rob. Soft conversation had lifted in the late night while Sam stewed quietly on the front porch, a cigar in his mouth.

Minnie and DooRay had sat nearby in the porch rockers and watched clouds brush across the waning July moon. The paddle fans whirled slowly and moved the night air into soft puffs, capturing the aroma of Sam's honeyed Montecristo cigar.

DooRay had begun to hum, his baritone voice rising and falling as though singing to the angels. The words followed . . . *It is well, it is well with my soul.*

Remembering the moment, Sam had shifted in his chair and felt himself moved by DooRay's lyrical words. *It is well, it is well with my soul.* He had left the porch and walked out into the farmyard, and felt the steadiness of his beating heart. He turned and gazed at the lighted windows in the Donnelly house. He saw Essie and the Irish doctor talking, their faces close. Then, Essie smiled. The doctor laughed.

From the darkness of the farmyard, Sam had watched as Rob Gray lifted Essie's chin with his hand, almost saw his breath on her face. The moment was surreal, standing still in time.

Sam's jaw clenched, then a breath released. He saw Essie reach up and gently remove Rob's hand from her chin. His entire body shaking, Sam stepped closer to the house. Looking through the lighted window, he read Rob Gray's lips. *I love you, Essie.*

# CHAPTER SIXTY-NINE

K iller spent the entire morning with one eye cocked to the sky. Murphy stood nearby, diligently watching for the return of the marauding hawk. The two banded together, inseparable. After all, they had survived a lightning strike at DooRay's house the previous summer, as well as a knife-welding crazy man who had cut off Murphy's ear and Killer's glorious tail feathers during the past summer's harrowing events.

Killer's reputation as a snake-killing rooster had proved accurate when he ravaged a fat moccasin in the chicken pen. The pair's prominence on the Donnelly farm had been well-earned.

And, now, as late morning approached, they strolled the farm lane, a peaceful journey without the presence of a killer hawk.

Essie and Minnie cleaned Jewell's room in preparation for Rose and her mother's visit, placing fresh linens on the bed, and arranging a vase of pink roses on the bedside table. The scent of on-coming rain filled the room, the windows wide open as warm wind brought the dark clouds from the west.

"Minnie, when we finish here, let's go down the hall to my mother and father's room and freshen it for Rose's mother. She'll love mother's ceramics."

"Yes, she will. Those are the prettiest things I've ever seen. She'll love those family pictures, too."

The food for their guests had been prepared except for the ham. Essie planned to bake the seven pound shank cut first thing in the morning. Delectable potato salad, deviled eggs, a pot of fresh-picked green beans and yellow corn were stored in the refrigerator.

On the counter, a fresh baked buttered rum pound cake waited for a delectable rum glaze. Jewell's favorite china sat in formal place settings on the oval walnut dining table along with Swarovski crystal that their mother had bought in Switzerland.

By 1:00, the old house was ready for company. DooRay had mulched the shrubs and azaleas, raked the farmyard and swept the front porch. Periwinkles bloomed in wide clay pots next to the porch steps.

Crepe myrtles bloomed along the farm lane where a car eased slowly along and parked at the edge of the barn. A long-legged Rob Gray left his car and strode across the farmyard. He waved to DooRay. "That was great fish you fried last night, lad."

DooRay grinned. "Ole DooRay done got fat eatin' all those hushpuppies and cake."

"Me, too!" Rob yelled, as he rounded the corner of the house and found Essie in the porch swing. "Well, lassie, you're as lovely as summertime flowers. Afternoon to ye."

"Hello, Rob. Come sit a while." Essie watched the Irishman's face. Her words to him the previous evening had been quite candid, a reckoning that she had mulled over and finally expressed to the man she knew loved her. It was difficult for her, but a necessary task.

She could not deny her deep love for Sam any longer, and telling the Irishman had been the first step in getting off the fence she had been on for so long. Nonetheless, her heart ached as she looked into Rob's dark eyes and the smile that he sent to her.

"It would please me very much if we could remain good friends and be in each other's lives," she said, a catch in her throat.

"Oh, lassie. I'll always be around. Thomasville has me entwined in the care of its people. The Archbold folks have extraordinary medical facilities and, of course, it's a haven for doctors like myself. Can't imagine being anywhere else."

He grinned at her. "And the Pryor family is a big part of my heart. I can't envision a life without those fine boys. And, Ollie."

Essie nodded. Still, she heard a soft lingering in his words. Her eyes held his for a long moment. "It's possible Minnie will go to Thomasville after nursing school."

"Ah, so she will, for sure. I had a long chat with her about school. She's quite intelligent as well as committed to getting an education." He looked up at Essie and spoke softly. "They're our family, you know. Minnie, Ollie, Pitch and Orland." He paused. "And DooRay."

Tears welled in Essie's eyes and she looked away. The Irishman was right. Together, they had assimilated their lives into the lives of the small Boston, Georgia, family. The Pryor's needs had been great, and together they had mended hurts, filled needs and, in the end, restored a broken family.

Her voice cracking, Essie turned back to Rob. "You have made a difference in our lives. For that, we shall always be grateful."

Rob lowered his head and rocked slowly. Without looking at Essie, he leaned forward and spoke in a whisper. "And there I was – across that giant sea from Ireland, in a little Southern town . . . " he faltered. "And, in the dead of winter, this beautiful barefooted woman knocked on my door at 3:00 in the morning and demanded I follow her to the Pryor farm."

He looked up at Essie. "And, my life changed. I became part of a *family. Minnie, Pitch, Orland and Ollie.*" He laughed. "And that family included hogs, a mean rooster, and Miss Areba Wright, the purple lady. *Life*, Essie. It was about living life and it was a beautiful thing. I am thankful for the opportunity to be a part of not only their lives, but your life,too."

A tear rolled down Essie's cheek. She blinked and another one found its way to the bottom of her chin. Through the tears, she gathered enough composure to speak, although haltingly.

"I shall always treasure you, Rob."

The rain that had threatened earlier blew in like a devil on horseback, the raindrops fat and heavy, and swirling within the sudden wrath of wind. The tin roof of the barn exploded with pounding rain, the water flooding down the eaves and into the farmyard.

Lightning flashed to the west and left shards of bright light splitting the sky.

From the end of the lane, a car turned onto the drive and parked at the edge of the front porch. The windshield wipers worked furiously, the car lights shining against the side of the barn. Suddenly, the car door opened and a figure, hidden under a large black umbrella, dashed up the porch steps.

Cursing loudly, Lola LaRue threw her umbrella into the yard. "My new Italian shoes are soaked!" She swiped a wet hand across her head and yanked the bright pink hat from her head and threw it in the same direction as the umbrella.

"Haven't you folks in this God-forsaken place ever heard of a portico? Hell, you probably don't even know what a portico is!"

Miss LaRue slapped the water from her skirt. "I'll be danged. Look at this! My skirt is dry clean only!"

Rob jumped from his chair and extended his hand to Lola. "Here, Lassie. Sit down and I'll get you a towel."

At that moment, Lola stilled, her eyes wide and questioning as she focused on the Irishman. "Well, now, Handsome. Aren't you a Prince Charming?"

Essie rolled her eyes. The New Yorker had returned. The brassy, red-lipped editor from the Thomas H. Fox Literary Agency. "There's a towel in the linen closet at the top of the stairs, Rob."

Rob dashed into the house and left a dripping Lola LaRue on the porch, her mascara running down her cheeks. It seemed her outfit was beginning to shrink from the dousing it had received. Lola's cleavage spilled from her v-necked blouse, while her long legs stretched forever from the bottom of her skirt. *The redhead was back.*

"Miss LaRue, I don't believe I received word that you were paying a visit," said Essie, unsmiling.

"Oh, hell, Essie. Do you realize you're out in the middle of nowhere. Closest airport is Tallahassee. Telephones don't work. Roads aren't paved. Only two gas stations between here and the airport. You might as well be on the moon."

Lola looked around disapprovingly. "And that damn rooster and goat. Are they still here or did you barbecue them? Hope so anyway."

Rob bounded down the stairs and onto the porch. Instead of handing Lola the towel, he began drying off the tall redhead, pressing the towel on her arms, then across her chest and down her legs. He worked quickly, catching every wet spot he could find. "There you go," he said, stepping back and checking his handiwork.

His eyes met Lola's. The redhead was posed like a New York model, her wet clothes plastered to her body, her gaze telling the Irishman that he had missed a spot or two.

Flustered, Rob handed Lola the towel. "Maybe I'd better get another dry towel." He spun around, almost plowing through the screen door. He flew up the stairs to the linen closet, leaving a dripping Lola LaRue on the porch.

Essie seemed unconcerned about Lola's dripping state and pushed the swing while she admired Lola's plastered hair and running mascara.

"I will assume you're here on business." She paused, a slight smile forming. "Although I notice you're not exactly wearing business attire."

Lola slipped off her expensive Italian shoes and threw them in a corner of the porch. "I told you I'd be back. You have some decisions to make."

"What decisions?"

"You need to approve the manuscript's layout and book cover. And, a few minor things. Like a schedule for book promotions." Lola, irritated, glared at Essie.

"Book promotions?" asked Essie.

"Don't play dumb with me, country girl. You knew you had to do this at some point. So get over that look on your face. I shoulda had you come to New York."

Essie chuckled. "Oh, Lola. You will never warm my heart. I haven't forgotten your blatant lies to me when you were here last. Farm girl? What a story you told. Mr. Fox assured me you were born in New York City and had never even seen a cow, much less raised on a farm."

Lola grinned. "I could be a writer myself. That was a good story, wasn't it?"

"A good story, but a deceitful one." Essie's face hardened. "Do you ever tell the truth?"

Lola grinned even wider. "Only when I have to."

Rob bounded out the door and handed Lola a dry towel. "Here you go."

Her eyes seductive, she began slowly wiping her legs and arms. Then, wrapped the towel around her and sat in a nearby chair.

"So, I like your towel service, Essie. Who is this handsome man?" She smiled at Rob. Even in her wet disarray, she was movie-star beautiful. *Oh, if only she was Southern.*

Rob dipped his chin. "Robert Gray from Thomasville, Georgia."

"That Irish accent is not from Thomasville, Georgia, my dear. I'd say you're from across the pond."

Essie rose from the swing and leaned against the porch rail, mist from the rain on her back.

"This is Dr. Robert Gray from Ireland. I met him while on a trip to Boston, Georgia. He's a dear friend." Lola smiled at Rob, her eyes and face softening, the New York patina sliding off, perhaps revealing a woman whose heart carried a slight promise of tenderness.

Lola's smile was sincere. "It is a pleasure to meet you, Dr. Robert Gray from Ireland."

Rob nodded. "Thank you. Shall I fix you a hot cup of tea?" He bowed slightly. The Irishman was also a gentleman.

"Lovely," said Lola. "That would be lovely."

Rob turned to Essie. "How about you, Essie. Would you enjoy a cup of tea?"

"Yes, I would. Let's go inside until the rain is over."

They left the porch and the pounding rain. Across the Bellville road, Lum Townsend's cows lowered their heads, the rain blowing across their backs and waited for the storm to end.

While tea brewed, Essie and the Thomas H. Fox literary agent discussed the details of the publication of her novel. Due for release in April 1958, the novel's debut would require Essie's participation in book signing tours in at least five major cities in the northeast. Her Southern tour was yet to be decided.

The Thomas H. Fox Literary Agency, enamoured with Essie's novel *Watermelon Queen of Madison County,* hired a renowned marketing group to promote the novel's debut. No doubt about it, the Madison County farm girl was slated to become the next literary star.

Lola, her business mode in high gear, rattled off the details of the publishing process to Essie. "And, then, on to a New York Times book review. You'll be up there with *Auntie Mame!*"

Essie approved the last change to her manuscript with her initials. "I'd like to debut my novel in the South, not New York."

"The South?" Lola shrieked. "Honey, this is not just a *Southern* book. Any book debut worth having, is worth having in New York."

Lola gathered her papers and stuffed them in her briefcase. "You don't have to worry about a thing, Essie. All the details will be handled by Thomas Fox and me. Absolutely, no worries."

Essie glanced at Rob. "Please pour us some tea, Rob."

Dr. Robert Gray carried one of Edith Donnelly's bone China teapots to the table, along with teacups and saucers. "Come on, lassies. Let's enjoy."

Essie leaned back in her chair and gave Lola a discerning look. "Since the story takes place in Madison County, why wouldn't its debut be held here? The grand premiere of *Gone With the Wind* was held in Atlanta, not Hollywood or New York."

Sipping her tea, Lola sputtered, sending tea across the table. Almost choking, she sat her cup into her saucer.

"In Madison County? Of course! And all fourteen people who live here can attend. Why, we'll set up the event in some old barn somewhere, off a wet clay road, where that damn goat and rooster can attend!"

Lola stood from the table. She closed her eyes and lifted her arms into the air. "I can see it all now. We'll haul in thousands of watermelons and use them as seating for the thousands that will attend. And, we can build a throne for the 'watermelon queen' out of corn stalks. What an extraordinary sight it will be. We'll serve sliced watermelon and corn liquor, along with grandma's okra and tomatoes."

The literary agent clasped her arms to her chest, smiling, then opened her eyes and smirked at Essie.

Suddenly, Essie stood and grabbed Lola's briefcase. "Tell you what, Lola. I'm gonna throw your briefcase out into the chicken pen. And, if you think you can retrieve it, I'll agree to the debut in New York."

Rob jerked his head from Essie to Lola, alarm across his face. "Oh, lassie's, let's settle this more amicably. You see, we have a wee bit of talking to do."

"I'm through talking!" said Essie, through hardened lips.

Lola eased herself from her chair. "Oh, my. I feel I have been quite disrespectful." Her face melted into remorse, her entire body withdrawing into contrition, pangs of conscience with her every breath.

"Go on," said Essie, with firmness. "Let's see how repentant you are?" Essie's stone-like posture sent a message to the woman whose reputation garnered no sympathy. Essie grasped the briefcase closer and tighter.

Haltingly, Lola spoke. The black streaks of mascara on her cheeks lay somewhat humorous, along with her strands of misguided hair.

In a soft, humble voice, Lola spoke. "When I get back to New York, I'll talk with Mr. Fox and we'll work it out. I can't promise the premiere will take place in Madison County, but I can promise the premiere will be followed by a grand debut right here in Madison County."

Lola hesitated, a half smile playing along her red lips. "Guess that means you'll have to grow a hell of a lot of watermelons next summer." She paused and grinned wide. "We'll need them for seating, of course."

Somehow, someway, the bright copper-hair, the long false eyelashes, the painted nails and the luminous green eyes beckoned a camaraderie to be formed, a meeting of minds that put both sides on even ground.

For a second time since first meeting the flamboyant red-head, Essie was moved by the literary agent's heartfelt dissertation. Beyond the brash persona of the New Yorker, she recognized a brimming softness in Lola's character, a trait that was, for whatever reason, hidden behind her abrasive personality.

In the quiet room, Essie slid Lola's briefcase across the table. Slowly, she removed her hand from the leather handle, trailing her fingers across the table.

"I'll hold you to that promise, Lola."

Lola lifted her chin, holding Essie's gaze for a long, thoughtful moment. "That story I told you a while back about me being raised on a farm was true. Thomas Fox just doesn't know it."

Essie flinched slightly, her gaze rolling around the room in thought. "Okay, then. What do you call a baby pig?"

"Piglets."

"What's a Rhode Island red?"

"A chicken."

"What's a Holstein?"

"A cow."

Essie narrowed her eyes, a hardness returning. She gritted her teeth and spoke with an arrogant finality. "What is NPK?"

Lola blinked several times, a slight confusion. Her breathing shallow, she stepped in front of Essie.

She raised her chin and in a commanding voice, said, "NPK? Miss Donnelly, do you think you can stump this Illinois farm girl? NPK are macro-nutrients that make up fertilizer. Nitrogen, phosphorus and potassium." Lola raised her eyebrows and gave Essie a smug glance.

Essie slowly nodded her head. "Well done."

The rain moved east, the sparse clouds leaving room for abundant sunshine across Madison County's landscape. At the Donnelly farm, Essie wrapped a piece of buttered rum pound cake in waxed paper for Lola LaRue.

"Here, Lola. Tuck this into your handbag. It will make your plane ride more enjoyable."

Lola smiled sweetly. "Thank you for lunch, Essie. You'll have to teach me how to make corn fritters one day." She hesitated. "I *am* coming back, you know."

"You're always welcome, Lola. Business or not."

Nearby, Rob picked up Lola's briefcase. "Don't forget this."

"Ah, those are important papers. Thank you." Her gaze lingered on the dark eyes of Dr. Gray. "Do you visit Madison County often?"

Rob handed Lola her briefcase and, at the same time, smelled the red-head's lovely perfume. Lola had washed her face of smeared mascara, her lips absent of lipstick and was all at once an Illinois farm girl, her skin pink with only a few freckles across her nose.

"Not often enough, I assure you," he said. His voice lowered, almost conspiratorially. "I must invite you to visit Thomasville. It's a lovely town and not too far from the airport in Tallahassee."

Rob paused and glanced at Essie, then back to Lola. "When you return to Madison County for the Watermelon Queen's debut, you must let me know, lassie."

Lola reached out and gathered Rob's hand into hers. "It has been a pleasure meeting you. Come to New York and I'll show you the City. We'll see a Broadway play. Or even better, you can attend *Watermelon Queen of Madison County's* premiere. "

Rob grasped Lola's hand a moment longer. "I shall be there."

They waved good-bye to the New Yorker from the Donnelly front porch, both smiling as Lola's arm shot out the car window, waving heartily when she turned onto the Bellville road. A lock of her hair escaped the open window, twisting into a long strand. When the sun rays found it, it turned into a trailing red flame.

# CHAPTER SEVENTY

Long evening shadows stretched across the Donnelly farm and gathered dusk into the softness of a summer night. Less than an hour after sunset, Jupiter brightened in the southeast sky while a waning moon hovered nearby.

Essie took a plate of leftovers to the tack room and sat on an overturned bucket while DooRay nibbled on corn fritters and a pork chop.

"Miss Essie, I declare your cookin' gets better and better. These corn fritters taste like Mama's. You gots to show ole DooRay how to make 'em."

"Just mix together some flour, egg, milk, a little sugar. I took two ears of corn and cut off the kernels, then added that to the mixture."

DooRay smacked loudly, a deviled egg disappearing into his mouth. "Ain't nothin' like good ole country cookin'."

Essie stood and reached into her shirt pocket and pulled out cake wrapped in waxed paper. "Here's a slice of that rum cake for dessert."

"Oh, you're spoilin' ole DooRay." The black man grinned and reached for his cake. "Miss Essie, I'll be sure and get the lane all raked up 'fore Miss Rose and her mama get here."

"That'd be nice, DooRay. After you finish, our guests will think they've arrived at *Tara*."

"Tara?" DooRay scrunched his face in question.

"Tara was the name of the plantation in the movie *Gone With the Wind.*"

"That right?" DooRay nodded. "Never did see that movie, Miss Essie. Just knowed they be lots of slaves in it." He looked up at Essie. "Might even be some of my kinfolks in that movie."

In DooRay's face, Essie saw the beauty of his heart, his kindness. But, most of all, she saw his love for his fellow man. If anybody was to get to Heaven, it would be DooRay Aikens.

"Good night, DooRay. I'll make us coffee in the morning."

The aroma of a Montecristo cigar rode on the soft breeze coming from the west, across the Donnelly front porch and into the farmyard. The familiarity of the fragrance was like going home, like finding a pot of warm beef stew on the stove.

In the middle of the farm yard, Essie gazed at the night sky, and found Venus sitting high over the eastern horizon, a brilliant light beckoning one to discover its magic.

She rounded the corner of the house and stepped onto the porch and saw the lighted tip of Sam's cigar. He was in the swing. Waiting for her.

"Well, hello," she called. She walked the length of the porch and sat beside him. A natural thing to do. After all, he had loved her since the homecoming parade of 1939. Perhaps it was time to love him back.

"Hello, Miss Donnelly," he said, after a short puff on his cigar. His words were low and husky, much like Gary Cooper in *Friendly Persuasion. I will pleasure you in a hundred ways.*

Essie pushed the swing and listened to the whippoorwills in the nearby fields. Their song was a love song.

"Your doctor friend return to Thomasville?"

"Yes. Late this afternoon."

"Ya'll make love in the barn? In that stack of hay Murphy sleeps in?"

Essie's foot stopped the swing. "No, we didn't. We did, however, run naked through the rain around 3:00."

Sam relit his cigar. "No surprises there."

"Shoulda been here."

"Wasn't invited."

"If it was raining now, we could try it ourselves."

"Does it have to be raining?"

"No." Essie closed her eyes and wondered how she had wandered away from Sam Washington. He'd been there all along.

Sam stubbed his cigar on the porch rail and flipped it into an empty flower pot. His arm went around Essie and he pulled her closer. Her head rested on his chest, the fragrance of her hair floating in whispers around him.

The swing moved back and forth with a gentle motion, the creak of the chain soothing. A firefly drifted past, then another. And another.

"What time will Rose and her mother arrive on Wednesday?"

Essie stirred. "They'll be here in time for lunch."

"I'm glad she's coming. Wish she'd known Jewell." Sam paused, a deep sigh coming from his chest. "She would have made a fine mother."

Yes, thought Essie. If only Jewell had been given the chance to be a mother. But, Edith Donnelly had thought differently. *There would be no illegitimate children in the Donnelly family.*

The great conspiracy to give away Jewell's baby was orchestrated by Jewell's mother without the least bit of compunction. No guilt, no regrets. *Whatever it takes to preserve the purity of the Donnelly name.*

"I hope you'll come by to meet them. Maybe, for dinner?"

"I'll be here."

Sam reached down and lifted Essie's chin. His kiss was long and tender, a sweetness that held all the memories of past pleasures.

Sam gently pulled away, his heart racing. "Ah, Essie."

The swing stilled while the stars blinked in the far away sky. Deep in the woods, a panther screamed, followed by a thumping sound from the north pasture.

Essie stirred in Sam's arms, her breathing soft. After Rose's visit, she'd tell Sam many things. Tell him she loved him. Tell him she wanted to get married. Tell him she wanted children. Tell him all the things he'd been wanting to hear for so long.

But, first, she'd have to settle with the bad people. She'd take DooRay with her and, together, they would settle the score. She was not afraid, not even anxious. It was a Donnelly thing. She learned it from her Daddy. Soon, she'd right a wrong. It was always about righting a wrong.

Sam pushed the swing and whispered. "I'd better go. Early morning courtroom appearance. Don't want to be late in Judge Earp's court."

Essie watched Sam walk to his car. A match struck and the cigar tip flared as he opened his car door. "I love you, Essie Donnelly."

Sam gave the farm girl one last glance and wondered if she had heard his loving words.

# CHAPTER SEVENTY-ONE

The summer sunrise seemed reluctant. Clouds covered its arrival as though barricading the day and preventing its entry into the waiting sky.

The rock that was thrown high onto the roof of the Donnelly house struck loudly and rolled off the roof onto the ground. Tayki picked it up and threw it again, this time hitting the window in Essie's bedroom.

The Indian woman stepped back and watched the window. At last, Essie appeared. Her hair tousled around her face. Sleepiness lingering, she searched the yard.

"Here I am." Tayki shouted.

Essie saw a gray figure with stringy hair in the front yard, hopping like a rabbit. "Tayki! What is it?" Her words were not sweet.

"You come down. Tayki want coffee." Tayki disappeared under the eaves of the porch.

Upstairs, Essie grumbled as she slipped on her dungarees and shirt and clobbered down the stairs in an old pair of yard shoes. "Sun's not even up."

The kitchen was dark, the remnants of Lola LaRue's visit still on the kitchen table. Scattered papers lay everywhere as well as empty tea cups and saucers.

At the back door, Tayki pressed her face against the screen. "Tayki want sugar."

Essie cleared the kitchen table and filled the coffee pot with water and measured out the coffee. "Come on in, Tayki, but don't steal anything."

Tayki opened the screen door and slowly eased into the kitchen. "Tayki no steal," she said, irritation in her words.

Essie turned around and gave the Miccosukee woman a hard stare. "You know that's not true. All those years when things came up missing, you had them all along."

Miffed, Tayki put her nose in the air and turned her face away. "Tayki gave back."

"Yes, you did. And I thank you for that. However, you must understand that you cannot just take things because you want them or like them."

Tayki continued to turn her face to the wall. "Tayki give you things."

Essie walked to the kitchen table and cleared away the dirty tea cups. Gently, she said, "Yes, you do. I love your rocks and feathers . . . and . . . turtle shells."

Tayki turned her face to Essie and grinned. "I bring you snakeskin soon."

Essie blinked. "A snake skin?"

The Indian woman nodded vigorously. "Oh, yes! Big skin. Long as One-arm."

Essie cringed. "I don't want a snakeskin, Tayki. You keep it."

Tayki turned toward the wall once more. "You hurt Tayki."

Essie huffed out a breath. "Would a slice of rum cake make you feel better, Tayki."

The old woman zipped around to face Essie. "Big cake."

Essie left the table and poured coffee. She used the Glenlea pattern of China, and placed a cup and saucer in front of Tayki. "There's sugar in the sugar bowl." She pointed to a small round bowl in the center of the table.

Tayki twisted the cup and saucer in her hands. "Pretty."

"That was Jewell's favorite China pattern."

"Jewell pretty, too."

Essie stilled, holding a cake plate. "Yes, she was," she said softly.

At the kitchen counter, Essie sliced a large piece of cake and placed it on a cake plate. "Here you go, Tayki. Enjoy."

Essie watched the old woman dump five teaspoons of sugar into her coffee, then pour as much cream as the cup would hold. Tayki's face shone with happiness, her eyes bright, a smile on her thin mouth.

"Tayki, where's the hair clasp I gave you?" Tayki's hair hung across her face in snarled layers.

Tayki shrugged. "In bird nest."

"In bird nest?"

Tayki nodded while cake crumbs tumbled from her toothless mouth. "Big blue bird picked it up and flew away."

"A Blue Jay?"

Tayki stared blankly at Essie. "Bird had blue feathers."

Essie rose from the table. "I'll be back."

Upstairs, Essie found a bright yellow clasp with an edging of pink flowers. *Thank you, Jewell. Tayki will love this hair clasp.*

Once more, Essie presented Tayki with a lovely hair clasp. "Don't let the birds get this one, Tayki." She lifted Tayki's hair from her face and pinned it in place. "Lovely."

Tayki smiled sweetly. "Tayki pretty?"

"Yes. Very pretty," said Essie as she returned to her chair and watched Tayki's cake disappear.

Tayki added more sugar to her coffee and glanced at Essie. "Bad men on sandbar."

Essie stiffened. "Go on."

"They drunk and whoop and holler like crazy white people."

"Did they see you?"

Tayki laughed out loud, her mouth opening wide to reveal her pink gums. "What you think? You think Tayki stupid? I climb tree and sit on limb. I spit on them."

Wide-eyed, Essie leaned closer. "Did you see any guns?"

Tayki frowned. "I tell Tail and Cat to hide. Men have big guns."

An ominous air filled the kitchen. Essie's mind wandered. With a sense of foreboding flooding her thoughts, she envisioned the dangers she would face. And how could she subject DooRay to the consequences of a face-to-face meeting with Spit and his cohort and their powerful guns?

Her heart flitted this way and that, like it was confused. One minute she felt calm, the next minute an uneasiness found her. Yet, in the end, she settled into a sixth sense, one that forecast a preeminent verdict – a verdict that would satisfy her innate need to right a wrong.

"How many guns? Where do they keep them?"

Tayki frowned and held up three fingers.

"Three guns?"

Tayki nodded. "Guns in truck?"

"Truck? They're in the truck?" Essie almost shouted.

Tayki nodded. "Truck not locked." She grinned slyly. "Tayki steal bullets."

Essie jumped from the table and squealed. "You stole the bullets?"

Tayki grinned her widest grin. "Tayki steal good."

"Where are they?"

"Bottom of Withlacoochee."

Essie clapped her hands together. "Oh, Tayki! You did good. Very, very good!"

The Miccosukee woman looked up at Essie. "More cake."

"Oh, of course. Yes!" Essie rushed to the counter and sliced another piece of cake. Dashing to the refrigerator, she placed some whipped cream on the cake and proudly handed it to Tayki.

A beaming Tayki devoured her cake, mumbling strange words as the whipped cream smeared around her mouth and nose. Essie wanted to laugh but dared not.

"Tayki go now."

"Okay, Tayki. Thank you for telling me about the guns . . . and the bullets."

Tayki bounded out the back door and down the porch steps. Essie watched her leave and, in a flash, Tayki disappeared into the nearby woods, heading for the Witchlacoochee.

Essie breathed a sigh of relief. *The bullets.* How can Spit shoot his gun if he doesn't have bullets? Essie wanted to shout to the heavens.

Returning to the kitchen, Essie began to clear the table and instantly saw that Tayki's cup and saucer were missing. "Damn that woman!" she said under her breath.

# CHAPTER SEVENTY-TWO

The Westminster chimes on Edith Donnelly's Seth Thomas clock sounded seven times as Essie stepped from the back porch and carried coffee to DooRay. She had tucked biscuits and blackberry jam along side the coffee on the John Deere tin tray she carried.

Killer, standing regal atop the well house, delivered an exuberant crow, almost as melodic as the grandfather clock. He fluffed his feathers and jumped to the ground in search of Murphy.

The soft glow of a July sunrise eased over the tall cypress that lined the banks of the Withlacoochee and promised a magnificent day. The sound of Lum Townsend's truck in the pasture across the Bellville road meant hay for his prized cows.

Essie found DooRay shaving, the soft tune he hummed welcome in the quiet morning. He had already made his bed and tidied his cozy tack room house.

"Good morning, DooRay. Brought you coffee and biscuits."

"Oh, Miss Essie, I done smelled that coffee a long time ago. I reckon you had a visitor? That old Indian woman?"

Essie found a seat on an overturned bucket. "Yes, it was Tayki. She threw rocks at the house around 5:00. Had to get up before she threw one through my bedroom window."

DooRay wiped his face and cleaned his razor. A chuckle came from deep within his chest. "That woman be everywhere and you never knowed it. She like a ghost. Sometime, I listen real careful and hear her all the way from the river. She sing to other peoples, I think."

Essie contemplated DooRay's words. "She told me she sat in a tree and watched those men from Alabama Seed. Said she was close enough to spit on them." Essie glanced at DooRay. "You do know those men are camping on that big sandbar."

DooRay's wide eyes turned to Essie. "Uh, huh. Them bad mens see her, they shoot her, for sure."

Essie nodded. "She knows how dangerous they are."

From the tack room, Essie heard a car drive down the lane. "Someone's here, DooRay. Let me know if you want more coffee."

Essie rounded the edge of the barn, almost bumped into Murphy, and found Simmie Moore and Son Stokely standing in the farm lane. "Good morning," she called, a little uneasiness in her words.

"Hello, Essie. Hope it's not too early for a short visit." The sheriff of Madison County smiled and walked a few steps closer. Son Stokely followed a step behind, his large body moving with amazing finesse. Essie noticed he wore his badge.

"You know I have fresh coffee, Simmie. Meet you two on the porch."

Her mind running rampant, Essie wondered the purpose of Simmie's visit. Had he discovered more information on the evil-doers who assaulted DooRay? She felt a tinge of guilt: the culprits were only two miles away on a sandbar in the middle of the Withlacoochee River. *Tell Simmie where they are, Essie. Let him handle their arrest. Let him do his job, Essie. You are obstructing due process.*

In the kitchen, Essie poured two mugs of coffee and sliced two pieces of rum cake. She filled a tray with cream and sugar, forks and napkins, walked through the parlor and stepped onto the front porch. "Here you go. Bet you haven't had breakfast, have you?"

Simmie laughed. "Essie, Son and I have been roaming this county since 3:00 this morning. Had some cattle rustlers pinned down near the Hixtown swamp. Lost their trail."

Son looked down at his boots. They were soaked and muddy. His pant legs were wet to his knees.

The two men were thankful for their hot coffee. The rum cake disappeared in minutes and the plates set empty. Simmie pulled his pipe from his shirt pocket and packed it with his special mixture of Carter Hall and Captain Black tobacco. Some early mornings, Simmie would spread the tobaccos, along with thin slices of apple, on a cookie sheet and slide the pan into a warm oven for several hours.

The sheriff leaned back in his favorite Adirondack chair and puffed his pipe. In moments, the aroma of vanilla and a subtle fruitiness traveled the porch and sweetened the early morning air.

"Got information from the Lowndes County sheriff that the red truck has pretty much disappeared. No sign of it for about three days."

*The red truck is in the woods, about two miles from here. Unlocked. Guns inside. The men are camping on a large sandbar in the middle of the Withlacoochee. Tayki hunkered down in a nearby tree and spit on them. The old woman threw their cartridges into the river.*

Essie averted Simmie's stare. Finally, she glanced his way. "So, what's next?"

"Oh, we're not giving up. Have a few more clues to work on."

"Really?"

While blowing smoke into the air, Simmie locked eyes with Essie. "Yes. Small clues, but worthy of investigation."

Essie fiddled with the buttons on her shirt, her hand shaking slightly. She gathered enough courage to lean forward and look at Simmie directly.

*She was a liar, a deceiver, a woman who refused to deny DooRay, as well as herself, the opportunity to settle a score. She couldn't let go. No matter the consequences, she would not let go.*

Essie smiled. "I'm certain you'll be successful, Simmie."

Essie heard eight chimes from the grandfather clock as she waved goodbye to Simmie Moore and Son Stokely. Their visit had been impromptu, a little unnerving, especially in light of her knowledge of Spit's whereabouts.

The dark '56 Ford turned west down the Bellville road and toward Highway 53. Simmie would probably stop at Lon Terry's general store and discuss birddogs with the Irishman.

Essie shuddered slightly. Simmie Moore was one of the sharpest lawmen in northeast Florida, and he always knew more than he let on.

# CHAPTER SEVENTY-THREE

On Wednesday, Essie dusted furniture, put fresh flowers into tall vases and swept the front porch. She glanced across the yard. DooRay had, indeed, recreated *Tara,* raking pine straw and mulching the azaleas. All the fallen leaves had been gathered and burned. Not a twig was out of place.

The crepe myrtle blooms were vibrant, as well as the roses in the small rose garden at the end of the front porch. Periwinkles lay scattered among the ferns, their colors mixed, the tall stems bobbing in the breeze. Begonias peeked out from around the caladiums lining the front of the porch. Geraniums in clay pots were arranged between the trees along the lane.

Nearing Noon, Essie glanced out the dining room window.

Perhaps she was hallucinating. She stood on tiptoe, hardly breathing.

No! It was not an apparition – it was Jewell walking down the lane, the breeze blowing her dark hair, her green eyes sparkling. The hem of her yellow dress was caught by the warm air and flitted this way and that.

Essie's heart beat wildly. She ran to the front porch and down the steps and into the yard. Panting, she took a step forward. *Jewell?* She felt tears puddling on her cheeks and dripping from her chin.

"Hello, Aunt Essie," Rose called across the yard, her face luminous, her lips spread in a big smile. Her mother walked behind, hesitant, but joyful. Rose ran the last few steps and landed in Essie's arms.

*Oh, Jewell. Your daughter's here, in my arms. I'm holding her tightly and wishing you were here, too. Finally, she's home.*

"Oh, my," said Essie. She pulled away from her niece. "I . . . I'm sorry for all these tears. It's just . . . just so wonderful. Thank you for coming."

The young girl stared at Essie. "I've never had an aunt before." Laughing, she threw herself into Essie's arms once more.

Annalee stood back and waited. She and her husband had adopted Rose when she was only weeks old, never dreaming they would one day learn about Rose's birth mother, Jewell Donnelly.

"Come to the house. I have a wonderful lunch for you." Essie reached over and hugged Annalee. "Thank you, Annalee. This means so much to me."

"It means a lot to Rose, also."

The three women stepped onto the long wooden porch that fronted the grand, two-story Donnelly house. Earlier in the week, Essie and Minnie had placed large ferns in tall pots all along the edge of the porch. DooRay had painted the two Adirondack chairs a gleaming white. New floral cushions depicting bright red geraniums and yellow daylilies invited one to sit back and relax.

The three rockers had also been repainted and stood tall, their seats soft with plush cushions. Of course, at the end of the porch, the old wooden swing with the squeaky chain reminded one of days gone by. The swing would forever overflow with poignant memories of those who found comfort in its gentle movement.

"Please find a seat and I'll bring out a pitcher of fresh peach tea."

Essie left the porch and busied herself in the kitchen, returning with a tray of ice-filled glasses brimming with peach tea. "Enjoy!" she said, handing out napkins.

At the opposite end of the porch, Rose had sat in Jewell's chair, and Essie found herself staring at the young girl. *It was Jewell, through and through.* Every detail identical. The shining black hair, the bright green eyes and the lovely face.

Essie felt her throat tighten, her thoughts returning to the previous summer, the homecoming of Autrey Browning, the father Rose would never know. She felt the pain of discovering that Jewell had had a baby when she was eighteen. Then, the revelation that their mother had orchestrated the taking of the baby and then concealed its existence.

Had it not been for Bootsey Birthright, her mother's best friend, and her 'slip of the tongue,' Essie would have never known about Rose.

Essie's anger resurfaced. Her mother's grand plan to hide the birth had failed, but she had deprived the Donnelly family of knowing about Rose for eighteen years.

Soon after the birth, Jewell had nearly drowned in Cherry Lake, her mind forever damaged, and the memory of the birth hidden away forever.

*No, no, I'll not ruin this lovely day.* Essie pushed away her angry thoughts and smiled at her niece.

"See this swing, Rose? Your great grandfather built it out of cypress from the pond. Lots of your kinfolk have sat in this swing."

"What kinfolk?"

"Oh, my goodness. Let me think. Your mother, of course. Your grandmother, Edith, and your grandfather, Hubert. Your Uncle Lester and Aunt Shelly. And, many family friends.

"Most every Sunday after church, this porch would be full of ladies with grand hats and dresses. It was a big tea party every Sunday. Lots of delicious food. Your grandmother Edith was quite the hostess."

"Am I like my grandmother?"

"No. No, not at all. You're exactly like Jewell. You look like her and your mannerisms are very much like hers. I'm sure when I spend more time with you, I'll see more similarities."

Rose, her cheeks flushed, looked around the porch. "Which chair did my mother like the best?"

Essie's heart skipped a beat. She closed her eyes for a moment and saw Jewell in her favorite chair, reading her Bible.

"The chair you're sitting in was your mother's chair."

Rose's eyes widened. "I knew it! Somehow, I just *knew* this was my mother's chair."

Annalee, nestled in a rocker, sipped her tea. "This is a grand house, Essie."

"Thank you. My grandfather built this house over a hundred years ago. Come inside and we'll have some lunch."

Soft light filled the parlor, where Edith Donnelly's grand furniture displayed her many collections, as well as family pictures. Rose immediately rushed to the pictures of Jewell.

"Here she is! This is my mother!" Rose picked up a framed photograph of Jewell, then glanced quickly at Annalee and smiled. "You're my mother. This is the woman who birthed me."

Annalees nodded. "It's okay, honey. I understand. Please relish this moment. Your mother was born in this house, grew up here and lived here until she died. It's important for you to be here."

Essie served lunch in the formal dining room. Edith Donnelly would have been proud to see her fine China and crystal arranged perfectly on her solid mahogany table. The tablecloth was a crisp white, scalloped eyelets all along the edge. Napkins the color of an Alfred Carriere rose lay beautifully folded next to the plate. A vase of yard flowers, a mix of ferns, day lilies and hydrangeas, was arranged and sat in the middle of the table.

Essie had baked a ham, the aroma of cloves wafting throughout the kitchen. Minnie prepared scalloped potatoes and deviled eggs. Sliced tomatoes, a brilliant red, along with sliced cucumbers, filled a platter that had belonged to Essie's grandmother.

Jewell was in the room. Essie could smell the fragrance of her perfume, see the yellow ribbon in her hair, and feel the warmth of her breath. *She's here, Jewell. Your daughter. She looks just like you, doesn't she? Come sit down at the table with us, Jewell.*

After lunch, Rose climbed the stairs and found her mother's bedroom at the end of the long hall, the afternoon sun sending shafts of light through the sheer curtains and casting a yellow glow across the room.

At the doorway, Rose simply waited. Tears beckoned while she imagined her mother spending her entire life in this house, this room.

A dressing table, adorned with a silver hand mirror and hairbrush, sat across the room, near the north window. Perfume bottles, a vase of pink silk flowers and a basket of colorful hair ribbons were arranged on one end of the table. A picture of Jewell's mother and father was placed on the opposite end, leaving just enough room for a small white Bible.

Rose stepped into the room and ran her hand along the softness of the yellow bedspread, touching the embroidered pillows with her fingers. She hesitated and read the inscription on one of the pillows. *Praise Be The Lord* was written in script, the color blue contrasting with the bright white linen of the pillow.

*Jewell was everywhere.* Tidbits of memories lay on a tall chest. Pictures, a pom-pom, a treasure box filled with high school paraphernalia. A bookcase lined the wall opposite the bed. Yearbooks, journals, novels and scrapbooks filled the shelves.

The lamp on the bedside table was a small Chinoiserie, a combination of soft blues and yellows. The rug by the bed was white, oval shaped and trimmed in yellow fringe.

Rose sat on the bed and leaned back onto a pillow. She would sleep in Jewell's room, and during the night, when the house was dark and quiet, she would talk to Jewel and tell her she loved her and that she was sorry they had never met. She would thank her for giving her life. She would also thank her for her Aunt Essie.

Essie called from the bottom of the stairs. "Rose, shall we visit the cemetery?"

Rose jumped from the bed. "I'll be down in a minute." Jewell's daughter took one last look at the room. *I'll be back . . . and we'll talk some more.*

A hush seemed to fall over the Mt. Horeb cemetery as Essie and her guests walked past the little white church and along the fence line. The tombstones stood like sentinels across a three acre plot of land and held more than several hundred years of history.

The large oak trees, their limbs magnificent and stretching outward just five or six feet above the ground, provided cool shade and beckoned one to lean against its strong trunk and rest.

Essie, followed by Rose and Annalee, approached the Donnelly section of the cemetery, which lay in the southwest corner, only a few yards from the back of the small church. Tombstones of different heights and sizes were gathered together like a family should be – one next to the other and displaying the names of its occupant.

The tombstones of Edith and Hubert Donnelly, Essie and Jewell's parents, were side by side. Tall and regal, they were almost ostentatious, chosen by the pretentious matriarch of the family.

Jewell's tombstone rose gently from the earth. The marble was smooth, almost glowing. Jewell's name was written in script: *Jewell Agnes Donnelly Born August 4, 1921* and *Died July 15, 1956. An Angel on Earth*

Rose had gathered flowers from the Donnelly yard and placed them in a vase. She kneeled at Jewell's tombstone and placed the vase nearby.

Essie and Annalee remained a few feet away and were silent as Rose settled herself on the grass, her hands folded in her lap. A breeze caught the ends of her hair and ruffled the sleeves of her dress.

Rose leaned closer to her mother's tombstone and whispered. *Hello. It's me - Rose. I'm so happy to be here. I wish I could have known you, heard you sing to me, seen your smile and heard your laugh. I know you would have kept me if you could have. Cared for me. Loved me. Please remember that I'll always love you.*

Evening at the Donnelly farm came softly, a whisper of night sounds, the pale light of a three-quarter moon, the fragrance of night blooming jasmine and the squeak of the porch swing.

"That was a lovely dinner, Essie." Annalee leaned back in her rocker and closed her eyes. "Don't know when I've ever felt so relaxed."

Rose, in Jewell's chair, dreamy-eyed, chimed in. "The day was wonderful."

From the corner of the house, DooRay walked along the path and to the steps of the porch. "Good evenin', ever'body."

Essie jumped from the swing. "DooRay! You must meet my niece and her mother." She swung her arm toward Annalee. "This is Annalee Montgomery. I met her in Thomasville at the Rose Parade."

Essie glanced at Rose. "And this is her daughter, Rose. Also my niece."

DooRay grinned. "Such lovely ladies. Welcome."

"I've heard so much about you, DooRay." Annalee stood and held out her hand.

DooRay shook her hand. "Thank you, Miss Annalee. So glad you're visitin' Miss Essie."

"Please join us, DooRay." Essie pointed at a rocker.

"Well, I'll stay a while. Ole Murphy's ready for bed. Killer done flew up on the wellhouse. Sound asleep already."

DooRay glanced at Essie. "That was mighty good ham and potatoes, Miss Essie. I thank you for a plate."

"I'll send you home with some buttered rum pound cake, too."

They were a family, held together by love, their lives entwined for many different reasons, all treasures of the heart. Annalee satisfied her daughter's need to see her birth mother's home. Rose fulfilled her desire to acknowledge her link to the Donnelly dynasty, her need to know her lineage. It was a starting place for all that mattered to her.

*And Essie?* Essie basked in the knowledge that Jewell's daughter had come home. Had seen the place where her mother was born and lived.

Rose had slept in the big house, in Jewell's bedroom, in Jewell's bed, and dreamed of the same things of which Jewell had dreamed.

That's what it was, a coming together. The grief over Jewell's death would never go away, but it had faded with the arrival of her daughter into Essie's life.

They travelled down the farm lane and turned left at the Bellville road. They would cross the Withlacoochee, and pass through Valdosta on their way to Thomasville.

Rose opened the car window and waved. "We'll be back soon!"

The last thing Essie saw was Rose's gleaming black hair, pinned with one of Jewell's yellow hair ribbons, and caught by the Madison County wind.

# CHAPTER SEVENTY-FOUR

The sun crept westward, leaving behind long shadows that fell across the Donnelly farm and its grand house. The tall cypress at Grassy Pond hovered like guardians over the swampy water, their tops a rusty orange.

Essie rested in the swing, one foot pushing it slowly back and forth. Her copy of *The Heart is a Lonely Hunter* lay untouched next to her, her thoughts not on reading, but reminiscing. After Rose's visit, she felt peaceful. A calm that had eluded her for so long seemed to surround her and pledge endless tranquility.

*Tranquility?* Would Essie, the hard woman whose accuracy with a pistol or .22 rifle was unsurpassed, ever achieve a state of tranquility?

Lum Townsend's cows gathered at the fence along the Bellville road, across from the Donnelly house. Curious and apprehensive at the same time, they pushed together and snorted, their heads bobbing up and down with anxiety. Tails switched furiously back and forth like a metronome out of control.

Perplexed, Essie left the swing and walked down the farm lane toward the Bellville road, closer so she could observe the strange behavior of the cows. Almost to the road, she stopped and glanced in both directions, east and west.

Something was out of place, a peculiarity, an anomaly that caused Essie to pause. Her gaze found a lump of gray at the edge of the woods next to a large pine tree. She squinted her eyes and stared.

"Tayki!" she screamed. Essie ran along the edge of the road, about thirty yards, and fell to her knees at the strange gray pile that was Tayki.

She gently pushed the old woman to her side. "Tayki, talk to me."

Blood smeared Tayki's face, a cut lay open above her eyebrow. One eye was swollen and closed. A large purple bruise ran from her cheekbone down to her jawline.

"Tayki," Essie said. "Please talk to me."

Tayki moaned, her lips blue with bruising. Blood oozed from her nostrils.

Essie stood and yelled across the woods. "DooRay! Help!"

She dropped back down to the ground and cradled Tayki's head. "It's okay, Tayki. We'll take you up to the house and call Dr. Bush."

"DooRay," she called again. She leaned over and whispered in Tayki's ear. "Everything will be okay, Tayki."

Essie heard DooRay's shout from the woods. "Where you be, Miss Essie. I don't see you nowhere."

"On the road, DooRay," she hollered. "East, toward the river."

Essie heard thrashing coming from the woods and suddenly, from the brush and trees, a worried DooRay appeared. "Oh, Miss Essie. What done happened now?" He rushed toward her and knelt by Tayki.

"Oh, my goodness, Miss Essie. This old woman fall out of a tree or somethin'?"

"I don't know, DooRay. I just know she's hurt bad. Let's get her up somehow and take her to the house. Dr. Bush needs to see her, for sure."

"I reckon she be alive, Miss Essie. Ain't no dead person bleed like that."

With just one arm, DooRay's incredible strength lifted Tayki over his shoulder. The old Indian weighed a meager hundred pounds or so. All skin and bones, she hung across DooRay's shoulder while he walked down the edge of the road, then onto the farm lane toward the house.

Tayki cried out in her secret language, mumbling words and shrieking with pain. DooRay hurried along the farm lane, then up the porch steps. He felt Tayki's body become limp, no movement. No sound.

"Where you want me to put her, Miss Essie." Perspiration dripped from DooRay's face, quick breaths from his open mouth.

"In the house, DooRay. I'll lay a sheet across the sofa, then call Dr. Bush." Essie held the door and DooRay carried Tayki inside.

Dr. Frederick Bush pushed the needle into Tayki's arm, the morphine lessening her pain in just moments. He spoke to her softly, in a low soothing voice that assured her he'd make her whole again. The doctor reached into his bag, and pulled out the tools he'd need to suture the laceration above her eye.

"Can you open your eyes for me, Tayki?"

Tayki growled. "One eye."

It was true. The right eye was swollen shut, leaving only the left eye moveable. Dr. Bush examined her left eye, his small light scanning the pupil. He appraised the wounds on her face, her head, her neck, finally checking her limbs.

"I've determined you have no broken bones," he said, as he ran his hands along her arms and legs. Suddenly, his hand stopped mid-thigh on her right leg. After a moment, he reached in his bag and pulled out a pair of scissors and cut the bottom half of Tayki's pants away. "What have we got here?" he said, throwing the bloody pants to the floor.

Nearby, Essie paced the room. DooRay stood anxiously by the door-way. Both of them stared at Dr. Bush. "What is it, Dr. Bush?" Essie moved closer and leaned over the doctor.

"This woman's been shot."

# CHAPTER SEVENTY-FIVE

M adison County's beloved doctor closed his small black bag, worry lines across his forehead. "You rest, Tayki. I'm leaving medication with Essie and she'll see that you take it." He patted Tayki on the shoulder. "I'll check back with you tomorrow."

Tayki barely nodded, then fell into a deep sleep, her face misshapen and colored with bruises the color of an angry sky. Twelve stitches lined her right eyebrow, above her swollen eye. The abrasions on her body were many, scrapes and scratches on her arms, hands and neck.

Essie walked Dr. Bush to the door and onto the porch. "What do I need to know, Dr. Bush?"

Dr. Bush exhaled as if he had been holding his breath. He shook his head. "I'm quite surprised Tayki didn't have a concussion. I found one large knot on her head. But, her pupils are clear. I was able to pull up her eyelids, but saw no blood. Her eyes are showing no signs of trauma.

"As far as internal injuries, I'm not sure. If she had been more cognizant, perhaps I could have determined more about how this happened."

Dr. Bush handed Essie a small bottle of capsules. "This is pain medication for Tayki. Give her one every four hours throughout the day and night. You have enough for six doses, beginning at 8:00 tonight."

"When she wakes up, can I give her a little bit of soup?"

Dr. Bush nodded, "That would be good. Liquids are important, too. The importance of rest cannot be over-emphasized.

"Needless to say, if she were to cough up blood, call me right away. But, I don't see that happening. I'll come by late tomorrow afternoon. Meantime, stay close by in case she needs something. Have her sit up for a few minutes throughout the night, if you can."

The gray-haired doctor swiped his hand across his face and rested his chin in his hand. He looked hard at Essie. Then, he held out his hand. "I found this lodged in her thigh."

Essie flinched while she stared at the spent bullet, her heart beginning to race. A cold fear crept up her spine, and onto her neck.

Dr. Bush slipped the bullet back into his pocket, stepped from the porch and looked up at Essie, his face solemn.

"Essie, you know I'll have to report this to Simmie in the morning."

# CHAPTER SEVENTY-SIX

E ssie heard the screen door open behind her while she watched Dr.
Bush drive down the farm lane and turn right at the Bellville road.
DooRay leaned against the porch rail and saw Murphy standing by the
oak tree at the end of the porch, watching him with sad eyes.

"Go on to bed, you ole goat. Me and Miss Essie got some talkin' to
do." He left the porch rail and sat in a rocker.

Essie found the swing and glanced at DooRay. "It's them, DooRay. I
just know it. They shot Tayki."

DooRay's head began a slow nod. Deliberate and contemplating, he
turned and found Essie's hard stare. He'd seen her like this before – the
wild look. Her jaws steel hard, her teeth clamped together.

"Now, now, Miss Essie. We gone be careful here. Gots to think this
through," he said, with as much calmness as possible. "We gots to talk
with that old Indian woman. See what's happened."

Essie drew a deep breath, her words brittle. "DooRay, I know what
happened! And at daylight, I'm going down to that river with my daddy's
gun, fully loaded, and no one is going to stop me."

The farm girl jumped from the swing and paced the porch, her head
swinging from side to side, venom filling her mind. "They could have
killed her. Murdered her." She threw her fist in the air. "If you hadn't

floated down that river when they threw you in, you'd be over at the graveyard right now!"

Her hand flew out and knocked a plant from the porch rail. She kicked a potted fern, then threw a tea glass into the yard.

"Miss Essie." DooRay stilled the rocker, his large brown eyes fixed on hers. "You is a mighty fine woman. Smart and wise. Ain't no anger gone fix anythin' that's going on here. What we's got to do is be calm."

Essie placed her face in her hands. DooRay was right. She had to reel herself in, think clearly. And, as DooRay said, let Tayki tell them what happened.

The grandfather clock chimed eight times. Time for Tayki's medicine. "I understand, DooRay. We can't be impulsive. But, we can be prepared. I'm loading daddy's gun tonight."

She turned and opened the screen door. "Come on, let's take care of Tayki.

Inside the house, Essie kneeled beside Tayki and grasped her hand. Softly, "Tayki. It's time for your medicine."

One eye opened, its pupil moving back and forth searching the room, confused.

"It's Essie. You're in my house. You've been injured, but Dr. Bush says you'll be fine." Essie squeezed Tayki's hand. "Can you talk to me?"

Tayki flipped open her left eye wider and stared at Essie. "Tea. Big sugars."

Essie and DooRay laughed. "Big sugars!" Essie got to her feet and grinned at Tayki. "I'll make you some good soup, too. Chop some of that ham left over from yesterday, add some potatoes and carrots. A few onions, too."

DooRay placed a light blanket over Tayki. "DooRay gone make you some biscuits with lots of butter and corn cobb jelly."

The old woman smiled through her swollen lips. "One-Arm make good biscuits."

"Uh, huh. I surely does."

Sounds of soup making came from the kitchen, along with the aroma of onions and ham. The tea kettle whistled and Essie made Tayki's tea, sweetened with five teaspoons of sugar.

Essie rounded the corner from the kitchen carrying a tray. "Ready for your medicine, Tayki?"

Tayki dutifully swallowed her pain tablet, drinking a glass of water, then releasing a loud burp. She glanced at Essie and DooRay, a half grin showing her toothless pink gums. "Tea," she commanded.

While the soup simmered, Essie tucked another pillow under Tayki's head. "Dr. Bush wants you to sit up a little while. Keeps your lungs clear."

Tayki obliged and wriggled her body into a semi-sitting position. Essie placed the small tray in her lap, the tea hot and heavily sugared.

Tayki lifted the teacup, wincing a little. She slurped the tea loudly, a sucking sound that could be heard all the way to the barn.

"Tayki," Essie began. "Can you tell us what happened to you?" She sat on the floor next to Tayki's make-shift bed, crossed her legs and waited.

DooRay stood in a darkened corner of the room, his back against the wall. Waiting. He breath was steady, an in and out that brought a much-needed calm.

The Indian woman licked her lips and turned her lopsided face to Essie. "Tayki in tree on river. I see men on sandbar, much whiskey and shooting Tayki's squirrels. They laugh and holler and shoot gun everywhere."

Tayki paused. Remembering, she closed her good eye. She rocked back and forth, a conjuring up of images that made her catch her breath. Her left eye opened while a diatribe of gibberish poured from her mouth, an obvious tirade that admonished something or someone.

Essie waited a moment. "Go on, Tayki. Tell us."

Tayki opened her good eye. "Men see Tayki in tree and gun found me, too. Many bullets. Then, no more bullets. I fall from tree. Then, run." Tayki's body slumped. "I run like the wind. All I hear is men's laughing in my ears."

Essie looked over her shoulder and glanced at DooRay. One, long knowing look that made DooRay shiver and look away.

The bad people had found a new sport. While they drank their whiskey, they loaded their guns and aimed them at the trees along the river, killing squirrels and anything else that moved.

They had bellowed with laughter as the sound of their gunfire shattered the peace of the Withlacoochee and sent the smell of acrid cordite into the perfect, clear air.

Somehow, their bleary eyes had found the old Miccosukee woman hiding in a nearby tree and their sport became even more exciting.

Essie watched as Tayki's face softened, slipping into a peaceful place, the pain medication taking away all her hurts. When she woke again, Essie would give her warm soup. If it was near midnight, she'd give her another dose of the painkiller Dr. Bush had prescribed. She eased her down to her pillow and pulled her hair away from her face.

While Tayki slept, Essie and DooRay sat on the front porch and watched the bright moon move westward, carrying wispy clouds with it and promising a new day was on the horizon.

DooRay placed his empty bowl on the porch rail. "That was mighty good soup, Miss Essie. You made it just like my mama did. Lots of salt and pepper. Little bits of onion."

"Thank you, DooRay. Those were good biscuits, as always. Glad we saved some for Tayki."

"We gots to feed her, for sure." DooRay leaned his head on the back of the rocker and closed his eyes.

An owl flew low across the farm lane, his wings flapping smoothly and landed in the top of a maple tree. After a few moments, it screeched loudly.

A night breeze ran down the porch and carried with it the smell of fresh plowed farmland from Emmett Gaston's cornfield. Dried corn stalks had been plowed under weeks ago. It was time to plant peas for a late fall crop.

The creak of the swing's chain stopped, the swing still, Essie a breath away from the hard woman who was about to right a wrong.

"DooRay. At 4:00 o'clock, after I give Tayki her pain medication, I'm going to go to the river. Then, swim out to the sandbar and untie those Alabama boys' Jon boat."

Essie heard DooRay lean forward in the rocker. She knew he was incredulous, glaring at her in the dark, but she refused to look his way. "I'm not sure if it's anchored or just tied up, but either way, I'll get it loose.

"Then, I'm going to pull that boat down the river, out of sight. When those boys wake up, the only way they can get off that sandbar is to swim." Essie stood and walked to the porch rail and looked out over the farmyard. "And, I'll be waiting for them."

If DooRay could have seen Essie's face in the near-midnight darkness, he would have seen her smiling. It was the hard woman's devilish smile, the one that held a villainous intent. *It was time to right the wrong.*

Essie continued, her words somewhat softer. "Tayki said she threw their cartridges in the river. I'm sure she did, but that didn't include the cartridges in their guns. I think they ran out of ammunition when they went on a squirrel killing rampage."

Essie turned and faced DooRay. "If they hadn't run out of cartridges, I'm certain they would have killed Tayki. As it turned out, she was able to jump or fall from the tree and run."

DooRay, the man who had survived World War II, had led his squad to safety during a siege in Italy, and had returned home with only one arm, remained still, no words to say. He merely kept his eyes on the shadowed face of Essie Donnelly.

Without a doubt, he knew he'd never change her mind. His intellect told him it would be like a sortie, a strike against the enemy. Only he wouldn't be leading the attack this time. He'd have to follow the hard woman.

# CHAPTER SEVENTY-SEVEN

After her midnight medication, Tayki ate a small bowl of soup. At 4:00 a.m., Essie awakened her again. "Tayki, time for your medicine."

Tayki eased into a sitting position and drank a glass of water, looked around the room, swallowed her medicine and then snuggled back into her pillow. She would sleep hard for another four hours. Perhaps she would dream of tying a rope around the ankles of two bad men and dragging them behind the racing hooves of her favorite Appaloosa horse.

Essie lingered a moment and watched the face of the old woman, waited for her breathing to become deep and steady. She marveled at the petiteness of Tayki, her fine bones, her thin, long fingers. She saw the corners of her mouth turn upward slightly. Yes, she was definitely dreaming.

Outside, the night was wet with dew, the air's humidity thick. DooRay ambled around the yard, swept his foot through the acorns and mumbled to himself. "Lord, what's we gone do? DooRay ain't never fight with no white men 'fore."

A sudden chill followed him across the yard. "Ain't no way I can help Miss Essie. Only gots one arm. All these long skinny legs can do is run."

The black man glanced over his shoulder when he heard the screen door open and shut. There she was – a pistol in one hand and a rifle in the other. DooRay thought about Italy, the Germans. He'd used a rifle the entire four years he was in the Army, not willingly, but to survive. *DooRay's through killin' peoples,* he thought, as his eyes narrowed and watched the hard woman.

Essie stepped from the porch, her left hand holding her daddy's Colt Python, a revolver Hubert Donnelly had bought just before he died. Essie had become expert within days of its purchase. Now, as she walked toward DooRay, she felt the strength in her hands and her arms, her entire body and mind primed for her encounter with the bad people

The double-action .357 revolver could shoot anything two-hundred yards away, and, with her deadly aim, Essie felt the gun would handle any conflict.

The Winchester .22 short, slide action, semi-automatic in her right hand had been a favorite. Only a few feet from DooRay, she lifted it and offered it to him. So casual, like it was a glass of iced tea.

"Here you go, DooRay. It's loaded and ready to go."

DooRay shuddered. "Go where, Miss Essie?"

Essie pulled back and gave DooRay a hard stare. "DooRay," she said softly, "you don't have to go with me. You can stay here and watch over Tayki. I'll be okay." She turned and walked to the Pontiac.

"Miss Essie," DooRay called after her. "Let's call Sheriff Moore and let him help us."

Essie called over her shoulder. "I can handle this, DooRay."

"No, you cain't, Miss Essie. Them men's gone hurt you, for sho." The thin black man walked a few steps closer. "Please, Miss Essie. We cain't do this. DooRay cain't stand to see somethin' happen to you."

Essie stared through the dark, seeing DooRay's silhouette, the rifle, his thin body, the wide shoulders. She couldn't see his face, but she knew it was filled with anxiety.

"Come with me, DooRay," she half-whispered.

They slipped inside the Pontiac and traveled the dark, clay road to the river. No running lights, they parked an eighth of a mile from the river in a farm gate lane at the end of Lum Townsend's field.

In only five minutes, they had walked to the Bellville road bridge, the night calm, the river flowing quietly, flowing south. Their gaze scanned the river, no words between them, as they gathered their thoughts and prepared for an encounter with Spit and Freddie.

It was a crooked river, the water the color of dark rum, but pure, with springs hiding deep along its hundred and thirty mile trek.

Essie and DooRay left the bridge and entered the woods and walked among the trees and brush until they were opposite the large sandbar. Essie sat on her haunches and watched the camp. A large tent had been pitched in the center, the front opening facing north, a cold campfire nearby. Fishing poles leaned against the tent on the south side of the sandbar, where an eleven foot Jon boat had been shoved onto the sand.

"You hear what I hear, DooRay?" Essie cocked her ear toward the river, and leaned the Winchester against a tree.

"Somebody done been snorin' like a big ole bear."

"They're sleeping good after all that whiskey." Essie stood and handed DooRay the Colt revolver. "DooRay, meet me down the river, about a half mile, around the next big bend.

Right then, the tent flap opened and a large figure walked to the edge of the sandbar and stood while a stream of pee shot across the water.

Essie and DooRay stilled while the figure crawled back into the tent and, in a few minutes, heavy snoring resumed.

Easing down the limestone bank and to the water's edge, Essie took off her shoes and bluejeans, then slipped into the warm waters of the Withlacoochee. With long, quiet strokes, she was at the boat's edge in less than a minute, her last stroke reaching out and touching the edge of the boat.

She tugged on the boat, but it wouldn't move. There was no anchor, the boat had been merely shoved onto the sandbar. Essie left the water and crawled to the front of the boat, and pushed with all her might. The boat gave way and slid into the water.

Down river, DooRay waited while Essie reentered the water and pulled the boat away from the sandbar. The boat glided into the river, Essie behind it, propelling it with the kick of her legs.

As the boat rounded the bend, DooRay entered the river's edge. "Over here, Miss Essie," he whispered.

The boat moved like a ghost boat, empty and quiet. Essie steered it toward the bank and wondered if Tail was somewhere watching her, wondering where Tayki was. She was certain the old alligator remembered her from DooRay's rescue at the sandbar a month ago.

At the riverbank, the two maneuvered the boat into a small cutout in the limestone where the current couldn't carry it away. They wedged it carefully against the bank, the river lapping its sides gently.

"DooRay, I'm going to swim back. You go on along the woods and look for Tayki's shack. Just stay there and out of sight. Don't think anybody'd see you, but just be careful. Keep those guns handy."

DooRay nodded, his hand grasping the rifle, the revolver tucked in his armpit of his right arm and watched as Essie swam out into the river and headed north, back toward the sandbar and the two sleeping men.

Essie's arms worked smoothly, moving her body through the water, her legs giving strong kicks. Her eyes had adjusted to the darkness, and the sky seemed closer, the stars and waning moon bright as she gently moved along.

To her left, about ten yards away, she saw movement at the top of the water. Perhaps a floating log.

Then, the quick flip of a tail. The alligator moved closer, its body long and skimming the top of the water, its head exposed. *Tail!*

Almost to Tayki's shack, she passed the sandbar. No movement from the tent. Essie cut to her left across the water toward the riverbank, watching Tail. Then, the alligator dipped beneath the water and was gone.

A nightbird screeched loudly and flew across the river, its wings wide. An egret, its white body skimming across the water, shone pearl-like in the night.

At the river's edge, Essie slid on her bluejeans and shook the water from her hair. "DooRay," she whispered.

"Yes, ma'am. DooRay's right here waitin'."

Pulling herself up the riverbank, Essie grabbed the trunks and limbs of small trees and landed only a few feet from Tayki's shack.

"What we gone do now, Miss Essie?" DooRay had calmed. His body leaned against a tree, the rifle by his side. He was a soldier again.

"Wait, DooRay. We're going to wait."

# CHAPTER SEVENTY-EIGHT

It was the sound of squawking birds and the splash of fish that heralded the arrival of a new day. The rising sun brought a soft pale light to the eastern horizon, filtering through the tall cypress and casting warm shadows on the river.

Essie spun the cylinder on her daddy's Colt Python for the hundredth time and watched the sandbar. DooRay sat nearby, staring at the tree above him. Cat stretched out along a big limb, his eyes closed, every now and then yawning and then opening one eye to look at DooRay.

"That dang cat," he said, disgust filling his words. "Ain't nothin' but an ole flea bag. I reckon fleas is jumpin' off him right now and fallin' on my head."

"Shhhhh," said Essie.

DooRay sighed and glared at Cat. The panther was waiting for Tayki. After all, the old Indian had raised him since he was a newborn kitten.

He jerked and shrunk back. Slick eased down the tree trunk, only a few feet from DooRay. The black snake crawled into the shack, also waiting for Tayki.

Out in the river, close to shore, Tail skimmed the water now and then. Waiting.

From the sandbar, the flap of the tent opened and Spit stumbled out, unzipping his fly, and sending pee downriver.

The heavy man walked to the campfire and placed a few small sticks across the spent coals and lit it. A coffee pot sat nearby on a small rock. The flames caught and smoke lifted into the morning air.

Spit stretched and yawned and ambled around the tent, to the south side, and immediately saw the Jon boat was gone.

"Hey, Freddie," he called. "Our boat's missin'. Ain't nowhere."

Freddie, a chunky fellow, slow moving and slow talking, traipsed out of the tent. "What'd you say, Spit?"

"Look here. Boat's gone." Spit glanced down the river.

"Dang. What we gone do? We're in the middle of this here river."

"Hell, if I know." Spit kicked the coffee pot and stomped to the north side of the sandbar. "That's a deep river and I cain't swim a lick."

Freddie coughed and spit into the river. "I can swim, Spit. But, they's alligators in this river. I seen one swimming around all day yesterday evenin', not too far from this sandbar."

"How come you didn't shoot 'em?" Spit hurled his *Alabama Seeds* hat into the river." His face red with anger, he picked up his rifle. "I'll shoot 'em."

Freddie shook his head. "We're outta cartridges, Spit. Killed all them squirrels yesterday." Freddie's face sobered. "Might have hit that ole Indian woman."

"Shit! Ain't nobody gone come this way on the river. We'll be stuck for days if you don't swim to shore."

Freddie dipped his head and searched the river. "Look! There he is! Look at that thing. He's eight foot long."

While the two men watched Tail, Essie and DooRay scrambled down the bank, Cat hovering nearby. And waited.

Tail moved closer to the sandbar, his head half submerged, his eyes popping up every few minutes. He was a patient alligator.

"Go on, Freddie. We got to do somethin'." Spit lingered along the edge of the sandbar. "You reckon somebody done stole our Jon boat?"

Freddie stared at Spit. "Who'd steal our boat?"

"Don't know. But, the only way we're gonna git outta here is for you to swim on over to the river bank."

Freddie hesitated. "I ain't no olympic swimmer, Spit. Ain't no way I can outswim that alligator." The man's face was pale.

From thirty yards out, Tail eased below the surface and disappeared, the water rippling behind him. In only seconds, he resurfaced near the sandbar, about five yards away.

Both Spit and Freddie saw the gator and shrank back from the edge of the sandbar. Barely audible, Freddie whispered to Spit. "That gator's gone eat us, for sure."

# CHAPTER SEVENTY-NINE

At that moment, Essie stood, holding her rifle and walking to the water's edge, DooRay beside her. "You boys having a little difficulty?" she called, using her hog-calling voice, the one that made the devil shiver.

The two men jumped and peered across the river, their mouths open. Spit squinted at DooRay. "Freddie, is that the one-armed nigger we done throwed in the Withlacoochee a while back?" he whispered.

*The woman? He'd seen her before. But, where?* One eye on the gator and one eye on Essie, Spit cleared his throat. "Yep. Reckon we are. You think you can get a boat and get us off this sandbar?"

Essie grinned. "Why don't you swim to shore?" She grasped the rifle tighter. The Colt, stuck at the top of her bluejeans, seemed hot with anticipation.

Spit squirmed and bit his lip. "I cain't swim." He swung his head to Freddie. "Freddie can swim, but there's an alligator over there." He pointed to Tail, who had moved closer. Only a few yards away, the gator watched the two men.

Essie nodded. "Well, I reckon you'll rot on that sandbar," she said.

Spit scowled at Essie, his uneasiness evident. His fingers played along his pants leg, perhaps looking for a weapon he didn't have. "Who are you?"

*At last, the reckoning. Who was she? Who was the black man by her side?* Essie removed the Colt from her waistband and rubbed the grip with her thumb. The two men jerked back near the tent. Spit licked his lips, a tremble in his body. Freddie froze.

"Who am I?" Essie yelled. The birds in the trees flew farther into the woods away from her anger. She gestured to DooRay. "I'm this man's family."

At once, Spit hooted with laughter, leaned over and slapped his knee with his hand. Freddie cackled like a laying hen.

The bullet left the muzzle of the Colt Python and kicked the sand only three feet from Spit. The sound of the .357 magnum's blast exploded into the air, the noise echoing across the river and into the woods.

The two men cowered. No place to hide, no place to run, they held up their hands. "Now, wait just a minute. You cain't shoot at us like that." Spit pumped himself up and angrily shook his fist.

A second bullet tore into the coffee pot, only inches from Spit. The pot danced into the air and landed into the small fire.

Essie moved to the river's edge. The words came slowly, a biting anger reaching out and finding the men on the sandbar. "You can't throw a one-armed man into the river."

Realization flushed the faces of Spit and Freddie. Neither moved.

The hard woman from Madison County raised the revolver for the third time. "And you can't shoot an old Indian woman out of a tree."

"We ain't shot at nobody. Ain't throwed anybody in the river, either. You don't have no proof of nothin'."

Four bullets slammed into the sandbar, inches from the bad people. Essie flipped open the cylinder and slipped six more cartridges into her daddy's gun, in full view of the terrified men.

Even with one arm, DooRay pressed the rifle against the trunk of a sapling with his left shoulder, grasped the trigger with his right hand and aimed at the sandbar. He became the soldier he was during World War II, in the fields of Italy where men died all around him. He fired fifteen rounds, each one precisely where he wanted it.

The two men fell to the ground and huddled against one another, the bullets closing in on them. Freddie moaned loudly, his hands over his head. Spit's head was pressed into the sand.

The stillness that followed the barrage of bullets seemed other-worldly, as if the wrath of God had rained down upon the two men who had tried to drown DooRay and kill Tayki.

Essie and DooRay stood quietly along the riverbank. A calmness had enveloped them, perhaps an ending to their suffering.

Finally, Essie shouted across the water. "See that alligator over there? He's a maneater. He'll tear you to pieces if you step into the water so I'd stay on the sandbar if I were you."

The men didn't move or speak.

Essie tucked the Colt back into the waist of her dungarees as DooRay handed her the rifle. "Keep hold of that rifle, DooRay." She noticed a slight smile on DooRay's face, a satisfaction that spread from ear to ear.

She turned toward the sandbar and left one last message for the bad people.

"I called the sheriff of Madison County this morning. He'll be out here anytime to arrest both of you for attempted murder. 'Course, you can leave the sandbar before he gets here with his deputy, and then you won't have to worry about life in prison. Not after that alligator has you for dinner."

Essie and DooRay left the river and the two men on the sandbar. They left Cat in the oak tree, his tail swiping back and forth, watching the two men. They left Tail patrolling around the sandbar, his body visible on the top of the water and his long white teeth showing along his jaws. *And Slick?* Slick lay curled inside Tayki's shack, beneath her pillow, his thin black tail protruding an inch or two.

Just as they left the woods and stepped onto the Bellville road, a dark 1956 Ford passed them, but braked and backed up. The car's window rolled down, and Simmie Moore smiled at them. Son Stokely was in the passenger seat.

"Had a busy morning?" he casually asked, his eyes curious.

Essie nodded. "An interesting morning."

Simmie grinned. "Is that cordite I smell in the air?"

Essie raised her eyebrows and looked at DooRay, then back at Simmie. "Could be."

Simmie deliberated a moment. "Anything you need to tell me?"

Essie shrugged and took a deep breath. "Nothing special. 'Cept maybe that a boat is tucked away a half mile from the sandbar, if you need it."

Simmie and Son ignored the revolver stuffed in Essie's bluejeans and the rifle DooRay was carrying. The sheriff nodded. "Guess I'll be by a little later. Got any buttered rum pound cake?"

"I do."

Essie and DooRay watched the sheriff's car continue down the narrow clay road and park at the end of the bridge. The two lawmen left the car and entered the woods, Simmie whistling an old melody from days gone by while lighting his favorite pipe.

# CHAPTER EIGHTY

The sun had cleared the trees along the horizon, leaving the glitter of sunlight across the tin roof of the Donnelly barn. Essie parked the Pontiac at the end of the front porch, near the big oak and walked up the steps, her body weary, her mind spent. DooRay wasn't far behind, his shoulders slumped. The night had been long.

"I'll get some breakfast going, DooRay. Can you make biscuits?"

"I sho' can, Miss Essie. Some good pear butter Miss Mary Chamblin done made. Maybe a hot cup of coffee would taste good."

"Yes. Come on in. I'll put up these guns, then check on Tayki."

The house sat quiet. The grandfather clock chimed on the half hour and reminded Essie of her mother. In the kitchen, the small table was strewn with sugar, the sugar bowl on its side, the top nearby. Remnants of the buttered rum pound cake lay in the cake platter, crumbs scattered across the table and on the floor.

Tayki might have been medicated, but she was certainly well enough to find the sugar and the pound cake. Essie peeked around the corner of the kitchen and saw Tayki in a fetal position on the couch, a blanket covering her. She snored softly.

The old woman's face seemed peaceful despite the abrasions on her face, despite her swollen eye and twelve stitches. Tayki had missed out on the *'great gunfight at the Withlacoochee river sandbar.'* But, Essie would tell her all about it one day.

The clock read 8:35, thirty minutes past due for Tayki's medicine. Essie eased beside the sleeping woman and gently stroked her back. "Tayki, time for your medicine."

Tayki stirred and opened her one good eye and croaked. "Hot tea. Sugar, too." She grinned wide even though her lips were cut and puffy.

Essie frowned, a playful look. "I see you found the pound cake."

Tayki ducked her head. "Doctor said eat pound cake."

"Dr. Bush?" Essie laughed. "Let's take your medicine. DooRay's cooking breakfast."

The two women walked into the kitchen where DooRay had scooped flour into his favorite biscuit bowl. A jug of buttermilk and a can of lard sat nearby. He hummed softly, a little jig in his feet while his one hand mixed the dough.

Tayki eyed the sugar bowl while Essie made coffee. Outside, Murphy climbed up the back porch steps as if to say "where have you been?"

Killer, running along the fence, talked to his hens, a soft caw that said he'd not let a hawk get them as long as *he* ruled the farmyard.

At breakfast, Tayki ate heartily. She was a strong woman and falling from a tree and receiving a gunshot wound had not deterred her appetite.

DooRay sipped a second cup of coffee, irritation covering his face. He scratched his head. "Dang fleas, again. Done dropped on DooRay's head from that ole panther."

"Cat no have fleas," Tayki barked. She scowled at DooRay, her one good eye oozing contempt. Her lopsided face was almost humorous, the bruises and abrasions the colors of an artist's pallet.

Breakfast settled into a blissful few minutes, another pot of coffee perking, and the jar of pear butter wiped empty by Tayki.

"Miss Essie, Mr. Sam ain't been here for a few days. A casual question, but one that aroused his curiosity. DooRay Aikens' capacity to observe the goings-on at the Donnelly farm was his favorite pastime.

"That's true. He's been in Tallahassee handling Stan Barnwell's trial. He'll be back late tonight."

"Sure have missed Mr. Sam," said DooRay, taking another biscuit. He opened the jar of corn cobb jelly.

Tayki sat back. "Tayki go home."

"Go home? You can't go home, Tayki. You've got three more does of medicine. Besides that, Dr. Bush will be here this afternoon to check on you."

"I go home after medicine." She crossed her arms and sent a sullen look to Essie.

Essie shrugged. "Okay. After Dr. Bush checks you and your last dose of medicine."

The morning eased into a divine revelation, one filled with tranquility, and the desire to exchange love for love, an awakening that garnered peace at the Donnelly farm.

The farm resonated with the sounds of life. Emmett Gaston's tractor moved back and forth across the field to the west, pulling a disc bedder, hilling up rows for the next crop. Cattle egrets followed the tractor and gorged on the thousands of insects in the overturned soil.

Lum Townsend's cows grazed across the Bellville road in a field of lush green pasture grass. To the south, the Townsend's pond teemed with fish, a fish fry in the making. One of his horses neighed loudly, then pranced along the fence, his tail arched high.

The chicken hawk soared above, in a sky clear and endless. Down below, Killer cocked his eye and a warning escaped his throat. He was king of the farmyard.

Murphy had found the perfect spot along the fence line where blackberry bushes had tumbled out of control and left runaway branches just right for munching. Despite the absence of one ear, he would always be the most handsome goat in Madison County.

DooRay napped in his little cot in the tack room, not a care in the world, except maybe fleas from Tayki's son, *Cat*. A warm breeze drifted through the barn and the open door of his tiny room, a wren popping in and flitting along the rafters. Most likely, a nest lay tucked away in the small crevices.

In the upstairs bedroom, Essie slept after a long, warm bath. While she slept, she dreamed of Sam and, now and then, called out in her sleep. She kicked her legs and laughed out loud. Yes, she was dreaming of Sam.

Along about 3:00, Dr. Bush ambled up the porch steps, his black bag in his hand. The old doctor never seemed weary, his energy stored for helping those in need, his dedication to heal the sick a fervent reality.

"Essie, how about a glass of tea," he called. He opened the front screen door and peeked inside. "Essie," he called again.

"I'll be right down, Dr. Bush."

Tayki was sitting upright on the sofa, her good eye scrutinizing the doctor. "Tayki go home."

Frederick Bush nodded. "Let's take a look at you first. How're you feeling?" He pulled a nearby chair to the edge of the sofa.

Tayki grinned. "Like medicine."

"I bet you do, Tayki. It's good medicine. Takes your pain away." He took his small flashlight out of his bag and swiped the light across her face. The stitches looked perfect, no gaping of the skin. No more bleeding. Swelling kept her right eye closed, but that, too, would heal.

Essie bounded down the stairs. "Glad you're here, Dr. Bush," she said, brushing past to pour him a glass of tea.

"Good to see you, Essie. Tayki's vital signs are good. She's coming along just fine."

"She's certainly slept well," said Essie, placing the glass of tea on a small table. "She hasn't complained."

"That's good. We'll check on her again in a few days. Her last dose of pain medication will be enough. I'm sure she'll be sore for a few days, but she's a strong woman."

Dr. Frederick Bush said his goodbyes and followed the Bellville road back to Madison. He had a baby to deliver. His favorite part of doctoring. After he delivered , he'd ride out to the Washington farm and visit with Tillman and Julia, maybe fish a little in their pond. If he was lucky, Julia would ask him if he wanted some of her famous peanut brittle.

# CHAPTER EIGHTY-ONE

Tayki's 4:00 medicine was given right on time, easing her into a comfortable sleep, but only after a bowl of soup and her request for Essie to make another pound cake.

The porch had cooled somewhat, the last of the sun on the late July day easing over Madison County's rolling hills, clouds causing soft gray shadows.

Essie heard DooRay's baritone voice lift high in the twilight sky. She pushed the swing slowly and closed her eyes and listened to the words of *Jesus Is A Wonderful Savior* drift across the farm and maybe even to the Mt. Horeb cemetery.

Tires crunched across the fallen acorns as Simmie Moore parked his car under the massive limbs of an oak tree her grandfather had planted. She knew he'd come, a lot of questions would surely follow.

"Evenin', Essie." he said, removing his hat and reaching for his pipe. He stepped onto the porch and found his favorite rocker and meticulously filled his pipe, all the while harboring a soft smile. Before he lit his pipe, Essie smelled the sweet aroma of tobacco drifting down the porch, somehow pushing twilight nearer, the end of a day that would be long remembered.

"Hello, Simmie. She watched his face and marveled at the man he was – the man who made everything alright, kept his wits and somehow presided over the County without raising his voice.

She felt the tears come and turned her face away, finding interest in nothing but the remains of the day. When she looked at him again, he was watching her, a steady look that promised no judgment. Nor admonishment.

"I'm sorry, Simmie. I just wanted to let those men know I could have killed them if I wanted to." Essie wiped her nose, took a gulp of air and glanced at Simmie. "You arrest them?"

Simmie puffed on his pipe for a few moments, watching the cows across the road, becoming thoughtful. When he turned to Essie, his face held a look of resignation. "Yes. Charged them with attempted murder. Not only DooRay but also Tayki. Dr. Bush told me about Tayki and gave me the bullet."

"Simmie, I –."

"No need to explain, Essie. Your heart is in the right place." He smiled at her, a slight sadness in his eyes. He knew she had agonized over the near-drowning of DooRay as well as Tayki's life-threatening injuries.

Essie nodded. "Do you need anything from me?"

Simmie nodded. "I'll need a sworn statement from you. We'll take care of that next week. Need one from DooRay and Tayki, too. All of you will be the State's main witnesses and will testify at trial."

Essie took a deep breath. "Thank you, Simmie."

Simmie relit his pipe and pushed his rocker, the Donnelly front porch like a cocoon that wrapped itself around those who came, calming their fears and offering a semblance of solitude.

He spoke softly, "Your daddy's guns fairly accurate?"

Essie smiled. She knew what Simmie Moore was asking. "Especially the Colt."

Simmie leaned forward and sent Essie a grin. "Thanks for being a good citizen, Essie."

"You're welcome, Simmie."

The darkness came swiftly and carried with it the sound of whippoorwills, of owls, of crickets, of Lum Townsend's cows lowing across the Bellville road and finally the rise of the summer moon and its nearby stars. Essie watched Simmie travel down the farm lane and turn toward Pinetta, leaving behind the aroma of his pipe, the wisdom of his words and the joy of a priceless friendship.

Tayki burst through the screen door. "Tayki go home! Now!"

"Settle down, Tayki. You have one more pain pill to take."

"No medicine. Tayki feel good." Limping slightly, she stomped down the steps and into the night, the words of the Miccosukee following her.

Essie listened as Tayki called her ancestors, the moon, the stars and finally her son, *Cat*. Tail was nearby and anxiously waited for the Indian woman at the riverbank, just below her shack. He flipped his tail when he heard Tayki's cry, a far away song, the words completely understood by all the creatures who lived on the Withlacoochee River.

# CHAPTER EIGHTY-TWO

In the quiet of the late night, Essie, dressed in a cotton nightshirt and carrying a light blanket, settled in the porch swing, the light of the moon casting shadows across the stately Donnelly house.

Jewell's little plastic radio picked up the station from Valdosta, WAPB, the words of Billie Holiday's *I'll Be Seeing You* floating into the night, a feeling of melancholia sweeping the air. Somehow, it felt like the end. The end of what, Essie didn't know. Just below the surface, tears threatened and lingered there.

All was well on the Bellville road. A few deer crossed at the end of the farm lane, their silhouettes magical, a nighttime jaunt would have them soon jumping Lum Townsend's fence and frolicking with the cows.

*Lost. That's what she felt.* An empty feeling that brewed heavily in her heart and pushed its way outward, spilling over into regret.

Essie pushed the swing and looked up when car lights flashed down the drive, the beams sweeping the farmyard and slowly moving to the edge of the front porch.

She saw the glow at the end of his cigar first, then the Panama straw hat. It was then that a handsome, tall man wearing bluejeans and a crisp long-sleeved white shirt stepped from the car. He stood a moment at the edge of the oak tree, watching her.

Essie's long legs ran from the bottom of her short nightshirt, her feet stretched out from the swing, her skin shining in the moonlight. Not buttoned all the way to the top, the nightshirt revealed the soft curves of her breasts, a delicate cleavage that whispered *let me pleasure you in a hundred ways.*

Sam's hesitation fevered her, her heart pounding as she stilled the swing and stood. Sam remained still, an occasional puff on his cigar. Still watching her.

Essie slowly walked across the porch and leaned against a white column, a slight smile playing gently across her lips. She folded her arms and cocked her head.

"Mr. Washington," she whispered, in a husky, longing voice that crept down the steps and to the man in the Panama hat.

"Miss Donnelly," he said, his words teasing, seductive, like a hot flame that flicked across the yard and found her totally defenseless.

In the night, they stared at one another, a longing that crossed each other and entwined itself together and pulled tight so neither could escape.

"My darling," Essie said, taking one step closer. "I have missed you so."

Sam grinned wide. "Did I hear you call me *darling*?"

Had there been more light, Sam would have seen Essie's blush. Her voice, softer than an angel's, moved through the night air and cast a spell on him.

"Yes, you'll always be my darling."

Sam covered the few feet to the porch in one giant step and swept Essie Donnelly into his arms. He buried his face in her hair, felt her smooth, warm body beneath her nightshirt and held her like he'd never let her go.

Essie leaned back and looked into Sam's blue eyes. "I love you, Sam Washington."

# THE DONNELLY'S SISTERS'
# BUTTERED RUM POUND CAKE

1 cup butter, softened (2 sticks)
2 ½ cups of sugar
4 large eggs
3 ¼ cups all-purpose flour
1 teaspoon baking powder
½ teaspoon baking soda
1 teaspoon salt
1 cup of buttermilk
2 teaspoons vanilla

**Cake**: Cream butter until light and fluffy. Gradually add sugar and beat at medium speed for five minutes. Add eggs one at a time, beating well after each. In another bowl, combine flour, baking powder, baking soda and salt. Whisk until blended. Add dry mix to butter mix, alternating with buttermilk until well blended. Stir in two teaspoons vanilla.

Use a 10-inch tube pan or a 12-cup Bundt pan. Grease and flour well. Pour in batter. Bake at 325 degrees for one hour. Cool in pan for 15 minutes. Then, remove onto cake plate. Pour 2/3 of sauce mixture over cake that has been pricked with toothpick and allow to soak in for about 15 minutes. Pour remaining butter rum sauce over cake.

**Sauce:** Combine 1 cup sugar, 1/2 cup butter and ¼ cup water in a small saucepan and cook over medium heat until sugar melts. Stir constantly. Once thickened, remove from heat and stir in ¼ or ½ cup rum. (Rum flavoring works well!) Essie and Jewell dust with confectioners sugar and chopped pecans and most certainly serve on their mother's fine china – the Glenlea pattern. They beg you not to use paper plates or plastic dinnerware. P. S. Sam, indeed, learned to make this wonderful cake.

*www.suechamblinfrederick.com*   Order books through Amazon – print or e-books.

# ABOUT THE AUTHOR

***Sue Chamblin Frederick***. She is known as a sweet Southern belle, a woman whose eyelashes are longer than her fingers, her lips as red as a Georgia sunset. Yet, behind the feminine facade of a Scarlett-like ingénue lies an absolute and utterly calculating mind – a mind that harbors hints of genius – a genius she uses to write books that will leave you spellbound.

A warning! She's dangerous – when she writes spy thrillers she's only six degrees from a life filled with unimaginable adventures – journeys that will plunge her readers into a world of breath-taking intrigue. Put a Walther PPK pistol in her hand and she will kill you. Her German is so precise she'd fool Hitler. Her amorous prowess? If you have a secret, she will discover it – one way or the other.

When she writes romance, her readers rejoice as they read her delightful stories about the women from Venus and the men from Mars!

The author was born in north Florida in the little town of Live Oak, where the nearby Suwannee River flows the color of warm caramel, in a three-room, tin-roofed house named "poor." Her Irish mother's and English father's voices can be heard even today as they sweep across the hot tobacco fields of Suwannee County, "Susie, child, you must stop telling all those wild stories."

She lives with her Yankee husband in the piney woods of north Florida, where she is compelled to write about far away places and people whose hearts require a voice. Her two daughters live their lives hiding from their mother, whose rampant imagination keeps their lives in constant turmoil with stories of apple-rotten characters and plots that cause the devil to smile.